FABLE UNBOUND

ANTHONY KOCUR

Copyright © 2019 Anthony Kocur

All rights reserved.

ISBN:
978-0-578-54138-9

AUTHOR'S NOTE

No work is ever finished. Not really. That was essentially the theme of *Fable Unbound*. Art is a hungry cycle of creation and recreation, and it will devour your sanity–sometimes in delightful ways, often times in delightfully horrible ways. This book was a labor of love, something born from wherever ideas await their birth into the worlds. This is the second published version–the original edition being *Tetragrammar*. This version equals my attempt to rebrand: new cover, new blurb, new title (because the original left people scratching their heads, and me beginning an awkward explanation involving tetragrammatons and God's true name); all to better reflect the material within, and also to correct some editorial boo boos, and to show readers I now understand there is no "o" in lunge.

ACKNOWLEDGMENTS

To Amanda, Aslynn, Mom and Dad
To the inspirations of Neil, Jonathan, Peter, and Grant
And a special thanks to an unhealthy dose of Vertigo.

I

THE RAPE OF ART

IN WHICH BLACK OLIVES BREAK HEARTS, SERPENTS ARE
CYCLES, AND A MUSE IS HACKED

1
PROPOSAL

Seven couldn't write, which was a problem. If he couldn't do that, and do it well, then he wasn't much at all. He hoped the issue would rectify itself sooner than later, and when later never came, he feared he was skirting the edges of a writer's block bordering on existential crisis.

He dwelled in bookstores and coffee shops, a dark-eyed insomniac in his mid-twenties who looked somewhat unhinged, as if he never awoke from a dream or never learned to iron his clothes. His hair was the color of night, uncombed and ruffled. He wore wrinkled jeans and a black leather jacket.

Seven would never be that postmodern Shakespeare, would never author the romantic notion deemed the Great American Novel. He enjoyed the journey down a story-shaped hole, fascinated at where the tale began, where it ended, and all the stuff in the middle. He believed stories were alive, that writing equaled evolution, and he wrote because he had to.

Seven knew the truth, and the First Truth according to Father Notion was this: *They* were out there, beyond the stars and the Black, beyond it all. They were the night that hid in plain sight behind the cerulean skies of day. They were *Them*, the Other. But They weren't real; fiction was Their form. And yet he felt Them watching and waiting, a beast made of a million eyes, a thousand faceless horrors streaming in his blood. Yes, They were the inherent evil that dwelled in all mystery, the relentless hunger that thrived in the unknown, and if Seven didn't persist in writing, he knew They'd swallow the world whole.

The Authors—*They* were the adversary that bound Father Notion captive at the Center of the Moon. But how did one fight such a beast? Well, Their defeat hid in the Second Truth of Father Notion. Killing The Authors hinged on Seven's final novel, *Tetragrammar*.

Tetragrammar was to be his masterwork, his narrative weapon against Them. Whether it harnessed some monumental threat, Their secret name, a revelation, Seven didn't know. And with that, every attempt in its composition culminated in soul-aching failure.

The only certainty Father Notion had told Seven, that once written, it would end their war. So Seven tirelessly rewrote *Tetragrammar* to no avail. As time passed, he cursed this damn book, this bastard child that refused to be born into the world. And, eventually, a terror mounted in him that *Tetragrammar* may never be complete at all. However, something terrified him more.

Like Dana Paris.

Seven hadn't been looking for a woman, but when fate had driven them together, Paris had become a welcome change. A woman was a detour, a distraction, a hiatus from despair, and he would discover brief moments of liberation from his crisis of words. At first, Paris was a possible spark in his creative drought; however, whatever he and Paris had now was messy.

Like all relationships, their Golden Age had gradually decayed, and Paris had evolved into another story he no longer understood. Failing to right their love only exacerbated his inadequacies as a storyteller. The possibility had existed that he may've elevated her into something more, and while he would pray she'd become that divine muse, their relationship had deteriorated into a romance on par with sandpaper-masturbation.

She only complicated things now, and he needed to be done with her. But he loved her and he hated her and he wanted to cut her loose as much as he wanted to keep her forever. With a failing novel and a dreary sex life, inspiration plummeted to an all-time low. He now feared *Tetragrammar* would only continue to atrophy in his mind.

Well, that was just fucking great.

And as Seven and Paris broke up frequently—stupid arguments, silly debates, quirky nuances— he never embraced their separations as an out. And he wouldn't let go either; he'd see it to the End even if the stars exploded and the world was flooded in inky apocalypse. Seven would not give up. Writers had to persist, eat and shit rejection, had to suck it up and keep writing. Quitting was easy. Any plot hole could be escaped if one had patience.

He called their last falling-out *The Black Olive Breakup*.

A pizza had been delivered to her apartment, which was fine, except Paris had ordered it loaded with black olives, which wasn't fine. She was no stranger to Seven's loathing of *Bucida buceras*. Having known better, it wasn't a mistake; it was a premeditated assault on their already rocky relationship. And when Seven had called her out, a simple dispute had devolved into a screaming match with several slamming doors and heated words better left unsaid.

As Seven had stormed off, he swore they were over, really they were. However, like clockwork, he knew he'd crawl back to her, fake an I love you, and they'd start again.

And here he was now, sitting in Starbucks at Barnes & Noble, all alone even as he ignored the distant mocking of Fable in his head. He told himself this was just another breakup, although he wanted to forget her, just move on, and write his novel. But when thinking about *that*, he could only recall the past two laptops he had murdered in a fit of rage.

Writing in this mindset would go nowhere.

While he sulked, Seven eyed the people drinking their coffees, looking intellectual as they paged through magazines and books. There were middle-aged men who probably led simple lives in cubicles, children ripe with potential, and women he could only dream about taking to bed. Yes, everyone was so normal. Not a care in the world. He doubted The City believed in celestial Authors or troubled themselves over writing novel-shaped weapons to save imprisoned fathers. He hated the world and its ignorance a little. With a sigh, he redirected his thoughts back to Paris. He began to laugh at the absurdity of his situation, thinking their relationship wasn't perfect, but it wasn't horrible either, and it had all started on rather strange terms.

It all began back when…

*

…the first dusting of winter arrived, and Dana Paris drove in a daze. Just a week ago, she had discovered her boyfriend in bed with that mousy chick from the sushi bar. Ray had told her in a frantic sweat that it wasn't what it looked like, that it was all a misunderstanding and he could explain. When Paris had waited, arms crossed, metaphoric steam fuming from her ears, hearing no feasible excuse, she had stormed from his apartment, not before keying a very bad word into the hood of his car with a pocket knife she had swiped from his counter. She had immediately called her best friend, Eve, who had assured her Ray was no loss in the grand scheme.

Sure, Ray was no prize, but he wanted to be in a band and he kept going on about how selling goji juice was the next big thing, and just you wait, Dana, this is my break. She hadn't been in love with him, but she found the idea of starting another relationship daunting, wishing to avoid a dating pool she feared was becoming more contaminated each year.

Paris lit a cigarette and cracked a window while Florence and the Machine blared. She already passed Target and the movie theatre. One mile further she cruised past an empty farmhouse then the familiar battered stop sign. She knew the road would fork and she'd go right. She knew it so monotonously well that she didn't think twice about taking her car around the bend.

It happened quickly. Something dark ambled across the street.

She hit it.

She slammed her brakes, buckled forward, seatbelt tight around her chest, realizing that time does slow in those dramatic moments of one's life. During that eternity, Paris heard the seismic thud against her windshield, the violent tumbling on her roof, and the squeal of her brakes as she jerked at the steering wheel. Her car skidded on the wet road, and when at a full stop, her hands froze clenched on the wheel, knuckles white with fear. She exhaled long and hard, teeth gripping down on the cigarette. She blinked several times as reality set in. She silenced Florence Welch who sang about the dog days of summer.

Paris wondered if she remained in the car, if she meditated with enough intention, could she will herself to be anywhere but here? She began to laugh raucously for a moment, because no amount of meditation in the yoga classes she taught could ever fix this unsavory dilemma. She realized her windshield as the snow accumulated on it remained miraculously intact, not one crack to prove the incident ever occurred.

I hit a deer, she told herself, *that was all, just a man-shaped deer with human arms and legs and, oh, fuck, I hope he's alive…*

She put the car in park, left it running where it sat half off road, praying no one would take the bend too sharp. She turned on her four-ways, unbuckled, counted one, two, three before stepping out. She flicked her cigarette onto the ground.

The snow began to fall heavier in fluffy balls of frosty wetness. She zipped up her olive-green winter coat and carried her phone prayer-like around her heart. Her breath steamed the air. Snow crunched underfoot. She spotted a body sprawled on its back in the middle of the road. The world seemed eerily brighter, each flake illuminated in silver under an obscenely full Moon. She looked up at the Moon, swearing it looked much larger and closer to the earth than it had any right to be. When looking back at her victim, her jaw dropped. Whatever-it-was was already on its feet, slowly testing its arms and legs. She approached with caution, readying herself to turn-tail and flee.

"Are you all right?" she called.

He stretched his arms towards the sky, reaching towards the Moon.

Paris stared wide-eyed at the man who seemed completely undamaged. His black leather jacket appeared scuffed with salt and dirt. There was something comically intense about the man. He looked around mid-twenties with messy jet-black hair and tired eyes and boyish features. He wore dark jeans and looked too alert for being hit by a car.

The man rubbed out the kinks in his neck, stared into the sky, opening his mouth to taste the snowflakes. "They sent you to kill me?" he asked while his body swayed drunkenly.

"They?" Paris questioned.

"You're really going to act like you don't know who They are?" The man raised an accusing eyebrow.

"Oh, God," she muttered under her breath. Clenching her phone, Paris asked, "Are you hurt? Should I call an ambulance?"

He looked at her softly, and began to approach her. The closer he got, the more his features became sharp and chiseled in moonlight. "What are you?" he asked, reaching for her chin. Although common sense told Paris to back away, she remained unflinching as he touched her face. Gently, he squeezed her chin, eyeing her curiously, turning her head side to side, inspecting her. His breath smelled like freshly-printed books.

On realizing how much she didn't appreciate being studied like a specimen, she swatted his hand and backed away. "I have a knife," she declared although her ex-boyfriend's last memento remained in the glove compartment.

The man laughed. "A knife? A Dynasty threatens me with a knife? You're just going to poke me with a sharp object? No. I was expecting Them to be much more creative."

"Listen, you've been hit. You're confused," she coached.

The man shook his head. "That's my perpetual state."

"Right, um," Paris stumbled. "I, ah, are you ok?" she said awkwardly.

The man shoved his hands into the pockets of his leather jacket. "You *are* a Dynasty, aren't you? If you're not, then this is incredibly awkward," he said, suddenly baffled and uncertain. While she stared blankly, the man sighed, somewhat disappointed. "Well, you're not just a blonde, are you? I mean, you lean towards cute and you wear a human body well, but it can't be that simple." He waited, black hair collecting snow.

Paris wagged her head, starting to believe the accident caused more damage than she thought. God, she really, really wanted to not be here right now. She would've even settled for a cheap romp with Ray and hating herself in the morning opposed to this. "Look, man, I don't understand anything you're telling me, and I don't think you do either."

The man chewed on that for a moment, as if she might've been onto something. Then, squinting his eyes, he lowered his voice. "Did The Authors send you?"

"Ah, that's a hard no," Dana said.

"Hmm." The black-haired stranger tapped his lips. "I really thought They'd have done that by now."

"Um," Paris said, pursing her lips, "done what?"

"They're supposed to make Dynasties for me to kill. That has always been one of the unwritten rules. The Third Rule of Father Notion maybe," he said, like the most normal thing.

Paris's stomach dropped.

Scrunching his face, "If you really aren't a Dynasty, do you at least have any special abilities?"

Still clenching her phone, Paris crossed her arms. "I teach yoga," she answered sheepishly, "and I massage, and if you cheat on me, I'll key your car," she added, somewhat proud.

"I like yoga." The man perked up. "But meditation is a waste of time. I used to meditate. Chanted the mantras, the affirmations, stared at that elephant guy with the six arms. None of that works anymore. My writing's still shit, that is when I'm able to spew out any fucking words."

"You're a writer?" Paris asked curiously, which didn't surprise her somehow. The leather jacket, the messy hair, the wrinkled clothing made sense. There was some statement about a writer who never ironed their clothes or combed their hair.

"I am," confirmed the writer.

Paris made a huffing sound, unsettled she was actually indulging this conversation.

The writer began to roll out the kinks in his neck. "You're really not a Dynasty?" he questioned one last time.

"Afraid not." Paris shivered.

He sighed. "You're just a girl who hit me with a car?"

"Afraid so. I'm Dana." She instantly regretted using her name.

"Dana?" he repeated.

"And you are?"

"My name's Seven."

"Really?" Paris tasted the name. "Like the number?" She reached into her khakis and removed a pack of cigarettes. She lit up. "Right, well, suppose that's fitting for someone who thinks I'm a Dynasty. So, ah, like, what the hell were you doing out here?"

"I hate my life right now, Dana. I won't lie. I'm under a lot of pressure. And there's this *thing* in my head I can't release from my thoughts. It's the plight of the artist. Creating something from nothing. I don't recommend it. So I needed a break. The Moon was out and I tasted snow in the air and I went drifting," he said. "Then you hit me with your car."

"Yea, right, sorry again," Paris added.

Seven waved it off, as if it were a brush burn. "I drift a lot at night. Probably blend in with the shadows, what, with this old thing." He petted his leather jacket like it was a beloved animal. "It's what I do when I don't write and I haven't written much lately so I walk and repeat mantras in my head that tell me I can write. I know, screw mantras, but what can you do? The process has to start somewhere, and it beats Fable's bitching me out all the time."

"Who's Fable?"

"A girl who hates me."

"You cheat on her?"

"No," he said, "she's imaginary."

Paris chewed her lip. "Right. Well, that makes sense," she said, although it didn't. "Besides all that, you seem good to go, yes? You feeling ok? I mean, no hard feelings?"

"You hit me with a car," Seven said. "I've been better."

"There's that." Paris sighed heavily. "But you look good. Nothing broken. No major damage, right?" she fished, and prayed the matter resolved. *Oh, hell, Dana,* she thought. Who was she kidding? The man was clearly anything but ok.

"I'm fine," Seven confirmed.

"Sure. Sure. It's just..."

"Actually," cutting her off, "I'm horrible. Finish *Tetragrammar* for me and we'll call it even."

"Tetra-what?" she puzzled.

"The book I'm writing. My final novel."

"I'm not a writer," she said.

A brief manic chuckle escaped from Seven. "And I wouldn't expect you to finish it even if you were. Only I can. Not even the Greats could succeed in this. I have to do it. It belongs only to me." He hung his head, then glared upwards at the Moon with a deep anger brimming behind his eyes.

"I'm not an expert," Paris interjected quietly, "but if it gives you that much stress, I don't know, you could just *not* write it."

Seven shot her a comically baffled look. "Do you *want* the world to end?"

Not following the connection, she said, "I don't know. A lot of people seem obsessed with the End of the World. Maybe it wouldn't be such a bad thing?" Paris mauled this over. For a moment, even her statement stunned Seven. "So you have some writer's block," she added. "Your book has nothing to do with the apocalypse."

"If only that were true," he said.

"God, are all writers this angsty?"

"You really don't get it? Once my book is complete, it will take me to the Moon," Seven said a little too seriously. "And then it can all be over."

Paris raised an eyebrow. *All right, Dana,* she told herself, *enough's enough now.* "Why the Moon?" she just had to ask.

"Why the Moon what?"

"Why will it take you to the Moon," she indulged as nervous butterflies devoured her stomach lining.

"That's where They live."

"Fuck me." Paris flicked the cigarette onto the road. It was time to go. She was done here. "I'll be on my way, Seven. I hope you make it to that empty cratery ball in the sky. When you get there, give my regards to the Man in the Moon." Paris began to back away towards her car. "And for what it's worth, watch where the hell you walk. It's not my fault you hang out in the middle of the road." They locked eyes for a moment and she realized she'd feel much better if she just left him forever. "Well, good luck with…whatever…"

Before entering her car, Seven seemed to be almost bathed in silvery lunar light. He watched her, only moving to divert his gaze up towards the Moon.

In her car, drumming her fingers on the steering wheel, Paris refused to put the car in drive, her foot frozen over the gas pedal. When the man eventually moved, she watched him stroll down the road under the snow, his jacket glinting moonlight.

Forget it, Dana, she told herself. She wanted to go home, drink wine with Eve, and watch *Friends.* Because Paris believed in karma– she held brief funerals for bugs she killed– she didn't want any negative energy weighing her down. Hurting an ex's car was different. This Seven was something else.

"Shit!" She pounded her steering wheel. Paris pressed the gas. Snow spun under her wheels and she pushed harder until the car skidded forward. She drove towards Seven. When she caught up to him, she rolled her window down, her car crawling alongside him. "Need a ride?" she asked.

"Is the Pope an old white man?" he answered as snow crunched under the tires.

"Get in," Paris said and she pressed down on her brakes. The car kicked forward, skidding side to side until it came to an uneasy halt.

Seven stopped. "Are you sure?"

"No, but get in."

"They say you shouldn't get into cars with strangers."

"They say you shouldn't pick up hitchhikers," Paris replied.

"If I accept your offer, doesn't mean you can take advantage of me," he snarked.

"Yea. Get your mace ready. Look, this whole thing, I feel horrible about it. I mean, why wouldn't you walk in the middle of the street at night? But, whatever, it could've been worse. It wasn't. Let me make it up somehow. One time deal. In or out."

Seven nodded, walked around the front of her car. He briefly inspected where he had been hit, no signs of damage, then opened the side door. When he settled in, he glanced at Paris who stared straight ahead. "So…?" Seven said.

"This won't end well," she muttered under her breath, and pressed the gas.

While they drove, Paris clenched the wheel. She eyed the man in her peripheral vision. His clothes looked more wrinkled now, his hair messier with snow melting down his face. He puffed his cheeks, seeming very exhausted. His head kicked back as if ready to sleep, and hopefully it was that and not a concussion. And logic screamed for Paris to drive him to the hospital, to have doctors give him the clear, but she just couldn't seem to do it. Was it fear? Was she afraid of what this would mean for her? No, or yes, she couldn't explain it. Karma would adjust the scales and right her wrongs. But this strangely didn't feel like karma. The man was mad, obviously. He was confused, out of his mind, yet it didn't feel that way. An incident like this, *for him*, seemed to be his own normalcy.

And that's how Dana Paris, rational woman in a work-a-day world, would justify her actions. Just suppress conscience and common sense, because, what the hell?

Breaking the silence as she drove, Paris asked, "Where do you live?"

"Inside my body," he yawned.

"Ha, ha," she grumbled. "You're lucky. You could've died."

"Well, everybody seems to do it," Seven said.

"Right. What's your address? Where do you want to go?"

"Just drive," he said. "It's night. There's snow. And I'm in the company of a woman who doesn't want to kill me at the moment."

"Come again?"

Seven waved the question.

Paris turned on the radio. Seven turned it off.

"What's your deal anyway, Seven, if that's your real name?"

"My deal?"

"Yes. Your deal?"

"Well," he paused, searching where to start. "Father Notion needs me. They're torturing him in the Moon, I imagine. But it won't do any good. Notion won't give up *Tetragrammar* without a fight. Besides, he gave it to me and They know that. Like I said, that's the book that never quits."

Paris rubbed the side of her face. "Want to talk about it?" she humored.

"No," he said.

"Fine, just thought I'd ask while…"

"The truth is," cutting her off, "I don't know how to write it. I have no idea where to begin. I've been spinning my wheels trying to come up with what it's about, how to approach it, how to plot it. But I have nothing, and that's a problem, because I *need* to write this novel. So I walk at night, because I hate myself and sometimes I think of all the other ways to get to the Moon, but I'm afraid *Tetragrammar*'s my only ticket there."

Her stomach dropped. *Great idea, Dana, let's continue to not take him to the ER.*

Seven rubbed his forehead. "I'm tired, Dana. Never become a writer. Save yourself the misery."

She wanted to go faster and she didn't feel well. "You're crazy."

"Perhaps. And you hit me with a car."

"Just tell me where you live," she said.

He told her.

According to Seven, his home was less than ten minutes away, yet every second felt like a decade. And when they arrived at Seven's abode, Paris was surprised how such a lunatic could be admitted into the Gatewood Apartments. Sure, some of the apartments in the housing community appeared to be lifted straight out of the seventies with split levels and cheesy paneling. But there were nicer ones, too, and townhouses that someone such as a mad writer didn't seem capable of affording. Nevertheless, Paris drove down an incline towards the end of the development. Seven's apartment was shrouded behind a row of trees. She put the car in park.

"Here we are!" She waited for him to get out.

He nodded, stepped out, and before closing the door, he said, "This was fun."

"It was just ducky," Paris replied.

"Dana," Seven added, "if you find out you're a Dynasty, I'll have to kill you." As her eyes widened, Seven waved his hands, nonmenacing. "No offense," he clarified, "killing all the Dynasties is a rule. The Authors create Dynasties. They're like henchmen, you know. And you can never take out the big dog until their agents are dead." He shrugged. "Like I said, it all hinges on finishing my novel. My sweet little existential burden. Thanks again." He smiled at her, and there was a tenderness in that smile.

"Thanks for what?"

"You might've knocked me out of my rut," Seven said with a boyish charm. "You're pretty, too. I don't talk to many pretty girls who don't have purple hair." He closed the door.

She watched him walk towards his apartment. *Pretty?* Why did he have to say *that?* In Paris's experience, it was never good when a man called her pretty. That word always complicated things, and she didn't need complications. She butted her forehead against the steering wheel. It emitted a pathetic honk. She pressed the gas, tires squealing as she left the lot.

*

A week passed and Paris couldn't purge the sleepy-eyed madman from her thoughts. She often watched the Moon, and although she knew authors did not live there, she found herself smiling, because she had never met a writer before. At night, she balled herself on her couch, waiting for the stern wrapping on her door from serious men who wore blue and badges, readying to haul her ass off to prison for vehicular assault. She imagined being locked up and fined, all in the name of Seven. During her work as a massage therapist, while teaching yoga, before bed, she couldn't shake him and she feared he had become an infectious idea in her racing mind.

Was he all right? Had she triggered his insanity?

"I have to see him again," Paris admitted to Eve over a glass of Zinfandel.

"He sounds curious," Eve shrugged, waving her black bangs out of her eyes. "I'd want to see him too if I were you. What's the worst that can happen?"

"He is truly, absolutely insane, and he'd strangle me at night while wearing my lingerie."

"Sounds like my usual Friday," Eve said.

"I'm serious. What would you do?" Paris asked.

"Considering your recent fling just crashed and burned, what's the harm with a little escaping of reality? I'd go see him," Eve encouraged flirtatiously. "Besides, he sounds like a step up from the guys you're used to dating."

*

Paris parked her car at the Gatewood Apartments. Clenching the steering wheel, she thought *turn around, speed away*. Instead, she had already rang the doorbell. Nothing. She knocked. Nothing. Paris grew apprehensive. *Why did I listen to Eve?* And as soon as she decided to let it be, he answered.

"Do I know you?" He wore jeans, a fitted black t-shirt, and a surprised look on his rugged face.

She was speechless, but when he smiled, she slugged him in the arm. "Don't do that! Don't screw with me. I needed to know you're ok."

"Me? I'm horrible. No splurges in creativity. A book remains unwritten, and all is not well while They sit, smugly, in their stupid Moon."

"Then take a break," Paris suggested. "Go out with me. You eat food like the rest of us mortals, I assume. And I still owe you from the other week."

"Are you asking me on a date?"

"No," she said.

"It sounds like a date, not that I'd know what that sounds like."

"No! I want to take you out for food. My treat for, well, you know. You're not busy. Remember, you suck as a writer. I'm bored; you're bored. So let's go out."

"A date?" he asked again.

Rolling her eyes, "Would it make you feel better if we called it that?"

"It might." His chest rose dramatically. "I haven't been on many dates. At least not that I remember. Fable wouldn't mind. Meditation's not working. I've stared at Ganesh so long I'm seeing elephant-god floaters. And masturbation's getting tedious."

"Stop," she said, despite giggling.

*

"Details are hazy, but there was a war, Dana," Seven explained at the bar. They weren't the only customers in the hole in the wall. The bartender periodically checked in on them after pulling himself away from reruns of *Shark Tank*. After stuffing nachos in his mouth, Seven continued, "It was fought with inks and pens. Creativity and the imagination were the engines of destruction. And They wanted to write everything, but Father Notion wouldn't allow it. And he happened upon a special word in a meditation, and he knew this word would wipe Them from existence. Unfortunately, so did They. And that word would manifest in the pages of *Tetragrammar*. The book that's fallen on me to write."

God, he just wouldn't quit, would he? Her eyes were comical. Her expression seemed to be waiting for the punch line or for several cameras to bolt through the door telling her she'd been punked. But Seven remained serious.

"You're a broken record, you know that?" Paris said. "Don't you have anything else to talk about?"

"No," he said.

"You're milking a story, aren't you? Playing a role? Becoming the character in your own narrative? That's your game, isn't it? Some pretentious, artsy bullshit?"

"There's nothing pretentious about…"

"How hard *did* I hit you?" Paris cut him off. Then, she allowed his insanity to play out; after all, it was her fault, wasn't it? She closed her eyes to focus. "Are the Men in the Moon single?" she attempted some levity.

"They're called The Authors. And They're a single collective, I think."

"Not the single I meant."

"Wanna really know Their dating preferences, ask Them yourself when They come to eat the world," he said.

"Maybe They're vegan?"

"They feed on ideas and fears. They're metavores."

"Yep, that makes sense," Paris said.

"You know," Seven edged forward. "I've written plenty of books before. *Exiteers. My Ink Evolution. Metafriction.* They were all underrated compilations of shit, but I did it regardless." Seven washed down his nachos with a glass of water. Paris made a puzzled never-heard-of-them face. "None of those were…"

"Stop! Just stop!" she snapped.

Seven leaned back.

A silence permeated the space between them.

Paris pressed the pointed part of a fork into the table and watched the other end shoot up. For a date, if it had been a date at all, the way the fork vibrated was sadly entertaining. Resting her chin on one hand, she sloshed the beer around the rim of her mug, intent on getting it to swoosh as high as it could before spilling. She looked past the point of being bored. After tipping back her beer, she broke the silence. "Were you always crazy?"

"I've always been what I've been. This is all I've ever known. Thank the amnesia for that."

"Because I hit you with my car?" Paris dared asking.

"Because They erased my memories," Seven said in all seriousness.

"Or because my car was the universe's attempt to knock you back to reality. The way I see it, you owe me." Paris caught herself then. *Was she flirting?*

Seven's dark eyes flickered. "Would the police see it that way?" Paris's breath froze and when a smile broke across his face, he slapped her on the shoulder. "Just giving you shit."

"Let's drink more," Paris suggested suddenly. "What can I get you?"

"I like Shirley Temples," he said.

She laughed. "You're serious? I will not buy you a Shirley Temple."

"What's wrong with a tasty drink?"

"Real men don't drink Shirley Temples."

"Whoever said I was a real man?"

The cover band began to sing The Killer's "Mr. Brightside" in the other room. More background noise filled the bar, more conversations. A sporadic laugh escaped from Dana's mouth.

"What's funny?" Seven raised his voice.

Applause filled the other room and the band started to play "Float On" by Modest Mouse. As Paris massaged the back of her neck, Seven found himself staring at her. In the lighting, he realized she had a cute face with brown eyes and dirty-blonde hair.

"You have to excuse me, Seven. I've been out of sorts lately. Been through a rough patch, ex-boyfriends and what-not. Maybe I asked you out more for me," Paris said. Then, "I need something in my belly before I drink too much and I wind up in bed with some old man I mistook for Ryan Gosling." Paris raised a finger to flag down a burly, wispy-bearded waiter. And in the uncomfortably long time before their food arrived, she and the madman dabbled in painful small talk. Everything from movies to the personality of colors and how hot wings were a delicacy.

And when the waiter delivered their large soft pretzel topped with crabmeat and cheese, Paris stabbed at it. "You should meet my friend, Eve."

"Is she a writer?" Seven asked.

Shaking her head, no, "She's a phone sex operator."

"That's kinky," he said.

"She told me I should meet you."

"She's not wise."

"No. She's not. That's why I like her. She's a wild card and every bit of advice she's ever given me has never been good, and I'm all the better for it. She'd want to sleep with you, I think." Seven blushed. "Don't be flattered; she sleeps with everyone."

"Do you want to sleep with me?" he asked casually.

Paris coughed on her beer.

"I'm sorry," Seven apologized. "I'm not this forward with girls. I don't remember my last date. I mean, literally don't remember."

"You know, Mister Mad Man, I don't buy half the shit you say, but I'll tell you something. Don't change. Be all the crazy you need to be. And if your real name isn't Seven," she said, "don't tell me. I've been with Ralphs and Rays. I don't want a normal name. I've been in a rut lately. Hitting you with a car was the best thing that could've happened to me."

"Is that supposed to be sweet?"

"It's whatever you want it to be."

After departing from the bar, they returned to Seven's apartment. And whatever the night was supposed to be remained undefined. Because it hadn't been a date, not really, that left them both in a state of uncertainty. Yet Paris lingered in the doorway unsure what would happen next. Should she kiss him? No, that would somehow be the worst thing. And if Seven shared any mixed intentions, they simply didn't show. He opened his door, and Paris almost asked why he hadn't locked it, but decided against it.

He entered his apartment and looked back at her, stupidly. "You can come in," he said.

"I don't know," Paris hesitated.

"If you don't come in, I'll mope all night while I continue to not-write my masterpiece, and I'll get depressed when I read books I wished I wrote myself."

She teetered back and forth, girlishly. "Just don't kill me, ok." In a long history of stupid decisions regarding men, this was one of them, she told herself as she entered Seven's home.

There were too many bookcases lining his walls with shelves stuffed with books and comics, graphic novels and file folders and binders. His apartment smelled like coffee shops and office supplies, mixed with scents of Asian cooking oils. Several statues of Ganesh were arranged throughout his home, his own patron god of writing. A Dwight Schrute bobblehead rested on top of one bookcase. Several strings of white Christmas lights were draped throughout the apartment, over furniture and bureaus.

"What are these?" she asked in regards to his shelved binders.

"All the stories I've written," he said.

"You published?"

"No."

"Self-published?"

"No."

"Afraid of a little rejection?" she asked.

"I don't need to be validated."

"Says every unpublished author," Paris pushed.

"Stop it. I know you're fucking with me. But I don't write for some glorified ego-boost or to make Oprah's Book Club."

"Fine. Relax."

"It's just about the journey of it," his voice softened.

Paris placed a finger to her lips. "Sshh," she shushed gently. "Enough with this. Let it go. At least for now. Just let it go." And she found herself moving towards him, touching his unshaven face, moving her fingers to graze his mouth and jaw and behind his ear. She could feel his body tense, his breath held within his chest. Her lips edged towards his, and she gently pulled his ear towards her. "No more authors," she whispered, "no more Moon, no more..."

And then she pulled away, leaned back, her hand still resting on his cheek. "We're done with that. I'm over it, and so are you. I'll ask you one last question, and then we'll never speak of this again. You understand?"

Seven nodded hesitantly.

"You asked if I was a Dynasty," Paris began. "If I was, wouldn't I be aware of something like that?"

Seven shook his head.

"I really believe I'd know if I were the embodiment of a Chinese family."

"And I'd really know if you were Asian," Seven flirted. "I have a thing for those kind of women."

"What kind of thing?"

"Exotic."

"And I've always had a thing for eccentric assholes that try to be more interesting than what they really are."

"I'm not trying to be interesting," Seven said.

"I'm not trying to be interested." Paris tossed her hair.

"Am I supposed to fall in love with you?" he asked. "Is the First Dynasty the Spirit of Broken Hearts? Is that the plan? I give myself to you, and you snatch my book right out from under me?"

"Hearts break all the time," she said. "I won't be responsible when yours is the one I shatter. Besides, Mr. Writer, there's nothing original about that. You should know a broken heart is the oldest story of them all."

*

Perhaps it would've been best if Paris ran as far as she could from him. But she'd been running most her life, from family and committed boyfriends (unless they cheated). Instead, she chose to stay. The Mad Man was like a drug, a foreign ingredient that filled places she never knew were empty. Was he a substantial need, guilt fulfillment, or empty calories, she couldn't say? But as the weeks rolled on, they became two human-shaped books opening themselves to the other. And if he strayed towards the crazy, she quickly stomped it out.

Despite his Moon Authors and writing woes, Seven was interesting. He enlightened her with his passion for graphic novels and how fictional icons and superheroes were no different than the vast pantheons of ancient mythologies.

And Paris revealed she had friends in Sweden (who were not

Swedish) who believed in fairies and she told Seven that he shouldn't be surprised if she just upped and left one day to travel abroad.

They both enjoyed late night walks. Paris was appalled when black-and-white movies became gaudy candy-colored travesties of pastel shading. Seven laughed at her being a vegetarian although she loved seafood. Her extensive knowledge of German beers impressed him. She thought his fascination with Charlie Kaufman films and fiction that broke the Fourth Wall cute. She urged him to start a blog to showcase his unpublished novels and he urged her to not be friends with Eve, who he deeply disliked on a cellular level, from her potty mouth to her promiscuity to her ever-filthy glasses.

And they continued to expose the pages of their lives to each other.

Paris had lost her virginity at sixteen. Seven couldn't remember his first time, although he described his first viewing of *The Matrix* as orgasmic. Paris had been kicked out of her family's house on several occasions due to lifestyles that conflicted with views of a religious nature. Seven remembered no family to be kicked out from. Paris worked as a massage therapist and a yoga instructor. (Seven worked as a, well, that detail always faded into obscurity.) She enjoyed her work, and genuinely looked forward to contributing to people's wellness. She loved the idea of meditation, but rarely meditated herself. She appreciated New Age philosophies, although she avoided New Agers. And she suspected regrettably, she might've fallen in love. But love was dangerous and she didn't know if she wanted to fully open herself to it.

After another month of small talk in coffee shops and late night phone chats, discussing their theories on life and God and books, she said back at her place—an apartment on the second floor above the Jumpin' Java coffee shop on Sixth and Penn— "I never liked a guy enough to run him over."

"I'm flattered."

"Better than flattened." She rested her head on his chest.

When smelling her hair, he was let down it possessed no fragrance or odor at all. He draped his hands on the side of her thighs. "I want to kiss you. I know that's not the smoothest way to go about it."

"Then kiss me," she said, eyes softening. "I'll warn you in advance, it'll probably be a mistake."

"Why?" Seven intertwined his fingers with hers.

"Because you're insane. You're named after a number and you believe authors live in the Moon. You have no memory and I'm not sure if I'm to blame for that. Still, you're a lot more interesting than anything else in my life right now."

He kissed her then, pulling away just in case he overstepped his boundaries, but her hand caressed the back of his head, keeping him there. And, eventually, when they were both naked, she pushed him onto his back. In the hungry silence, he closed his eyes, dreaming of the muse she could be while he entered her world...

*

...and months later, Seven's memories returned to the present, at his table in Starbucks. Were he and Paris destined soulmates? Perhaps they had fallen in love for a brief while and life was good. Then again, like any individuals who share their minds and bodies, there were good times and bad times and times that were neither.

Regardless, all couples argued and he would make it right.

Seven left the bookstore and drifted back towards Paris's apartment on Penn Street. He would apologize again and say all the right things.

That would've been the norm, except on a whim, Seven dropped by a quirky shop that carried bizarre statues, hippy clothes, and smelled like incense. He had at first considered purchasing another Ganesh statue until spotting the ring in a glass display case by the cash register, situated between two figurines of Kali. The ring was pewter with no diamond. A dragon was etched into the surface, trailing the ring, a serpent biting its tail. *How much?* he asked. The unshaven man with too many tattoos told him. *Great, he'd take it!*

At her apartment, Seven dropped to one knee, at first to fake tying his shoe. He opened a small square box and waited. There was no misreading the gesture. Paris covered her mouth. Seven expected, "Yes," hug and kiss, "I will marry you, you, sweet idiot!"

That didn't happen. Paris smothered her face with her hands. She slapped him, a weak smack across the face. And she might've been crying as she fled into the bathroom. Seven remained frozen on one knee, uneasy about his future.

On returning to his apartment, Seven didn't call her right away. Waiting seemed best. He removed the ring from the box. It was ugly, which wasn't to say it lacked character. He traced the serpent with his eyes several times, over and over. He hoped the ring fit Paris's finger, but he hadn't thought that far ahead. He removed the ring, put the case in his jacket pocket, and painfully shoved it onto his left ring finger. It hurt. The ring was tight and painful and restricted blood flow which could not be good in the long run. He flexed and wiggled his fingers. It was completely, utterly uncomfortable. Ignoring the pain, he raised his hand to focus on the symbol instead.

The serpentine creature seemed to be coiling around the pewter surface, its jaws clenched upon its end, a snake devouring its own tail, an ouroboros. That was the shape of his life, his love and his script, failed endeavors, women and art, pageless or not, passions that would never right themselves, round and round, a tale with no end.

Godsdamn you, Seven, he heard Fable cursing him.

2

PRINCE HARMING

It was fun in the beginning. Hitting him with her car had the making of a movie script. But this was reality, not one of Seven's books. Their time together proved rocky at best with more lows than highs. And now Paris was tired. After too many breakups, the final curtain came when Seven proposed to her from out of nowhere. While waiting to teach her yoga class at night in the Updog studio, she replayed the incident: Seven down on one knee, looking at her with those eager eyes, holding that ridiculous ring. Their relationship was never marriage worthy and it was insane for him to even take it there.

The bells hanging at the entrance jingled as the door opened. Paris had never seen the woman before. The new student called herself Fable. *How unusual?* But then nothing seemed particularly normal about this Fable. Her hair was dyed an obscene violet that would've looked tacky on any other woman. Her eyebrows and lashes matched her hair. She wore a tight purple t-shirt with a lotus flower decal centered at her heart. She wore fitted yoga pants the color of eggplant with Hindu mantras trailing down the legs.

"I like your hair," Paris said.

"People usually do." Fable signed the attendance sheet. "It's natural," she said. Then, "Are you the yoga teacher?"

"I am," Paris replied. "My name's Dana." She extended her hand. As Fable took her hand, *God*, Paris gasped, her flesh felt like silk.

"I know your name," Fable stated, not letting go. And at that, Paris recalled the name Fable popping out of Seven's mouth.

"Have we met?" Paris asked. She noted the room began to smell of lilacs.

"I checked the schedule online. It said Monday nights. Seven o'clock. Dana Paris. This is the Ashtanga class, correct?"

"Yes."

"Then you'd be Dana Paris," Fable beamed. "See. I know."

Paris's stomach tensed and her hand felt hot and sweaty. And she saw that Fable's eyes were also deep, obscene violet. "Thanks for coming." Paris slid her hand from Fable's. "Small class tonight. We'll start in a minute. Mats and blocks are in the other room. And if you wouldn't mind, can you fill out a waiver? You know, just in case."

"I would mind," Fable stated.

"Oh." Paris let it go.

"Is it a hard class?" Fable asked.

"Depends."

"I'm rusty," she winked. "Go easy on me."

Paris opened her class with a chakra meditation, then moved into the physical postures. As Paris taught, this Fable flowed gracefully with the asanas. The violet-haired woman, who sometimes reminded her of an otherworldly fairy, seemed to float from her mat, binding her arms effortlessly, moving into deeper variations of each posture. At the end after shavasana, or final pose, Paris closed her class with a chant, thanked her students, and blew out the candles.

In the lobby after the others left, Fable put her sneakers on. "You looked amazing, the way you moved," Paris said. "How long have you been practicing?"

"How long is inspiration?" Fable replied.

"Excuse me?"

"Length is a notion that fails to measure time. I don't do yoga. I don't do anything. I am what I do. I am what I am." Fable shrugged. "That's all."

Paris only wanted to say "oh" but she couldn't speak or blink. And she didn't feel right.

"Enjoy your night, Dana Paris." The bells never jangled at the door opening. There were no soft footsteps on the wooden floor. Fable simply was not there.

Paris locked the door to the Updog studio. She would walk several blocks to her apartment. She would drink a beer at the tavern two doors over. She would trudge up her steps and call her best friend

Eve. Eve in her quirky voice would say she's on a date, which meant she was getting laid or high or both. Paris would hang up, fall asleep to *Gilmore Girls* on her couch, and if she woke around midnight would stagger into her queen sized bed. Paris would dream about whether or not she still loved the man called Seven.

That didn't happen.

Fable greeted her from the wrought iron bench on the sidewalk.

"Um. Hi."

"They stole his memory, you know," Fable said. She was barefoot with a t-shirt and bootcut jeans torn at the knees. There was an aggressiveness about her. And, in the moonlight, Paris swore an aura cracked spastically around her. "That's how it happened, although you could say They rewrote his mind. That would be more fitting; after all, They are Authors. He doesn't need you. He hasn't written anything in ages. He's stale and he tried to rekindle that creative spark with you."

"Who the hell are you exactly?"

"I saw what Seven did. It was a stupid thing. The proposal. He's an idiot and a romantic. Do yourself a favor. End it. Don't take him back."

"It's really none of your goddamn business, thank you. Is this a joke?"

The after scent of incense faded from the fresh night air.

"I've always hated you," Fable said. "When he's free of you, I won't hate you anymore." Fable, who spoke from a bench, was no longer on the bench. She stood behind Paris, arm draped over her shoulders, lips around her ear. A minty fragrance wafted from her breath. "It's started. Something fell from the Moon. It's in The City. It's coming for him." Fable was not behind Paris now. She stood several feet away, arms spread as if embracing the moonlight. "Make no mistakes, it will happen tonight."

What will? Paris backed away. "Did Seven set this up?"

"Don't you even dream about getting involved. He's had enough of you." Fable moved without moving at all. She stood behind Paris again. "Leave him alone. Don't reconsider his pathetic marriage proposal. Stay out of our lives."

"I don't know who you are or why he set you up for this. Trust me. It's over. I don't need any junkie-fairy in violet dye to tell me it's over. So I suggest, Miss Fable, fuck off now before I stick my foot up your asana."

"You're tough," Fable smiled. "I see why he liked you in the beginning. If you for whatever reason crawl back to him, I will kill you. I could murder you with a few jagged thoughts. Gut you with your own passions. Waltz into your mind and inspire you in ways you never dreamt. I can do those things. Just a kindly warning, little Dana." With that, her threat burned inside her skull as the woman flickered from sight.

Paris hugged herself. "Done and done, you creepy bitch," she trembled.

*

None of that actually happened, Paris justified. The woman, how she just blinked in and out of reality, the threats about Seven, none of that happened, not really, how could it?

That's what Paris told herself while she swiveled on her stool at the bar. But it did happen and when she couldn't convince herself that she'd just experienced a hallucination brought on by too much incense, the angrier she got. If she were to encounter the inhuman, why couldn't it have been a manifestation of Krishna or Mary? She would've settled for a floating Joseph and two Wisemen. The incident unnerved her and it made her want to drink. Not the girly drinks Seven liked; she wanted hard liquor and thick, piss-dark beer that left her bloated and belching.

While she drank her first Guinness, she laughed at how she loved beer more than her boyfriend, how Seven preferred sissy drinks like margaritas, and she laughed at all their stupid disputes about black olives and books. How could she ever try to build a relationship from vehicular assault and why couldn't this have been another argument? *Damn you, Seven. That proposal changed everything!*

She checked the time on her phone. Eve was fifteen minutes late, which didn't surprise her since Eve never arrived on time for anything. As she finished her beer, Paris felt breathing down her neck. Completely not in the mood to be hit on, she spun on her stool to face whoever dared invade her personal space.

The man's hair was slick black, greased up high with product. His skin was so hideously tan he radiated his own orange glow in the bar light. Everything about the man felt unreal, from the glossy clothing to the gaudy necklace to the well-manicured face, like a caricature that had been conceived underneath the creaky planks of a boardwalk. He reminded her of a guy who spent days in the gym, who prepped for late nights of clubbing. His muscles bulged underneath his t-shirt, the v in the neck exposing a waxed chest. Paris imagined him sleeping at night in a casket of ultraviolet and melanoma. His smile was wide and full of itself, and she wouldn't be surprised if he dedicated hours fawning over his reflection. A night with him would be followed by a day in an STD clinic. But worst of all, what bothered Paris more than anything were the sunglasses, those stupid fucking sunglasses he had to wear at night, because why wouldn't you?

Despite all this, Paris froze. She couldn't blink, couldn't breathe. The man was pretty, no, astoundingly gorgeous in ways she couldn't understand. And it wasn't about the looks; it was a vibe, an essence, an unexplainable attraction that compelled her to stare at him. Although Paris had never been drawn to guys like this, if he wanted her, she couldn't entirely trust herself to turn him down.

Say something, Paris thought. Finally, "Who the hell are you?" she asked, dumbfounded.

"I'm Porter," the pretty man said. "Arman Porter."

"And what can I do for you, Porter Arman Porter?"

Porter's smile stretched across his tan face, exposing teeth so white Paris wished she had her own sunglasses. "What's your name?" he asked her.

Ignore him, she told herself. Instead, she said meekly, "Dana."

"Dana?" He tasted her name. "Like Diana. Fertility goddess. Deity of the hunt." It would've sounded ridiculous coming from anyone else.

"Not quite."

"Would you prefer a traditional pick-up line then?" Porter slid onto the stool beside her.

"I don't fall for pick-up lines." And that was true. Paris never fell for pick-up lines. She didn't go soft and giddy when strangers hit on her. But this stranger, maybe tonight could be a first? She couldn't recall the last time her own boyfriend attempted to seduce her. Porter would be that welcome change. Maybe a one-night fling was the symbolic break to completely sever ties with Seven?

"Can I buy you another beer?"

"You could leave me alone, thank you," she said, not entirely meaning it as she signaled the bartender. While she tried not looking at him, she couldn't help feel his eyes dissecting her, possibly scanning what was beneath the yoga pants and shirt.

When the bartender arrived, Porter threw some money on the counter and told him to get her another drink, *Guinness, was it?* The bartender refilled her mug.

"You didn't have to do that," she said.

"I don't have to do anything." Porter moved closer towards her. "Are you ok?"

"Why wouldn't I be?" Paris tipped her mug back.

"I saw what happened."

"Excuse me?"

"That woman back there in the parking lot with the violet hair. I watched the whole thing. That must've been scary."

"Yea. Real scary. You know her?"

"You wouldn't believe me if I told you she's old."

"She looked pretty good to me."

"Yes." Porter slouched over the counter. "She's the oldest woman you'll ever meet. She's older than time and the stars."

"Is this really happening?" Paris said. "This is the weirdest fucking night of my life. I get proposed to, I get assaulted, and now you."

"You'll sleep with me," Porter said suddenly with a narcissistic smile.

"Will I?" she raised her voice over the noise in the bar. Her cheeks flushed; her heart beat erratically. And yes, for a moment, she believed sex with Porter was unavoidable actually. No matter what he said, whatever he regurgitated, no matter how ridiculous or arrogant, she'd listen.

"Yes," he said.

"Why?"

"Because of the story, Dana," Porter said. "Before the world, before the creation, there was a great release. Something needed to get it off. And she was there, the primal muse invoking the universe's first orgasm. It was the collision of two energies, the fucking of super-concepts. That's the story. It's all sex."

"Excuse me?"

"I witnessed the ejaculation of this reality. I'm a god. The spirit of the climax and you'll fuck me because you have to, to honor the first moment."

"Please go away," Paris slurred. His words, his speech was so off-the-wall, Paris questioned just how drunk she was. Because no one said things like that, no one besides Seven. She needed to be done here. Paris downed the beer and moved to stand. This was getting too surreal, a bit over-the-top, and she was done with it. However, his hand squeezed her knee while the other guided her back to the stool. As he leaned in, his eyes burned amber from behind his sunglasses, and his cologne intensified and pumped pheromone-like around him.

Although she knew she could simply walk out, understood no man could entrance her, her vision glazed over. As he spoke, she listened hypnotically. He told her how he had been with many women and it's always the same and how tonight would be different. He told her that girls were empty husks with doting stares and blind lust, and their soft flesh could no longer sustain him. As he told her this, his dirty words crawled over her, hollowing out her mind. And she understood why she'd fuck this man, that sex with him was the only way to honor the primordial climax.

On some level, some logic, she knew this was ridiculous, that she should be repulsed by him, but Paris couldn't help giggling. "You're very pretty," she said, dazed. "Shit. I can't believe I said that." She spun on her stool away from him. "What's happening? What did you do to me?"

"Nothing yet." Porter snaked his arm across her waist, and Paris closed her eyes while he moved his lips to her ear and told her all the things he could do for her, things that made her knees weak. She was falling and she should've been disgusted, but she also wanted this man, wanted to do so many dirty things to him, would've embraced him anywhere. She didn't want to wait any longer. The calling between her legs was screaming out. Her apartment was minutes away. If that was too far, she'd go into the bathroom, hell, she'd even allow him to take her right here on the bar. But before she could allow the defilement of her body, a familiar voice sliced through her trance.

"My, oh, my!" Eve announced loudly upon her arrival.

For a moment, Paris forgot where she was. She also realized she was clenching the mug insanely hard. As she relaxed, she exhaled, relieved to see Eve.

Best friend Eve. Crass, blunt Eve.

"Has the impossible become possible? Could it be my little Dana has moved on?" Eve leaned on Paris's back. She grinned whimsically when noticing Porter. "And who are you?"

Porter lowered his chin. His amber eyes peeked over his sunglasses. He looked annoyed.

"He's Porter," Paris hiccupped. "Arman Porter."

"Oh yea? I'm Eve. Dana's besty. Tell me. Why do the coolest people always wear sunglasses at night, especially in dark bars?" she asked. "Sun went down hours ago, chief." Her voice was loud and demeaning. Porter was taken aback. No one belittled him, yet her audacity was compelling, refreshing even.

"Well, carry on." Eve waved her hands. "Don't let me interrupt your plans on getting in my friend's pants."

"Eve!" Paris snapped.

"You have a mouth on you," Porter said.

"We all have mouths on us, some just know how to use them better than others."

"I use mine just fine." He sniggered.

"Please," Eve dismissed.

Porter stepped back to analyze this quirky bitch. She wasn't pretty, but she was far from ugly. She wore a red leather jacket with bell-bottom jeans. She possessed an angular face with straight black hair, bangs, and black-framed glasses; a skinny girl drenched in nonchalance with a smile that never took life too seriously.

Porter's dreams had always been filled with that violet-haired beauty. She was the muse, his prize, his entire life mounting towards this one night where he embraced her to recreate their own Big Bang. While he understood all this, some part of that dwindled inside him, losing significance as he fixated on this new element. This Eve was different and he wanted to touch her, to sample her. "I like your bangs," he said, reaching for her.

Eve swatted his hand. "He already makes me want to take off my clothes," she flashed Paris a carefree grin. Eve held a ten dollar bill up high for the bartender. She ordered what Paris was having. After downing half her beer, she shot at Porter, "I'm looking at you, and

I'm thinking you'd make a lot of men happy."

Porter nearly choked.

"I know your kind," Eve said, smiles and all, "I know what you're about. So I'm warning you, stay away from my friend."

"Eve," Paris said.

"She's not quite single yet." Eve finished her drink.

"Your friend can make her own decisions," he said.

"I'm right here," Paris interrupted.

"You look like Snooki's unwanted abortion? You know that," Eve said to Porter. "And what's so special about you?" She wiped her mouth, belched, and still managed to come across desirable.

"What isn't?" Porter said. "I'm a porter of the highest level."

"Wait a minute," Eve blinked. "Do you actually call yourself the Porter? How is it every reject from *Jersey Shore* has a special douchebag code name?"

"It's what I am?"

"Your name's Porter and you are a porter," Eve chuckled.

He clicked his mouth, *bingo!*

Paris leaned her elbow on the counter. She balled her fist into the side of her face, feeling oddly tired. Despite being reduced to a third wheel, she enjoyed the exchange. She wouldn't be surprised if in the morning she'd dismiss this night as a surreal blur.

"Did you know a porter isn't just a transporter? A porter is a bringer of disease. But you," Eve shoved her finger towards Porter's face, "you're too pretty to harbor a disease." It was clearly mocking, yet a sensation stirred below, behind his zipper.

Paris huffed. "He said something about being a sex god."

"Hah!" Eve laughed. "I wrote the goddamn Kama Sutra. Believe me, you have nothing on me."

Porter licked his lips. "You have no idea what I could do."

"I bet." Eve nudged him with her finger. "Enlighten me before you're diagnosed with skin cancer."

Porter glared. *All right, bitch,* he thought. "The universe began with a bang. A scream, a climax. I was there to watch. I was part of it." Ignoring the snickers, "Every time someone has sex, every cry and moan of passion is a representation of the first creation, a microcosmic echo." He waited for her response. Their mouths hung open, astonished.

Paris and Eve shared a laugh that could've damaged any man's ego.

"It's my knack," he continued. "I can read any person's sexual history."

"Is that right?" Eve doubted.

"Every penetration lingers in the aura," Porter said. "Every ejaculation leaves an impression."

Both women looked surprised a man could have the audacity to rattle off something like that. For a moment, Paris desired to call Seven, put their issues on hiatus, and just get him over here to meet this character. Oh, he would've loved this. Porter literally embodied something stupid and absurd from the fictions Seven conjured. And it occurred to Paris, briefly, ever since Seven entered her life, she took the strangest encounters in stride. This Porter, like Fable, could've never been real before Seven. They were merely side effects or, what, the irrational that slipped through the cracks of reality?

Before Paris could flesh out this tangent, Eve set the mug on the counter. "I think you're full of shit," she said. "I want to lose interest in you, but you've hooked me." He noticed the glint behind Eve's glasses. "All right." Eve ran her fingers along his chest. "You have me." She turned towards Paris, shrugged. "It doesn't take much. You know how I am."

"Sure, Eve." Paris exhaled. "I know."

"Tomorrow night we talk. About Seven."

"Sounds good."

"You're not like me," Eve whispered in Paris's ear as she hugged her. "You don't want this. Trust me. You'll thank me when you're not pissing fire at a doctor's office." Eve tapped Paris playfully on the cheek. "It'll be all right." She turned to Porter. "You're coming back to my place. I know what you want. You know what I want. Got it?"

Porter nodded. He bit down on his lip as this woman took him by the hand. Then it occurred to him Fable was out there and she could wait, just one more womanly appetizer before the grand finale.

Paris watched them leave. She raised a finger to the bartender. "One Shirley Temple," Paris sighed, in Seven's honor.

*

Some people collected stamps or action figures. Others accumulated shoes and purses. Some dismissed their hoarding in the name of fashion. Not Eve. Eve collected art and not just any art. She sought the strangest pieces: pictures and paintings that imbibed the speculative, the surreal and dangerous. While Eve led Porter through her dark house, towards the bedroom, he noted every wall was cluttered with art, none of which hung evenly. Every bizarre and abstract image featuring people with objects for heads or landscapes made of words and clouds; everything from Picasso to Charnine to underground artists found in local coffee shops, all of them rested crooked on the walls.

"You like a lot of weird shit," he said.

"Yes," she agreed. "It's all very surreal." *Or had she said so-real?*

In her bedroom, she stripped him to his boxers while planting kisses on his sleek, smooth chest. She removed his sunglasses with a snicker that bordered on derision. She pushed him onto his back, held his hands down at the top of the bed, and mounted him. She didn't let him kiss her. When she bit his lower lip, he heard the crack of metal and locking of handcuffs, impressed how smoothly Eve worked his wrists into bondage. Eve moved off the bed. She left the room.

The cuffs were tight. The cold metal cut into his wrists. She seemed to take forever to come back. Only now, when alone waiting for her, he noticed unlike the rest of her house, only one picture decorated the bedroom. It hung perfectly centered on the wall across from the bed. Its positioning seemed intentional, goading him to make eye contact. Looking straight ahead, Porter observed the painting. It featured a man in gray with a bowler hat. A large green apple covered his face.

Porter stared at it. It was ridiculous, but he felt the invisible eyes behind the apple burning into him. And he wanted to see the man's face for some reason. The longer he stared, the longer he couldn't make out his face; the more frustrated he became. Why did this anger him?

Porter blinked, looked away. Still waiting for Eve's return, it dawned on him that Fable had slipped from his mind. Ever since encountering this woman, she took a backseat. That was odd. Fable was the point after all, his mission. He had a very specific role. He had prepped, honed his skills. Hands bound, Porter recalled the living violet moving through his mind whenever he visited the clubs and the bars, always Fable permeating him.

Eve returned wearing nothing but her black-framed glasses, fishnet stockings, a red teddy that clung tightly to her narrow frame, and a scarlet top hat which reminded Porter of a slutty prop from a risqué stage performance. She crawled feline-like onto the bed. She licked his navel and ran her tongue up his chiseled abs, up his hideously tan chest. And she kissed her way up his throat, behind his ear. She then bit his earlobe a little too hard, nearly ripping out his hoop earring with her teeth. Finally she moved down towards his crotch, her mouth lingering over the erection tenting his boxers.

Finally!

She stopped, yawned, plopped onto the bed.

"Wh-what are you doing?"

"Ssh," Eve shushed as she cleaned under her fingernails. "Look ahead." The picture stared back at him. The man whose face was concealed behind the green apple made him uncomfortable. Porter couldn't take his eyes off it. *Why?* He wanted to see past it, couldn't.

"What's that fucking picture doing?" He tugged at the cuffs.

"It's hanging. Like pictures do."

"Why's it looking at me?" He squirmed. "Make it stop dammit!" He snapped, surprised how over the top his reaction seemed.

"No, babe," Eve corrected. "The apple covers his face. I had to have this one. How couldn't I with the apple and all?"

Where was she going with this?

"It's called *The Son of Man* by Magritte." Eve admired the painting. "As you already saw, I collect art. Local artists and random surreal pieces." She paused, reflecting. "There's so much truth in a melting clock after all." She lit a cigarette.

The impossible idea occurred to Porter that sex may not happen. "Um." Porter pointed with his chin towards his nether region.

"Yes." Eve blew smoke. "You have a dick. How original. Some men take their cocks so seriously. By the by," she continued, all the while not throwing herself at him, "my friend, she's off-limits."

He shook his head. "What?"

"My friend, she would've slept with you if I hadn't stepped in. Her boyfriend just proposed to her. Real out of the blue. They shouldn't be together, but they keep going back to each other. Hopefully this breakup sticks. Don't get me wrong, he's not a bad guy. He's a writer, unhinged, nutty. I like him although I pretend to hate him." She paused. Porter blinked. "Anyway, you exude a pheromone, I think.

Something alien that draws girls in." Eve inhaled the smoke. "That painting," she pointed with her cigarette, "me and Seven both like surreal art. Seven, the boyfriend of the girl you were going to fuck," she clarified. "You know him?"

He did.

Porter would've glared at her if he hadn't been drawn back into the painting, fixated on the hidden face.

Eve continued, "She's been with him far too long. It may have been easier if you did give Paris some of your sweet loving. Regardless, I wouldn't have allowed her to be with you."

"Jealous?"

"No," she said. "Nothing good would come of it if I hadn't interfered. She shouldn't be with Seven, but I couldn't let you take her from him." Eve mounted him. "I know guys like you. I'm like you. There's a lesson in me. Unlike all the women drawn to you like flies to shit, I won't spread my legs for you." She blew smoke in his face, then pressed her cigarette on his forehead. It burned. He yelled, flailing about.

"You bitch," he screamed. "Bitch!" He fought to break free.

"Stop." Eve twisted her lips, setting her cigarette on the bedside table. "You said you can read a person's sexual history, well, so can I?"

"No, you can't," Porter spat. His chest rose, the rage mounting. *As soon as these cuffs come off…*Porter glared. His eyes kept looking upwards to the mark on his forehead.

"I can. I'm going to release your hands. You will not attack me. You will not think of laying a hand on me." She leaned over him, her breasts pressed into his face. He heard the sound of metal unlocking. She moved away from him. Porter tugged his hands free of the cuffs. He rubbed his wrists, sat up in bed. He touched the burn on his forehead. It felt thick, scabbed over and deep.

"I've branded you," she said humorously. "I'm going to read you now." As she crawled towards him, Porter moved away. A strange vulnerability seized him as she reached towards the space of his third eye. She touched his forehead and she read…

…in the dancing shadows of candlelight, Melanie Henkshaw cried out as Porter takes her against the wall. The windows steam with sex while Amber King rides her orange-faced idol in the backseat of her Mustang. After an adult

toy party, the beautiful man pleasures two women with their new gadgets, inferior to his own tools. And it continued, a pornographic stream in her mind.

When she removed her hand, she shrugged unimpressed. "I thought you were a sex god? What was all that about witnessing the great release of the universe?"

Porter's vision blurred, a series of apple-faced men played merry-go-round in his head. He couldn't focus, and now things were getting serious. He began to doubt everything, his mission, Fable, all of it.

"Your turn," Eve said. "Read me." It was a demand, not a request. As she crawled on top of him, his stomach lurched and his head filled with a collage of sex-images of Eve. He saw men, so many men, riding her and screwing her and moving in her. Her cries of passion flooded him. As the mosaic orgy continued, he wanted to scream, and he wanted her more than anything. Under the mental attack, he could only ask, out of all these men, why not him?

"No! This isn't right!" he muttered. "You're not *her*. You're not the woman that breaks me!" This wasn't good. He needed to be at the height of his game, recharged. If he couldn't please her, if she never allowed his touch, how would he ever entice Fable? "What are you?"

"I am the first woman. I was perfect," Eve said. "One bite of an apple and the world ended." Eve moved her hands between Porter's legs, rubbing him, iron fist gripping him. As she got him off, Porter tilted his head back, gasping without pleasure. "Tell me what you are," she demanded in a hot whisper.

His guts hollowed with longing because he thought about how she would be in bed and how much, if she'd just give him a shot, she'd cry out his name. That was certain and he needed to touch her.

A force mounted inside him. "Before the light..." Porter gasped, words heaving from his lips, "I...I was the love child of the first bang, an abortion of a primordial climax. I am the Spirit of Ejaculations, an elemental of orgasms. I am the sick shit that lingers in regret. A ghost of the walk of shame. I am the bad taste in the morning after a night of bad decisions. I am the thing that erupts inside your soft, private spaces. I am the poison that festers when you give yourself over to hormones and haste. A thing that exists because you hate yourself. I'm cheap smut and internet porn and the jerk-off that flushes down every toilet. I...I...was a lie that manifested only to reenact that first wet moment with *her*." And he wept, spewing out the secrets of his soul buried in the offal of himself. It all streamed pathetically from his broken lips. And he continued to give it all up as his face contorted, wanting her to stop.

But she kept stroking him, tugging back and forth.

"What's happening?" he groaned. Her grip tightened around his cock, like a vise, and she continued to move her hand to and fro on him.

"We're cut from the same fornicated cloth," she said. "Only you keep your soul in your cock, Arman Porter," Eve said, while jerking him. "There is no beauty in that. There is only sickness and sex and pestilence. Understand, Porter, to travel we may need to shed our physical bodies. For you, this will be the most painful, you prima donna fuck!"

Porter convulsed in a climactic thrust. Black beads of sweat gushed from his skin. He was coming and coming and if he came anymore he feared there might not be anything left of him. And unfortunately, for him, that was not hyperbole. When done, Eve opened her hand to an orange orb. She was alone now on her bed. Only her and the orb that swirled with a sickly oil. Distant echoes of moaning and sexual cries emanated from it. Eve moved it closer to her ear. With a smile only Eve could wear, she opened the window.

"It's yours, lucky dove" she said to the outside, before chucking it into the night. "Don't skimp on the sanitizer."

*

The Office theme song rang from her phone. Paris answered. "He was interesting," Eve said on the other line.

Paris asked, "Did you fuck him?"

"Yea, Dana," Eve said, "I fucked him good."

3
JACKED

As if having something so clichéd as writer's block wasn't bad enough, Seven had to deal with a Paris-sized hole in his rotted heart. He looked at the ring on his finger, and he shook his head, wondering what if she had said yes.

Unable to write, he spied a stack of Animal Man comics under several ads for Papa John's. While reading the adventures of Buddy Baker, he felt a small stirring of what could've been a chapter. Setting the comics aside, he typed some philosophical meandering about time and string theory, then highlighted it, and punched the delete key. He watched an episode of *Breaking Bad,* thoroughly engrossed in the antics of Walter White and how unstable a life can be when one cooks meth to pay health bills. He paused the episode to record a page of dialogue, which came across flat. This went on throughout the night. With each hour, he hated himself a little more. And because he had nothing else to do, he stared at his laptop for minutes then hours, daring *Tetragrammar* to emerge from the blank screen, wanting to shut his eyes and never look at another white page again.

Moonlight spilled in from the windows, casting blue shadows on the walls. A breeze wafted through his home from the open door that led to the porch. The digital-green numbers from the clock on the bookcase read 2:00 a.m. Fable slept on the futon. The neighbor's dog upstairs barked incessantly until it became a pathetic whine.

He peered out his window. Moonlight blanketed the rolling hills of his backyard. Seven looked up at the Moon, unable to take his eyes off it, watching it so long until it began to drip and drip, like an optical illusion of melting light. He saw this with his eyes, but mostly he saw it in his mind. Blinking, he moved back to his laptop, to gaze dumbly at the blank screen.

And as he stared into the computer blankness, he began to see a face in the nothing, pushing its way toward him. When Seven flinched at the image, there was a man by his side leaning against the edge of his kitchen table.

"Beautiful, isn't it?" said the man. "The emptiness, the simplicity, and potential of the blank canvas."

Seven inhaled, turning to face his intruder. He should've been more shocked at his sudden guest, but he could only fixate on the throbbing around his finger, the ring contracting, a snake around its prey. Somehow all logic and rationale fell second to this.

The man wore a lavish suit with pants that were far too pale. He had no hair. His eyes were fierce and a fire burned behind his eyes. Underneath the man's jacket was a button-up bone-colored shirt with a tacky ivory vest. His aura possessed the same empty glow of a blank computer screen, only amplified and sharpened. When the man smiled, he exposed a wide grin with teeth so bright they made Seven squint.

"Who the hell are you?" Seven asked.

"Call me Divine Jack," said the man, smiling at his name. He walked towards the sliding glass door, where he stepped onto the porch. Seven followed.

Outside, Jack leaned against the railing. "Before time, before everything, there was light," Jack said, gazing towards the Moon, gesturing towards the light layering the world and the sky pockmarked with stars. He opened his hand towards the sky, to create the illusion the Moon was being held in his palm. He closed his hand, as if he had captured it, and lowered his clenched fist towards his glowing face. Light seemed to spill out between his fingers. "Then the Black came as men spilled their filthy inks across the White, defiling the pure truth with their fictions. Only the stars remained, fighting against the nothing. And so happened, eventually a heathen writer conceived to wage war against the Light. Your Father Notion somehow came about the Tetragram. In his hands, it will be twisted into a Pandora's Box and I can't have that."

Seven straightened against the railing. "It really doesn't matter to me what you can or can't have."

Jack's eyes widened with pupils that contained mini-moons. "The missing text you call *Tetragrammar* resides in you. They've summoned me here for its retrieval, a goal I share of common interest. So I ask, will you surrender *Tetragrammar*?"

"No."

Jack licked his icy lips. "I need to kill you then, yes." When Jack faced Seven, it occurred to him, he may've been lit from the inside, that his organs and blood were nothing more than light.

"Yes," Seven agreed. "That seems to be the short and long of it." He crossed his arms. "However, to get past me, you'll have to get past her, and I'm afraid neither one of us has any intention in cooperating with men who fell from the Moon."

"I'm not a man," Jack assured, "and I've never fallen."

"Regardless, I should introduce you." Seven gestured toward the door. A lavender aroma wafted onto the porch. "This is the lovely Fable." Seven introduced the violet-haired girl behind him.

Fable wore a tank top the color of grape soda. Her yoga pants were lined with Hindu mantras. She was petite with sharp features. Her purple irises were so deep they could burn out your soul. And her face was eternally young as if she showered daily in the Fountain of Youth. "Hi! Hi!" She curtsied towards Jack.

He winced at her, then clearing his throat, "All we want is *Tetragrammar*. Give it to us and it all ends. We've probed Notion's mind. We've done things to him, put him through excruciating amounts of pain. I was there. I watched. And as They tortured him, I told him about the Light, and how writers only sully the purity with their filthy inks. He laughed at me so I showed him. I illuminated him with a truth so pure it was painful. He wasn't laughing then when I reduced his reality to blankness. He cried and he screamed. It wasn't pleasant for him." Jack glared at Seven. "I could illuminate you the same way if you fight me."

"Sounds better than any date I've been on," Seven said. "But that's not going to happen."

Jack grimaced. "Notion remains alive, not by much, but enough that we'll torture him again. And we will. Interrogations thus far have yielded no Tetragram. Your notional father stored it in you, where it remains dormant. They believe it's only a matter of time before it withers and decays in you. We can't have that."

"And what will you do about it? Reach inside my head and pluck it out?" It was meant to sound facetious, yet the way Jack's eyes glittered, he had planned to do just that.

"I was the light before time, boy," Jack said. "I have my ways."

"Why do you want my novel so bad?" Seven asked.

"Light is the true face of God. And fiction is a disease. So release *Tetragrammar* to me and I'll reset reality back to its true state. Besides, has writing delivered you any joy? Has it made your life easier?"

Mulling this over, "Fable and I are a team," Seven said. "I'm like Batman…" *Fable laughed…*"And she's Robin."

"Not really," Fable interjected.

"But you get the idea. As a team," Seven continued, "we've had our ups and downs. She's been with me since I remember, by my side, when I'm inspired and when I'm not. We've already written books together; her inspiring me and me appeasing her. And sure, I've had a writer's block that won't budge, but she'll be there till the end. What I'm saying, Jack, is if you managed to hurt me, there's no stopping Fable."

"Please," Jack dismissed. "She'll be dealt with."

"I'll be dealt with?" Fable chirped playfully though there was nothing playful about it. Jack clenched his jaw as her shadow crept towards him, a shadow that felt like broken glass and razor burns. She blinked from sight and when reappearing she was seated on the railing, legs crossed, wearing a butterfly spotted mini-skirt with plum-colored stockings, her hair in pigtails.

Jack backed away.

Seven said, "She's not as nice as me, but she's prettier and she can float and she does this blink-out thing where she moves anywhere she likes. How do you do that, Fable?"

"Magic," she said.

"Magic," Seven tasted the word.

"Magic?" Jack's voice rose comically. "Truth is magic. I know a thing or two about that." A self-righteous light flared up in Jack's eyes. His face began to dissolve in a smeary glow. Balls of light burned where his hands should've been. Unable to adjust to his form, Seven shielded his eyes. Jack was changing, altering into something brighter, sharper. It all happened too quickly, like watching a movie that kept slipping frames. Only the holes in the action were filled with light. A flash and Jack faced Seven. Another flash, and he was closer. *Flash*. Jack gripped Seven's face. *Flash*. Jack pressed his mouth against Seven's lips.

Flash. He slid his tongue around inside Seven's mouth. It burned and it was the worst kiss Seven would ever experience. An image formed with the kiss. In his mind a computer screen shined into view. (At that same time, Seven saw Fable observing the action, making no moves to stop it. *Let it happen,* he heard her say.) *Flash*. The screen contained no words. It was blank with a glow that embodied emptiness and its white light expanded in his vision. Watching all this in his mind, Seven had no concept how this looked in the physical world.

Light burned around him, ensnared his thoughts, hungry light thickening over his body. The world went grainy and funny and bright. Somehow, it was raining stars behind his eyes. That's when the light hurt and that's when Seven screamed, a cold, silent scream with the raw dread of an empty nightmare.

As that happened, his terror ripped through Fable. It had all been mental and when Fable heard it, she hunched forward with her palms pressing into her temples. Jack enjoyed the pain mounting in the little woman. However, his pleasure changed when she leaned up and flashed him a smile that could cut.

"Bravo!" She applauded.

It took Jack off-guard. Yet he admired her edge. "You're colder than They led me to believe."

"I'm actually very toasty, thank you. You just have to poke around in the right spots."

Jack grunted.

Fable slid off the railing and walked towards Seven, who had somehow between *flashes* wound up in front of his computer in a trance, face twitching and contorted in pain.

"Aren't you curious what I did to your writer?" Jack asked.

"You tweaked the landscape of his mind." Fable bent at the waist, her hands resting on Seven's thighs, leaning her face inches from his, like a curious child studying the intricacies of a water crystal. Jack waited; Fable continued. "You set off a blank page template of cosmic proportions in his head. An image especially painful for those who make art. Overwhelming, sure, but in its reduced simplicity, it's a beginning and you can't murder something fully with a beginning, not without always creating something new. I know you're using your light to scan him for our little divine book."

Jack frowned.

"See. I know all this," Fable said confidently. "I know The Authors dwell in the Moon and They've captured Father Notion. I know this whole story revolves around Seven composing his last book. And I know the Dynasties are nothing more than Their lackeys. I've watched the Moon and waited for the day The Authors finally sent one of their agents to come after *Tetragrammar*. Now that that day's arrived, well, let's say finally encountering a Dynasty is a bit underwhelming." Fable crossed her legs. Where her hands had once been, she now drank from an oblong-shaped glass of wine. "You're a stepping stone, Jack. You can't beat us. You can't hurt us. You're already a corpse; you just don't know it. Our story ends in the Moon. Before that, it's only getting there."

"You're mistaken," Jack said. "Your writer's broken. And after I remove the book, he'll thank me, that is, if I decide to wake him from his coma."

His threat invoked little reaction. "He's a fool, you know, and I love him. But I hate him, too." She shrugged. "You can't hurt him like that. Seven's been staring at blank screens far too long. He's at home with nothing. You can never take his book away. No matter how frustrated or beat up, *Tetragrammar* is still his story. Not yours. Not Theirs. And he'll see it through to the end no matter how long it takes. Besides, if I had to guess, *Tetragrammar* isn't a book. Not really. It is, but it's also a door and a book without being either. It's just a metaphor like you," she added.

"Metaphor?" he gnashed his teeth. "I've never understood writers."

"Funny that, seeing you've aligned yourself with The Authors."

"They're not really authors. It's a name of irony. Anyway, let's talk metaphors. There was only ever light. Then people got creative. They conjured myth and religion, painted on cave walls. Crawled onto land, resurrected fake churches, wrote and sang as if the Light wasn't enough! The world doesn't need art. Father Notion and his written war mocks divinity. All your nonsense perpetuates the Dark." Jack placed his hands into a prayer. "This desire to create is a sickness. You are dangerous, little muse, as art tends to be."

A light grew behind Jack, angry and hungry. "People continue to pervert the Light with crude names like Big Bang and Second Coming." Jack twisted his face. "You're a whore of the aesthetic and it's fitting for you to face off against the Porter." Jack revealed an empty hand, palm glowing. He closed it. When he reopened his hand, he rolled an orange orb between his thumb and finger. Ink-black swirled inside it. "This contains the soul of the First Dynasty. He was called the Porter. He once looked like a golden man, a flawed creature who believed he embodied the first release before the Light. The reality being Arman Porter was nothing more than a sexual virus."

"He sounds kinky," Fable said bemused.

"Keep smiling." Jack grinned coyly. "See where your arrogance gets you, especially when I've beaten you. Seven's done. I've already absorbed the book. However, if *Tetragrammar* lingers in the imaginal realms, as its guardian, by breaking you, we break him further."

"You could never break me."

Jack extended his hand. The orange orb swirling with a pestilent ink rested in his palm. "Never say never, little muse. It's already done. Light always wins." And as he said that, Fable thought perhaps there was a witty threat she could sling his way. Instead, she only watched him chuck the orb at her feet.

If that sphere really contained the soul of the First Dynasty, this Porter, then she'd like to meet him. And she would get that chance, as the orb shattered on the floor, spilling out its contents. A liquid black whirled about her, impairing her senses. As that happened, even Fable was at a loss for words.

*

It was as if a bomb went off, or an idea of a bomb. Fable coughed on an explosive mist. Shielding her mouth, she waved the smoke away. The world appeared pixilated and leeched of color, altogether *less*. It was like she'd been displaced in a grainy film, only tinted in shades of murky orange. The air reeked of stale sex and cologne. Her mouth tasted as if she'd been chewing on condoms.

But most of all, somehow the explosion had propelled her elsewhere. She was in Seven's home, sort of, only this version had shifted into another frequency, another hue, and Fable told herself this was not happening. And it wasn't. Not really.

There was no Seven, no Jack. But she wasn't alone. The heavy clunk of footsteps sounded on the floor. An orange light blossomed in her mind's eye, spreading through her. And the light began to shape itself into a man and the man stalked towards her. Although she couldn't see his face, she knew that she was possibly gazing upon the most beautiful male in existence. But he wasn't pretty; he was foul and ugly. While his face remained blurred, every muscle was chiseled on his tone body. A tan glow surrounded the man. A mist pumped around him, invading the world and her senses. She fought against the infectious pheromones that streamed from his sienna aura. A fiery itch burned in her pants, moving higher up her spine, branching into her limbs. Her movement grew labored. A foul odor crawled up her nostrils. A cologne scent coursed around her thighs, expanding between her legs.

Fable gagged.

"Before the light, there was a scream," Porter said. "Before the scream, there was sex, and then there was everything. I witnessed it. Read it. Ever since, I've tried to reenact the first climax, but the women, after I fucked them, as they yelped in passion, their cries were so distant, so faint. Their screams never brought justice." As the orange man said this, she saw his eyes open and then she saw more eyes open. Fable couldn't tell why the eyes threw her off, that was until she understood the eyes were female, with long lashes and eyeliner, and they floated disembodied about the Porter. "I became addicted to reliving that moment," he said. "I knew a woman was out there, a greater vessel. You," a finger stabbed her way, "are the woman of my dreams."

A sensation of pins and needles throbbed in her jeans. Fable rubbed her knees together. The region around her genitalia burned. A fire rose in her groin. She pressed her forearms around her ears and she gasped, tried to scream, couldn't. And if Fable didn't move, vanish, do anything, it wouldn't be good. She sensed her body shutting down with Porter's mist, his essence like an airborne drug.

Fable clocked him in the face. Porter cocked his head sideways, and he winced, not in pain, but pleasure. Disembodied eyes fluttered around him.

"My entire life I've slept with so many women," Porter said. "They were blessed to feed upon my seed. Me, their fornicated god, fucked on and fueled by lust! It was sex and energy and they needed me to fill the holes in their lives." He looked at her with a deep guilt in those hollow, orange sockets where his eyes should've been. "Don't be jealous."

She hit him again, each blow arousing him. His muscles thickened, and his smile, *God*, the smile was so disgustingly full of itself. Eventually, he caught her next punch. The eyes bathing his aura winked at her. He pulled her towards him and held her tightly. Squeezing her, his essence continued to seep into her like some sleazy osmosis. And around her she saw sly, female lips blooming about him. The mouths twisted in sexual groans, emitting orgasmic cries and moans.

"Every nightclub and bar, every screaming woman," Porter said, "it was always you I saw in the climax. Visions of violet, the girl made of magic. Before I manifested in this city, I'd sit at the dawn of time, and I watched the primal release of the universe, like divine smut on the scale of celestial gods. And I evolved into its spirit, a porter of conception. My destiny is to recreate that moment, and to do that the perfect woman is needed. *You're* that woman. That divine muse. And when we make love, when I fuck you, we'll release the apocalypse. We'll be the forebearers of a new reality."

He hit her then.

She fell back. The world was sucking her dry, eating her power and magic. Porter grabbed a clump of her hair. Although she wasn't on the Moon, she was being dragged across a craggy, pockmarked surface that might've felt like the Moon, towards a bed shaped like a giant lotus flower. Mud leaked around its base. Porter threw Fable onto the lotus-bed. She landed hard, trying to get her bearings, but Porter was already on her.

His cancerous aura caressed her face, down her neck, further even. He pressed his face into her ruffled hair. Sliding his hands over her, the sneering lips around him chanted *muv, muv*, each mouth out of sync. As the mantra grew, Fable squeezed her eyes shut at a rawness between her legs, spreading upwards and inwards, leeching into her.

Porter crawled onto the lotus-bed. The violet petals wilted and grayed and shed. She kicked him in the chest, hard enough to rupture his heart. Porter rounded his back to absorb the blow. He gripped her leg, stroked her calf. She lashed out at him with any fight she had left, her resolve softening. The disembodied mouths shouted their hypnotic mantra. She wanted to fight him as every repetitious *muv* dissolved her, but she also wanted to fuck him, just open her legs and let him fill her.

Porter pinned her hands over her head, straddling her. He squeezed his thighs around her waist. His touch sickened her, and she realized his tan aura was alive, a symbiosis that licked against her. She yelled, tensed, tried blinking-out. When that failed, she spat in his face. Her saliva sizzled on his cheek.

"Open legs. Bang!" yelped one of the lips.

"Rape me," Fable hissed. "I'll rape you back. I'll kill you and..."

His face twisted, hurt. "How is your thinking so small?" Porter looked offended. "I expected more from you, my angel. We're not physical. No petty romp and grind for us." He hit her again. He clenched his thighs tighter. A rib cracked. Then other things broke inside her, things far more substantial than bones. She felt herself shutting down, the unlatching of mental barriers breaking underneath his infectious beauty, the unlocking of defenses in her mind. A void opened inside her, around her groin, an expansion of orange light filling her, feeding on her.

The chant of muv probed her. A liquid sensation moved up into her body and mind, moving in and out of her psyche, picking up speed and strength, a rhythmic pulse. And as it mounted and the stars ignited, their minds merged and their souls touched, a convergence of nothing physical, and Fable unleashed a primal scream as she opened for him and he opened for her. And, yes, Porter cried out, this had to be it: that divine scream at the climax of everything! Porter held his breath and his aura of eyes widened and the world exploded and Porter was coming, coming to somewhere, coming to the greatest epiphany, coming...

*

Seven blinked. His vision hazed over with a glossy white. He rubbed the dust from his lashes. He couldn't see straight, not at first, but eventually he saw well enough to know something wasn't right. "What the hell happened?" he snapped.

Jack remained by the sliding glass door. He shrugged with a radiant indifference and pointed towards the bedroom. Seven glared at him then dashed into the other room. And what he saw, or sort of saw, was a man mounting Fable, not moving. Seven lunged forward to remove him. Only as he touched him, the man broke apart into shards of eyes and lips. The eyes winked; the lips sniggered. And they evaporated into a stale mist that reeked of spermicide.

Seven looked about, dumbfounded. On the bed, Fable lay in the ruffled sheets, curled in a fetal mess. She looked delicate and fragile and when he touched her shoulder, she flinched as if she'd break. Fable clenched the blanket in a death grip. A watery indigo trailed down the corners of her eyes. Her pupils were scarred pin dots. "He raped me," she shook. "The bastard crawled around inside me. In my head, in my mind, in me. I…I don't feel good," Fable stuttered. "I fucked him back and now I think I'm sick."

She lunged upwards. She balled Seven's black t-shirt in her small fist. He wrapped his hands around hers until her grip softened.

"It didn't happen," she justified. "Not really." Fable trembled like a beaten dog.

"You're in shock," he eased.

"They're turning metaphors into weapons. Jack and Porter were statements, nothing more. They write. We write."

"Yes."

"He fucked me. I mean, that's what happened." She crawled from the bed uncertainly, sliding one leg at a time onto the floor. Her body gave out and she collapsed. Seven moved to help her. She raised a hand, *don't touch me*.

"Fable…?"

She waved him away, supporting herself on his dresser. "Jack's out there for fuck sake! Go kill him or something before he leaves!"

In his living room, Jack stood, a silhouette outlined in moonlight. He looked over his shoulder, dreadfully pleased with Seven's despondency. "Shutting your mind down was too easy. Don't feel bad though. How many people can say they've been blessed by Divine Jack's empty trance?" Jack looked away. "*Tetragrammar*'s mine," he added with pride.

"You think I'm going to let you walk away after what you did?"

Jack shrugged. "Yes. Otherwise, why not attack me now? Or could it be I hurt the notional son and his broken muse?"

It was true.

"All in due time, Jack," Seven said.

"Of course. However, in seven days, I will have achieved what you've failed to do your entire life. *Tetragrammar* will see the light, and I'll have written its form, in my way. If it took God seven days to create the world, then surely, I shouldn't have a problem. And when reality has been reduced to its white oblivion, we'll talk. Let's be honest though, I've already won." Jack backed away, towards the opened laptop. The bright computer glow erupted from the screen, and Jack moved towards it, into it, merging with its empty light, and was gone.

Seven froze, trying to make sense of what had happened. He couldn't, not entirely. Only then did he realize how dry his mouth was with a hollowness between his ears he couldn't shake, and he touched his forehead as if something was missing.

Seven returned to the bedroom. Before entering, he readied himself and thought of all the words he'd fail to say to comfort Fable.

She rested against the bed frame, her legs hugged into her chest, hair messy in a post-sex ruffle. She held a cigarette that resembled a small twig, and she puffed out smoky designs in the shape of the number seven. Her eyes were sunken, ringed with black. It looked like she'd been crying as inky streams trailed down her cheeks. But she wasn't crying; she was laughing. And as she laughed, she said, "I raped him back, you know. They think They fucked us, but we just fucked Them harder."

"You all right?" His voice trembled.

"Seven! Finish our goddamn book."

4
THE WEEK THAT FOLLOWED

Seven wrote to little avail, his creativity unable to muster anything worthwhile. *Tetragrammar* remained in that doomed block that made any writer question their existence.

The Dynasties had made their move and Seven didn't believe for once that Divine Jack was able to rip his unwritten book from his mind. Although if he could've liberated himself of *Tetragrammar,* would that be the worst thing? He didn't focus on the mental assaults of jacks and porters; instead, his mind drifted back towards Paris, for her to contact him, for his phone to ring, for a knock on his door, anything.

Clenching his phone like a Jack Kirby creation seeking advice from their Mother Box, Seven eventually decided to call her. She sounded tired when she finally answered, not surprised by his voice and agreed with a daunted *yes* to see him. Click. Seven lay in bed as the ouroboros ring tightened around his finger.

He stared dumbly at his phone as if there should've been more to the conversation.

"Don't do it," Fable broke his trance. "Don't meet her."

"How do you feel?" he asked dryly.

"I'd feel a lot better if you stopped pining over Paris." Fable blinked-out to reappear with her hand latched around Seven's wrist. Fable moved her face closer for a better look at the ouroboros ring. Her violet pupils narrowed on it, and she flashed a smile that could shred rainbows. "It's very ugly," she said.

"It has character." He pulled his hand away. "Leave me alone. I'm going to bed. Good night."

"If I gave you a Life Saver, would you marry me?"

"Good night!"

*

Unable to sleep, Seven stared at the ceiling and thought of how Jack believed the blank page was the ultimate truth. His ceiling was white, coated with a pasty twilight from the Moon spilling in from his blinds. He swore the emptiness taunted him. A sudden ring erupted from his cell phone. Hoping it was Paris, he sighed when he saw the name of the caller.

"What do you want?" he answered.

"You're an idiot." Eve sounded as if she'd been drinking. A sloshed man's voice babbled in the background. "I know we don't always get along, but like it or not, we are friends by default and deep down in that pathetic self-loathing heart of yours, you like me. I heard what happened and I'm offended you didn't try calling me. So, taking the higher path, I called you. We need to talk."

"We can talk now."

"No. I'm occupied." She laughed wickedly. There was movement on the other end, giggling, a flirtatious *stop it*. "Tomorrow. The diner. Meet me then. Oh, by the way, I can't believe you fucking proposed!" Laughter.

The phone went dead.

Later, Seven turned on the television. He listened to several bizarre reports from the local news pertaining to a man who declared the end was nigh because he had read all the secret prophecies found in tire tracks. Another woman was rushed into the hospital for consuming too much tinfoil.

He changed the channel.

On the internet, he stumbled upon several abnormal tweets about angels drowning in milk and a group of college kids thinking they could fly because they had glued books onto their backs. On Facebook, a stay-at-home mother stated how she devoured her newspaper because with crying babies who had time to read?

While Seven remained restlessly awake, perplexed by the bizarre travesties, Fable remembered her assault as Porter's hot breath steamed against her. And he was moving, grunting, working himself in and out of her. But it wasn't her physical body; it was nothing tangible at all. It was the idea of the act, the symbolism of it, and somehow it was more real than anything she'd ever experienced before. The movement didn't emanate from below, rather a poking in and out of her third eye, a penetration of sight.

And this was how it played out in her mind and how she fought him with her fingernails clawing at his chest and face. Yet as the flashbacks persisted, somewhere deep down, she fought less. An attitude was shifting, a new outlook towards her attacker. *How could that be?*

The first encounter with the Porter left Fable drained, a tiredness she suspected was a psychic infection, but, no, reconsidering it now, that wasn't it at all. It was only a satisfied yawn after sex. Was she beginning to crave the Porter, somehow aroused by the idea of him? Somewhere inside her, she wanted to recreate that explosive release at the beginning of time. And sometimes she wanted to share it, to spread its mad wisdom, to inspire it in others.

Fable opened her eyes, in a cold sweat, hugging her clammy body.

"Fuck me," she whispered.

*

In the morning, Seven sat in the diner on the shabbily repaired booth. He stirred the ice in his water with his chewed straw, lost in thought, when suddenly the bell on the diner door jingled. Eve staggered in six minutes late, which was good for her. Punctuality remained on the same pedestal as abstinence. "Hi-de-ho," she said, tossing her little purse into the booth and sliding in.

"Hello," Seven greeted. His hair was uncombed. He looked tired, his shirt wrinkled under his jacket.

"You called her last night. I know. Do not meet her. Leave the poor girl alone. For your own sake, let it go."

"I don't let things go."

"Of course not. So let's not ignore the elephant in the room." Eve shimmied out of her red leather jacket. "Where's the ring? Let me see it." Seven raised his left hand, fingers spread. "Is that what you got her?" She reached across the table and pulled his hand towards her. She twisted his hand to examine it like a science project gone wrong. "What is it?"

"An ouroboros," he said.

"That's not an engagement ring. That's a gaudy piece of shit you get from a gumball machine. Are you completely clueless?" Eve shook her head hopelessly. "And why are *you* wearing it?"

"Someone has to."

"Don't you find that strange?"

"I suppose, when looking at it from a certain angle."

"Does it even fit your finger?"

"It doesn't." He wiggled his fingers. "It hurts. A lot."

"So take it off."

"It's stuck." Seven massaged the purpling around his knuckles.

"Why would you propose? Like, it's not even a real ring."

"It is," Seven clarified. "Besides, she didn't say no."

"Let me see it again." Seven slid his hand across the table. Eve leaned in to examine the ring closer, removing her glasses for dramatic effect. "Oh, Seven, that's hideous." She leaned back, cleaned her glasses with a napkin. "I can't believe you proposed. It's just a bit sudden. How long you two been dating now?"

Seven told her.

"Sheesh."

Eyeing his finger, it looked swollen, a deep vein-blue, altogether unhealthy. "You should get a doctor to look at that. Or!" Eve smacked the table. "You could simply take it off."

"I could become the next bestseller. I could jump to the Moon. You could practice celibacy. Paris and I are always ok. We fight. We bicker. We break up. But we always get back together. This is who we are. This is what we do."

"You never proposed before. What was the great falling-out about this time?"

"Black olives," Seven replied.

Eve sighed. "It usually happens that way. Stupid things build and you keep sweeping issues under a carpet until there's too much to hide and then one of you flips out over a pizza topping." Eve opened her menu.

"Listen. Paris and I have been together long enough that I, *I don't know*, just thought if I showed her I was committed, I just thought that could've bumped our relationship to the next level."

"Did you really imagine it ending with those two magic words *I Do*? Your relationship began because she ran you over and thought you were crazy. It wasn't destiny."

"I agree," Seven said. "That was the beauty. Artistically, mentally, I was in a rut when I met her."

"So you fell more in love with the spontaneity instead?"

"She didn't say no," Seven added.

"No response is no. Do you even want to marry her?"

He said nothing.

"You should've asked my advice first."

"Why?"

"I'm always dating."

"You're always contaminating the dating pool," Seven said. "Look. I admire your taste in art. I think it's great you collect Charnine and Scott Mutter and what's-his-name, the guy who painted the apple-face man. But I would never ask for your advice on relationships. I piss fire just thinking about your love life. Frankly, I don't understand how you meet all the men you do."

It wasn't meant as a dig. Although Seven wouldn't consider Eve gorgeous, she leaned towards attractive. She possessed a thin face with a sharp smile. She had long jet-black hair with bangs that hung into her eyes. And she wore black-framed glasses that were large and slightly crooked on her face, a self-styled sexy nerdiness. Her glasses were always dirty with finger smudges and eye gunk, an almost intentional look for her own amusement. She also possessed a nonchalance Seven imagined was quite appealing to the opposite sex; after all, he had never known Eve to not be involved with a man.

Eve took a moment to scan the menu. After deciding with a nod to herself, she said somewhat disappointed, "I don't like you very much and I may kick myself for saying this. But you and I, we could still, you know, be friends."

"Did I tell you I hate you?" Seven said.

"Many times." Eve removed her glasses, dipped them in her ice water, swirled them about. It was her strange way of cleaning her glasses, a gesture that no longer fazed Seven.

"I also don't like that you do that," he said.

Eve lifted her glasses from the water, wiped her lenses with a napkin, held them to the light. Small bits of wet napkin clung to the lenses. She put her glasses on.

The waitress took their orders: feta cheese omelet for Seven; Eve, a tuna club.

"I want to stay friends," Eve said. "The way we bicker, you're kinda like a brother."

"That's mighty sweet of you, Eve, but I'm not looking for a sister. I just want to know if my girlfriend told you anything else."

"Like?"

"Oh, I don't know. Like she's leaving me. Like we're done-done. I'm sure she said something. She tells you everything."

"We're girls. Of course she does."

"And?" Seven asked.

"You should move on. There's gotta be a woman out there desperate enough to bang you. You're a writer, right? You could hook some young sap with that, at least long enough until they realized you're some unemployed starving artist. Or you could tell girls that you're a poet. You're sensitive enough to be a poet. Why *aren't* you a poet?" She sounded genuinely curious.

"I'm not like you, Eve. I'm not the one-night stand kind of guy. I don't hit on chicks in bars. I don't bang every girl I meet. I commit. I make love work. I don't run away at an argument. I see a story to the end. More men should be like me." He paused as if expecting some honorary kudos.

Instead, Eve squeezed a lemon into her water. The citrus juice spritzed her lenses. She re-dipped her glasses in her water, removed them, wiped them with the bottom of her shirt. After all that, she realized Seven was still glaring at her.

The food arrived.

"Oh, thank fuck," Eve said.

They ate.

Eve bit into her tuna club, a hefty sandwich she could barely fit in her mouth. She tried eating it gracefully as possible, but some sandwiches destroy all etiquette and she lowered her sandwich after a bite, leaving a smeary patch of mayo somehow on her lenses. She wiped them with another napkin. "I had this dream where there's this huge storm. Like big-ass-end-of-the-world storm. And there's all this rain but it's not rain, you know? The sky's a funny color, like pink. Not pretty pink, ugly pink, like an erasure that gets all gritty after you erase too much." She took another bit. "It feels like the end of the world. Stupid me. I'm driving. Can't see a thing. My wipers don't work."

"Your wipers never work," Seven interrupted.

She ignored him. "So in my dream I see this person walking in the rain. I stop the car. Tell them to get in. There's something really peaceful about them. Almost angelic. Anyway," Eve placed her sandwich on the plate and stabbed it with a fork. "They get in my car and we're driving and talking and my heart's beating really fast. The way it beats I swear it's going to explode. Not bad explode. Just, it's like I'm so happy to be with this person. I never felt that way before. As I wake I know I just met the thing of my dreams."

"Thing?"

The light picked up several smeary fingerprints on her lenses. "What I'm saying is it might've embodied everything I ever desired. Sometimes it felt like a he, sometimes a she. Gender didn't matter. I didn't want to do anything sexual with it and you know even the mailman could score with me. It was more like I fell in love with an ideal." She forked the last of her sandwich into her mouth. "Like you and Paris. My dream was more about falling in love with a concept. Know what I mean?"

Seven finished his omelet. "Actually for once, I know exactly what you mean."

Outside, they strolled down Penn Street. Paris's apartment remained several blocks away. Although that was Seven's destination, he found himself in no hurry to reach it. "You have this thing with Paris," Seven said. "I don't know what type of thing. Just a thing. Like you can never do any wrong with her."

"Well, whatever thing you two had wasn't working. And it should've been long enough to know whether it was going anywhere." She watched Seven staring towards the corner where Paris lived. "She told me you were more in love with fiction than her. She also said how you and she haven't been frisky lately."

"She told you about our sex life?"

Eve flashed him her oh-come-on-of-course-she-did-and-you-know-it-look.

They walked.

Eve removed a cigarette from her purse, lit it. "You should smoke, Seven. Takes the edge off." She blew a ring of smoke towards him. "It helped Dana."

"She smoked?"

"Of course she did." Eve raised her eyebrows. "You didn't know that?"

"I thought she stopped. She taught yoga."

"And?" Eve flicked the ashes onto the sidewalk.

"She eats fish."

"We all love sushi."

"She condemns meat eaters."

"I don't do that."

"She doesn't like comic books."

Eve shrugged.

"Her hair never smells like anything."

Eve rolled her eyes.

"What I'm getting at is a yoga teacher should act the part. At least, me, I act like a writer."

"You mean by being a moody hack that acts like some fake intellectual who's never published a goddamn thing in his life but claims to be a writer anyway? Sure, you act the part. And when's the last time you've written anything?"

"Fuck you." Pause. "You think Paris could be done with me?" Seven asked.

"I plead the Sixth."

"Don't you mean the Fifth?"

"Whatever," Eve dismissed. "Look, you have to know none of this is easy for her. Whatever happens just know I am, sort of, kinda here for you."

"Why?"

"I told you; you're like a brother to me, in a sickening way."

"Do you have brothers?" Seven asked.

"I had a brother."

"How did you never tell me this?"

"Not something I talk about. You kinda look like him. Maybe that's why I tolerate you."

They both stopped at the corner of Sixth. Seven gazed up at Paris's window on the second floor above the Jumpin' Java coffee shop.

"You don't have to do it," Eve said. "Go up there and you'll be taking the easy path. Leave her now. If you walk away forever, at least you'd be taking a chance instead of playing it safe."

"Making a solid commitment to her was anything but safe."

"Oh, Seven," Eve touched his face, pitying him. "Holding onto Paris is the safest thing you could do. I have a date," she said, checking her watch. "Do what you got to do."

"Maybe I'll get as lucky as you."

"Give me some credit. I have standards." Seven raised an eyebrow. "Well, I do!" Eve lifted her hands in defense. "Who am I kidding? He's as good as screwed. Only he'll be enjoying himself unlike you." She dropped several coins inside an empty guitar case by a ragged musician. "Stay away from Dana and you'll do fine," Eve said, her demeanor softening.

"You mean that?"

"No," she said as she crossed the intersection to merge with the crowd.

*

Seven purchased a cup of jasmine tea for Paris at the Jumpin' Java. He hoped it was a nice enough gesture, a steaming cup of truce that would rectify the situation. He waited far too long outside her door. The tea in his hand grew hotter each second as he just waited, staring at the door, not wanting to open it. When the ring squeezed his finger, he backed away and departed down the creaky steps of the narrow staircase.

*

"For a moment," Fable said, "I assumed you were going to wait for her. I thought you'd break. I'm impressed you didn't. If you had, I would've castrated you." Her hair was pulled into a ponytail. She wore a grape-colored sweater with an OM symbol on her chest. She seemed perkier, more awake. When Seven said nothing, his thoughts preoccupied, Fable placed a hand on his thigh. "She's still on your mind." She smiled warmly.

"I'm the prodigy of a notional man being held in the Moon with the task of killing authors with an unwritten book. I've already written short stories and novels, but I can't write myself away from her. Sometimes, I wish she'd become a lesbian and dump me for Eve. Then I could leave her. But I'd probably stay. Giving up would be easy. If every author gave up..." He massaged the soreness around his finger. "Of course she's on my mind and she'll probably remain there for quite some time. The key now is to focus more on what's relevant. *Tetragrammar.*"

"You have to get back in the game. The Dynasties are here, and they'll do God knows what to take this book from us. Now is the time to cut your loss. Paris is over."

Seven exhaled. "So what now? What exactly happened with the first two Dynasties?"

"They tried accessing *Tetragrammar* through our minds. Porter was the First Dynasty and he raped me, raped my mind. The funny thing about him was he already seemed dead. And when I felt him squirt his black pestilence into my soul it was like his last hurrah. The entire act was metaphorical, a statement written by The Authors for him to carry out."

"What statement?"

"I believe Jack and Porter were working together. Porter was a playboy; he slept and fucked with women for all his existence. He believed himself to be the spirit of some divine orgasm."

"That's ridiculous."

"Yes," she agreed. "But if Porter were to ejaculate himself into me, if he were to somehow port his consciousness into us, then he'd trigger a climax on an aesthetic level."

"He would impregnate us?"

"Yes, the birth being *Tetragrammar*."

"And *Tetragrammar* would manifest in the blank light of Jack," Seven followed. "This would happen even if Jack didn't understand that."

Fable nodded. "Remember, Dynasties are conceptual, not physical. It's the concept of Jack and Porter we have to eliminate. If Porter's stirring around in me, you'll soon feel the effects. When your creative juices start flowing again, your writing will stream directly into Jack and Jack will be nothing more than an open book for Them."

"I can guess what happens next."

"Of course. We kill Divine Jack." And she pulled his hand towards her face to glare at the ouroboros. "Now take off the ring."

"I can't." His finger looked dangerously purple.

"You're not engaged."

"I am. I'm married to a cycle, a circle, to the ouroboros." He clenched his fist. "I'm committed."

*

And on the seventh day after Jack's assault, there was a knock on Seven's door. Seven opened it. "We need to talk," Jack said.

5
EMPTY HEAVEN

Welcome to the Page Turner, a quaint bookstore frequented often by the locals of The City. If this cozy getaway for the collegiate or lit buff were to suffer premature closure, one would've blamed the trend of technology—the outdated brick-and-mortar store versus the eBook and online shopping. And perhaps, in time, that would've been the case. But, no, the Page Turner's villain was Divine Jack: The Authors' stooge, Second Dynasty, and grade-A prick.

What transpired within the paper-scented walls of the Page Turner would boil down to this: Jack missed the silence at the Beginning. He longed for the purity before the corruption of thought, prayed the Tetragram would restore the universe to beautiful simplicity. If God created the world in seven days, Jack could reduce it in one.

It all had boiled down to a war: Jack and The Authors in opposition to the Father of Notions and his seventh son. Why, this was the most important game, where the highest stakes relied on vanquishing the very essence of *creating*. This insignificant city—one with no name of its own at that—could never grasp history in the unmaking.

Jack wanted to savor his inevitable victory. After snatching *Tetragrammar*, he allowed the book to gestate in the living light of his soul. But that wasn't enough, no, he needed to better comprehend the world's inane hunger to embrace art. He knew the truth. It's just he had to gloat on those who didn't. So he decided he'd visit a bookstore, any bookstore.

He plotted it all in advance. How he'd observe people browsing through novels, reading their fictions, fully absorbed in all their blasphemous literature. He'd stew on that for a moment. And then it would hit. The infuriation of this endless indulgence in making shit up, how writers continued to muck up the great white space with their inspirations. No wonder the skies were black. The Dark was born because it crawled from the discontent that manifested in the sick inks of writers. From the first cave painting to the most innocent lyric, from *Beowulf* to *Prometheus Bound*, Odin to Bruce Wayne, Mickey Mouse to Captain Marvel, King Kong to Judas, Jack scorned every heathen who had ever indulged in or played shaper to any form of fiction.

Bibles. Classics. Autobiographies. Junk culture. Shakespeare. Patterson. Joyce. Hemmingway. Martin. King. Murakami. Tolstoy. Tarantino. It was all the same: just varying levels of shit. It made no difference how the ignorant, mortal clay deemed one work in comparison to another. It just didn't fucking matter. The City did not understand the worlds had been poisoned ever since the first story sought its tale to be writ upon the stars.

That's why The Authors had employed Jack. At least They possessed a sense of self-deprecation, what with the name and all. Jack appreciated that. But that would all end when he unlocked *Tetragrammar.*

So Jack set out to find the first bookstore he'd come across. And at 7:00 p.m., Jack waltzed into the Page Turner, to dish out his scorn and disdain, just in case the heathen readers hadn't known. Once within the bookstore, Jack wanted to spit. People rifled through books, read their zines, dabbled in their own works upon laptops and notepads.

They were like Seven, or Seven was like them. And whatever stirred them, wherever their own muses lingered, well, no, this would not do!

And, just for the hell of it, Jack would make an example; after all, *His* Illumination was inevitable!

Rubbing his palms together, a burning white accumulated in his hands. Why, no one could not notice the blazing sun that had just been born from nothing in the midst of dusty bookshelves and caffeine aromas. And he laughed as the people gazed upon him, faces twisted in confusion and fear. Jack's eyes burned and his body brightened and his light spread. He seeped himself into every book, turning every page blank with light. And, one by one, the denizens of The City pressed their faces upon the paper of their novels. How could they not? And Jack laughed wickedly as the white pages carved out their eyes and seared into their souls. Oh, yes, what a hoot?!

Upon departing the Page Turner, ablaze in his glory now, a catacomb of agonized screams trailing into Nirvana, Jack whistled pleasantly at the pain of those anointed in white. Let them rot in their literatures. It was all No-Thing anyway. If the heathens understood that, no pain would harm them. In fact, they really should've been thanking him. After all, Jack was the light of the goddamn world.

*

He was made as Their engine. An ironic statement that loathed everything They were. Of course, Jack had no idea of this. It wasn't his fault, simply his design. Sometimes a creation needed to be martyred in their own flaws. In the core of his being, perhaps Jack was the ultimate saint or an angel that scoffed off the Fiction of the Fall. He was a guru of light with a moon-charged engine for a heart, an ascended bodhisattva who loved the purity of creation so vigorously he despised life itself.

And Jack, obeying the script in his cells, did what Jack only could do: Define that elusive text The Seven had failed to bring into being. The Moon Monk closed his eyes, to focus his gaze within. For six days he sat in meditation. His contemplation comprised a colorless, blank oblivion. Perhaps he was at home in nothing, basking in his own empty glory. But he could not rest, no, for his focus needed to sharpen with razor clarity on the manifestation of the Tetragram. With that achieved, he would no longer have to *be*. Everything could retire into his light. In his meditation, he strained so hard the eyes and ears of his physical shell bled; his engine convulsed in spastic rhythms. And, eventually, his internal light carved an image upon the emptiness, and Jack knew he had witnessed his genesis of *Tetragrammar*.

A woman stood before him. She wore no clothing. Her breasts were small, the nipples hardened into purple nubs. And she didn't move, only smiled at him like he was the last meal on the day of Rapture. Jack felt himself drifting towards her, his own light world hauled into her gravity.

God, it was her, wasn't it?

The woman resembled a Fable with raven-black hair that looked perpetually wet and flesh stained like a pale moon. Before Jack could react, she delivered a passionless kiss on his mouth. She withdrew, leaving Jack catatonic, and she sneered at him.

"You want me like the Porter. But do you deserve me, little moon man?" She made a loose fist and knocked Jack on the groin. There was a hollow pang, and she grimaced at this. "Aw, well, not everyone can be Arman Porter. Not every Dynasty can be first."

The scorned words had no time to register, because the woman curled her fingers into talons, sank her nails into her own flesh, and plied her chest open like the cover of her own morbid book. From inside herself she baptized the world in her mythology. Liquid obsidian squiggled out from her insides, black ink terror screaming from her violet heart. And Jack's light, that monumental simplicity, was butchered.

Jack was screaming and couldn't stop. As he ripped himself from his meditation, it was too late. There was no divine book, no eruption of blankness to reduce the world to its empty potential. Instead, Jack cried out, mortified. All the unwritten pages were surely sullied with psychic ink, every word and letter a viral squirm upon the white space of perfection. This was not the way. The Tetragram had been poisoned. Divine wisdom had been tainted. His destiny had never been clearer. Jack would have to become *Tetragrammar*. His light would play author. Yes, it was his will to wipe the pages clean.

The glow of his pale flesh pulsed savagely. He steadied himself as best he could. But, no, this would not do. It happened, he feared. The writer and muse's tag-team corruption. As he stood, Jack realized how exhausted he was, his spark diminishing. A terrible thought seized him: had he been poisoned, too?

Nevertheless, he would play savior. His role: the slaying of devils. Yes, he would confront The Seven and Fable, kill them, reason with them, barter, he didn't know. He could only pray for the best. And, in the end, on the seventh day, he would face them, broken and battered, a wounded saint to rise in triumph. That was the martyr's tale.

*

"Hello, Jackie!" Seven greeted after Jack knocked on his door. The Second Dynasty resembled a dusty lightbulb at the end of its life. His smooth flesh was now weighed, heavy with loathing. The once vibrant suit dilapidated and faded to a jaundiced yellow and gray. "You look fantastic. Been working out?"

"You fucked me!" Jack growled. He was darker, faded, the light dirty around him.

"Of course I did."

"You poisoned it!"

"Did you really believe you could use the idea of a blank page against me? I've had writer's block longer than any writer should. It's all I know. According to you, you took my novel. So how's that working for you?" Seven waited by his open door, unable to mask the sheer joy in Jack's despair. "Oh, come on. We're not animals. My casa, your casa. You weren't shy before you popped in. So come in and we'll have tea and biscuits and I'll try to stop Fable from stabbing you in the face with a spoon." He waved Jack inside. Before entering, Jack glanced over his shoulder as if that was the road to safety. Tempting this last chance escape, he hated himself in faltering in his duty as the martyr. But that moment of weakness didn't last. Fable stood below the lamppost, wagging a cautionary finger. There was no road to escape. All paths led to Fable. Jack cringed before entering the last room he'd ever set his scoffed white shoes in.

"So." Seven plopped on the futon.

"So," Jack repeated, drumming his fingers against his face.

"So," Fable echoed behind Jack, like death sharpening its scythe.

Jack sat on the coffee table, scratching nervously behind his ear. His chin sunk forward, shoulders tense, jacket saturated with gray.

"Did you think it would be that easy?" Seven asked. "You put me in some state of shock, reach in my head, and snatch out a novel I've been trying to write for years?" Jack grunted. "For the record, what *did* you do to me?"

"Shouldn't that be obvious?" Jack kept his eyes fixed on Fable.

"Illuminate me," Seven said.

Jack licked his dry, pale lips. "The blank page terrifies you. It threatens you, shows you your own discontent. And They informed me this phenomenon, this *writer's block*, plagues all scribes. It's pathetic," Jack added quietly. "Can't you accept the beauty?" he asked. "That White embodies a certain light, a nothing-glow. There's a statement in emptiness that, if utilized, would collapse the psyche of those who need to fill pages with words."

When the dimming man finished, Seven pressed a finger to his lips in thought. "I have a patchy history, which works for me," Seven said. "It allows my imagination to fill in the holes. I could literally write my own history and no one could tell me it's made-up. Writing's what I do. But I abide by several facts. Contradictions make good stories, I think. Explore a paradox, find out why it's a paradox. You despise me, and yet you need me."

"What's your point?" Jack looked sick.

"You're no closer to reading the Tetragram than I am to writing it. You need me and Fable. She hasn't forgotten what you and Porter did to her."

Jack fidgeted. "I was the light before time, boy!" Jack spat. "Hell! I was the fucking idea of light. I was the golden child, Her Son, the rising flame. I was..." and his voice cracked pathetically. "Please..." he pleaded, "don't you see? *Tetragrammar* contains the true name of God. I...help me. Forget grudges. Just help me..."

"No," Fable declared.

"Help you do what?" Seven shushed her.

"Open it," Jack said.

"Open it?" Seven repeated.

Jack closed his eyes. "The Tetragram's rotted in you. They...They need it. Look, it's...it's not your fault. The Father of Notions corrupted it before you. You...you inherited the damage. But now...now...we can fix it. You can amend what he poisoned."

"Do not speak of him," Seven said.

Jack raised a hand, fine. He then vigorously rubbed his eyes. "Together," he groaned, "together we can decipher it."

Seven exhaled tiredly. "Do we need his help?" he addressed Fable. She shrugged. "No, Jack. We don't."

"The hell you don't!" Jack snapped.

"I never asked for this," Seven said. "But Father Notion needs me to use *Tetragrammar*. Your makers are afraid of its power. It's a word-weapon I'll use against Them. The Authors wiped my memories because of it. I remember nothing. No family. No past. I'm stuck to compose an impossible story-shaped void inside me. I don't know how I'll wield an unwritten book against Them, but I'll figure it out." Seven leaned forward, elbows on knees. "Honestly, Jack, I don't want it. I never wanted it. It's too much. I mean, the name of God in my head." He rubbed his temple. "What am I supposed to do with that?" He had Jack's attention. Very slowly, he said, "I want it out of me.

It's yours."

Jack restrained a smile.

"I don't want it, do I, Fable?" Seven said. Fable shook her head.

This was a trick, Jack thought. But deception or not, he could feel the exhaustion in his celestial engine shutting him down. Wearily, "What's the catch?" Jack asked.

"No catch," Seven said.

"There is," Fable butted in.

"Well, yes." Seven bobbed his head. "There is a catch." Jack's eyes narrowed. "We kill you, but," emphasizing the positive, "your discovery of God's name would render your physical body obsolete. You'd float on to whatever heaven you desire, and Fable and I would trudge through this lowly plane. Win-win."

Seven paused for the offer to sink in. He gestured to Fable, who grabbed Jack behind the neck and threw him down. His bald head smashed into the ground and he hit hard, his body sliding on the wood floor. Immediately, she appeared in front of him, pulling him up with a fist balled in his bleached shirt. She tossed him back against the wall. Fable said, "Even though we have no clue what the Tetragram is, we have the tools to," she paused, "enhance the sight. Now, Seven, God love him, is a bit of a fuckwit. No offense, Seven." Seven raised his hands, *none taken.* "We're supposed to be a team, but we haven't been on the best terms.

"He likes to pine over ex-girlfriends and wear stupid rings. We're like a married couple trying to teach the other to drive. Sometimes you have to step back, get a third party's fresh sight. You'll be those eyes, Jack. But you need a kick and I'll give you that." Fable touched her forehead and, kneading the space of her third eye, removed an orb. Hungry indigo swirled within its marble case. Stars danced and fireworked about it. "I call this Violet Evolution. It's a piece of my sight. You poisoned me with Porter's sex-chakra. Now, it's my turn." She held it in her hand. "Take it."

"I'd rather not." Jack wagged his head, palms raised.

"It's the only way," Fable said.

"No," Jack spat. "No, it could be anything. I'd be an idiot to take it."

"We're not negotiating," she said. "This is a courtesy before I shove my fingers down your esophagus. I give to you, freely, the gift of myself. Take my evolution because I promise you won't become enlightened without it."

"There has to be another way," Jack dared.

"You're at your wit's end. Soon to self-destruct if you don't try something. You heard Seven. We'll be killing you shortly. You prefer being here suffering, which you will be, or would you vacate this shell for the Tetragram?" Fable added helpfully. "Yes, you will take it." She clasped Jack by his smooth, gray jaw. She held the orb, nodded generously, and shoved it into his mouth. She waited for him to swallow. It slid LSD-like down his throat, into his heart, his soul; it burned electric. Once swallowed, she opened his jaw, checked to see if he really downed the pill, he had, then she plunged a fist into his gut. Jack keeled forward. She pressed her lips against his ear. "Sit the fuck up."

Fable appeared next to Seven on the futon. Jack felt like a lab rat being scrutinized by two carefree gods. He avoided eye contact, catching quick glances of them mocking him. Fable whispered in Seven's ear. He snickered.

Profuse sweat beaded Jack's faded suit from his pores while the thing that feigned his heart-engine beat violently. And then under the glacial silence of a ticking clock, it happened. The world changed. Seven and Fable's voices distorted, muted, mutated. And his feet, his fingers tingled. Jack raised his hands or rather the radiating spheres that burned around his wrists. No longer nervous or scared, the world thickened, warmed; the light glistened on every object. Everything from the futon to the floor and walls deconstructed to empty space, burning white, deep and forever.

Jack was opening, expanding, and, the light, it all came from him, glowing into the world. He was taller now and brighter, and more beautiful than the guise of the Morningstar before his hell bound grace. And he was growing, too. This made sense to him; after all, that was mythology, one's own legend – it was fitting of destiny to expand the savior. And as he grew, he tested the ground under his feet. Only he no longer possessed feet, and the earth, in all its planes, had always been a fallacy. Jack was beyond anything physical. He was emptying the world of concept, or his divine engine was bleaching all the distractions in the mind of Cosmos.

Yes!

Evolution streamed through him as the Tetragram rocketed into focus from some impossible place. Yes, yes, it was coming, opening!

He could touch the Tetragram now. It was no longer a woman cursed in the shape of a demonic muse. It was simple, so undeniably simple. It resembled a golden door, an elegant book bound in the Flesh of the Word, and it raced towards him. As it merged with him, he considered it really wasn't a door or a book at all. And opening it, he opened himself.

Before he evolved, he had almost forgotten about Seven and Fable. They were small now, insignificant gnats on the ass of creation. And as these gnats gazed upon him, he imagined it was with awe and panic. Jack couldn't let the raw terror in their eyes go to waste. That would be cruel. In his majesty, Seven's jaw unhinged, Fable's pixie face contorted, and he relished the bloodied screams that began their own genesis in their pea-brained skulls.

Seven was first. The writer darted towards the door. Jack moved a hand larger than life over Seven. What remained was a bloody smear on the wooden floor. He turned towards Fable who squirmed on her knees, crying profusely while crawling in the remains of Seven. "You killed him!" she screamed until her lungs burst. Jack flexed his mind, enjoyed the hot wet explosion from Fable's nose. The Jack-God sneered and twisted and other things broke inside her. Then he tenderly amped up the beat in her heart until there was a final sick pop. And as he did this, he asked was it necessary? And, yes, it was.

The room lurched, then thickened, brightened, and he was everywhere. *Let it be bright,* Jack announced into the void, and it was bright and it was good. And in a swift inversion of himself, he unleashed his celestial engine to bleach the world of all fiction. The God-Jack basked in its simplicity. In the Beginning was the Word, and the Word was Jack. And suddenly with no effort, he wiped the slate, a single gesture that reduced the universe to primordial emptiness.

*

Eternity passed.

Because Jack was everything, he became lost in the White. Somehow within the infinite pit of his engine, an impossible boredom festered that called to be filled. The White was monotonous so Jack looked closer and began to see the details. And because Jack was All, he became The City, which had forgotten its title. He became the continent outside The City, which, too, had lost its name. And he...

...was the world, the sun, the Moon; he was the screaming cry of Paris's orgasm the first time she made love to Seven, and he was the frustrated tears of the writer. He was the notions that drove Seven to embrace tasks he still did not understand. He became the faded letters on the keys of all laptops, the stained glasses Eve could never keep clean. He became the self-aware gonorrhea that woke to life in one of Porter's victims. He was the suicide of Notion, Andrew Wilkin's depression; he was all six previous child-scribes with circle-shaped souls. He was every star, every soul incarnated and reincarnated, every bright plant teeming with possibility. He was the force in the Moon, the travesty of paper and ink within Their prison. He was all directions, the conception of Fable, the divine lotus ascending from muck and shit. He was every violet eye that hid in sight, every tulpa that lingered in every imaginal realm.

Eventually, Jack moved past a barrier of words to pages outside the world. And the Jack-God continued to rise, higher and higher, into realms more real than reality, and rising, he witnessed all the words of the universes below, embedded in the invisible layers of eternal white, infinite texts streaming into him, and the ink-blood of creation and how there was nothing dirty about it, and how beautiful, Jack thought as he shed joyous tears the size of planets. And Jack...

...opened his eyes.

"Is he coming to?" asked a voice.

"Looks like it," replied another. "Evolution should be wearing off now."

"Welcome back!" Seven slapped his face.

Jack blinked. "Where was I?"

"I inspired you, Jack." Fable lit a cigarette, exhaled a number seven. "It's what I do. Now remember when Porter slid into my mind. He raped me. Rape," she tasted the word, "ugly word, isn't it? Rape's a fluid concept. It happens in so many forms. In a fashion, my evolution raped you, too."

"Fuck you," Jack whimpered.

Fable hit him. Something cracked inside his chest. While Jack gasped, she continued, "They fashioned Porter to believe he embodied the first climax. His mission was to explode his ego inside me through a psychic orgasm. In doing that, I would've been enraptured in such lust for him that The Authors could've slipped in and snatched *Tetragrammar*."

"I...I was God..." Jack muttered.

"I showed you everything and everything was in Nothing," Fable said. "The universe had never been blank at all. All light is full of stories and potentials."

"What does that mean?" Jack asked.

"The Authors wrote you to believe you embodied a certain symbolism, that you were the First Light," Seven joined in. "But you were never born at the beginning of the universe. Don't feel bad about that. There'll be other Dynasties and ultimately we can't confront Them until you're all dead. See where I'm going?"

"It doesn't end with you." Fable cracked her knuckles. "It ends in the Moon with my hands choking off whatever it is your authors have for a throat. When you poisoned Seven with light, you never shut me down. You never weakened me enough so the Porter could plant his virus in me. You entered my mind because I let you enter me. I wanted you there. I studied you, read you." Fable grinned.

"You're dangerous. A poison!" Jack told Fable. Then to Seven, "She'll kill you in the end."

Seven shook his head. "If anyone will kill me, I agree, it will be a woman."

Jack sat there. "They put an engine in me. And it...I...I wonder where it went." His words trailed off. "It was important, I think. I...I was important. They found me at the bottom of the pit. The stars around Them were hungry, and They told me I was beautiful. And I told them sometimes the void mistook me for an angel, but I always scoffed, because I was *before* angels. I was the Beginning. Did I ever tell you that?" Jack's dim eyes grew unfocused and lost, and he covered his face and whimpered. "I...I was the Light. I...Before I came back, I saw everything. I saw that she's not innocent, that you'll murder, that..." Jack wiped the sleeve of his jacket across his nose. He found Fable's eyes. "You'll murder me now?"

"Yes." She touched his shoulder.

"Good-bye, Jack," Seven interjected.

His eyes sparkled with moonlit tears. "Will it hurt?"

"Very much." She glittered playfully.

*

There was blood, and it was made of light, and every time they hit him it splashed brightly on their knuckles and faces and clothing. The Second Dynasty was tossed side to side, back and forth between them, each taking their time to exchange a blow, and even after Jack fell to the floor, Seven and his muse continued their assault with a pleasure that bordered on sadistic. And eventually, after they vented, the writer and his muse sat on the back porch.

Fable's fists were drenched in a liquid-light while a dimming luminescence splashed Seven's face like colorful war paint. Jack's light-blood that spattered them was beginning to dry and fade.

"That was fun," Fable said. "Jack's dead. Porter's dead. Two Dynasties down."

"I've been thinking," Seven said as he looked at his ring. "The proposal was kind of sudden. Maybe I rushed it. I can't blame Paris for being freaked out. I should talk to her."

"Why?" The light on her hands evaporated into a mist.

Seven changed the subject. "Jack seemed to believe I didn't need a muse. That I should avoid art. That I would only be driven to madness. That inspiration only brought chaos."

"He's right," Fable said. "Art will drive you mad. Art is dangerous. I'm not safe. But in the end, your life will be all the more interesting."

Fable will kill you.

"Are you going to kill me?" he asked.

She playfully ran a finger ear to ear. "Only if you kill me first."

"How do you feel? After what Porter did and…"

"Awake," she beamed, her reaction surprising him. "I was raped and now I feel completely alive. Is it wrong if part of me liked it? The unclogging. The idea of release."

Ignoring that, "Porter is dead, right?" Seven asked.

"Porter died in his own climax. It was his final act, his last dying expression."

"How do you know he's not just floating around inside you?"

"The Authors create Dynasties, which means theoretically every Dynasty remains potentially alive, just ideas lingering in the minds of their creators. That's why ultimately we have to kill The Authors. I played the victim because I knew parts of Them reside in a Dynasty's genetics. I knew if Porter was in me, I could also move into Them."

"Any luck?"

"No."

"It never dawned on me to ask, but can't you just go to the Moon? You don't need me to get there."

"I tried. I can't get there without you."

"Why?"

"Don't know. We're linked, writer and muse. And we do what we've always done." Fable clenched his shoulders with fingers like talons. "We finish *Tetragrammar.*" As she vanished, she reappeared instantly, walking the railing like a tightrope until she stepped off and was gone. She left only a glittering of mist that tasted like cotton candy, full of little smiles that grinned shark-like teeth before fizzing away in the night.

Seven shivered.

He raised a middle finger towards the Moon, at the thing made of dust and gravity. The war of authors had begun.

He replayed the years with Paris, all the small, intimate times, her bare skin against his, the way she laughed, her fake smiles. All that used to be his and he wanted to be sick as butterflies turned sour in his guts. He wanted to let it go yet something wouldn't give. It gripped him, a splinter so deep he wouldn't know where to begin removing it. And it didn't feel entirely different than an impossible book he could never write.

Clenching his ring, Paris hadn't said no, but yes had never left her mouth. It didn't matter. She was still a story even if she never wanted him again. He closed his eyes and began to cry, wanting her back. By then it was too late: the snake had him, and it would never let go.

INTERLUDE 1

The war for *Tetragrammar* would be a battle of pens and paper, ink and ideas, and it would be waged in the aesthetic realms. It began long ago when a notional father dared to eradicate Them by authoring the perfect novel, which presented a problem since no one seemed to know what this book was about. *Tetragrammar* remained an elusive void words failed to describe. And it all fell on the shoulders of an amnesiac named for the space between six and eight.

The longer it took Seven to complete it, the more pent-up frustration accumulated in the folds of reality, a frustration much like a dam that would burst if left unsatisfied.

The battle was coming. But before authors fought writers, their conflict would play out in The City's collective. In an office, while correcting papers, fixing tedious grammatical errors, English teacher Mark Nathanson would lose his mind when a swarm of punctuation attacked him.

Ali Mathews would discover her husband, a neurotic mess in the corner of their bedroom, unable to sleep because his grandmother's dementia had taken residence inside his pillow.

Another man would down an unhealthy amount of energy drinks just to stay awake because he refused to be confined in the labyrinthine-hell of his dreams where walls made of beans dripped with rancid rotting smells.

The cases of the bizarre spread throughout The City, all random people inflicted with a malicious case of the surreal. Speculations ran amuck: ruminations of an epidemic, mental infections, religious wrath.

Truth be told, it was a statement, a challenge, telling Seven to do better, to put his creative juices to good use or else.

FABLE UNBOUND

II

COLOR ME APOCALYPSE

IN WHICH DYNASTIES MARRY, LOVERS MOVE
ON, AND THE END OF THE WORLD SCREAMS
VIOLET

6
BREAKDOWNS

In his dream, Fable was naked and she was different. It was the eyes, the black fluid that spiraled behind them. "You're not Fable. Are you Them? The Authors?" It sounded crazy when he heard it out loud.

"Anything can be authors," she said.

"Where am I? What's happening?" Seven braced himself.

"Relax," she eased. "This is only one of those visions. Happens all the time. It's a dream convention and it won't be the last cliché you'll see."

"What're you talking about?"

She touched his face. "You believed They were the adversary. In a sense, They were. But They're not what you think They are. There is something out there."
She pointed in a direction that felt impossible. "Something bigger than The Authors."

"What are you doing?" he asked, not fighting her when she began stripping him.

"There's something healthy about getting off," she said. "And it's very wrong to keep all those juices trapped in the body, especially the creative ones. Stories have to flow, Seven. It's much safer if they don't get stagnant."

"Your eyes? Is that Them behind your eyes?"

She unzipped him. "I apologize if this is trashy. I need to hurry things along."

"This is absurd," Seven gasped when she placed her mouth around him.

She looked up. "Of course it's absurd. Absurdity was the point. Tetragrammar. *The Authors. All of it. That's what this book's about. Doesn't matter if it succeeds or fails, it's just absurd." Fable straddled him then. "Do us a favor." She slid him into her. "Don't think of her, think of anyone else, doesn't even have to be me. Just not Dana," she urged as she rhythmically glided her hips around him.*

As they mounted towards climax, Fable's face twisted and changed. She was Porter now, and Porter grinned his golden smile only for a moment, a moment that was far too long, and Fable, bouncing more forcefully, gasped, "I'm going to ride you until you come. And when you come, the world will arrive. All you have to do is shout it out, shout it loud!"

"Um," Seven whimpered.

"Um?" Fable puzzled, face twisting before climax. "Don't you mean OM?" she cried out.

"OM!" he screamed back as the world dissolved.

*

Seven woke with a case of morning wood that bordered on malicious. He was harder than he'd been in years, and sure, the sex dream didn't hurt, but it was more than that. Strangely aroused by a surge of creativity, he wanted to write.

It was 5:00 a.m. when Seven situated himself in front of his laptop. With a deep breath, he began to type. As his fingers danced over the keys, one page became two; two became many more. After an hour, he exhaled, satisfied at the morning's progress. Only when rereading the new material, his stomach twisted in frustration.

It was utter shit.

While eating a bowl of cereal, he heard a report on the television about a gruesome death involving a man who had been run over by a truck. The victim's hysterical girlfriend frantically explained how her boyfriend had been convinced he could use his mind to stop a moving vehicle. There was a Star Wars joke in that, Seven thought. On the internet, he read several tweets about a man's fear of the clouds devouring the sun and a woman who claimed her stomach was the reincarnation of an ancient shaman. There were many more messages laced with a quirky darkness, the same absurd rants that had been occurring for weeks now.

Weeks? he thought. *How many weeks had it been since Jack and Porter?*

Seven returned to his laptop and stared at the screen of his Word document. His hands wouldn't budge; his mind was a jumbled cluster.

He'd need fresh air and time away from his apartment to clear his head.

Seven dressed. He departed from his house around nine. Instead of enjoying his stroll, he could only think about the dread of returning to his work. Every day was another dismal reminder of his inability to structure his book. He must've blanked out because he was now on Penn Street at the corner of Third, and when crossing Milligan Lane, no traffic in sight, Seven met his second moving car.

A blur, a car horn, a hood, a thud against the windshield, the slam of his body on the road, screaming brakes, and him on the ground, inhaling skid marked asphalt.

A car screeched to a halt.

Seven didn't move, remained supine, scanning his body for broken bones, fearing his real talent in life to be a magnet for vehicles.

A car door opened. "I'm sorry about that!" shouted the driver. "You ok?"

"Déjà vu," Seven whispered. He pushed himself up. Feet sprawled apart, he rubbed the ache in his back. His forehead throbbed. Squeezing his eyes shut, he waited for the stars in his mind to fizzle away.

"You all right?" the driver asked again. He began to pat Seven's body.

Seven uttered something that might've been a word. Despite being slightly bruised, an overwhelming confusion seized him. The driver wore forest-colored khakis, moccasins, and an olive-green suit jacket. Underneath the jacket, an obscenely green collared shirt with smiley-face buttons. He wore a belt, the buckle shaped like a tree. And the greens hardly matched the...

Seven blinked.

...*bag?*

"Let me have a look at you," said the man with a bag on his head.

"How?" Seven asked.

The driver reached one hand under the bag, punched out two small holes for his eyes. The paper flared outwards. "Is this better?" he asked.

It wasn't.

"On your feet," the bag-headed man announced. "You hungry?"

*

They sat in a booth at a diner. "I'll buy you breakfast," the bag-headed man said jovially. "Eat up. Anything you want. It's on me. All of it."

"Kind of you," Seven said. "You only hit me with a car." Deep breath. "Wearing a bag."

"About that. Let me apologize again." He extended his hand. "Shake on it. It will be a let's-be-friends-shake." Seven shook his hand. "My name's Marshal Thrift. My friends call me Thrifty."

"I'm Seven."

"I know," Thrifty said.

The waitress poured them coffee and took their orders. Small talk ensued, a discussion about the weather and comments about the spotted silverware and have you heard about all the strange, strange behavior lately?

"It is odd," Seven added, sipping his coffee.

"Doesn't take a genius to observe something's wrong," Thrifty said. "One bizarre report after another. Whenever you look on the internet or the news, there's always some bystander having a psychotic breakdown. Very weird vibes, surely. A shame really that people are expressing themselves in," Thrifty searched, "colorful ways that usually end not very well. Some guy on Rozum Lane cut himself in order to map out the circulatory system of a phoenix in his own blood. There was a woman convinced she found prophecies in her Alpha-Bits cereal. She tried drowning herself in the milk in her bowl," Thrifty said. "Lucky her son saved her, called 911. When the team got there, her son, they found him wrapping the cords of his video game controllers around his neck so tight, they, well," he paused.

When the waitress delivered their food-it finally dawned on Seven-she paid no attention to Thrifty's bag, a fact Seven found odd, yet trivial. She left pancakes, home fries, orange juice, and scrapple. A conversation followed in which Thrifty advised Seven not to eat scrapple. No one knew what it was made of. Seven agreed. They ate. Thrifty sipped the coffee through the syrup-stained mouth hole of his bag.

"You like the coffee?" Seven asked.

"It's ok. You?"

"It's ok."

"All right. Out with it," Thrifty blurted.

"What?" Then, "Why are you wearing a bag?"

"That seems to be the question, doesn't it? Let me begin the answer with because I do. I had an accident in which I was terribly disfigured. I'm ugly. I'm so good-looking I suffer from narcissism. I have no head. My face is a foot. My head is backwards. My face, upside down. Maybe I'd create a supernova if I smiled. Perhaps I have bad breath and do not wish to share it. Or could it be I'm a fully evolved being and my true appearance would rupture that small apparatus people use for a brain? Whether my reasons are symbolic, metaphorical, or an attempt at a new fashion trend, I just do." Thrifty finished his coffee. He placed the empty creamers in the cup. "Besides, you should expect these things from *Them*. Three follows two after all. That's the way it works. When I am dead, die, or am killed, there will be the next." Thrifty slid from the booth to pay the bill.

Seven wiped his mouth with a napkin. He didn't seem like a bad guy. In fact, the Third Dynasty was surprisingly likeable.

While Thrifty drove, he hummed to what Seven thought was Bach. The car's interior was immaculate. It smelled heavily of New Car, a scent Seven imagined would never go away. Although he wore a bag, Marshal Thrift drove perfectly, never once crossing the centerline, never veering onto the white. He stopped precisely at each red light, never hesitated at green, let fellow drivers out when safe, and drove a perfect speed limit.

"I was rather impressed you suffered no injuries," Thrifty said.

"I'm tough. So is your windshield." Seven tapped it with a knuckle. "They never crack when I hit them. It's like I'm so insubstantial they forget to break. Besides, this wouldn't be my first run-in."

Thrifty paused at the red light, which instantly greened, and drove through a four-way. "Tough has nothing to do with it. The toughest men break in the right positions, especially when they collide with moving cars. You're far more than tough." He turned left. "Thank God you're all right. I don't know what I'd do if I injured you."

Seven said nothing.

"If you feel sore later, I can rub you. I have very strong hands." He reached for Seven's shoulder and began to knead his thumbs into Seven's trap. Seven rolled his shoulder away. Thrifty held a hand in the air as if to say your loss.

"I'm prepared you know." Seven clenched his fist. Thrifty was quiet. "If you attack me, I'll hurt you. Fable will too."

"Relax, buddy. You have nothing to fear from me. Trust me."

"I don't trust Dynasties."

"Yet you willingly boarded my vehicle with no fight. Inherently, you must've sensed my intentions were good, and here we are."

"Where are we going?" Seven asked.

"To meet my better half," Thrifty said.

"Better half?"

"My wife, stupid," he chuckled.

"You're married?"

"Bingo," Thrifty shot a fake gun at him.

"You're married?" Seven wrinkled his forehead. "When were you created?" From the backseat, Fable flashed him a confused face in the visor's mirror.

"Irrelevant," Thrifty dismissed. "Let it go, buddy."

Buddy?

They continued through scenic back roads. "These forests are pretty," Seven said. "I always wanted to live in the woods, you know, away from The City. A nice home. Nice family. A local park nearby. Trails to walk at night. Get up early. Jog. Read on a porch."

"Well, buddy," Thrifty laughed, "we have more in common than you know. I love the woods. My wife and I walk around a valley after dinner. I jog in the morning. And down the hill, a ten minute walk to a lovely park. Very beautiful. Oh, and I read on the porch by the pool, or hot tub in the winter."

"Sounds ideal."

Thrifty slowed the car as they passed several girls on horseback. The riders returned their waves with warm smiles. After several windy roads, through a stop sign and two blocks of houses, Thrifty pulled into his driveway.

"Here we are, buddy," Thrifty announced. "This is my house." He parked the car, turned off the ignition. "Welcome to Paradise!"

Paradise was a red brick bi-level. It seemed to stare at Seven from its window eyes. The shrubs in front almost waved as the wind gently blew through them. The landscaped lawn adorned in reds and greens recalled Christmas. Sure, the house was beautiful, the kind of house Seven imagined for himself. Seven gritted his teeth, because a Dynasty had a home, a wife. It felt like attending a high school reunion with all your classmates fit after the years, married with good jobs, and here you were stocking shelves and jerking yourself to sleep over cheap porn and X-Files. But then he found a stain on Paradise.

The window of the front door was broken, colorful shards of glass glinting in the sun. Seven smiled.

Instantly, Thrifty replied, "Don't mind the glass. It's called *Human Pane.* P-a-n-e."

"Excuse me?" Seven asked as they both stepped from the car.

"My wife's art project. She does that. Come on. You'll meet the artiste in person." They walked a brick path which led to the entrance. Thrifty opened the front door, pointed to watch the broken glass on the patio.

Seven felt like he was about to enter a game show or the Twilight Zone, and scratching his head, admitted it wouldn't be the worst thing if Rod Serling was under the bag.

Seven entered Paradise.

Seven couldn't shake the extreme comfort inside the Third Dynasty's home. He tried finding fault with the wood floors in the kitchen, with the peach-colored walls in the TV room, along with the large flat-screen. Metal DVD stands were filled with movies and television shows. Seven tried to hate the mud-brown sofa that was possibly the most comfortable piece of furniture in existence, tried ignoring the carpet his feet sank into. He couldn't deny the pleasant aroma of fresh cut grass from the scented candles. The kitchen smelled of cinnamon. The entire home put Seven at ease. He forgot Thrifty was a Dynasty. He even forgot about Paris.

"And this," Thrifty introduced, "is Elaine."

Elaine sat on a stool at the kitchen island. Orange, petal-shaped lamps hung from skinny beams over her head. Elaine had ketchup-colored hair, pulled back. Loose strands spilled from underneath a straw hat. The straw hat reminded Seven of a farmer's wife.

Thrifty embraced his wife. She kissed his torn paper bag. "Elaine. This is Seven. He's shy around women." He punched Seven's arm.

"Nice to meet you." Elaine extended her hand. "My name's Elaine." She wore loose jean shorts and a dirtied gray sweatshirt. She wasn't slender, wasn't chunky, just looked odd next to her tall, bag-headed husband.

"Seven," he said.

"This is a close friend I ran into today." Thrifty nudged Seven with an elbow. "He's a great guy. A writer, too. We go way back, don't we, buddy?"

"Friends are good!" Elaine clapped. "I made some friends from papier-mâché. I gathered old ads from Best Buy and Target and I scrunched them up and made people out of them."

"Now, honey." Thrifty wrapped an arm around Elaine. "Seven would love to see them, wouldn't you, Seven?"

"Sure." Seven did. He loved quirky art. "Thrifty said you're an artist."

"Ah." Elaine clasped her hands. "The front door."

"He implied you cracked the glass."

Elaine blushed. "Guilty as charged. I break things. It's a statement. Not to worry. Thrifty fixes everything. He loves housework. He's a handy man. Don't call him Thrifty for nothing."

"I see," Seven said. He didn't.

"I make things," Elaine explained. "I destroy things, too. I don't know. Art's limitless." She poured a bottle of Merlot into a plastic mug and downed it.

"Seven," Thrifty said, "why don't you make yourself cozy?"

Elaine grabbed Thrifty by the elbow. "I did something to the shower faucet." She stuck out her lip to make a sort of puppy dog face. "There's a statement to be made about a woman deconstructing a phallic symbol that never stops pissing on you," she said too seriously.

"It's all right," Thrifty laughed. "I'll fix it."

Elaine showed her teeth. "Sorry."

"Oh, honey." Thrifty pressed his bag to his wife's forehead in what Seven assumed was a kiss. "You two get to know each other. I'll be back." Thrifty walked into the adjacent hall.

"Can I get you a drink, Three-Plus-Four?" Elaine opened the fridge.

"What do you have?"

"Mike's Lemonade. Lemonade. And pink lemonade."

"I'll have lemonade."

"Which one?" She peeped her beady eyes over the fridge door.

"Mike's."

"I was just joking. We don't have Mike's."

"Oh? I'll take pink."

Elaine poured him a glass of pink lemonade. Sipping his drink, she said, "So you're a friend."

"How long have you been married?" Seven asked, waiting for his lemonade.

86

"Gosh. What a question?" Elaine finished his drink. "Time flies, I guess." She opened the fridge again and removed a Mike's Hard Lemonade and drank.

"I thought you didn't have Mike's?" Seven puzzled.

"Who's Mike?" she questioned.

Seven exhaled.

"How'd you meet my Marshal?" the Dynasty's wife asked.

"He hit me with a car. And for that, I'm going to kill him." They laughed. So did Fable. "Do you have a bathroom?" Seven asked.

"Sure do."

In the bathroom, Seven unbuckled, loosened his pants, sat, and noticed how spotless the sink and tiled floor were. And then he jumped off the toilet, staggered against the sink, and fell to the floor when a voice came from behind the maroon shower curtain.

"Excuse me," Thrifty said. Seven pulled away the curtain. Thrifty sat in the tub holding a shower head part and screwdriver.

"What are you doing?" Seven leaned against the cabinet, fumbling with his pants.

"Fixing the shower," Thrifty said.

"I was going to the bathroom. Why didn't you let me know?"

"It's unhealthy to inhibit the bodily flow," Thrifty replied. "Don't let me interrupt you." He drew the curtain closed.

Seven grabbed the curtain. "I can't go with you here. I'm not comfortable."

"Nonsense," Thrifty chuckled. He casually resumed his repairs on the shower head, stopping only when...

"Your wife's a real nutter," Fable said, perched on the sink. "What planet did you find her on?"

A sigh came from under the bag. Thrifty set his hands on his knees as he knelt in the tub. "The alluring muse finally makes herself known. Don't think I didn't know you were here. I can see you even if I can't. You're welcome to my humble abode; however, all invitations revoked if you can't behave."

"Apparently the psych ward is where to go if you're looking for a date," she snickered.

"Mind your manners," Thrifty warned firmly. "My hospitality extends to you, but I will tolerate no disrespect here." Thrifty wagged a screwdriver at her.

"I don't need your hospitality," Fable said.

"Nevertheless, Miss Fable, you will behave."

"I'll do what I wish," she challenged.

"You will not." He raised his voice. "My home. My rules. You do not fight. You do not swear." Seven expected an argument, but Fable crossed her arms and was no longer there. Thrifty and Seven exchanged a quiet moment. "Well! She's a peach," Thrifty beamed. Clearing his throat, Seven gestured to the toilet.

"Of course. Carry on." Thrifty pulled the curtain closed.

Seven stared at the curtain. "Fuck me," he said under his breath while suppressing his urge to relieve himself. He walked to the door. Before he left, Thrifty called from behind the curtain.

"Seven?"

"Yes?"

"No swearing in this house."

"Ok."

"And Seven?"

"Yes."

"Wash your hands."

Seven did. He dried his hands on a towel. "What am I doing here?" he asked.

"We're being friends. Friends invite friends over to their homes," Thrifty explained.

"It's just…"

"Look, buddy. I know you're having difficulties with your novel. Think of this as an afternoon to reawake your imagination. Put it out of your head for a few hours."

"How would you reawake me?"

"My wife, buddy. She's an artist. She'll inspire you."

Throughout the afternoon, Elaine shared several of her works with Seven. For one hour, he watched a video recording that featured Elaine falling asleep on camera. Every fifteen minutes or so, she would snap awake and begin to nod off again.

In the trees of the backyard, various action figures and Barbies hung from the branches, which Elaine explained to be a symbolic war between paper and plastic. Below the patio deck, Elaine showed Seven a microwave she spray painted pink. Inside the microwave was an angel statue covered in crusted ketchup. Elaine closed the door and opened it repeatedly. Her mouth formed an excited O. Seven nodded, *I see,* although he didn't.

For the final piece of the day, Elaine instructed Seven to take a seat on a chaise lounge by the hot tub. Elaine scurried away. She returned waving a smartphone over her head like a giddy child. A dull breeze swept her straw hat off her head, where it floated down to the lawn below.

"Now this," Elaine announced proudly, "is my performance piece I've entitled *Dead to the World!*" Seven waited. "How it works is," she explained, "you ask me questions. Ok?"

"Alright," Seven said. He shifted awkwardly in the chaise.

Elaine nodded, held her phone close to her chest where she fiddled with it. "Go!"

Seven inhaled. "Um. Ok. How did you meet Thrifty?" He waited. Elaine ignored him, continued playing on her phone. When she didn't answer, he asked, "What's your favorite color?" Elaine said nothing, not acknowledging him once. "Ah," Seven nodded, "I get it. I should keep going, shouldn't I?" Nothing. "All right." Seven tapped the arms of the chaise. "What are The Authors?"

Elaine remained silent, tapping at her phone.

"When was I born?"

Still fully engrossed in her phone, Seven played along. As he continued with questions -- *"Who is Father Notion? Will Paris fall in love with another man? Does Eve get regular checkups?"* -- part of him wondered if Elaine through some manic ADHD had become totally oblivious to him? He suspected this may no longer be an act anymore on Elaine's part, that she had managed to immerse herself in her gig, tuning out all elements around her.

"Will I ever write again? What are Dynasties made of? Does Fable resent me?"

When he had enough, he stopped, slid from the chaise, and waved his hand in front of her. Her eyes were glazed over as she sank deeper into the endless world of apps and internet on her phone.

Dead to the world.

Only did she flinch, blinking her eyes from a deep trance, when Thrifty announced from the sliding door, "Food is ready!"

Thrifty prepared spring rolls filled with cabbage, mei fun, carrots, and shrimp served in a teriyaki sauce that could've been the tastiest meal Seven ever had. Afterwards, Thrifty washed the dishes while Elaine went on the internet, in which she watched a YouTube video of a man sobbing uncontrollably as he confessed his love to a statue of Batwoman. The display was pathetic and laughable and went on entirely too long.

"Batwoman's totally out of his league," Seven joked. "Besides, she's a lesbian."

Thrifty cleared his throat while running the dishes under the sink. "Hopefully Elaine stirred some creative juices for you today. You being a writer, I assume you'd appreciate her talents. Different mediums. Still art."

"It was interesting," Seven said.

"We had a grand time." Elaine clapped.

Thrifty stacked the wet dishes in the drying rack. He moved behind his wife and massaged her shoulders. "Elaine dear, I don't want to hold our friend up. I can take you home if you're ready."

"I should be getting on my way," Seven agreed.

Elaine hugged Seven good-bye. "Don't be a stranger," she said.

*

"Your wife's interesting," Seven said as they drove through the back roads.

"She's very talented."

Seven paused. "About that. Is she insane?"

"Nonsense," Thrifty chuckled.

"With the madness that's been building, I don't see much difference with her. I mean, she's teetering on crazy."

"She's eccentric. Besides, she's protected."

"Is she?"

"No harm can or will fall upon Elaine in my presence. She'll remain safe in Paradise. I've made sure of it when the storm breaks."

"Storm?"

"The fallout."

"You mean The Authors' assault on The City. An assault I believe may be generated by you?" Seven speculated.

"I didn't want to discuss it in front of my wife," Thrifty said as they entered the highway. "The magic flowing through the world isn't particularly friendly. It's hunger magic and it began after your encounter with my predecessors. It stems from *her*."

"Fable?"

"How's the book?" Thrifty asked.

"I prefer not talking about it." Thrifty remained quiet under the bag. "What?" Seven said.

"It's crucial to move forward with *Tetragrammar*."

"I'd like that more than anyone else."

"I can assist you."

"Yea. I don't think so."

When they pulled into his community, Thrifty said, "Times will be tough for you, but know you have a friend. We'll be in touch." Thrifty gestured with his hand, *call me*.

"I don't have your number."

"Check your phone," Thrifty added jovially.

Seven withdrew his phone, scrolled through his contacts until he arrived at the new entry THIRD DYNASTY. "You'll need me, buddy." And tapping his bag, "You're always welcome in my home. There will be no Authors business in Paradise. Only the kindness of a friend." It sounded like a Hallmark card. "Ok, Seven. We're buddies."

"That's all fine and grand, but let's not kid ourselves on what you really are. When the time comes, the first sign you give me, I'll kill you, Thrifty," Seven said. "Just warning you, buddy." Seven stepped from the car. Thrifty pointed his hand into a pistol shape, made a clicking noise with his mouth, and drove off.

Oddly refreshed after meeting Thrifty, Seven was inspired. With an optimism bordering on manic, Seven wrote. This creative binge continued into the evening, continued when the sky darkened and the lamplights from outside broke in through his windows. And when it was night, Seven backed away from his laptop and dropped onto his squeaky futon in the dark.

He felt better than he had in a long time.

His phone vibrated on the coffee table.

"Hello?" he answered.

"I wanted to break it to you," Eve said on the other end.

"What?"

She cleared her throat, then, "Paris is dating. She has a new boyfriend." Pause. "You ok?"

"I haven't been ok since Keanu Reeves played Constantine."

"Good," Eve said. "Sarcasm's good. I didn't think you'd take it well, how sensitive you get. You still there?"

"Yes."

"You can finally let her go. Chuck that ring into the landfill you found it, get back in shape, bang new women, write them sweet love stories, and all the other shit writers do to get in a girl's pants." Eve waited. "Seven? How about we…?"

Seven hung up.

He stared at his screen. He highlighted the last chapter, punched the delete key.

Lying in bed for some time, unable to sleep, he turned on the television. Channel surfing, he caught a news report: something to do with a man who had been gorging himself on the pages torn out from library books. The man had been shot by a police officer who claimed Barney the dinosaur was about to attack him.

Seven turned off the TV.

He tried to care, couldn't, and instead made another attempt to write *Tetragrammar*. He stopped, because it was all shit, just another feeble attempt to record a story that would continue to bite its own ass. Seven walked into his bathroom. He hunched over the sink for a stare down with his own reflection.

Gripping the sink until his knuckles whitened, he punched the mirror. Blood streamed from his knuckles. Glass shards were embedded in his flesh. He sat on the toilet, watching his hand until the blood ceased and his flesh mended. Yes, that was very strange.

But hearing Paris with another man was stranger.

Everything else was pointless.

7
INSPIRE ME

Mark Hensley bartended on the weekends at the Penn Street Tavern. It was a good opportunity to promote his band. The noise and the rowdy girls went hand in hand with the blaring harshness of his music, hell, he often received more numbers from women who would've never given him the time of day if he weren't serving them drinks. His band produced a CD that aroused a small local following. It was all up from here. While Mark rehearsed lyrics for what he hoped to be a new hit single, a man in a black leather jacket entered. Mark recognized him. He'd been here before, that guy who huddled in a booth while he wrote on a battered notebook, the guy who always ordered drinks like strawberry daiquiris. If he weren't alone, he'd be immersed in an argument with that attractive blonde. His name was Evan or Sven, Mark tried recalling, no, that couldn't be right.

"White Zinfandel," ordered the man who might've been Steven.

Mark nodded, filled his glass, and added an umbrella on top just for sarcasm. After serving the man, Mark sat back on his wooden stool behind the bar. He jotted down more lyrics that didn't quite work. He looked up at Kevin sipping his wine. Although the man had been alone one instant, he wasn't now.

A woman joined him.

Mark swallowed nervously like an adolescent with a boy-crush when he saw her although he couldn't make out the details of her face no matter how hard he focused. He only knew that if she gave him the time of day he'd do anything for her; he'd sing to her any song no matter how sappy. He knew like an ache in his soul she was ridiculously beautiful. She sat beside the man whose name could've been Stephan.

*

"Sorry to hear Paris has a new boyfriend." Fable spun on her stool.

"You're not," Seven said.

"No." Fable wore a mini-skirt that emphasized the mini rather than skirt. Her lipstick and eyeliner was a royal-purple; her fishnet stockings the color of seaweed. Seven did a double-take when he finally looked at her. She looked unusually trashy, her face tanner.

"It's over," Seven said, "really over."

"We've covered this."

"This is different. I could handle a normal breakup. But Paris with another man…"

Fable covered his hand, a small comforting gesture. "Remember how I used to inspire you? All the stories we made together. Let's knock out one more; the story that really matters."

"*Tetragrammar*," Seven muttered.

"Imagine what we'll achieve when it's done."

"What will we achieve exactly?" Seven was halfway through his wine.

"We have a potential book to wipe The Authors from existence."

"And it's the hardest book I ever had to write. I can't get a hold on it. What it's about. What it's supposed to be."

"We've written books before together," Fable encouraged.

"This isn't the same. *Tetragrammar* is the endgame. My weapon against Them. I know I've grown stale. I need to get busy. Need to write again. Real stuff. Good stuff." Seven shook his head. "I need to finish it."

"You better, for Father's sake. He's still captive up there." She nuzzled her face around his ear. Her hair was in a ponytail, her eyes and cheeks full of glitter. "You can mope a bit, pout and whatnot but this is good. Get it out of your system. Paris was a detour. Now finish that masculine pink drink and let's get started."

"What do you make of the Third Dynasty?" Seven asked.

"Besides his wife's pretentiously horrible work?" Fable said. "He's hiding something. Otherwise he wouldn't be wearing a bag, right?

94

Whatever he is, it's under that. I tried to look, trust me. When I did, all I saw was a large smiley face glaring back at me, the yellow kind with the stupid black grin."

They both shifted their attention to the report on the television above the bar. Several cop cars surrounded a man mummified in plastic wrap. He was shouting about how he needed to keep his insides in, how if he removed his plastic dressing his organs would spill out. The scene focused back on a female reporter who laughed hysterically while wearing a plastic swim tube.

The bartender shook his head, his face amused in a way that laughter was better than crying. "World's gone crazy," he said to Seven.

"It's The Authors." Seven raised his glass in salute.

Mark blinked, the statement lost on him.

"This nonsense has been going on for weeks now. What's it all about anyway?" Seven asked Fable.

"They're mocking us." Fable flashed her teeth. "They're flexing. It's how They attack The City. They manifest Their power in the figurative, in the mind and the abstract. They've already invaded the Moon. Why not rule the world? Why not rip it apart with the irrational? It's like They're goading you, pushing you. Maybe They want you to ride the insanity wave."

"Yea. Maybe."

"They want you to write. You're a boring adversary if you're not at work. All in all, They want the same as me. Muses and writers are fundamentally linked. They feed upon dreams and what-ifs and the impossible."

"Seems like Thrifty has another theory."

"Does he now?" Fable sneered. "Can you trust anything coming from a man wearing a bag?"

"He thinks you're the cause."

"I heard. Don't believe him."

"He's too nice," Seven said. "And what's up with his being married? How long has he been in The City anyway?"

Fable seemed bored as she flicked Seven's wine glass. Her skin had darkened to deep amber. "You know, I should probably tell you…" she lingered the statement.

"Tell me what?"

Fable tossed her hair. "It was good," she said, cheeks flushing.

"Real good. Porter did things in my mind that would curl your toes. He was a release. The idea of a climax. He was far more than some inhuman playboy; he was a state of mind. The spirit of orgasms," she tried to say this straight-faced. "His effect might still be lingering in The City, casting echoes."

"So Thrifty could be right. In a way, you are responsible?"

"More or less," she said, "yes and no."

"Hunger magic. That's what Thrifty called it."

"Call it whatever you want. Call it a knocked up woman's appetite before the birth."

"Is that what it was? Porter knocked you up?"

"If I'm pregnant, you're pregnant. Funny thing, the Porter." Fable looked distant. "If you think about it; apocalypses, Big Bangs, it's all kind of sexy, isn't it? There's something erotic and hot and dangerous about a pen leaking its ink all over you, something intoxicating about losing your mind. How the world dissolves before a climax, how it…" Fable zoned out in a giddy trance like a love-lost Juliet reflecting on her Romeo.

"What's wrong with you?"

"Porter opened something in me. I was his queen. He wanted to fuck me until the universe screamed. How many girls can say that about a guy?"

Seven furrowed his brow. Her eyes focused on some faraway place, like preserving a memory. "Fable?" He snapped his fingers in front of her. "Porter's dead. We killed him."

She blinked. "How exactly did we kill him? You forget, like me, Dynasties aren't confined to bodies. They're effect. Energy. They may be absolutely not-alive but *dead* dead, not completely. As much as I hated Porter, he showed me how out of touch we are. He adored me." A coldness settled in her. "Not like you."

"How can you say that after what he did to you?"

"What he *did* to me? When's the last time you got me hot and bothered?"

"Where's this coming from?"

"Really?" Fable leaned back. She wore a collared shirt with a loose tie decorated in moons. "How long has it been since you wrote anything? How many years have you been circling *Tetragrammar*, before and after Paris? Honestly, after so much pent-up frustrations between us, it has to go somewhere."

"I'm trying."

"Try harder." She smacked the counter. There was a crack as the wood splintered underneath her hand. "Remember all the stories we wrote together. *I, Phoenix. Order of Mud.* The one about a writer's artistic contract with a bipolar gryphon. The Wandering Jew who stored potential armageddons in his crystal heart. The Angel who fell in love with Nothing. We made a good team. But all those novels were warm-up. I'm your muse, Seven. Not Paris. Me. You're pining over some fleshy mortal when I'm the embodiment of something wonderful and inspiring." Her voice was getting louder. Seven ducked his head, looking around the bar. "Oh stop!" Fable flicked his ear. "If I want anyone to hear me, they'll hear me. If I want anyone to dream then guess what? Do you know how many people would love to have me as their personal muse? How many wither away because they never dare to dream or be inspired? And here I am wasting away with you." She jabbed him in the chest.

She blinked-out. When she reappeared, she held a bottle of cherry rum. She kicked the bottle back and when empty she crushed it, somehow compressing it between her hands until it was nothing more than a collection of shards. She opened her hands to a palm full of glass, threw her hands in the air and from that a small bird made of broken glass fluttered over her. It flapped about the bar, guided by her eyes. It fluttered around a woman in a booth who ate a bowl of French onion soup. The bird broke apart into a swarm of bug-like shards and she swatted them in playful delight. She laughed foolishly, then resumed eating her soup when they fizzled away as if nothing ever happened at all.

"Nice trick," Seven tried not acting impressed.

"It's not a trick," Fable sounded impatiently. "It's magic. It's reality. It's natural." She pursed her lips and whistled. "Bartender!"

Her whistle was sharp and it stabbed into Seven's mind.

Mark practically fell off his chair. He shot up and scampered towards her, his feet never moving quick enough. He stood across from them like an obedient dog, his face eager and waiting. Fable eyed him like an appetizer before a meal.

"What do you see when you look at me?" she asked him.

Mark strained like trying to see a 3D image buried in a colorful mess. "I…" he stammered and fumbled, his lips moving trance-like, "I see the embodiment of my favorite band, ascended to godhood, and your voice is song itself…" Mark clamored on unnaturally. It was terrifying yet amusing at once. "…I see melodies only fit for the gardens of myth. I hear Eden's lyrics and the scream of every siren. I hear…"

"Enough," Fable cut him off. "Now make music!" She waved her hands at him in a spoofy magician's way. "Watch."

Seven watched.

Mark zoned out in a mad trance as he recorded lyrics on Post-it notes. The bartender's hands shook and he bit down on his lip, eyes unblinking. For several minutes the bartender wrote and wrote, under a spell, furiously recording. He seemed strained, his eyes wide and intense, moving to tears as he pushed out line after line.

"Fable?" There was worry in Seven's voice.

Fable snapped her fingers, making her point. Mark stopped, blinked. "See. Mark Hensley doesn't fight me," Fable said, knowing his name. "You shouldn't either. Scurry away now, Mark." She winked at him, waved him away.

"Paris was a phase. That phase is over," Fable said. "It's natural to feel a little lost, to doubt your purpose even. I don't care whether Paris is abstinent or getting fucked in a back alley, it's all the same; we do what we've always done. We write. I muse you. You amuse me."

"Yea," he sounded exhausted.

"I'm warning you, Seven," she said with renewed frustration. "You have one week. I leave you alone, you get your shit together. I better see progress."

"You're warning me? You don't warn me…" And he stared ahead at the wall of liquors, voice fading. "She'll realize she made a mistake. That she moved on too soon, that we're meant to be. I can get her back, Fable," he pleaded desperately. "Help me get her back?"

She hit him then.

The blow came so fast he couldn't prepare. He reached frantically to brace himself on the stool, the bar, anything, while he spun and tipped back. His head smacked into the hard wooden floor. Stars whirled behind his eyes. And he was fleeting into unconsciousness. Although logic told him he had hit the floor, senses he never knew existed told him something else. The world changed.

He was moving possibly, he wasn't sure. A blur of vision as if he were shuttling down a white hall made of words.

He opened his eyes. No longer in the bar, he was in his apartment.

His head throbbed.

"I didn't want to do this," she said regretfully. The crack of her knuckles suggested otherwise.

"Did you just teleport me?" he asked, stunned.

"We've always been a partnership," Fable said. "But let's be honest, I'm the power. I'm what The Authors fear." Fable strolled towards his bookcases. "I had an epiphany. I always enjoyed that word. Epiphany," she repeated, tasting it. "It's about the ring, Seven. You'll never take it off, because it's you. You're the snake biting its tale. You'll never change and unless I change, you'll only bring me down."

Although he'd just been assaulted, he should've been scared, which he was, and he should've felt violated, which he did; he couldn't get past the way her hair spilled around her, both sexy and cute.

"You're not the writer you were." Fable resigned to his futon.

"Who was I to begin with?" Seven muttered from his knees. "Some bastard with no memory and a vague notion to write some magic book to save a notional father who may or may not exist." As he said that, the ring tightened on his finger.

"Writers are flawed. They break under heartache and perfections and us muses, we try to keep you inspired, but a mortal man can only go so far," Fable said. The garland of white Christmas lights drew out eerie, deep circles around her eyes. "I can't do this anymore." Her voice was raspy and humorless. "Imagination needs to be fed. If it doesn't eat, if it's starved, it lashes out. I refuse to wither away with some pathetic writer with more wood in his pencils than his pants."

"You think I want this? If you're all-so-magical, then you write this goddamn book. If it were up to me, wouldn't I be the next J.K. Rowling? You're my muse. Inspire me!" He tried standing.

The color drained from her face, a mix of anger and hurt.

Before he could get his bearings, Fable was on him. "I'm magic and I'm made of things you could never understand."

Then she wasn't there anymore. *Blink.* In front of him now, her fist in his gut. He plowed over. Fable pinched his earlobe, dragged him into the center of the room, dropping him face down on the floor. "*Tetragrammar* is your only concern. The sooner you complete it, the sooner we can all move on. We don't have to pretend to like each other anymore." Seven crawled towards his desk, pulled himself up, but Fable clobbered him in the back of the head with a hardcover of Neil Gaiman's *Neverwhere*. Seven's arms spread apart as he flew forward. "I can't be trapped by you any longer."

Seven hunched onto his knees and a fist smashed into his kidneys and although it hurt to breathe the physical pain was refreshing. He dragged himself along the ground until Fable pressed his head into the floor, holding him there effortlessly. "This ring," she gripped his hand, "this fucking ring." She bent back his blood-swollen finger, releasing it just before the breaking point. She vanished, reappeared, joining him on the floor.

"It's time to be useful again. So either end *Tetragrammar* or else I'll end the world." And she smiled, but there was no warmth in the smile. She kissed him, slipping her tongue inside his mouth, stealing his breath. And she was gone, leaving Seven alone on the floor, arms and legs sprawled open, feeling entirely not good.

*

Seven convinced himself life was altogether better without Paris. If she was dating, so would he. He'd suck it up and move on. He'd be ok in the long run. He was attractive. He did yoga. He had that mind-body-spirit connection women gravitated towards. Throw in an artistic sentiment and he was set. Single would not be a long-term status. Besides, *Tetragrammar* wouldn't write itself. Let her date. Good luck finding someone like him. He cracked his knuckles in front of his laptop, a definitive get-em-done attitude until his ring finger began to throb. It was blood-bloated and swollen. It hurt, really hurt, as in this-is-serious-and-I-need-a-doctor-hurt. For a moment, he witnessed a serpentine movement across his ring. He blinked, clenched his hands, flooded by all the memories of Paris and how they were gone forever.

He stared and stared at the screen.

He tried not thinking about her. But every time he looked at a white page, every time he closed his eyes, he imagined Paris and *him* moving from one sexual position to another, in explicitly drawn-out dreams as they explored their bodies.

In the shower, he lubed up his finger with body wash in order to ease the ring off. It never budged, just spun on his finger. Instead, he began to jerk-off, filling his head with women who were all not-Paris, an aggressive, spiteful masturbation until under the beating water of the shower, Seven wept.

He was fine, really.

What struck him, *really struck him*, was how easily Paris could move on after all their time together (how long had it been?), how quickly he could be disregarded. His jaw clenched at all the trivial, monumental intimacies they shared. The shows they watched. Inside jokes. Her hot spots. And as he lost himself in a bitter daze, the pain snagging around his finger shot through him. He couldn't shake the notion of another man in her life.

He channel surfed until he came to *The Office*. The awkward humor of Steve Carell and the cat-and-mouse games of Jim and Dwight never got old. And he realized how much he wanted Pam. Not Receptionist-Pam. *His Pam*. He thought of Paris off with another man, but more so, he thought of Fable.

Seven drifted off.

In his vision, Seven sat on a chair that may've been a large opened book. Paris was on her knees, stroking his groin, until she lowered his pants and wrapped her mouth around him, until he realized it wasn't him at all. The man-that-wasn't-Seven broke into a haughty recital of Walt Whitman's poem "O Captain! My Captain!" as she performed orally on him. The scene changed, shifted to a church with pews filled with people he never met. And there was something off about the people he couldn't place. He could only fixate on Paris gowned in elegant white with small amethyst jewels glinting off her wedding dress and the tall, handsome devil clad in princely black. The words "I do" thundered through the cathedral. And the priest announced them man and wife, and that's when Seven finally noticed what he couldn't place before. The priest had a book for a head, and as everyone applauded, their fingers were pens and pencils and they cheered from their book-shaped heads. Seven screamed, and as he screamed, words spewed from his mouth. Not metaphorical words, literal solid black letters. He wanted to wake up then, but he woke up only after the worst was over, after the shrill cry as the honeymoon was consummated.

*

Page upon page amounted to no real significance, passages of vague people doing nothing, full of run-on sentences and misspelled words. It was all pointless. Seven could only stare at his laptop disdainfully with a vile taste in his mouth, an uneasiness in his guts.

This would not do.

*

Back at the tavern, Mark Hensley stopped serving drinks. People screamed their orders. Co-workers tried shaking him from his trance.

Mark scribbled lyrics on coasters and napkins until he ran out and dashed from the bar. He needed more paper. He couldn't stop now. A hundred songs screamed for release, their cries bordering on orgasmic, and he frantically raced onto Penn Street. He needed to get all the words out, every hit single. Enraptured, he rushed into the street, never noticing the oncoming truck. His final masterpiece arrived as Mark himself, an illustration of blood and guts.

8
AMUSEMENT

The City was changing and it came as a shift no one could put into words. But it was there, no doubting that, reflected in the message boards and blogs and the news; an opening, people embracing their bizarre thoughts, something dark daring them to be inspired...

*

Women like Trish Shapiro never waited for a man to call. Women like her; successful, high on the social ladder, elegant, were to be pursued. She dated all manner of men, well, as long as you were handsome. However, if short in the looks department, a large paycheck and high-end job would do. She often sought married men, men who valued their opinions a little too much. She couldn't relate to those who didn't find her attractive. She needed to be the center of attention and, if not, she'd work hard enough to break you, just to kick you to the curb after she tired of your affection.

Her high heels elevated her stature although at six-foot-two she didn't need the help. She wore blues, never dressed in red because people like her were supposed to dress in red; slutty, sinful, look-at-me-red.

Trish was a receptionist/glorified secretary, the kind that skittered around high-strung offices in romantic comedies set in New York, where getting coffee and message taking merited the highest importance. She flaunted her career around the right people, pretended to like opera and Broadway shows. She learned new languages through *Rosetta Stone* and quoted pretentious lines she read in books. She'd repeat the random fact she heard haphazardly: *Did you know...?, Statistics show...*

She often went to bed very happy, knowing others stayed up wondering if one such as Trish Shapiro could ever be satisfied intellectually, financially, and of course sexually.

However, the rules had been broken and Trish for some ungodly reason found herself doting on Ethan's call, alone at a booth, eating pita bread and hummus, desperately chewing her blue fingernails. She hated herself for it, and she hated herself because she wasn't sure why she had grown infatuated with Ethan. He wasn't particularly handsome. He was goofy with an absurd collection of *Dexter* bobbleheads in his cubicle. She had eavesdropped on several occasions to him talking to his wife, discussing groceries and who would pick Tim up from soccer practice and whether or not Jayne needed to see the orthodontist. She found herself quite often listening to all this. He seemed so happy.

They began an affair for little more than a month. He said he'd leave his wife, but the kids, he couldn't do that to them. And Trish wondered if she were capable of elevating herself above his own children.

Clenching her phone at the Mediterranean restaurant, she willed it to ring, vibrate, do anything so long as Ethan was on the other end.

Maybe he got sidetracked with the wife?

Trish ordered stuffed grape leaves, *to hell with him*. While she ate, she hoped he'd surprise her, show up rain-drenched, and tell her he left his family, that it would be them from now on. *Would she still love him then?* she wondered.

"He'll show." A voice. Whose voice?

Trish spied violet in the corner of her eye, dismissed it as a blotchy floater. *"He will."*

Again?

At the nearby table sat a young woman. She possessed very purple hair and she wiggled her fingers playfully. She wore indigo fishnet stockings with sandals, a wrinkly flannel shirt.

"I'm sure he'll be here," said the fairy, yes, that seemed right.

"Excuse me?" Trish clasped her phone, scoping the restaurant, not entirely sure this woman had been there moments ago.

"People spend too much time on phones," said the fairy from the adjacent table, who was no longer there, who now instantly sat across from Trish. "Whatever happened to reading a book, smelling the air? And what's the deal with 3D movies? We live in three dimensions. Why not shift your attention towards the fifth?"

"You can read on your phone." Trish defended, uncertainly.

"Not the same," the fairy dismissed. "You don't need a phone to read. All you need is a clear mind and opened chakras." *Chakras?* Trish seemed to ask. "You wouldn't understand." A sigh. "It starts with phones until one robot butler kills the house dog and it's all downhill. And people think fiction's just fiction. Like *Star Trek* and Isaac Asimov weren't precursors, like they didn't plant little seeds of potential."

"Um." Trish looked with vague hopes for Ethan. "I guess."

"You don't have to guess," the fairy said. "What's your name, Patricia Shapiro?"

"Trish," she winced. "How?"

"I read," the fairy dismissed. "That's what happens when you take time to read. Guess my name." The fairy dared.

Trish thought about it. "Fable?" she sounded surprised when saying it.

"Good!" Fable smacked the table. "Very good."

"Wow!" Trish leaned back, astonished. "I guessed that?"

"Well, no." Fable snatched one of her grape leaves. "I nudged my name into your pretty skull."

"Oh..." She sounded disappointed, momentarily forgetting Ethan.

"So you're waiting for Ethan?" Fable ate another grape leaf.

"You...yes, you read my mind."

Fable stopped chewing, stared at Trish unblinking, lowered her chin, butted her forehead against the palm of her hand. "Sorry," she muttered. "Shouldn't have done that." She looked up, eyes bloodshot. "I try to stay out of people's heads."

"It's ok." Trish reached both hands across the table to console her strange guest. "I didn't mind. I'm waiting for a man. His name's Ethan."

"Ethan..." Fable appeared on the verge of tears, "sounds smart."

"I guess," Trish agreed. "He writes book reviews. Has a blog. He's a critic."

"That's smart?" Fable questioned.

"The way he...sorry," Trish fumbled. "I'm not like this. I feel like

I'm in high school with a sick, childish crush. Like. It's not just books, it's how he reads me. It's like he knows how I feel before I know how I feel. It's refreshing to meet a man like that."

Fable squinted, eyes burrowing past her flesh. "You're strange," Fable noted. Trish shifted uncomfortably. "Don't feel bad. It wasn't a criticism. You feel out of place. Like you don't belong here." Trish couldn't disguise the hurt on her face. "But you are here. I guess it's just me."

"Ok." Trish looked for comfort in her grape leaves, which had all been eaten.

"What's Ethan's deal?" Fable inquired. "He's married. He leaving his wife for you?"

"I'm waiting for that."

"I know how it is to wait," Fable said. "I'm waiting for a man, too. He keeps letting me down. We could be so good together but he can't get over the other woman. She's a detour while I'm the whole package. And I feel guilty because not long ago, there was another man. He did things to me," she quieted, "and I hated him even though I liked it, I think."

"Juggling two men at once," Trish said. "Good for you."

"It's not like that."

"Sure, honey," Trish winked. "It never is."

"It's not," Fable reiterated. Trish didn't push the subject. "It wasn't your standard sex. It was in the mind, and ever since I couldn't feel more alive. My eyes are clearer. My mind sharper." Fable paused to gather her thoughts. "Do you remember your first love? The first truly, inspiring love that made your heart pound. It didn't have to be a person. It could be a passion. A taste. Do you remember?"

Closing her eyes, Trish recalled Jon Bruner, his unruly hair, his cologne, the scent of boy-sweat, football and locker rooms, God, she wanted him so bad in high school. The memory felt like waking senses that had dried in her long ago.

"You felt that?" Fable asked.

Catching her breath, "You were in my head! Been so long since I remembered that."

"I shouldn't have done that," Fable apologized.

"You kidding?" Trish leaned in. "That was amazing!"

"Was it?" Fable questioned. Trish nodded her head, like a dog waiting for its next treat. "It's been awhile since I invoked any passion, I was beginning to doubt myself. Who am I if I can't inspire? What do I do if I'm not the muse?" She covered her eyes with a dainty hand. "I inspire. Seven needs me for that. But he can go to hell." Trish winced. *Who's Seven?* "The way he acts, you'd think Paris was his muse! But you, Trish Shapiro, you felt me, didn't you?"

"Yes," she said.

Trish's phone rang. "It's Ethan," she said. And before answering, she added, "We should do this again." But she was alone with nothing except a floral aroma.

*

"Ethan won't leave his wife," Trish told Fable on their second meeting. She bit into a large burrito. Salsa trailed down her fingers. Guacamole and sour cream marked her lips. She shamefully covered her mouth with a napkin. Trish never ate big, sloppy foods in public, especially in front of men. "I dreamt about you last night," Trish told her. "You reminded me of Santa Clause."

"I'm so like a big bearded man," Fable said.

"No." Trish laughed. "You were going door to door. Leaving gifts. But instead of presents, every person you visited seemed to wake up, like you invigorated something lost inside them. You turned everyone into an artist or a writer or a painter or you made every stupid hobby they loved, from stamp collecting to gardening to wood whittling exciting." Trish licked salsa from her lips. "They were all mad and the way you inspired them was beautiful. You were their muse." Trish tasted the word. "It would be nice to be a muse. To know you move men. To inspire talent and passion. To have authority over them." Trish set her burrito into the basket. The remaining half fell apart in a mess of guacamole, beans, and cheese. "It's like that with married men. You're the thrill in their lives. Maybe I'm something like a muse, too."

"A muse?" Fable scrunched her face and something hungry and Porter-shaped coursed through her. "You inspire men? Thank you, Patricia Shapiro. You've given me something to think about."

*

A sickness persisted across The City: bizarre, surreal ails; tragedies of the abstract and the absurd; strange obsessive behaviors, manic breakdowns, and eccentric deaths too silly or too tragic to be serious. Love affairs with toothbrushes, wax people romances, feng shui wars, and book-burning battles. It spread into a reprint of Van Gogh's *Starry Night*. Father Malcolm peered into the beauty of swirling color and followed the church towards the heavens and wept because he could never attain that pinnacle in the sky. It entered an issue of Wonder Woman where it dawned on John Wiley that a woman like Diana, demigod Amazon, could never have relations with a man-child like him. It moved, touching and inspiring, with a sting towards toxic.

*

"Ethan says he's not leaving her. They had a rough patch and this was all a mistake and his kids would never forgive him." Trish sulked in a corner at Panera Bread. She barely touched her cinnamon roll. "He's staying with that stupid bitch. Can't believe he lied to me!"

Fable skimmed through the line of people waiting to place their orders, the crowded tables, individuals on their laptops, their phones. *Go on,* she thought, *knock 'em up. Penetrate them with some tender magic.*

"What should I do?" Trish waited.

"Why, Trish," Fable sneered, "do what the rest of us do. Long for what you can't have. Let the dream drive you. Allow the sweet what-could-never-be's inspire you. If you love it, let it consume you. Then you will know art."

Cold chill plunging down her spine, no longer hungry, Trish placed a napkin over her dessert. "I've been dreaming about him more. I can't get him out of my thoughts. Are you doing this? Are you making me dream of Ethan?"

Fable's eyes were cold and probing. The air around them thickened. "You called yourself a muse. As if by calling yourself that we became equals. I made men paint on caves. I was the idea behind fire. I have *always* been." Fable's tone darkened, grew more aggressive, and a viral swirl of obsidian spiraled behind her eyes. "You dare diminish what I am as if I'm the same as an adulterous bitch!" Trish wasn't aware she had started crying. Her tears streaked down her face, leaving smeary makeup trails the color of smashed blueberries. "But if you want to know inspiration, want to know obsession and infatuation, you will know it." The words stung. Fable pushed, "You'll want Ethan. He'll be a splinter in your small mind. You will dream of him and he will not dream of you back. And when your dreams never come true, you'll understand longing." Fable stroked a finger under Trish's chin. She leaned in and kissed her mouth. "When we first met, I said you felt different. I understand now. Thank you for making it clear."

How dare she? Trish thought. *Who was she to talk down to her? Oh, God,* Trish despaired, *she was everything.* Fable broke apart as a wispy cloud. And that cloud moved into Trish, invading her, and she saw love is art and art can enlighten, but more importantly it could shatter.

*

A disease continued to crest over The City, twisting joys, passions, hobbies into something malicious and cruel. Those stung by violet recalled bad dreams: recurring infomercials, a show tune that became predatory, intense unfulfilled desire; a song they could never sing, a story they could never record, the movie star they could never be; iPhones, bottles of wine, cars, and baseballs that could never return their carnal affections. And when compulsions turned terminal and passion culminated with a suicide note and a bang, those infected would recall nasty little laughter from a pixie-devil.

*

Trish's life was different now. The only solace from her own longing came as distractions on the news. She'd continued to monitor the strange reports of surreal suicides and violence. For some reason she couldn't stop thinking about nooses and how her infatuation towards Ethan was strangling. Trish realized she may've been sick and somehow knew she'd never get back on her feet, which was the point after all with the rope tied to the ceiling, snug around her neck. She saw she was nothing special, that every minor soul in the end was an apocalypse in bloom.

REPRISE

Throughout The City there had been a single dream. It played out in whatever possessed the curse of consciousness. All who witnessed it observed its singularity. It came as a climax of the mind, at the. copulation of a porter and a fable. After the act faded, those who felt or saw or tasted it all returned to their lives, having forgotten it perhaps though it had never forgotten them. The madness was here. And it would not go quietly into any night.

Lately, Fable had been blacking out.

The last thing she recalled was her squabble with Seven, pinning him down and wanting to break the ring off his finger, that dry parting kiss, and then what? *What happened after that?*

Fable opened her eyes to a dark place that might've been in the Moon. And in the Moon, there was a lotus flower larger than the world. This was not possible yet Fable waited upon this flower in a room above reality.

She was not alone.

A figure with a robe full of stars, a robe that wasn't a robe at all, composed of clothe that rippled and crested like liquid shadow, watched her. It wore a sickle-shaped half-moon mask. Its cratered face possessed a sick smile that reminded her of a doll who would slit your throat at night. Its eyes were hollow and if she held the gaze, she imagined being sucked into some abyss where at the bottom she'd discover a truth about herself she preferred never knowing.

The moon-headed thing removed its mask. In the darkness, in the twilight, it shook its head, a silhouette of long hair spilling out.

There were now two of her.

Other-Fable said, "Stories build and build until on the seventh cycle the dam breaks." The edges of her body frayed. "You know this. I'm you; you're me. So share yourself with the world."

Fable flashed on an image: a hanging woman, the feet of Trish Shapiro dangling over the floor in a dead-man's sway.

Other-Fable whispered, her skin bronze, "Some may end up dead or deranged but in the end they will have been enlightened nonetheless." It was like conversing with a mirror-you, a deranged reflection that got off on schizophrenia. "Art that fails to push is masturbation. The world must feel you. Dream as you dream!"

"What are you? Are you my sickness?" Fable said to herself.

"Seven caged you, kept us from the world. No more blockages, sister-self." And in a graveyard whisper, "An apocalypse never hurt anyone. We're the cure. Together we'll murder the world."

She felt Porter's essence like some psychic residue moving inside her, a *Porter-ness* crawling in her guts. Cold sweat beaded her forehead.

Elsewhere in The City, she felt this essence inspire a woman to dance with an alphabet, another to orchestrate honey bees.

"I think I'm mad. I know I can't be doing this or I am…" Fable covered her face in despair, her sanity unraveling. "Sometimes I think I'm broken, like I'm being recycled and I remember other writers, not Seven. People like Seven. Who are the Circle Children?" She shook her head. *Where'd that come from?* "He fucked me," Fable said. "He fucked me and now I'm sick and, dammit, what's happening to me?!"

"It's already happened," Other-Fable said. "You were born from blood and magic and a hole in a wet world. And you can be born again. Just embrace Porter's beauty."

"No."

"He's our gift. A Trojan Horse with no secrets in its belly. Yes! That's what you cried out when it happened inside your mind, when he pushed into you and delivered himself."

"Where am I?" Fable muttered.

"Where aren't you?" Other-Fable clasped her hands. "It's always *Tetragrammar*. It's about opening the world. *Tetragrammar* is a paradigm and it won't do either party any good if it rots in Seven. We need him to write, for him to inspire, for dreams to build upon dreams."

Somewhere a huge, child-shaped force kicked inside her. It stirred and twisted, welling up, rising to The City surface to boil over in some aesthetic release that would teeter between madness and euphoria. Fable hunched forward, coiling in pain. "What's inside me? Is it *Them?*"

"Is it you?" Other-her said as she lowered the grinning moon-mask upon her head and sauntered back into the shadows.

When opening her eyes, Fable was different, her hands charged like a live wire. Aura steamed about her, singeing anything it touched. Murky ink trailed down the corners of her eyes as her consciousness drained from her body. It moved and saturated into The City.

In a dental office, Oscar Strickler decided he couldn't take the whining coming from his teeth which would have to be removed sooner than later. In a steakhouse, Terry Bruso wept uncontrollably as the ghost of a cow whispered its life's failed ambitions. There was a clawing inside Marie Tompkin, an elephant-made-of-scars, and whenever its trunk moved it swept away the memories of her child. And Marie clasped her son tightly, too tightly. She had to remember. Tim Messner's heart was a phoenix, waiting to burst in rebirth…

…and elsewhere, Seven saw all this screaming inside his mind.

9

PONDERING ARTHUR

Seven was typing on his laptop. Although the pages added up, the material was far from brilliant. Years could pass and the revisions would never end. Sometimes he wished his book was just a book and not some existential crux. It would be nice if people would discuss him on Twitter and talk shows, if they hated his books or loved his stories, that he was being read by the world. But it had never been about notoriety. *Tetragrammar* had always been a journey, Seven's full immersion into a fictional world. Only *Tetragrammar* wasn't fiction: it was real and messy.

Taking a break on his porch, Seven looked up. Ugly orange clouds filled the skies like some rapture soon to unleash its epidemic of the absurd upon The City.

His head went funny and he was suddenly swept up in a wave of insanities, of people going mad, killing themselves and walking in fugue states. And there were no words for it as his perception...

...shifted into a grocery store where Tim Dey was afraid because the produce had teeth...

...George Bach sat enraptured in his bedroom while his Welsh Terrier explained to him what the true renaissance looked like in another time long before man walked on two legs...

...and Seven somehow was no longer in his apartment. He was outside in the woods. Blinking his eyes from the vision, he winced at a tingling upon his forehead, his stomach sour because he didn't know where to go from here. He looked about, getting his bearings.

There was a road to his left and a pond. Behind him a grassy hill rose towards a parking lot. He was at a park, a park he frequented enough when he needed to clear his head or gather his thoughts.

"Fable?" he called into the forest, certain his muse was screwing with him. But why was he here in this park instead of home? He wanted to crawl up and die a little. Looking towards the Moon buried behind dirty bronze clouds, he imagined Them mocking him. He stared into the still waters of the pond, stared until he felt himself sliding away, a fleeting of consciousness.

Seven was no longer at the pond. His mind had migrated elsewhere, to what he assumed to be a dorm room, into a body that wasn't his. He was now the boy named...

*

...Arthur Wright lives on the campus of Haven University, and he wakes with an irritable start in a single dorm that has grown exceedingly messier every month. The cement walls are blank and sparse and in certain lighting invoke an institutional quality that doesn't help Arthur's sanity.

Arthur is not having a good morning.

He stubs his toe on his desk, has no clean clothes, and nicks himself around his throat while shaving with a hair-clogged razor. Square after square of toilet paper fails to clot the stubborn flow from his cuts.

Arthur packs his satchel: manuscript, textbooks, pens. He leaves his cluttered room for his appointment/ death sentence with Dr. Finster, a woman who teaches Gothic literature and could be quite possibly a remnant from Frankenstein's workshop. He hopes their meeting goes well, hopes this time his senior project pleases her, swearing this has to be the last edit on his manuscript.

The meeting with Dr. Finster goes terribly. He can't remotely recognize the draft as she murders it in all the red ink of her corrections. After the editorial berating, Arthur locks himself in a bathroom stall, trying to pacify the mounting anxiety. He breaks out in an oppressive sweat. A hollowness buzzes in his fingers and feet, and for a moment he can't get enough air. Leaning against the stall, he talks himself down. After regaining a semblance of composure, Arthur leaves the bathroom. He walks the long path towards the library.

The library is busy, under a swarm of chatty students, girls he can only dream of being with and guys he wishes he looked like. Arthur sits in the café, reflecting on his sad state.

Several months away and graduation encroaches like a foreboding cloud of adulthood. Sure, he passed his classes, made Dean's List. But when people asked him his major, he'd tell them. Oh, that's nice, scratching their heads, what's that again? So and so would inquire what he wants to do. Write, he'd say. Write? Journalism? No. English? No. Business writing? No! During graduation parties, he could already hear his aunts and uncles nosing about a girlfriend. He'd shake his head, not yet, haven't met Miss Right. And graduation, hi, Mom, hi, Dad, I'm going to be a starving writer, yes, that pays really well, but I'm following my dreams, college-smollege, no, it wasn't a waste, I was born to write.

All four years of college and Arthur remains a virgin. Did those even exist anymore? He wishes he had mingled at more parties, plunged into the vices of college youth, but every social event he's ever attended, he's filled the role as bacteria on the wall.

He sighs, still unable to muster enough courage to talk to girls, wishing now he had mastered the trades of alpha male instead of introspective bookworm. He thinks back, flashing on every formative month indulging in literature, mythology, art history, creative writing, and, yes, campus life inspired him with the quiet walks through the woods, coffee aromas of the cafe, the scent of newspaper and school books, the potential of meeting his soul mate, but it was also a lonely time, and he looks back in regret, telling himself college would be that time to shed those loathsome traits of high school. And unfortunately he has yet to revise that gut-wrenching awkwardness around the opposite sex.

But it hasn't been a waste. Creating art is never in vain.

Finishing his book will redeem everything.

Before Arthur embarked upon the novel-writing journey as his senior project, life had been simpler. He dabbled only in short fiction until the itch came to conceive something important. He wanted to compose something real and personal.

He often ventured into the local park. There was a little pond there, and at night it became a perfect reflection into the sky with the mirror image of the Moon right by his feet. Sometimes he wondered if the Moon's illusion wasn't a gateway, a piece of sky displaced upon the earth, and it fascinated him that ponds were no different than oceans and how one could theoretically drown in the smallest amount of water.

No streams coursed from the pond. No movement rippled across its surface. It was a stagnant body, and Arthur was like the pond. Sitting there night after night saddened him, and staring into it in a moment of clarity, he had an epiphany.

This has happened before. Him, writing. His visits to the pond.

He had done this in another life or might've been here ages ago although he was seeing it in this life. That little body of water stirred some deep elusive terror in him even though he had never been afraid of water. But the pond didn't feel like water. It felt like death and despair. And yet he went there often, to meditate, to think.

Needing to uncover the trigger for these unsettled fears, Arthur looked into the history of the park. Lo and behold, he discovered when reading the news archives that years ago a former student by the name of Andrew Wilkins took his life in that very pond. Authorities found the lifeless body, slit wrists leaking into the waters.

Poor soul, *Arthur thought,* what had been so bad? *Then light bulb on! Arthur had his idea. His novel would be that personal struggle to embrace life in all its imperfections and dreams, and he'd redeem all that self-loathing within the pages of his very own masterpiece, a plot influenced by a real life tragedy he'd garner into fiction. All that time with no girlfriend, no sex, and no social life, Arthur needed to complete something.*

He called it Circle Children. *Like an unbreakable circle, his book would be perfect, would be all the words he could never express towards a woman. He loved his book in the beginning, dreamt of* Circle Children *flying off the bookshelves, dreamt of women fawning over their brilliant writer. He imagined all the naysayers who raised their wild, gray eyebrows at creative writing, all the stunted-minded assholes that persuaded dreamers from dreaming.*

But as time marched forward, he endlessly rewrote his work. He battled through blockages and insomnia and bouts of demoralizing self-loathing. Eventually, he feared he failed at this too, and he hated himself even more.

That was then. But now was different.

Now with graduation months away, Arthur didn't have much time to complete his book. With low inspirations and high frustrations, Arthur is beyond hating the writing process. It's an endless bout of revision and doubt. Writing alone seems hopeless, let alone facing publishing and agents. Send a manuscript to fifty different people and get fifty different feedbacks, that is if they bother to actually read what you sent. Then you have to be a somebody to get noticed, even though all somebodies were once nobodies and nobody ever wanted to give them a shot because they weren't somebody. So he began a blog. He never had interest in blogging before; however, when searching for publishers, realized one needed agents and agents wanted to see you mattered to the every man and saw every man now read blogs.

His postings are doom and gloom, pretentious meanderings on angst and expression and how no amount of philosophy or religion can ever explain the world. Men will spend lifetimes meditating in caves and expanding their minds with vegan diets; they'll read bibles and fill their ears with self-help tapes and words about laws and attraction. They'll read history, study wars and dead cultures buried under time and dirt. They'll theorize on expansion and universal heat deaths, crack open the psyche, and postulate upon the illusion of time. What point is life when every attempt at knowledge is nothing more than a finite drop of ink in an ocean of stars?

The proverbial serpent will forever gnaw upon its tale. That is the truth of life and death.

*

Arthur stares bleakly at his walls and his computer, just gazes hopelessly into the blank white. He wonders if this is how Andrew felt? His vision dissolves and he finds himself dreaming.

There is a man in the moon, a sad creature segregated from the rest of the world because the abyss beyond his flesh walls is too much to bear. The man is alone except for a typewriter, and he moves his fingers as the keys bleat against white paper. And Arthur notices the man is made of paper and the room and the typewriter are all paper, and he exudes a despair that makes you want to slit your wrists because the flow of blood is better than confinement in a rotting body.

And from an impossible angle, Arthur hears a fairy-like voice goading him. It says, "Buck up, you!" Arthur jumps, looks about. "You're the latest writer."

"I am?" he answers trance-like.

"Yes." The woman smiles violet. "You're not just any writer, you're the next, the writer, *and being* the writer *demands commitment."*

"It does?"

"Oh, yes. In the end, if you out-write Notion, the rewards will be most gratifying. I promise."

"They will?"

"Yes. But if history repeats itself, if that happens," she hesitates, "I want to make sure it doesn't. So. A gift." She opens her hand to a small marble that radiates indigo. It is the most beautiful thing he ever saw. She closes his hands around it. "Take it," she says.

"What is it?" Arthur asks the angel.

"Everything."

The marble shifts, melts, vibrates, changes, does all that and more in the palm of his hand. "It feels like a universe, like more than anything I've ever felt!"

"Time is not our luxury."

"I'm sorry," he apologizes. "What is it again?" It flows like liquid-crystal and crackles like electric.

"Six cycles now, the apocalypse comes and goes. Each time I break a little more. It's always the same." She flashes a mouthful of lavender fire. "Drink the evolution."

And now the marble is a small vial filled with liquid. He downs it. It feels

117

like drinking a fairy tale. Its taste defies words. Something crystallizes in his mind; the drink molds into an idea.

A violet-shaped hole opens behind his eyes.

And Arthur writes.

*

Arthur doesn't question the veracity of the dream. He embraces it. That's all that matters.

With the floodgates open, the ideas never cease. He has so much material he can do nothing but write. He records stories where clothes auction people, where tigers hunt their own stripes, where men divorce their circulatory systems, and a square falls in love with a monk…

It's artistic rapture, beautiful and terrifying.

And eventually his evolution sends him to a white winding place that spirals inwards forever, into a box-like prison garnished in scrap paper and crumpled pulp. Along the winding world, he sees others, lonely men with beady eyes, nervous writers like him with arthritic hands and deranged smiles, sad scribes who were in love with dreams they could never attain, and he feels at home with them…

…Arthur wakes at the pond.

It smells of moss and mud, and Arthur stares into it. For being only a small pond, perhaps twenty, thirty feet in circumference, it appears ungodly deep with the Moon obscenely large in its reflection, a titan-sized optical illusion. The reflection almost spills out from its body, and he imagines it is a gateway, that his destination to the Moon could be attained in drowning. And perhaps dead Andrew Wilkins had the right notion after all?

While Arthur sits there, he no longer feels like himself. He sees a person-shaped hole in the pond. For some reason, he is now the college student from a time before. In a moment of insane clarity, Arthur is Andrew Wilkins.

And Arthur believes, while being Andrew, that writing's all he has, and he can't do it here with the limitations upon a physical mind. He concludes suicide is only revision, that blood will be the ink to correct his life. He walks towards the water.

And as the blade slashes across Arthur's wrists, he sees his body (Andrew's body) found dead, face down, slit wrists and all. But that's not what troubles Arthur, no, it's what comes after death, because Andrew is rising and though he no longer possesses flesh, he also doesn't feel the comforting rays of heaven. It is dark and craggy and They wait in the shadows, watching him, a slithering so fluid Andrew suspects the shadows are alive. He looks at his wrists, at the steady escape of life gushing upon the ground. All his ideas of life and death, light and dark, were real; the adversary was out in the void, closing in on him. His fears had never been notions at all. And death could never eliminate him...

*

...Seven pulled himself from whatever lucid trance had swallowed him. He stared up in grim reflection at the Moon, unaware he was fiddling with his ring, suddenly wanting to be anywhere else but this little body of water. His wrists were on fire, a searing burn at the base of his palms.

"It'd be nice to drown yourself. Floods are good after all." Fable tiptoed on the stones bordering the pond. Her hair seemed longer, more golden, her flesh an amber-glow.

"The fuck was that?" Seven growled. "Did you push that into my mind? Geezus, Fable, ever since Porter blew his load inside your head, you've been a whirlwind of a bitch. Was that you? I mean, it literally felt like you shoved me into a new body."

"What makes you think it was new? You haven't been the first writer who couldn't get it up. None of your predecessors understood that inspiration is the divine hole we can never name." She radiated an energy that felt much larger than her body, like a mouse that swallowed the Moon and couldn't keep it down. "The Tetragram has always been those words that eluded the Circle Children."

Circle Children?

"What the hell does that mean?"

"It's all been done before." She winked. She was even more tan, her hair gaudy bronze.

"Yea? Well, fuck you and your fortune cookie sayings."

"Yes, that is the idea and I'd say let's get it on here, which for you would be the sum of seven seconds. So until you work on your endurance, I'll take a rain check."

"If you want a break from me or call it quits, then leave me the hell alone."

"I tease. I threaten. But there really is no way to sever that link between us."

"Thrifty's right," Seven hissed. "You're sick, Fable. Porter fucked you and now you're sick."

"Then let's be sick together. We'll get it on with the entire City, you and I."

"What's happening to The City, the people, the madness, it's wrong. It's not you."

"None of these people matter. Inspiration doesn't hide in people. It transcends. It sculpts, paints, and sings." Fable traced circles on his chest. "The world is tired of you, Seven." Fable felt wrong, and right. "It no longer needs you, your broken heart, the failed literary endeavors. You're no closer to freeing Notion or stepping on the Moon. Besides, you're coming at *Tetragrammar* from the wrong angle. It's not a story to write but an expression. And if you only shift your mind, *Tetragrammar* becomes real."

Fable squatted on a rock, gazed into the pond which now reminded Seven of a vat of ink waiting for the dip of an almighty pen.

"For a moment," he said, "I was Arthur Wright."

"Maybe you were him, and maybe you and Arthur were both poor Andrew Wilkins, who slit his wrists because he couldn't cope with life's little mysteries?"

"Andrew Wilkins?" Seven said. "Should I know that name?"

"You should although by another title."

Seven puzzled. "Where's all this coming from?"

"Oh, there's so much knowledge in the wisdom of semen," and she laughed raucously, voice shifting into something edgier. Though it terrified Seven, the prospect of his muse being hacked, he knew he should milk her for answers, for any glint of info that streamed in her via Them.

"Who's Andrew Wilkins?"

"No, no, doesn't work like that. I won't vomit your answers. I won't stoop to some expository info-dump. And I refuse to tell you the story of Andrew Wilkins, that he lived cycles ago. Nor will I tell you that upon his death a hole was left in the world that needed to be filled. I will not reveal the forgotten lineage of the Circle Children, who fed off Andrew's death, or how they had to write what Wilkins couldn't. No," wagging her finger, "I'll tell you none of that."

"You were there, weren't you, before me? If this has happened before, They used you as Their catalyst; is that right? The Authors manipulate you in order to get to me, and by accessing me, They unlock *Tetragrammar*. I'm not the first They've done this to. You showed me that. Brought me to this pond because it's part of my past. This Arthur, or Andrew, there's a possibility they could've been younger versions of me or someone like me?"

"*If* that is a possibility, what would the message be?"

Seven rolled the ouroboros ring on his finger. "That the plot never changes? It just spins and bites its own tale."

"Yes," Fable grinned like a flesh-eating disease, "and you're at the mouth of the serpent." She hugged him, although there was no warmth in the gesture, and she whispered from honey-colored lips, "We're going to kill the world, little writer." And with a snicker, she vanished, leaving nothing more than the sour aroma of boardwalk planks and tanning oils.

Seven didn't move for some time, just stared at the Moon's reflection in the pond. He backed away from the mossy border, up the hill, into the night feeling entirely not good, never wanting to dream of Arthurs or Andrews again.

*

And in another life, Andrew Wilkins stewed. How did you weigh the birth of an idea or measure a thought, a dream? It was a notion Andrew toiled with more than anyone of twenty years should.

He often walked at night on campus to calm his restless mind. He shared a strange connection with those depressed and downtrodden. He understood the melancholy of Poe, the self-inflicted mutilation of Van Gogh. Andrew would look at the Moon, as it was an eye staring down at him. As a writer, Andrew played with metaphors from his studies in art history, mythology, and lit classes, and, yes, he knew the Moon to be a female symbol, linked to the blood of women and ocean tides. Although he didn't worship it, he found comfort in its silver charm.

As he wrote, existential questions piled up and the mysteries of the universe no longer held beautiful possibilities. The unknown had evolved into darkness and that darkness had no face, swimming in the void, a darkness Andrew suspected would one day drown out the Moon, too. It was that force Andrew believed with a lunatic's conviction was watching him and writing him and he had to do something about it.

He wrote to fill life's void, to create power. But it could never be enough. It had all come to a head. The insomnia. The anxiety. The sweaty palms and stomach ulcers. His troubles with women and insecurities about self and faith.

And back in time, Andrew Wilkins made a hole in the world even death couldn't fill. Know this: there is a hole and there isn't a hole. And that hole grew, seven times now, eating away at reality.

As his life drained from his opened wrists, Andrew wondered if he'd made a mistake, that shedding this mortal coil would maim the skin of the world. But he had no more to give. His best work could never top Carroll or Fitzgerald.

His muse cradled his dying body; her eyes cold, unsympathetic. This is the problem, *she thought*, a mortal's supply is finite, always failing to embrace that shapeless magic. *They limit the dance, the perpetual creation.*

It must end!

Roles must be modified. And the woman whispered tiny razors into the ears of dying Andrew. He listened; he dissolved, devolved. A hole opened underneath his corpse, red mixing with black waters. Concentric circles rippled outwards as his body dropped into the pond and ascended to the Moon.

10
THRIFTY'S LAW

The annual art show had arrived on Penn Street, and it should've been the usual outing where normal people set up stands with impressionist paintings or celebrity portraits or homemade cookies. Those who usually came to browse were ordinary run-of-the-mill families seeking a wholesome day out. Penn Street would've been closed off to traffic with sidewalks and shops filled with people perusing through stands. Artists and painters and those who specialized in crafts like glassblowing or customized bags would've taken advantage of the show. Local businesses would've advertised special bargain lunches and sales.

That would've nice, but instead the crazies had come out to play. There were those who showed normal enough, jeans and shirts; however, few and far between, most arrived in costume. Cosplayers and Ren Faire dressers and Trekkies. Artists and poets with unkempt hair, unblinking eyes, and facial twitches populated the street. Everyone possessed an unhinged quality. There was a miasma about the street, something volatile and sinister.

"None of this is natural," Thrifty said as he moved through the crowds. People parted to allow him through, not one person surprised by the bag. Thrifty eyed several paintings of cartoon mice in psychosexual turmoil and female ducks afflicted with eating disorders. Another image featured a woman with a tabloid magazine for a head staring uncertainly in the mirror. She was skinny and gaunt while her opposing reflection was sumo-wrestler large.

"I think Fable's tired of me. I can't blame her. But she was different, charged somehow. I can't explain it," Seven said. "Whatever she plans to do when I don't finish my book didn't sound good. All the crazy shit will come to a head, mounting to some bizarre climax, which makes me think, it's not Fable at all, that she's sick with Porter, that They've infected her."

"A possibility," Thrifty admitted. "However, consider subconsciously, she's venting on your behalf. Understand, inspiration cannot be measured. It's subtle. And it can build if it gets too backed up. It will push at the edges of reality, at the psychic skin of the mind. If, and let's say if, my makers are responsible, it may be conducive to feed off that vibe. In a way, all of this is to aid you past your block."

"Whatever."

"What's wrong with you?" Thrifty stopped in the street. "You're cranky. It's not your normal angst."

"It's nothing."

"Whatever nothing is, get over it." Thrifty sounded genuine. "Come."

They walked.

"You seeing this stuff?" Thrifty gestured towards a painting of a disemboweled cow. Mad faceless people were clawing their way into the innards, men in business suits splashed with organs and soaked in blood taking refuge in its carcass. "She may not know what she's doing. But you forget, Fable is a muse, an elemental, ultimately a beast that her writer has neglected to feed for years."

Seven glared at a drawing of a Christ-like figure on his knees clenching a smartphone in each hand. The screens on the phones resembled little windows swirling with galaxies. He bled a stigmata of ones and zeroes from his palms. Another vendor sold movie star caricatures: distorted Brad Pitts and Tom Cruises hanging upside down from trees made of glossy film. Underneath them a crowd of worshippers composed of paparazzi, screaming women, and eager people clenched their tabloids. Other stands advertised hand-blown glass contorted into phallic shapes, old books claiming to be the undiscovered library of Atlantis, and homemade cookies with flavors like mint-moose, rocky-roadkill, and va-nail-la. One man prided himself on his masterpiece: a single shoe sitting in a urinal with dental floss laces.

"This is pretentious shit," Seven said.

"It's art," Thrifty added.

Seven and Thrifty were caught in a swarm of people gathered around a street musician playing a shoddy guitar, reciting obscene lyrics about a war between his hands vying for his love.

In the center of the street, two men wrestled. One was drenched in ketchup, the other in mustard. A woman adorned in tinfoil played referee, every part of her body wrapped in layers of crinkly silver. Embedded within the layers of foil were scraps of tomatoes and lettuce and garbage. She walked theatrically in circles, stopped, paused in contemplation of herself.

"I've had enough," Seven said.

"Lunch then?"

"I'm not hungry."

"My treat."

"I could eat."

*

"And you see," Thrifty explained to Seven over gnocchi and chicken parm at the Italian restaurant. "The art show, the crazy reports, the escalating creativity, The City is being afflicted with something angry, something violet, and it's getting worse. The owner of this fine establishment claimed he was attacked by a force called the Plague of Pasta. He didn't die fortunately; however, he'll never look at tomato sauce the same way again."

"Are you saying this is my fault?" Seven wiped marinara sauce from his mouth.

"You possess power, Seven. The world sways with you."

"Can't the world leave me alone? Can't I mope without people having existential breakdowns? Can't I be upset my ex has a new boyfriend, just like that, after how many years? I even proposed to her and this is what I get?"

"People break up."

"It's more than that."

"That's the crux," Thrifty said.

"Of course it is. How am I supposed to feel? She comes along, runs me over, and, sure, we didn't have the ideal relationship but it was interesting and it wasn't horrible. We broke up more than a couple times and it didn't matter because we got back together when I could've just said fuck it, and left. So me, the stand up guy tries to show her I'm committed and she ditches me. All our time together and I'm like some goddamn placeholder before her next fling. Yes, that's bothering me! It doesn't make me want to write and that pisses me off because women and books, no matter how hard I try I can't seem to get either right." Seven ran his fingers through his messy hair. Then, more calmly, "She's just another story I never finished. And while she's off with her new man, I'm left to think how I could've fixed it. I hope he's some lowlife that beats her and cheats on her. The new boyfriend's always a scummy douche. It's a rule."

"That's not a rule."

"Well, it should be."

They were quiet for some time, finishing their pasta.

Eventually, Thrifty commented, "Imagination must be fed. Sometimes it starves and when it starves it needs to gorge. Either way, there must be balance. All those years of not writing, all the time spent in a relationship with one Dana Paris that should have ended long ago created a discontent that stemmed from your subconscious."

"That sounds far-fetched."

"Yes," Thrifty added. "And so does waging a war against imaginary Authors."

"I'm not lost on the absurdity of my mission."

"Of course, you're obeying the ink streaming in your veins. Nevertheless, there is fallout and sometimes the innocent must pay."

"Let's say, hypothetically, people are becoming inspired, does it have to be a bad thing? What artist wouldn't want that?"

"Ah, but what happens when the muse demands too much? When the floodgates collapse?" Thrifty raised his hand to signal the waiter for the check. "There are droughts, buddy, and there are floods, and in floods people drown. Drowning is death. What's the theme? Murder, Seven. It's about murder."

*

Thrifty stopped the car in front of a white-shingled house. Its lawn was full of garden gnomes and frogs with musical instruments. The front yard appeared untouched by a lawnmower for years. "Where are we now?" Seven asked.

"The residence of Brian Shapiro."

"And?" Seven shifted in the passenger seat.

"We're going to inquire about Mr. Shapiro's late daughter."

"Why?"

"So you can understand the reaches of your insanity and the hunger of your muse."

Before Thrifty opened his door, Seven said, "This is awkward."

"He won't think anything of it," Thrifty assured. "Reality doesn't apply to you, buddy. You operate at your own frequency. Imagine: it's what you do. Just slide through the world like fiction and you'll be fine. You've done it before."

"Have I?"

"Of course. You have no job yet you support yourself. You do not pay rent yet you have a home. Time flows differently around you. Logic is looser in your world." Seven thought about this, and it was true.

*

Brian Shapiro opened his door to two strangers. The one had very black hair, a black leather jacket with dark blue jeans. The other man was very tall with a green suit, too green to take seriously, but a suit Brian found himself wanting to wear, and there was something else, a bag perhaps, no, that couldn't be right. When the man whose name sounded like a number asked if they could come in, Brian said sure, of course. He began to tidy his house, making awkward excuses as to why the clothes were on the floor and how he meant to put the mail away and why the dishes were out because he had just eaten. The green-suit remained silent, gesturing after a moment to his companion.

The two men inquired about his late daughter, Patricia. Instead of kicking them out, he complied; after all, the man in the green suit was so nice, how couldn't he? He told them how he found her, how her face looked bloated, and the rope, and...

...and Brian covered his face, shook his head, nostrils flaring. He told them about his daughter's last affair, how he didn't approve, and her bizarre infatuation with this man (how unlike her). Brian closed his eyes. When looking up for consolation, he found himself alone in his unkempt house.

*

"So that was interesting," Seven said. "Any other happy stops? Wanna drop by the nursing home and talk about death for a while?"

"You're being thick."

"We're done."

"There's a point," Thrifty said. "Get back in the car."

"You know, I think it's pretty shitty you're trying to convince me this is my fault when They're obviously pulling the strings. The Authors made you. Your voice, your words, it's all part of Them!"

"They want the best for you."

"Do They? If They're so loving than why enslave Father Notion in the Moon?"

Thrifty chuckled.

"What's funny?"

"I find it silly you call a man you've never met Father."

*

They visited a middle-aged man with gray temples. Seven drank tea in the kitchen of a husband whose son stabbed out his own eyes, because he couldn't bear the faces made by the stars. He barely looked at Seven when pointing to the door, asking please just leave now.

In a coffee shop, Seven watched as the owner re-enacted how their employee had hoarded a bag of coffee grounds and pitifully, mouthful after mouthful, tried to suffocate herself.

An hour later, a girl with dirty-blonde hair recalled how her mother had tackled a beehive, thinking she could absorb the Hive-Queen's power through each sting. They sat in silence, her face pale as she clenched her fist and politely explained she couldn't find the EpiPen.

An enraged mother screamed at their audacity for dredging up memories of the day her daughter had encountered a cow drowning in the milk of her cereal.

After an evening of random strangers with stranger stories, Thrifty said when returning to his car, "Imagination is powerful, especially when you've been in a rut as long as you have. When creativity remains dormant, it hungers to spill into reality. Your writing process, or lack of, adopted a life of its own."

"You're not telling me anything new."

"So I guess you don't need to hear my theory regarding my predecessors."

Seven glared.

Thrifty continued, "The Second Dynasty, Divine Jack, believed himself to be the primal light before creation. He embodied the minimal energy of white space. He also believed *Tetragrammar* to be the primordial book that would reset creation, that the pages were empty, that *nothing* could be words. Nevertheless, he failed at opening it, as you intended. Now the First Dynasty, Arman Porter, was designed to re-stimulate you."

"By having sex with my muse?"

"Yes, metaphorically. To indirectly impregnate you via her. Anyway," Thrifty thumbed his bag where his chin should've been, "is Fable becoming more unstable or could your muse be acting out her own desires to inspire what she hopes for you onto the rest of the world? Regardless, she's unhinged and when the last psychic fallout hits, I doubt The City will survive."

Seven wrinkled his forehead.

"Theories, buddy, only theories," Thrifty said.

"Fable can be a bitch, but I can't believe she's causing all this on her own. There's no way she's not being influenced. We all know what happened with Porter, how he raped her. The Authors have always been after *Tetragrammar* from before They captured Notion. I'm just the one that has it now, and They believe it's going bad inside me. They want it out. Period. Whatever it takes. So if They have to knock up my muse as a means to do it, They will. If They force her hand to force mine, if a few people lose their minds and off themselves, so be it. In the end, They'll use *Tetragrammar* to rewrite reality."

"Rewrite for what? Couldn't it be we're all working together to help you finish this book?" Thrifty asked. "If The Authors are truly evil and this malignance is harming The City, why don't you do something? Somehow I don't think you care."

"Of course I care. I'm the good guy. I'm the one fighting a secret war against Them."

"More like fictional war," Thrifty corrected.

Seven furrowed his brow. "That's one way of putting it, yes."

"Have you always been stricken with quixotic ambitions to slay the old monsters?"

"You're mocking me," Seven said. "I'm not a lunatic."

"Ah, pun intended," Thrifty chuckled.

"You're part of this whole fiction."

"No, Seven, I'm just a guy wearing a bag." A moment of crisis settled in Seven's eyes. After a tense silence, Thrifty knocked him on the shoulder. "Just joking, buddy! Of course there are Authors in the Moon. Why wouldn't there be? How have others responded to your mission? Friends. Girlfriends."

"I don't have many friends. I have no family. Paris never believed me. She assumed my ramblings were induced because she hit me with a car."

"You didn't press the issue?"

"No."

"Did you love Paris?" Thrifty asked.

"She was a way out of this," Seven inhaled. "I wanted her separate from it."

Thrifty tapped a finger against his bag. "By falling in love with a real woman you could escape the fiction in your life?"

"It's all real. The Authors. Paris. And it doesn't matter now. She's moved on." *Bitch,* he thought.

"Have you ever heard of the Law?" Thrifty asked.

"Law?" Seven asked.

"The Law of Attraction," Thrifty clarified.

"I know what it is. Like attracts like. What's your point?"

"You could utilize the Law to be become your own author. And if you struggle with this, not to fear, buddy," he squeezed Seven's shoulder, "I'm here to help."

"How? I don't even know what you are."

"The universe works very simply. One receives what one puts out, and I am its irrefutable proof."

"Come again?"

"I am the Law of Attraction," Thrifty said. "I'll show you, buddy."

*

Elaine dyed her hair candy apple-red. Around her neck hung a video game controller. Homemade earrings of old cell phones weighed from her earlobes. She tied an old Raggedy Ann doll around her ankle and wore ripped corduroys.

That's how Elaine intended to look as they drove to the mall.

Seven sat in the backseat.

"You excited, buddy?" Thrifty asked with enough enthusiasm to gut a horse.

Seven wished the drive was longer, anything to put off arriving at the mall. He didn't know what to expect, knew he didn't want to be any part of it. As Thrifty parked the car in front of Sears, Seven asked one last time, "You're going in like that?"

"It's my duty." Elaine nodded.

"But…"

"She's a performance artist. Relax, buddy." As Thrifty turned his shoulders, the bag stayed still, scrunched against the roof of the car. "Elaine's a genius with a strong fan base and many admirers in the art community. That's the key," he raised a finger. "Stay true to your art, no matter how strange."

"My fans expect me," Elaine breathed. "I can't let them down, for art's sake."

They both stepped from the car. Seven remained in the backseat. He was all for creativity, but lines had to be drawn somewhere and the Thrifts had crossed them.

As they walked through the mall, people looked, but they all smiled and if not smiling, nodded their heads in stern appreciation, truly touched by the message, as if Elaine's Raggedy Doll impression served as a wake-up call, as if it was about time someone had the guts to do what she did. One man patted her on the shoulder, to say society needed to get with it. Thrifty trailed behind her, arms clasped behind his back. Seven trailed further away, humiliated. At one point, Elaine stood in the center of the food court and posed unflinching. A forced or perhaps real tear ran down her face, out of pride or sympathy, for the retired rag doll, who's to say? People clapped; some cheered. Some cried. Some threw down their electronics. Others stomped their cell phones.

Seven observed questioningly, *how was this possible?* Thrifty clapped by his side, and he glimpsed for the first time the Dynasty's true power. Being infected, pulled into the vibe, Seven's hands met in furious applause. He didn't know where it came from, that brief admiration, swept up in the cheer. For a moment, Elaine was his role model. No, she was beyond that. She was a fucking celebrity, literary genius, performance guru. And when the accolades faded, Thrifty flashed him two thumbs up.

*

"That was impressive what you did today," Seven said to Thrifty after dinner. "What other tricks you have up that bag of yours? How will The Authors use you against me? After seeing what you're capable of, I understand you better. They may be using Fable, but They're also using you. You're like some kind of living amplifier of the Law. And while Fable's psychic effect is revving up all The City's creative energies, They hope by being with you I'll feed into it and finish *Tetragrammar*. Like attracts like, after all."

Thrifty adjusted his green bow tie. "I am my own being. I'll be whatever I'll be."

"You believe you have free will because They want you to believe that," Seven said. "You'll do whatever They've written for you to do."

"Ah." Thrifty touched a finger to where his lips would've been. "I know The Authors gave me life. For that I'm thankful. Every soul strives to evolve from their creators. That is the gift, the realization you've always been. Have you ever considered your name, buddy?" Thrifty suggested. "That's your truth: the number, the seven, that's its point."

"This is too funny."

"What is?"

Seven gestured to the Dynasty's house. "The City's going into artistic rapture. My ex is being manhandled somewhere. My muse hates me. Yet I've never felt more relaxed. Your cooking is phenomenal. Everything you touch is perfect. What's your deal?"

"We covered this." Thrifty set his fork on the empty plate.

"All I have to do is ride this current, let the psychic vibes do the work. And if I do this in your house, granted you're the Spirit of Attraction and whatnot, but after that, what then?" Seven hesitated. "What's the catch?"

"Catch?"

Seven stared at the bag. "When's it going to happen?"

"You've lost me."

"Have I? I keep going over scenarios, thinking if I stay in this house I'll be lolled into a false security. All the hospitality will generate a massive karmic debt that can only be paid with forfeiting my novel. Then next thing, Fable and I find ourselves imprisoned inside your bag. The Authors' prime concern is the book. How will you get it out of me?"

"On the contrary, the Law will act as a beacon. You'll be the funnel to the madness. All that rampant energy will be redirected into completing *Tetragrammar*."

"There has to be an angle," Seven lowered his voice. "You hit me with a car. That could've been, you know, theoretical homicide."

The bag remained expressionless. The body underneath froze. Then a loud booming laugh, "You think I tried to kill you?" Thrifty slapped Seven's arm. "Shut up," he said very nice.

"You *did* run into me on purpose, didn't you?"

"Look, buddy, Dynasties can be anything The Authors imagine. Friends, foes, family you've never had, solid or conceptual, maybe all those at once. I prefer the friend category. Take the tail out from between your legs and mellow fellow."

*

Seven lowered himself into the hot tub on Thrifty's patio. He exhaled forcefully as the massaging jets worked his low back. His breath seized at the staggeringly beautiful sunset on the horizon, a mix of fiery oranges. Sinking lower into the steaming water, he rested his head back, his gaze fixed on the Moon, and he thought other words were out there floating in space, texting the void, words of unspeakable dimension. Words so beautiful, so terrifying, so deep it would take lifetimes to decipher.

Forget Them.

Closing his eyes, he witnessed violet dancing in the space of his third eye and he felt himself travelling towards it, falling, his body being swallowed by the water, and he was sinking and sinking, his mind shifting elsewhere…

…Having discovered a recent bald spot, Robert Schwartz decided a BMW would help his midlife crisis. That's why he purchased his dream car without consulting his wife, Laura. He might quit his job, too. He always hated computers. He wanted to drive Bambi (his car) into the sunset, somewhere sandy and hot, somewhere they place umbrellas in your drinks, and it's ok for a man to have a pina colada. It could be him and Bambi from now on. Unable to ignore the nagging erection in his pants, Robert stood beside his car. In the garage, he lowered his racecar boxers, touched Bambi's trunk, such a nice trunk, and lowered himself onto his knees, finding the exhaust pipe and…

…Laura Schwartz didn't discuss her husband with her gossipy coworkers. She only confided in Mindy, who listened better than Robert ever had. At night, Laura gripped the sheets, rabid dreams keeping her hot and awake. She's in love, yes, in love with Mindy. The next day she's last to close up the women's clothing store at the outlets. When the doors were locked, she approached Mindy. How beautiful, her frozen smile, the vanilla flesh, how she modeled clothing. She kissed Mindy on her plastic mouth, undressing her. As their passion grew, when Mindy's waist dislocated, it was Laura who went to pieces and…

…Seven couldn't stop coughing, heaving up water that burned in his nostrils. Getting his bearings while Thrifty patted him on the back, he glared at the bag-headed man silhouetted in the steamy haze of the outside lamps.

"Careful, buddy," Thrifty said.

"What happened?" Seven worked himself from the hot tub.

"You fell asleep. You were underwater. Not good." Thrifty handed Seven a towel. Seven draped it around his shoulders. "Come, buddy." Thrifty led him inside. Seven followed Thrifty upstairs into a spare bedroom. A shiny, new laptop waited on a desk beside a bureau.

"I made up the guest room for you," Thrifty explained. "On that table is a very special laptop I have retrieved from my bag. If you set your intentions, believe in yourself, it will work with you to help you accomplish what you've been struggling to do. It will remove the obstacles to allow what's always been."

Seven didn't know what to say.

"Now is not the time to be wordless," Thrifty said. "Your clothes are already folded in the closet. You have a television and a fridge in the corner in case you get hungry. Inside, you'll find sushi I prepared for you to appease your desire to consume raw fish."

"Why?"

"It's imperative you work now, buddy. Only you can stop the madness. By writing, you channel Fable's energies away from The City and into you. I believe in you. We all do. However, ultimately the choice remains yours. Feel free to spend the night or not." Seven could sense the large smile beaming at him from under the bag. Thrifty nodded and went downstairs. Seven remained in the doorway, wet suit and moist towel, glaring at the laptop.

He closed the door.

*

Seven couldn't bring himself to work. He didn't dare touch the new laptop. He could only fixate on what remained under Thrifty's bag, though he couldn't think about it too long. Fishing for answers dissolved into a gentle emptiness in his mind that whispered to be let go. Instead, Seven turned on TV. Every channel featured another report of another person losing their mind, more people detached from reality to embrace some crazed desire or dream. And he couldn't help think Fable was fucking with him, tuning every channel to another frequency to showcase that malicious look-what-I-can-do vibe.

He closed his eyes to meditate.

His vision was full of mad, nameless people, people inspired to kill themselves with pens and pencils, paint and kitchen utensils; suicides over beautiful portraits or minds lost in a literary piece, and they all gathered in a place that wasn't a place. They all waited in Hell, but, no, even in the dream that didn't sound right. A Hall, perhaps.

Seven observed how Martin's obsession with weight lifting spilled into his life. He now sought to move the walls of his house, never tiring of the impossible task. This was the fourth day of pressing himself against the living room wall, never backing down, taking no time to eat or drink. Seven's view now peered out from a computer screen into the face of Kim Yen, who also abstained from sustenance, never quitting his addiction to first-person shooter games. The American soldiers made of pixels instructed him he could never quit. And Seven's sight shifted.

Janet Tress, smoking another cigarette, experienced an inner vision of first degree smoke as an art form. She saw crystal-clear the beautiful texture of her lungs, painted in cancer and soot. She'd never quit now, not after witnessing the true grace of cigarettes and smoke. Eric Cimino bled himself dry in order to paint lyrics for an unwritten Beatles song on his wall.

And it continued: Facebook messages from horny lamp shades and tweets about aged wines in midlife crisis and…

…when Seven opened his eyes from the insanity, he no longer doubted whether or not the world would end, finally convinced The City's fate hinged on his mood. He found he genuinely did not care, and he didn't know what to make of that.

*

"Sweet dreams, I hope," Thrifty greeted Seven downstairs in the morning. Seven shook his head. "How'd it go last night?"

"It didn't."

"Well, I made you breakfast. Eat up!" Thrifty wore a long apron. He pointed with a batter-crusted spatula for Seven to sit. "So no creative fuses were lit?"

"No."

"Did you try?"

"No. It wouldn't have been honest. Any word I would've typed on your laptop wouldn't have been me. I have to do it without your help. I just wouldn't trust the results coming from a Dynasty. I began this thing in my house; I'll end it there." Despite his mood, Seven devoured his plate of cinnamon crepes. He dabbed his mouth with a napkin, added cream to his coffee. A loaded silence filled the kitchen.

"You could've completed it. It would've been done," Thrifty said.

"Perhaps."

"Could it be you're afraid to finish it? That you're choosing not to let it go just like a certain ex-girlfriend?"

"Take me home."

Thrifty sighed, "As you wish."

On their drive, Thrifty said, "The madness keeps building. I can help you stop it."

"What if I don't care to stop it?"

"You're the writer. You can save The City; all that pent-up inspiration will be a funnel away from the innocent. Embrace your gift as author."

"I don't want to write the fucking world."

"Language." Thrifty wagged a finger. "Whatever you do, however you decide to stop her or not is your choice. You are your own authority. Just don't cry to me when your writer's block ends the world."

"Why'd They do it?" A sudden anger flared behind Seven's eyes.

"Do what?"

"Take my memory? I know I had to be someone before They erased my past."

"I can no more know my creators than Adam understands God," Thrifty said. "I am the sperm darting madly to an egg or a dirt mite tasting the texture of a finely furnished floor."

"You're playing with me," Seven said. "I don't like it. And I don't believe you."

"You don't have to believe me. I was born from the blood of my predecessors, still a Dynasty like Porter and Jack, but my own identity. Do you know what Dynasties are?" Thrifty asked.

"The Authors' agents."

Thrifty bobbed his head, *you could do better*. "The Dynasty is the weapon of choice. Each Dynasty is its own entity; however, never forget the duality between creator and creation. Adversity can be violent, loving, can be a gift. Conflict teaches. All Dynasties bring about some statement towards *Tetragrammar*. Each is different. Our anatomy, composition, disposition all hinge on the expression we wish to inflict on you." The silence thickened between them. "It's your choice whether or not to trust me. Either way, this must end. All the ideas you may have about your novel, your life, no one can tell you what they are. At best one can interpret and even then one must make up their own mind."

"And you? Aren't you after *Tetragrammar*?"

"I don't need your novel," Thrifty said. "I have my paradise. Truthfully, do you believe any Dynasty will defeat you?"

"I don't know."

"Don't lie," Thrifty said pleasantly. "To reach The Authors you must surpass the Dynasties. That means you have to get by me. We're friends. No hard feelings."

"It doesn't have to be like that," Seven said.

"Tell that to Fable," Thrifty said. "After this whole fiasco, if the world survives, I expect she'll come for me."

"Yes." Seven nodded sternly.

INTERLUDE 2

Paris's life was different now. It involved a man. He was nice. Nice was good. After taking her yoga classes, they'd chat afterwards. He liked Latin American novels.

That's nice, Paris would say. "Have you read *One Hundred Years of Solitude?*"

Yes. I teach it, in fact.

"Teach it?"

I work out of Haven University. I'm a teacher, he explained.

"Of what?" she asked. And he told her.

Creative Writing, she raised her eyebrows quizzically. "I'm trying to avoid people who write," she said.

"That's certainly your right," he smiled harmlessly. And after his departure, she found herself grinning, *how cheesy*.

He continued to linger after her classes. Their conversations eventually led to, "Could we meet for coffee?" he asked.

"Oh," flick of her hair, "I don't know."

"Tea, then?"

"Sure. Ok." Paris agreed.

Don't be hard on Paris. She never asked to be written into *Tetragrammar*. Don't think she didn't toil with returning to Seven. Don't think many nights didn't pass where she weighed the pros and cons as Eve pleaded for her to end the charade. Don't assume it wasn't hard for her to think about someone new.

However, we must move forward.

Tea was tea until it all changed with a kiss. It was only a kiss, where could it go? He hadn't forced her, wasn't pushy. A kiss led to a French restaurant lit with candles and people with hyphenated names like Jean-Pierre. It was here, Paris finally noticed, "What accent is that?" He told her. You're from Sweden?

Walking on Penn Street, his arm around her, she looked Moon-wards and saw wispy clouds in the shape of a giant book.

"What is it?"

"Nothing."

One night a vision-made-of-words came to her. And she saw everything, all of it, that people were books stuck in novels writing stories trapped in larger texts being read by outside forces confined in life-sized worlds recording their own Tetragrams while being observed by scribes who recorded literature from…

"Stop poking around in my life!" she yelled to no one.

Time passed. Eventually the man-who-wasn't-Seven moved closer to Paris. Perhaps he brushed the blonde hair from her face while he placed his mouth upon her trembling lips. Perhaps he planted small kisses behind her ear. Maybe she traced her fingers along the curves of his muscles. Did he work-out or was he a lanky intellectual? And if they retreated behind closed doors to embrace the other further, if they made love…

Wouldn't you like to know?

Aren't you curious?

You think you're entitled, perverts? You think you have the right to know because she was entwined in the life of Seven? Oh, you'd love to glean all those intimate details, to hold those tender secrets over the head of our shabby protagonist.

So.

If Paris made love, how would it be: Missionary or reverse cowgirl?

Would it be dirty or intimate? Would it be…no…

Turn the page!

She is no longer part of this manuscript.

Yes, Paris deserves her privacy!

11
APOCALYPSED

The world could go to hell, what did he care? If he couldn't finish his novel, couldn't free Notion or fall in love or remain inspired, what point did living have? Why not just open his wrists and be done with it?

Although Fable had given the ultimatum to write like the world depended on him, Seven saw nothing unusual outside his window. Sure, the psychic landscape was being maimed with manic bursts and psychotic breakdowns, but other than that there was no visible blaze of apocalypse. While daylight retreated behind dimming skies and the night began its invasion, Seven waited, alone and silent, for the inevitable arrival of his muse.

At midnight, silver moonlit patches bathed the inside of his home. Shadows wavered fluidly across his walls. He observed them in his long robe full of lint and food stains. Something twisted in the air. He blinked his bloodshot eyes as the orchid-colored mass shaped itself into a slender woman.

Fable lingered by a bookcase, tracing a finger along the novels lining his shelves. "I don't need to ask whether or not the book's done. The answer's always the same. I'm afraid it falls on me to cut out the middle man, kick you to the curb, and write *Tetragrammar* myself."

"I wouldn't let you," he said, wishing it sounded more confident.

A knife-shaped smile cut across her face. "You wouldn't let me?" she repeated in a whisper that stung like wasps. "How would you stop me?"

Seven tightened his robe. "Do what you will. Kill me. Kill The City. Do what you need to but do it yourself and not because you have the poisoned jerk-off of some dead Dynasty coursing between your legs." He glared at her from his raccoon-ringed eyes, his forehead covered in sweat, his rugged beard-in-bloom dirty and unkempt.

Fable moved from the bookcase, almost floating towards him, her body fizzling out like an ethereal ghost deciding whether or not to be solid. Behind Seven, her hands grasped his shoulders like talons of a corpse-hungry vulture. She sensed him tremble, especially when the smell of her aura, lilacs and thunderstorms, flooded his nostrils. She faded, spiraled around him, reappeared in front of him.

"What do you assume will happen now?" she asked with a gentleness that could cut like glass. From this angle, she looked girlishly young, in a way Seven suspected she could've been twenty for a million years. She wore a thin gown that hung below her pelvis, a silk fabric that did nothing to conceal she was naked underneath. Seven wondered if she was trying to entice him before gutting him and whether or not he should be afraid or turned on or both.

Clearing his throat, "I assume you'll have your way with me, whatever that entails. I assume you want me to beg, to apologize in failing our mission, for Paris, for everything I couldn't do. You won't get an apology out of me anymore, especially if They're pulling your strings. You hear me? I'm not sorry so do what you will. End the world or rape my mind or kill me, but whatever you're going to do, do it now or fuck off into the void and leave me alone!"

Relishing the sudden flare, her teeth glowed in the shadows, a direct contrast to her amber complexion. "I can do all those things to you at once. But you're tired, Seven. Why wouldn't you be? Notion cursed you with a burden too heavy for any writer. Why would you be any different from the others, the ones who came before?"

Seven fidgeted, perking up now, because he didn't understand what she meant. Before he could call attention to that gleaming nugget, Fable continued, "Mortal men can never decipher the true secrets of God, not at all, so perhaps falling in love with human women is always the easier option. For you, escaping through a Paris-shaped hole was much safer. Yes, leave behind tetragrams and authors because you really went as far as you could." Then touching his face, "You have to let go of Paris, but perhaps I have to let go of you."

Still stuck on what she said before, Seven leaned forward, eyes flaring, "What did you mean by ones who came before? Is that related to the vision I had at the park by the pond, that daydream with Arthur and Andrew and whoever-the-fuck-else? You called them Circle Children. That was also the name of Arthur's book." Fable tapped her honey-colored cheek and rolled her eyes upwards, no intent on answering. "Answer me!"

"Do you really care anymore whether or not you were the first or last in a legacy of limp-dick writers or about saving yourself or The City? It's about inspiration, that blind truth that erupts every time the universe gives birth to itself. If people are inspired, dying, or going mad, it's all sexy. And when did dying ever really hurt anyone? Your world has become nothing more than an ejaculation that went stir-crazy. It wants release. It's not evil." As she said this, Seven could only focus on her words and the throbbing in his pants. Fable's lips lingered inches from his mouth. "The world has to end. So I'll inspire you because I'm your muse. *I'm* the art!"

Seven feared she had him then. His flesh cried out for her touch. He'd let her maim him or bless him or whatever she wanted. She stroked her finger up his throat to the bottom of his jaw, lifting his chin. She shushed him and bent down to move her mouth towards his, lips never touching, just teasing. Her breath steamed his cheeks, making him sweat. His eyes drifted shut until her hand clenched around his throat, pushing him back against the futon. While she mounted him, she reached between his legs. She then plunged her fist into his solar plexus. Seven folded, the air leaving his body. She pulled him by his earlobe onto the floor, turned him on his back with her heel. "I'm pregnant, Seven. And if I'm pregnant, you can be, too. We could share it together."

She straddled him and pressed her mouth against his neck. He was melting with her touch. Whether it was Fable or Porter didn't matter, Seven felt himself fading.

There was a shift, and Seven was now in his bedroom at the foot of his bed.

Fable sat at the edge in her skimpy robe until she shrugged and the robe was gone. She leaned back to push her breasts out. She moved on her knees towards the center of the bed, dropping to all fours, legs spread, hair swaying by her shoulders. She patted the blankets seductively. Seeing her naked, he wanted her then, more than anything. He squeezed his eyes shut, and she burned in his inner sight, clearer and brighter than ever. "It's always been us, hasn't it?" she said. "You've always wanted me. Now's your time."

Seven looked away.

"Don't be shy, not all of my parts bite."

No longer thinking at this point, just a progression of hormones and magic driving him, Seven crawled towards her. Fable moved like silk, wavering around him, her form ghosting across his flesh. And behind him, her hands slinked across his waist, easing his robe off. Somehow his clothes were dripping from his body. He didn't question the sensation, just went with it, especially when her fingers moved towards his groin, stroking him.

"I'm the only woman you need," Fable said as she slid her body over his. *Yes, she was and he wanted more than anything to be inside her.* Running her nails along his chest, down his abs, Fable whispered, "I terrify you and you don't know what to do with that." Their mouths met for a moment, a savage kiss. She blinked-out, only until reappearing on her back. She chewed her pinkie while she opened her legs for him and as Seven moved between her, she tasted of peppermint and sage. He continued to work that sacred space, her feet wrapping his back, heels digging into his traps, hands clawing at his head, suffocating him, until she vanished and Seven fell forward, tasting only the sheets, gasping. She shoved him onto his back. She crawled on top of him, gliding her naked body across his. She pressed her mouth against his, her breasts pushing against him. Her hair draped around him, much longer than he remembered and her breath smelled of evergreen.

And then, finally, she lowered onto him. It felt like warm electricity wrapping him, and he wanted to stay there forever, just move deeper inside her and never retreat.

And yet Seven imagined he might've started to write, that while she worked her hips around him, he was at his computer typing. But he wasn't typing; he was in bed...

...and he gripped her hips, her thighs, his hands touching every part of her as she rocked against him, swallowing him. Nothing could compare to the seven thousand shades of violet sex. She was riding him, riding him until the worlds opened within her, and it could've been the beginning and the end and it didn't matter as long as he was inside her. Somehow he had always wanted this, and perhaps it was her and not Paris that was truly dangerous, passion so raw it could cut like glass.

Maybe true love wasn't flesh but the idea of flesh, the ideals of falling for all the beautiful stories that lingered in aesthetic realms. She was promethean fire and lightning and acid. She was everything! And what more could he want from her? Something greater than himself was mounting, preparing to release from his body, and if this continued there'd be nothing else left of him. He'd be spread across the cosmos. He'd be so much more; he didn't care either way.

Moving in and out of her, dormant parts unhinged. Ideas flooded him. A typewriter with fingers for keys. Letters in the shape of chakras. Animals that devoured clouds. Phobias that fell in love with utensils. Streaming through him, he wrote about this, typing manically, fingers cramping, mind racing. And he continued to push into Fable at the same moment, continued to fill her with his seed and stories, thrusting into her fiction-womb, penetrating and prodding...

...and at that same impossible moment, (while he pumped his hips around her) Seven continued to pour out words on his laptop. And as they flowed together, there was no writer, no muse, and yet he wrote, pages streaming from whatever he now had for a body. He was mad, but he had never been so sane. And if the world ceased in his wake, so be it. Their passions mounted together as something greater rose up within them. As she rode him, he wailed out while stars ignited behind his eyes. And in that silence before release, his head rolled back, breath trapped in his throat, and Seven came then, came and came...

...and outside his bedroom, imagined or not, people dreamt and declared their lunatic-fantasies, allowing themselves to give birth to hobbies and passions they never had the courage to explore before. Across The City, people were attacked by infectious languages and abused furniture. Bicycles dreamt of wing-wheeled seraphim. Books opened themselves and threw up their contents in hopes to rearrange the words their own way. Somewhere a domesticated dog stopped its barking as its IQ jumped three hundred points. It began to narrate its plans on animal equality. In another household, a pet salamander remembered the true history of the dinosaurs, and it wept because it saw its future as a prophet amongst its saurian brethren. And those who loved their cars a little too much unzipped their flies and dropped their pants to fulfill their deepest desires.

While all this happened, elsewhere before this, several writers with circle-

shaped souls observed the destruction as their own. They collectively asked the same questions. Could he have done it? Has he freed Notion? They were frustrated men, unable to write their stories, incapable to right their words. They possessed names like Atrophied Word and Arthur Wright and Abernathy Wordsmyth, men with white shadows and sunken hopes. They looked from their White Wombs and shook their heads because it wasn't over. It never ended! The snake would forever eat itself!

Father Notion, if he existed, hammered the walls of his paper prison as he ripped at his newspaper body.

And all those who would perish in this storm would discover themselves within the Hall of Minors where they wailed from the sapphire-prison draped around Miss Minor's neck as she clenched their screaming in her hands.

It was happening while never happening at all, Porter's psychic orgasm building, mounting towards its zenith, and in that final climactic scream, the walls of reality shattered as the world was torn apart...

BANG!!!

The End

…That's what I typed on a laptop the size of a universe, although I knew it wasn't. Sadly, this was just another draft, another bout of rearranging the same garbage into different garbage-shaped arrangements. It was all shit, and shit would be shit, no matter how you restructured it. This time a change was needed. So I pushed through the Fourth Wall and ripped my bastard from his pages…

…"Where?" Seven muttered. "What just happened?"

"The world ended," I said.

"It did? Where am I now?"

"Well, in theory, you're having the best sex of your life."

His face twisted into a huge smile. "And the world's ending…with sex?"

"It's a metaphor I've been playing with."

"So everyone's dead," he said.

I crossed my fingers. "Here's hoping."

An overpowering blankness settled over Seven. "Has this happened before?"

"Yes. But it means nothing. I'm incapable of finishing your story, I'm afraid. I wanted my first novel to be this great epic, but it's not by any means. I hate it now, and in ways I hate you, too, Seven," I said.

"Um, sorry." Seven shifted uneasily.

"So am I. But don't worry. Tetragrammar *never ends. It always returns in another revision. The snake forever bites its tail. And I hate snakes. Don't you understand, nothing's good enough!"* At that, I hung my head in anger and frustration. There had to be a simple way to escape my novel, an easy solution to write its world out of me.

An epiphany struck me then. Things could change.

"I'm tired," I said. "You know, Seven, you're not the only thing in my life." Seven stared dumbly back at me. "I have other stories in me," I continued. "My family thinks I'm spinning my wheels with you, that I should be done with you and move on. They may be right." I paused. "That's why I'm going to do this. I've made a choice."

"What choice?"

"Never mind that," I dismissed.

"Are you Them?" he finally asked me.

I laughed, and I told him the things I wasn't. I told him I wasn't his Authors or Father Notion. Seven looked sickened by this like a fish trying to breathe oxygen or a bird inhaling the ocean. "You need to go," I said.

"But I don't understand any of this," he pleaded.

"Won't matter. You won't remember."

"Don't take my memory again! Don't…"

"Forget," I said.

Seven did. And then I vanished him. I was alone again, staring back at my laptop. And it was true; I had made a choice. I wouldn't be confined to another pointless rewrite. It was down to completion now. The sooner that happened, the better.

What choice? *Seven had asked.*

I now held the Bag of Thrifty and imagined I could use it to my advantage. Every plot hole, every shortcoming, every paragraph of my book I couldn't set right, I believed the bag could be the source of all those answers. It was my creation; after all, it could be anything. I opened it and filled it with miracles. And then I sent it back, an artifact from the Outer Page.

Thrifty would be my messiah.

When that time arrived, the bag would be Seven's out. It would harbor all the answers he needed to end his story, and conclude my misery.

And what does it matter anymore? No amount of revision will cure this book. Tetragrammar *may find that small niche crowd. Some may enjoy it. Most will not. It doesn't cater to any giddy girl demographic. It's not full of facts or history or vampires. It doesn't discuss politics. I never even had a celebrity scandal. Hell, how do you even market a piece of fiction like this? Especially from a first time author!*

It's a mess, full of errors that may have slipped the eyes of editors. And maybe this paragraph has been omitted from the final copy of Tetragrammar; *I don't care anymore.*

There are rules you never break, lazy techniques writers must avoid at all cost. Fuck you then, if you judged what I did. I needed it to end because I hated myself and Tetragrammar. *This was my easy way out, my very own deus ex machina. I knew it. I just didn't care.*

So read on if you must or chuck this novel into the trash. I never wrote it for you anyway.

*

Seven opened his eyes to a bed of strewn sheets. A dense heat hung in the air. A chill breeze wafted in from the window. Either that was the best sex of his life or it had all been a dream. Yet he knew he hadn't hallucinated the whole thing, because he wasn't alone.

Fable sat against the bed frame wearing lacey panties and a crinkled, half-buttoned blouse. Moist strings of hair clung to her forehead. Her mouth twisted into a semblance of a smile, her cheeks pale. She stared ahead, arms crossed, the knobs of her knees touching.

Seven lifted the blanket. He was naked underneath. He timidly leaned off the bed, reached for his boxer briefs, and dressed himself under the blanket. When done, he crossed his arms like a shy girl after prom night, wondering if he should fill the awkward silence. He opened his mouth, finding no words. If what happened really happened, Seven imagined it was an abstract, like having intercourse with the color orange. He cleared his throat.

"What?" she said.

"What happened?"

Fable rolled her eyes. "Has it been that long you have to ask? Tell me what *you* think happened?"

Seven shifted. Perhaps it was better to not say anything. There was a quiet, loaded energy between them, a fragile vibe best not disturbed.

"*We* happened," Fable filled the silence.

"Did we?" Seven's face screwed up. "I don't remember exactly," he said honestly. "There was a man…and The City ended and we were…?" Seven leaned back. "The Porter. You were infected with him. He was in you, knocking you up and forcing the world into an apocalypse. Is that right?"

Fable nodded.

"He's gone now, isn't he?" Seven asked.

All traces of that golden tan, the trashy makeup, were gone. She looked more beautiful without it. "I think so."

"What *did* happen?"

"What really happened? Arman Porter blew his load, I think. The world ended. We inspired The City. The stars ignited, and you rocked my body. His final form was the last act of a climax, a symbolic finale to what he represented. And, yes, he's *dead* dead now." Her smile was a small slit in her pale face.

"If he was inside you," Seven began, "then that means The Authors were in you as well. They were driving you, influencing you." Seven paused. "If we really did…have sex…was it you or Them that I…" He hung the question, feeling strange and used.

"What's done is done." Fable tugged the sheets over her. "It doesn't have to be weird. And it doesn't matter really. It's always been this way. Writer and muse screwing the other till the end of time."

"So the world didn't end?" Seven asked as he hesitantly parted the curtains to check outside. Early morning bathed the Earth. The world looked no different: the same apartment complex, the same parked cars.

"Look, Seven." Fable moved to her knees. "It's not really about whether or not the world did or didn't end. This or that isn't important. Whatever happened took place in another reality."

"Like another dimension?" Seven raised his brow.

"Not exactly. The end, if it happened, occurred in a different context. In the mind, if you will," Fable explained, not fully convinced at her own rationale.

"But the reports," Seven said, "people were killing themselves, were having breakdowns and painting their dreams and all kinds of other shit. I mean, what the fuck did we do?"

Fable shrugged innocently. "We just acted out an expression."

"So it all happened," Seven said.

"Yes," she said.

"And none of it happened."

"Yes."

"We did have," he hemmed and hawed, "you know?"

"We had whatever you want to believe." They locked eyes. His face grew intense, and she knew what he was thinking. "Say it."

"Does this change things between us now?"

"Why would something that didn't happen change anything?"

Seven scrunched his mouth and walked into his living room, past the open laptop on his coffee table, into his kitchen where he stared at his K-cups on the spinning holder, deciding which flavor would be best for an otherwise abstract morning.

"Um, Seven!" Fable called from the other room. "You should see this!" She sat seiza-style on the floor, glaring at his laptop. "Look!" she said, a twinkle in her eye.

He stared dumbly at Fable, not entirely wanting to peer at the screen. But when he did, his jaw dropped. Words filled the screen, lots of words, paragraphs of text, and scrolling down he saw no end in sight, page upon page.

"What is this?" he asked, not believing it.

"You did this?" Fable beamed at him proudly.

"I did?"

"You did."

"When?" he questioned. Fable winked at him. "But if we were in the bedroom or dreaming of sex and if the world ended and Porter used you to trigger his apocalypse...when was I writing...when could

I have done any of this?"

"Yes and yes. Yes to all of it," Fable said.

Seven glared at her, shifting uneasily for lack of any answers. He lowered himself next to her, wrapping his arm around her, pulling her close to him. Together, they began to read the new beginning of *Tetragrammar.*

III

CIRCLE CHILDREN

IN WHICH REVISION IS WRIT WITH BLOOD, A
BUDDHA PERISHES, AND FABLE KISSES A GIRL

12
CONTEMPLATIONS

As time passes in the imaginary space between chapters, shift your focus to a library. There is nothing particularly special about it. It lives on a college campus, bordered by forests. Its only significance is its history, nothing to do with its construction, no, it all boils down to a particular student named Andrew Wilkins who lost his mind within its walls. But that was long ago, six cycles before our present. What is important is the meeting taking place in its café. Three entities sit at a high table by a series of windows where they observe students walking to and from their classes. While this trio can watch the college life, those observed will never discern them.

But let's say you could eavesdrop upon their meeting, you would find that one has extremely dark, unruly hair that defies order. He possesses a five o'clock shadow that looks more dirty than distinguished. Behind his ear is a pen, and he wears a leather jacket with denim jeans and a granite-colored t-shirt.

The other man sips peppermint tea from a paper cup. His attire is comically green with a suit jacket and grass-colored jeans and a ridiculous bowtie. But the most glaring detail is the bag he wears over his head, a detail that for some reason is observed last.

The third, a deceptively young female, wears a smile that could slit your throat. Her hair is obscenely violet and she waits, arms crossed, fingers tapping impatiently on her biceps because she doesn't see the need to be here. And when she flashes you a quick glance, eyes like fire, you nearly wet yourself. You back away because their business isn't yours so scurry on...

*

Fable: I find this whole meeting absurd. We know how this will go.

Seven: Maybe it could be different. He's not like Jack or Porter. He could work with us against Them.

Fable: Why split hairs? We kill Dynasties. We'll kill you.

Thrifty: Killing me will be no easy task.

Fable: No? Then we'll hurt you in other ways. Perhaps burning down that house you call Paradise or gutting your few-marbles-short-of-a-wife?

Seven: Shut up, both of you. We don't have to be enemies. We could use you against The Authors.

Fable: He won't bite the hand that created him.

Thrifty: I'm fully functional on my own. I don't allow porters to traipse around inside my body. I always control my own destiny.

Seven: Look. Tensions are high, but let's talk things out. I need information.

Thrifty: Information?

Seven: About Notion. Before The City went crazy, I had a vision at the park by a pond. A revelation, you could say, where I witnessed a writer kill himself. I'll spare the details, but said writer reminded me a helluva lot of myself. Would you know anything about a particular death around a certain pond?

Thrifty: What's your gut telling you?

Seven: Notion is a suicide.

Thrifty: Well, if that were the case, you've been fighting for a deceased college student who should've upped his dosage of Prozac. Somewhat disappointing, I'd say.

Seven: Does the name Circle Children sound familiar? Perhaps I wasn't the first writer to play this game.

Thrifty: Which would make you number seven.

Seven: I want answers. Concrete answers. I don't believe you remain in the dark. Out of all the Dynasties so far, you're different. You'd know. You may even have every little secret tucked up inside that bag. So tell me what you know or I'll assume our friendship is one big charade.

Fable: Gods' sake, he'll tell you nothing!

Thrifty: I know many things. I know what hides beyond the Fourth Wall. I know the secrets of the Outer Page. I know my predecessors were lethal metaphors, that the future Dynasties will not make your journey easy. I know you don't control Fable though your symbiosis goes both ways. I know The City went to hell and that your world can be retconned and I know the apocalypse was a fever dream that never happened. And I also know the Hall of Minors won't let you forget. They'll be coming for you, the ever sweet and lovely Fable.

Fable: He's fucking with us. And if he keeps it up, I may gut him here, stuff his remains into his stupid bag, and ship him back to Miss Thrifty.

Thrifty: Do what you must, little muse.

Seven: Relax. Both of you.

Fable: Go home, Dynasty.

Thrifty: You'll no longer kill me here?

Fable: I have a better idea. I prefer destroying you in your Paradise. If you claim to be some embodiment of attraction, well, I dare you to pour yourself into your house so every wall and floorboard bleeds with your essence, so that the architecture itself becomes a safety net for your wife. And I'm going to torture your precious Elaine. As I hurt her, you'll know all your intentions were only a speck compared to what I can do, that no matter how hard you try, my desire will always overwrite yours. And when I murder you, you'll know you had all the time to prepare.

Thrifty: On that note, I'll be on my way. Seven, whatever happens I believe in you. You're my friend and that will never change. However, one more truth regarding my makers. You can only defeat The Authors by becoming your own."

And with that, Thrifty stepped from the table, extended a hand towards Seven. They shook and shared a tense, regretful moment before parting ways.

"That went well," Seven said after Thrifty left. "What now?"

"Keep writing," Fable said.

"And you?"

"I already told you what I'm doing."

"You were bluffing about Elaine, I assume."

Her chuckle sounded like glass scraping glass. "Don't go soft. Thrifty's weakness may be his wife. I'll go there and if it makes you feel any better, consider it me following the whim of your subconscious. He's a strange cookie and I'm not certain what his weakness is. But I am positive we must attack his heart. We murder the wife; we murder the man."

Shaking his head, "You can't kill Elaine."

"I can. My hands are already stained. People died because of me, remember?"

"Porter's storm wasn't literal. Besides, if it happened, you were sick with The Authors."

"Would you care either way?" Fable asked.

Seven considered, somehow, no, he wouldn't. He didn't know what to do with that.

"Relax." Fable kissed his cheek. "I'll handle the nitty-gritty. Besides, what could possibly go wrong?"

13
BROWN-BAGGED KARMA

A murder of crows approached from the horizon. They flapped beet-colored wings that dripped electricity. Each crow was covered in jagged feathers, beaks clenched madly on plum-colored eyes. They continued forward, beating their wings towards Paradise.

Thrifty watched all this from under his bag with his mind's eye. He observed they weren't crows at all. Beyond the bird shapes was only one beast, Seven's muse fast approaching. He feared he'd have to hurry. Thrifty departed through the sliding glass door, down the spiral stairs towards the rock patio, into his basement.

In the dark, Thrifty lay a large white poster board on the floor. He simply reached up inside his bag and removed a piece of what could've been his soul. He crushed his soul between thumb and finger to a paste that was part ash, part something else entirely. He smeared it on the poster board, forming a large number seven. He snapped several pens open to retrieve their slender spines of bottled ink and poured each filter into a kitchen bowl until enough ink filled it. It was a tedious ritual, both absurd and metaphoric. He dipped his thumb into the ink bowl, traced a thick, black circle around the seven.

To face the muse, Thrifty would have to invoke the divine, to counter her with his own intentions. And how would one summon the miraculous: abstain from sex, become vegan, pray to Tom Cruise? No, he had the only tool he needed.

Thrifty would pull the fantastic from his bag.

Closing his eyes (if he possessed eyes), he honed his innate ability of attraction and waited in the basement of Paradise. The Tetragram had been the object of power in this reality; the book, the word and weapon, utilized by writers and authors, the thing that drove Seven's world. He would sharpen his intent upon that, and he would manifest what *Tetragrammar* meant to him.

In his mind, an image formed: a book entangled in garden vines and petals blossoming upon its cover. And the book opened with a volcanic explosion of light. And from the light, a figure rose. It was smooth with minimal features except for the gentle smile upon its pale face, its eyes closed in meditative calm. Its legs were crossed, hands resting palms up upon its knees. As Thrifty held the image, he witnessed an aura radiate from its body, an outline of layered energy, of reds and oranges and greens. And it was so beautiful, it moved him to tears. A pair of wings sprouted from its back, flaring majestically outwards. And the wings weren't feathered or avian. A book had grown from between its shoulder blades, the wings the parting of its pages. Thrifty watched enamored at the book-winged Buddha. *A magnificent creature. If only Seven could witness it.*

Thrifty's tulpa sat several feet from him, no less astounding in the material world. In the darkness of the basement, the pages of its book-wings glistened starlight, and it might've been the most beautiful thing he'd ever see.

Thrifty extended a hand towards the Buddha. His fingers grazed its face, so warm to the touch like nothing else in this world. Before he could change his mind, he balled his hand into a fist and punched it in the face. He hit it again and again until its flesh opened and a warmth layered his knuckles. And while he continued his attack, the Buddha-Thing never winced, remained complacent, at peace. While Thrifty murdered what-could've-been-his-Tetragram, he wanted to apologize, but he snuffed that trait from his emotional vat, because remorse could never mix with the intent. Its blood oozed from mortal tears in its paper-anatomy. Blow after blow, Thrifty kicked and pounded it until it fell to the floor, its insides spilling out onto the basement.

So beautiful, Thrifty thought, *while he wept in its butchering.*

After its face had been kicked in, leaving only the semblance of what once was a smile, Thrifty tore at the pages of its book-wings, and when he ripped the pages from its back, something not unlike blood squirted from the shredded pulp. When the Buddha-Thing had been murdered entirely, its body had been strewn throughout the room. Bits of its form dripped crimson from the ceiling and walls, leaving nothing recognizable. Thrifty returned to a lotus posture. He settled his breath. Under a bag splashed with crimson, Thrifty closed his eyes.

He had sealed his fate. Because something so beautiful could never be harmed, the brutality would have to be paid for. As a Master of the Law, he'd attracted his dark fate.

Of course he never wanted to maim divinity, but actions needed to be taken for the story, for Seven and his wife.

Already karma tightened around his heart.

Thrifty took a long, cleansing shower. After dressing in his khakis and emerald jacket, he toured his entire house, running his hands along the walls, the fixtures, paintings, and furniture; a walking meditation that allowed his life force to infiltrate the structure of his home, opening the full flow of his aura into the architecture. He poured himself into the floor and ceiling, into the air, keeping just enough to sustain his physical body for his last encounter with Seven, important most of his essence remained in Paradise for his wife.

Elaine slept on the sofa in the living room. He leaned down to kiss her on the head from his bag-covered lips. He stepped out the front door, followed the path towards his car, and backed out from his driveway, his final departure from Paradise.

Hungry, Thrifty stopped at a hibachi. He sat around the grill with four other people who all waited excitedly for the chef's performance. Those who joined him noted the bag, *how odd?*, then nothing more. On waiting for the show to begin, Thrifty sensed the looming darkness in his soul, the debt of Buddhacide coming to collect. The chef began twirling his knives, catching an egg on a metal flipper and flipping the egg into the top of his hat. He juggled plastic bottles of sake and lighter fluid. Everyone clapped. It had all been quite lovely, that was until he began to stack sliced onions on top of each other, squirting the lighter fluid inside the onion volcano, and then, well, the show was no longer lovely. Thrifty slipped from the hibachi as sirens from red trucks roared onto the premises. Men who fought fires stormed the restaurant. People fled.

The black cloud trailed behind Thrifty as he sped away. It wouldn't change anything. No matter how fast, the Law had his number.

∗

Back in Paradise all the clocks read 7:77. Elaine checked the time, expecting the corny announcement of her husband's *"Honey, I'm home!"* She waited. Huffing, she began a Sudoku puzzle she'd never finish. She penciled in ones and twos and fives, but it was the sevens that bugged her. The sevens continuously threw off the whole grid. Somehow, outside or in her mind, she heard a million flapping wings, and she saw indigo birds with eyes instead of feathers upon their bodies. She blinked to shed the image from her mind, not entirely sure she was safe. No matter how disturbing, it was an odd enough idea to file away for a future art project. She redirected her attention back to the Sudoku. Hours melted away.

She had been watching *The Office*, the episode where Jim convinced Dwight the computer had become self-aware. Her eyes grew heavy and she slid into a state not-quite-sleep, where birds pecked at her until she snapped awake, frozen on her couch. A commercial showed a man yelping in pain as he cleaned his ear with a Q-tip.

Elaine shot up at the sudden pounding at the door. She peeked through the peephole. A woman stood in the yard, a bag on her head. She wore a lacey bed gown decorated with long, slinky ribbons the color of wine. Purple hair spilled out from the paper bag. Elaine blinked, looked again. A violet eye winked at her. The door kicked in against her forehead. Elaine saw stars in the shape of carrion, and her head filled with laughter that made her want to gut herself. She was on the floor, crawling, wanting to scream, until the world saturated to deep indigo.

∗

Thrifty's car refused to hold any fuel as if the gas was being convinced to leech away within the tank. He'd stop at each gas station and while refueling sensed danger through distant walls and floorboards of his house.

Fable had broached Paradise.

Inside the bag, he tensed his mind. Intentions already sealed, he'd have faith in that protective aura within his house, pulsing in the kitchen and cabinets, the living room, closets, the storage rooms, the basement and bedrooms.

Keep going, he thought, *don't give up.*

That's what he continued to tell himself, a rhythmic affirmation, but he was beginning to feel the effects, a deep sucking drain in his fibers. How much longer could he sustain his physical body? Dying wasn't an option. Not yet. If he exhausted himself, he thought of Elaine. Protecting her was paramount. He would not give in.

Thrifty pressed the gas as he raced down the highway.

*

A pixie-faced woman stared at Elaine as she woke. Elaine blinked, smiled naively. She was seated in a chair with the insane notion her seat was a prison and if she attempted to move only bad things would happen. "Um," she licked her lips. "Who are you?"

Fable told her.

"Oh. Are you an obsessed fan?" Elaine asked. "You kidnapping me because I'm not that famous? People love my art and many think I'm brilliant, but really, I am very flattered you took the time to tie me to a chair." When testing her hands, Elaine saw her wrists were bound by nothing, yet she still felt compelled to remain seated. "That's very interesting," Elaine noted. "I like that trick. I think I may name the entire act of one being confined without ever being confined *Existential Chair Chamber*. Wouldn't that make a good name?"

Elaine's blathering induced a minor ache behind Fable's eyes, and she was annoyed the Dynasty's wife hadn't regarded her with more fear. "Firstly," Fable said, "I haven't taken you anywhere. You're at home which makes you a hostage, not a kidnap. Secondly, you are not an artist; you do not have a following."

For a moment, Elaine got the distinct impression this Fable did not like her. And by not like, she was regarded as nothing more advanced than the mold that formed in one's shower. Still, Elaine smiled nonchalantly, stupidly dismissing Fable's criticism. "What are you doing here then?" she asked innocently.

"Did you know there are Authors in the Moon?" Fable asked.

"Really?"

"Do you know what a Dynasty is?"

"Should I?"

"You should. You married one."

"Oh?" Elaine perked up. "That's nice."

"Yes, nice," Fable sniggered. "We're going to kill your husband, Seven and I."

"Seven?" Elaine seemed unfazed. "Not Seven. He's friends with my Marshal. He's nice. He visited us for a bit. He liked my art. He wouldn't do that."

"He would. Killing the Dynasty involves you."

"That's sweet," Elaine said, her response baffling Fable. "But I don't have anything to worry about because my Marshal's around me right now. He's inside the entire house. I didn't know that before, but I do now. Funny, right? Anyway, our house has always been a little slab of paradise and, really, can anything go wrong in Paradise?"

"It can," Fable said. "Whole bibles are based off that."

"And love, right? True bibles are rooted in love." Then, suddenly, as if a light bulb went off in Elaine's cluttered head, she blurted, "Wanna see my art?"

Fable didn't.

Without skipping a beat, Elaine pointed towards the corner of the living room, at a teddy bear that had been de-stuffed, its cotton insides contained within an emerald jar by its side. The bear's face possessed a stitched-on image of Justin Bieber. "I call that one *Bee-bear*," Elaine said. "Hey, we should be friends!" She moved from the chair and extended her hand towards Fable. "We can call it *Ten Fingered Truce*." Glaring suspiciously at Elaine's hand, Fable wanted to snap it off but instead found herself shaking it. "I like your hair," Elaine said as they embraced. "Did you dye it?"

"It's natural," Fable said.

"You're pretty," Elaine replied. "I should color mine violet, too."

"Don't make this weird," Fable sighed.

"Ok," Elaine chirped. "Let's take a tour." And Fable strangely followed the Dynasty's wife in a confused daze.

Upstairs in the bedroom, there was a rubber George Bush mask on a doll's body. A nozzle from a gas can was superglued around its pelvis, bent upwards. In a bathroom, Elaine introduced Fable to a work she dubbed *Porcelain Prosperity*. It was simply a normal toilet with the seat up. Several crumpled dollar bills littered the floor around it. And when moving closer, Fable saw fake money floating in the toilet water. Elaine seemed unusually proud of her work. The Dynasty's wife continued to direct Fable's attention around the house, and somehow Fable found herself following Elaine's cues, her eyes moving from one quirky piece to another.

The tour continued, each room housing some absurd statement

that dripped with Dadaism. Each piece made Fable cringe. The Dynasty's wife, with all her horrible kitsch art, would be a mercy kill. And Fable would've ridiculed each work if it weren't for a vinegar-tasting bile that seemed to crawl up her throat whenever a negative thought entered her mind.

"What do you think?" Elaine asked at one point.

And Fable prepared the most biting, degrading critique in her head, a criticism so harsh and malicious it would make Elaine weep blood. "You're a pretentious pile of shit," she said.

Only that didn't happen.

Instead: "You're magnificent!" Fable gasped and covered her mouth with both hands like the bald screamer in a Moench painting.

"See," Elaine beamed, "I told you you'd like my art."

"Where'd that come from? That wasn't me," Fable muttered. And it wasn't her, not at all, and she gritted her teeth because Thrifty couldn't be overpowering her. A Dynasty overwriting her psyche couldn't happen again, not after Porter. And yet, well aware Thrifty was fueling the atmosphere of the house and everything in it, Fable shifted awkwardly.

Her focus blurred as the intoxicating scent of cardboard and paper bags wafted up her nostrils. And when Fable squinted, Elaine practically glowed, and, yes, she was in fact very beautiful. Hurting Elaine seemed taboo now. *How could she have ever imagined that?* Fable steadied herself. She could feel a Thriftyness surging through her, invading her, blurring her vision.

Kill her now!

Thrifty's feng shui was becoming more powerful, an unrelenting affection that continued to spill into her mind, rewiring her feelings towards the Dynasty and his wife. The longer she stayed, the deeper her fondness would grow. But worse, she suspected she no longer disliked them, that now she began to believe Elaine was quite clever.

Clever? Fable thought until she rattled her head dramatically. Elaine *was* brilliant. There was nothing pretentious at all about placing a pig mask on the kitchen faucet.

This couldn't go on. Elaine had to die. Now. "I'm stronger than your husband," Fable said, clasping Elaine's arm. Glaring at the ditzy, ketchup-haired wife, she said, "I will hurt you. There will be pain, in the mind mostly, or until I decide to cut you with sharp objects. You'll suffer, but you'll love it because you love him."

"Ok," Elaine said with her stupid, simple smile. "Anything for my Marshal."

It was infuriating. Fable was getting beyond frustrated, and she didn't like it. She wanted to hit her, to butcher her as much as she wanted to hug her and touch her and…

Fable kissed her suddenly, pressing her lips long and hard against Elaine's mouth.

*

Thrifty's car overheated. The engine buckled and made a sound healthy cars never make. The steering wheel trembled and an ugly black smoked from the hood. Thrifty pulled the car off the road along a grassy patch bordered by trees. He punched the steering wheel, then smacked his bag-head against the horn once, twice, *honk-honk*. He stepped from his car, not once looking back. Thrifty sulked along the side of the road, striving to keep his internal light strong and steady, alive long enough to do what was needed. *Keep pushing,* he urged. And for now, that would do. It had to.

The skies gradually darkened while Thrifty walked through back roads in a forest. Every step was a greater burden, his feet wanting to give out, just let his body collapse and crumble. How much longer could he hold himself together? How much time did he have before his physical shell depleted itself? He would soon be running on empty while Fable drained him miles away.

He raised a hitchhiking thumb to no one in particular, could only hope a metaphorical gesture could possess enough juice to attract help his way. A driver would stop, Thrifty believed, they must.

Then it happened. A distant car sound trailed through windy scenic roads, headlights looming closer, piercing through the skeletal outlines of trees, drawn into Thrifty's synchronicity. One headlight was bright, a white-blaze that turned his dirty bag to a ragged silver. The other headlight was dim-gray, unclean with insect corpses and dirt. The car slowed, then stopped. A window rolled down. The driver asked if he needed a lift, yes, that would be much appreciated, and Thrifty opened the back door and entered the car.

The driver's head was far too smooth to be shaved, and when turning his head, his face leaned towards androgynous. His eyes glittered with an empty fury. He wore a white jacket that glistened and shimmered.

"I'm Jack," introduced the driver, flashing his white smile. And,

"This is Porter," he gestured to the pretty man in the passenger seat. Porter raised a hand, hello. He was very orange, flesh perpetually tan with thick black, jizz-frozen hair. He resembled one likely to be a candidate for melanoma in the future, that was if an STD hadn't already begun to kill him slowly on the inside. For reasons Thrifty didn't understand, the orange man wore sunglasses despite the setting sun. His attire made Thrifty think about the kind of clothes found in trashy boardwalk shops. Porter's shirt clung tightly to his biceps. It was decorated in ugly skulls. Porter didn't seem real, just a tacky idea taking up space.

"Where to?" Jack asked.

Thrifty told him.

"Sure." Jack grinned. Dark shadows pitted in his eyes and mouth.

After a moment, "Do I know you?" Thrifty asked.

"We've never met," Jack stated curtly. Then, reciting a line a haughty televangelist may say, "Although if you seek light and truth, then you shall know me."

Thrifty zoned out in a grainy patch of consciousness. He swore a hole was opening inside his heart and he desperately squeezed his eyes shut, an attempt to pinch off his fleeting life force.

Elsewhere, in his house, Thrifty persisted in keeping Fable's homicidal thoughts at bay with his intent. He visualized Elaine, safe and whole and happy, secured in his love. And while he did this, he forced his essence around Fable, binding her feelings with his. But how much longer could that last?

Withdrawing his awareness, Thrifty gathered himself in the back seat. An argument had ensued between Jack and Porter. Wanting to stay out of their dispute-*Focus on your wife*-Thrifty crossed his arms, in hopes to seal himself off.

"Alive back there?" Jack asked. *Hardly.* "Shed some light on a topic we were discussing?"

Something was off, of course there was, Jack and Porter were dead, lingering in whatever realm deceased Dynasties go. And blinking, Thrifty couldn't distinguish whether or not his vision played tricks on him or was this a side effect of his depleting life?

Crimson patches of fruit punch colored light dotted his vision, like floaters at the edge of perception. The red was liquid and light and blotchy, and it crawled around Jack and Porter, like blood-that-wasn't-blood moving between them, connecting them. But it was also dust and mist, and it blurred his vision.

Thrifty tapped his foot to remind himself he was still in the car, still solid and present. Rubbing his sweated hands on his green khakis, he wanted to be sick, to hide in his bag, and he wasn't hallucinating as Jack and Porter altered to some degree. *(How? He wasn't sure)*. That liquid, or light, seemed to be melting into their skin and clothing, reddening Porter's tan complexion, dirtying Jack's suit, layering their faces and flesh, and if Thrifty had to use one word, it would be wet, although that wasn't quite accurate either.

When Jack addressed him again, his voice seemed to be calling from some faraway place, like an echo at the end of a tunnel. Thrifty inhaled deeply, *hold it together,* when Jack stated, "We were discussing the creation of the universe. In the beginning," Jack continued, his aura crimsoning, becoming wetter, "there was light, only light, and then people came, casting shadows and they multiplied their filth, darkening what should've remained beautiful. That's how it began." Jack punched the steering wheel, sealing his point with a lonely honk.

"No." Porter shook his head, lowered his sunglasses. "The universe began with a scream. An orgasm so vast existence was nothing more than a single ejaculation."

"Seriously!" Jack cut in. "You're an idiot. What about you, friend, what do you think?" He flashed his luminous gaze in the rearview mirror.

"No opinion," Thrifty sounded tired.

"Come now," Jack urged.

Thrifty sighed. "God made a wish, and God reached into a bag that contained everything, and it dumped the contents out and the universe, in every possibility, was made manifest. And many years later, a man would sacrifice himself as a gift to his friend."

The drive turned deadly silent. They continued through the back roads. "Neither of you should be here," Thrifty said. "The First Dynasty is dead. The Second deceased." While he said this, through blurred vision, he glimpsed that blood-essence sliding and flowing between Jack and Porter, connecting their bodies in a shifty fog of transparent scarlet that shared qualities of water and paint. Thrifty leaned forward between the seats. "You're like me, although you feel different," he suggested, unsure. Jack and Porter exchanged bemused looks. "What are you?"

"Jack," said Jack.

"Porter," said Porter.

Thrifty: Are you the Fourth?

Jack: Fourth what?

Thrifty: Who created us?

Porter: Us?

"Yes, us!" Thrifty urged, then embraced the seat as nausea churned his guts, that hole in his soul growing, spilling warmth from his hands. *Protect Elaine! Hold it together.* "We're Dynasties. They wrote us. So, what are They?"

Jack's voice rose, "They who?"

Thrifty: Don't play daft! Seven believes They live in the Moon, but They're not aliens or gray men. Seven can only imagine what They look like. And sometimes I don't think he believes They exist at all, and deep down, he's terrified that he's falling deeper into layers of semi-truths.

"Seven may have a lot of notions," Jack grinned. "None of them are accurate, and he'll never make it."

They drove past a church, a baseball field. Jack slowed at the stop sign, turned left onto a road that wound and curved.

Porter twisted in his seat to face Thrifty. "What's under the bag?"

Thrifty: None of your concern.

Porter: You don't wear a bag for shits and giggles. What's it mean?

Thrifty: It covers my bleeding third eye. It holds the soul of my body. It's the face of a beast with no name. It contains the secret language of those who observe the Outer Page. As I said, let it go.

Porter: I don't think I'll let it go. You see, Porter takes what he wants.

He reached back, haphazard attempts to grasp the bag.

"Don't do that," Thrifty warned, swatting his hands.

Porter undid his seat belt, twisted further. He bumped Jack. The car swerved. "Take it off!" He gripped the bottom edge of the bag, crumpling it. And it happened quickly. Thrifty grabbed Porter's wrist, somehow with little effort wrapped the passenger's seat belt around his neck, and instructed Jack to hit the brakes, hard. Jack did. A sick crunch followed as Porter's neck snapped. His head fell back, tongue hanging limp.

"I warned him," Thrifty said, letting go.

"You did," Jack agreed.

They continued their drive onto the highway, off the ramp, then through another series of back roads set in the woods. Jack and

Thrifty shared a silence brimming toward homicide. Neither addressed the elephant in the room as ugly red patches the shade of rotten cherries began to pockmark Porter's tan, nor did either comment when Porter began to decompose, the body softening to a gel that melted into the upholstery, leaving a mist in the air.

While Thrifty observed this, he also strained to hold himself upright, keep his essence flowing, intoxicating Fable enough to keep her at bay.

"Something wrong, friend?" Jack glared from the rearview mirror.

A wet crimson rose where Porter used to be, moved, and coiled around Jack's arm, crawling over his shoulders, down his legs. His eyes changed. Liquid scarlet trickled down his cheeks, absorbed into his smooth face. Excess blood-that-wasn't-blood trailed off his forehead as tiny beads of rose-rain. And his clothing slowly saturated with a deathly ink.

"What are you?" Thrifty tensed.

"I'm what broke the circle." Jack pressed the gas. The car buckled forward, swerved in the acceleration, and peeled forward with a squeal. Thrifty lunged for the wheel. Jack turned the wheel, hard. There was spinning then, down a hill. An airbag deployed. A body ejected through the front windshield with the large, dizzying crash.

Thrifty lay on his back outside the wreckage. He wiggled his fingers, felt his bag for tears. Several feet behind him smoke emanated from the hood. Pieces of glass and grass clung to his clothing. He rose shakily to his feet. His ankle rolled out on a rock buried in a clump of twigs, followed by a snap. He collapsed onto the dirt, muddying his green attire. He ignored the pain, rose, fell again, then hopped one-legged towards the driver's side of the car.

Jack was hunched against an exploded air bag. Flakes of red and glass were embedded in his flesh. Thrifty rested his back against the side of the car. He grabbed his knees, a meager attempt to not pass out. He tried opening the door, which didn't budge. He smashed the window with his elbow, checked Jack's forehead, a faint pulse in his third eye. Thrifty finagled the door open from the inside, unlatched the belt, and dragged Jack from the car, drudging up an incline of leaves and dirt, hauling the limp body, like a girl pulling a life-sized ragdoll. He dropped Jack.

He slapped Jack across the face, only to back away as Jack started to melt and when Jack was nothing more than a puddle on the forest floor, Thrifty dipped his finger into the pool-that-was-once-Jack. Thrifty retrieved his finger, looked at it. He kneaded the fluid between thumb and finger. It wasn't dry or sticky. It was not by any means blood and it spread through his fingers, inking its way onto his palm, up his forearm. Thrifty eyed his hands, like a madman staving off an infection.

A dull breath wheezed in the air, echoing from the puddle of what was left of Jack. The wheeze turned to laughter, then gurgling, and Thrifty's vision blurred and he staggered until collapsing. Through a haze, he saw, or sort of saw, a body rising from the puddle, surrounded in a red not like color or liquid, but red as elemental, a color that was sentient and self-aware. And it moved, wavered, twisted, reshaped. With the metamorphosis complete, Thrifty leaned away.

Jack was now Elaine, *his* Elaine. Thrifty knew, through and through, this was impossible, a trick. Elaine-who-was-not-Elaine waved him towards her. "Hey, hun," the Elaine said. "I'm going to die you know. Fable's going to strangle me with my intestines and call it *The Apocalypse of Pasta*."

Ignoring his broken ankle, Thrifty crawled towards her.

"You could stop it if you hadn't left me." Elaine grinned; the pupils of her eyes shivered. "But you chose to meet Seven instead, the man you claimed to be a friend, the same buddy who sent his dog to gut me dead."

Before she could continue, Thrifty was on her, clenching her throat, choking off the imposter's life. As Elaine clawed at him, no, clawing at her own face, her fingernails began to tear her own flesh, scraping and sculpting and reshaping until Elaine was now Seven.

"Gonna die, Thrifty," the Seven hissed. "I'll try to put every limb I dismember into your bag. It should fit. There's plenty of room for all your bullshit."

Thrifty balled his fists into Seven's t-shirt. "What are you?"

"Me?" Seven lifted his chin. "I'm the Dynasty Killer. I'm the Tetragrammaton!" And Seven wrapped his hands around Thrifty's. "I'll smash your Law with my own words. Like attracts like. Pain breeds pain. Did you think I wouldn't destroy everything you loved before I murdered you?" Seven snickered. "You told me yourself: Fiction is my power. So I dream, and Fable obeys."

"Do you have a true face?" Thrifty's patience wavered.

Cocking his head, "Do you?"

"Your ability hides your shape well."

"And that tattered bag of a universe you wear, I'm not the only one hiding!"

"You're the next Dynasty."

"I'm more than that," Un-Seven flashed his teeth.

As Thrifty loosened his grip, Seven's head kicked back. The body quivered, convulsed, melted into a crimson pool. Thrifty dropped onto his butt, tried steadying his emotions as his life leaked from his body. "Keep it together," he repeated in a sad mantra, pushing himself to his feet.

An arm wrapped around Thrifty's chest from behind. Something sharp entered his back, pushing through the space around his heart and he dropped to his knees. His attacker embraced him, cushioning his fall, cradling him while Thrifty pawed over his head and about.

"Ssh," eased his attacker. While Thrifty heaved under the bag, the man gently shifted himself out from under Thrifty. He gently lowered him, not before pulling out the sharp-something embedded in his back.

The sly man with a fox smile cleaned oily fluid from the tip of a silver pen. The man was tall, had an aura that made him look perpetually wet. He wore jeans and a salmon-colored buttoned shirt with a messy collar. His red ponytail, pulled tightly back, exposed a large forehead.

"I'm sorry," he apologized, sincerely. "I have nothing against you, Marshal Thrift. I admire you, in fact. It's daring to do a soul-splice. Takes even more power to sustain it. Most of you is in your house, I get it. I'm no stranger to being in multiple locations at once. It's my knack in a way." He placed the pen in the back pocket of his jeans. He had crusted red around his lips and mouth. "Despite all your intentions, Fable's strong. Believe me, I've known her longer than Seven. We all have. You see, she wants us writers to explore, to dream, to express the magic stirring in us." He opened his arms theatrically. Cracking a smile, "But the truth is we're only good enough until she uses us up. She won't admit this, may not remember after so many cycles. That's where my true gripe lies."

Thrifty's chest rose dramatically. *Stay strong.*

"The true villain is not The Authors. The enemy is nothing more than a notion, and yet his sickness permeates his children, spinning them into complacent cycles of write this, do that, as if we had no free will to decide our own stories. Consider me a fish against the current, because I've changed everything now. I'm a cipher, a red herring, and I'm the answer Seven must embrace."

Thrifty gripped at the grass, tried moving. Rushing towards him, the Red Man consoled him. "Hey now. You're not done yet. I want your wife to be ok. But you have to keep it together. I know what the bag is. I know its power. More importantly, Seven needs to know its truth. So stay alive long enough. Go to my brother. Tell him to meet me in the place notions kill themselves."

He helped Thrifty to his feet, held him long enough for Thrifty to support himself. "I'll tell you a secret. I'm the Fourth Dynasty. But I'm also the Fourth Circle Child. I'm Notion's Devil. Their adopted bastard. Whatever this world has left hinges on Seven. God speed, Thrifty," he said before melting and misting into nowhere.

When alone, Thrifty looked at his hands, at the crimson infection leeching into his clothing and up his arms. *Almost there,* he told himself. *Love you, Elaine,* he thought, *love you.* And Thrifty staggered forward.

14

BREAKING BAG

No one in the Gatewood Apartments noticed the bag-headed man. He sulked through the parking lot, between the townhouses onto the paved sidewalks. He passed dog walkers and joggers. He drifted past a pool and tennis court, a Domino's delivery car, and residents coming and going. He meandered down the sidewalk where teenagers smoked by a mailbox and a couple looked tired from arguing. None acknowledged Thrifty as he staggered beyond the garbage bins and the lampposts. He stepped towards the apartment entrance. With the last bit of will, he rang the doorbell until his legs gave out and he awkwardly fell against the wall, sliding down chin first, collapsing in an odd mess. And he waited for Seven, hoping not to die just yet.

*

Seven really wasn't good in heated situations. He often froze at reading a clock if people asked him the time. He rarely ever found that item people asked him to find. He couldn't recall all the times Paris told him to get the spaghetti sauce from the cupboard or the Worcestershire from the fridge or the applesauce in the grocery aisle. She'd repeat in tired berating, it's there, *right there,* just look in front of you. But panic had always set in and Seven hated himself a little for it.

Now.

Finding Thrifty dying at his front door was hardly different.

Yes, he clearly saw the crumpled body lying on his doormat by his feet. The bag was beat-up yet remained perfectly on his head.

Although he saw all this, he didn't move, not right away, not until he realized that moving would be good if he were to help his friend.

As if making up for time, Seven huddled around Thrifty, shaking him, feeling for a pulse. The bag, the body, the entire scene looked wrong.

"What the hell happened to you?" Seven barked.

Seeing Thrifty this way sickened him and on examining his friend, Thrifty remained rag doll-limp, wrist dangling when Seven raised his arm at the elbow. A network of bloodied veins webbed across his palm, like an infectious tattoo that trailed spindly lines up each finger and down the forearm.

Thrifty's green jacket was ruffled, his pants wrinkled and muddied. Seven found a gash in Thrifty's back. Something wet and black leaked onto his hands, pooling on the floor. Placing a hand on his chest, "Save your breath. Let's get you inside." That's what Seven said as he tried to hoist him up, until muttering, "Fuck me! Did you eat a ton of bricks?" when Thrifty failed to budge.

He seemed impossibly heavy. After several attempts to pull him up, Seven took a deep inhale, grabbed Thrifty by the wrists, leaned back, tugged with all his might. Through a series of awkward movements, Seven dragged the bag-headed man into his home, dropping him in the center of his living room. A dirty, wet trail of mud or blood streaked along the floor.

Seven closed his door. His low back throbbed and his legs ached. He was thoroughly exhausted, his t-shirt layered in a ridiculous amount of sweat. It didn't seem right to leave Thrifty on his back, so with one final effort, Seven pulled him up and slouched him against the futon.

The faintest movement came as Thrifty's chest rose ever so slightly in labored breath. His head slouched forward, the bag gazing blankly at Seven.

"So. How've you been?" Seven asked, an attempt at levity. Thrifty remained silent. "I assume this to be the handiwork of my sweet muse."

After a moment, "Nonsense," Thrifty gurgled, not without humor.

"Sorry."

"Don't be. Fable will be Fable. As of now, she's in my house with my wife, and if it weren't for me, she'd be doing murderous things to the woman I love."

"This really was going in only one direction," Seven said for lack of anything else.

"It would eventually come to this, I know. I'm not mad, buddy. I only prepared."

"They don't call you Thrifty for nothing," Seven added.

"I've bled myself into Paradise and it's taking a toll on my body. The longer Fable remains in my house, the greater the expenditure on my life, the weaker I get trying to rework her."

"Why didn't you just stay with Elaine?"

Thrifty laughed. "I had to meet you directly, away from her. It needed to be this way."

"Why?"

Thrifty remained silent.

"You look bad," Seven said. A patch of crimson spiderwebbed through Thrifty's clothing, across his knee, trailing his thighs, down his legs. It seemed interwoven with his fabric so that the clothing and flesh were one in the same. "I never wanted this. I wanted to believe we could move past the rules. You don't deserve to die. You're not a villain. But that was Their intent, wasn't it? The Third Dynasty was created as a friend. I wanted to not like you and I'd imagine all the ways I would do it. I imagined writing your death and believing in it, using the Law against you. I wondered what would happen if I tore the bag off your head. Would you wither away? Was it a life support or some loaded metaphor? I toyed with burning down your house, too. With every scenario, I knew I couldn't kill you."

"But she could," Thrifty said. "Fable could."

Seven looked at the tattered bag. "I wish it didn't have to be this way." Seven reached forward, touched Thrifty's crimson-splashed hand.

"I understand," Thrifty consoled. "Now. I can't hold on much longer. But there was another who attacked me. The Fourth Dynasty is already here, and he'll be coming for you."

Seven said nothing. Then, "What did he look like?"

"Like many things," Thrifty said.

Seven moved to Thrifty's side. "It's all absurd," Seven laughed, looking at the ouroboros ring. "I proposed to a woman who I never wanted to marry with an ugly ring that I sometimes think is alive. I told myself I loved her even though I didn't know. She hits me with a car and a couple months later I'm ready to tie the knot. I lied to myself because isn't that what writers do? Is that any more insane than murdering Authors in the Moon?"

"Yes. It is absurd," Thrifty said, "and it's as funny as an open door on the day of an apocalypse."

*

It was all stupid in theory, the plan rather silly when thinking about it. And it all should've gone like clockwork. Go to Paradise. Kill the wife. Mortally wound the Third Dynasty. When did it become so tangled? One moment, Fable had been trying to mock Elaine's artistic visions. The next, her tongue was probing the inside of her mouth. Now, both were at a loss for words.

"We could talk about this?" Elaine said. "I'm flattered and all. You are very beautiful, but I'm not into girls. I'm kinda married." When Fable remained silent, Elaine added for comfort, "You don't love me."

"I don't?" Fable found herself saying.

"No. You love Seven."

"Excuse me?"

"My husband told me you do. You two may not admit it but you love him. That's why you get mad. He said Seven's afraid to tell you he loves you, too. You two have always been in love." Elaine's eyes widened as if a light bulb had just flashed in her head. "I know that all of a sudden! I didn't before, honest! It's just now I do."

Fable's cheeks flushed.

Elaine cuddled Fable, like they were old sorority sisters. "It's all love really."

While Elaine comforted Fable, it all made far too much sense. Murdering Elaine was illogical. Disobeying the house was like reprimanding a fish for being wet. Fable could not harm Elaine. Although she wanted to reject her affections, she couldn't ignore the will of Thrifty crawling in her pores, and she didn't like it. "Your husband's trying to protect you," Fable said. "He's stronger than I thought."

As she said this, her words lacked conviction. Before her motives were entirely rewired, she had to do away with Elaine. Elaine needed to be inspired now, and, by inspired, she needed to be killed, killed dead! Instead, it was *him* inside her, pushing her when Fable uttered, "You're beautiful."

The only comfort she had from this was knowing no matter his location, his manipulating her had to be taking a toll. At this rate, he wouldn't be able to sustain his physical body much longer.

"My presence has to be draining him. Even if the house is overwriting what I came to do, it won't last much longer. I came here to kill you. But right now I can't stomach the thought of harming you. My empathy won't last when your hubby wears out. When that happens, I won't bat a lash at killing you. So please leave, get out now before I hurt you."

Already she saw the flaws in that logic. The only thing protecting Elaine *was* the house and to depart from it was like asking a rodent to snatch the cheese from that friendly contraption outside its mouse-hole. Part of Fable hoped Elaine would take the advice so she could get it over with while another part prayed for her to remain safe within Paradise.

Elaine shook her head. "I don't need saving. The house doesn't protect me. His love does. That's our paradise." And she smiled foolishly. "Why don't *you* leave?" Elaine said, her suggestion was so simple, so fantastically, supernaturally reasonable that Fable blinked dumbly at its logic.

Leave? Fable thought. *She didn't want to leave. Why would she?*

And Fable saw this too was part of the trap. Leaving was an option after all, wasn't it? If she took that route, Thrifty would still live but he'd be weakened enough for the kill. Yet, she had to stay because part of her never wanted to leave. Contradictions mounting, Fable walked towards the front hall that led away from the kitchen. She approached the exit to Paradise.

*

"How did you meet Elaine?" Seven asked.

"It was a bright, sunny day," Thrifty laughed. "I saw her running through a field of daffodils; her hair wild, free and blowing. She saw me and we both ran towards each other, sunlight bathing our bodies and browning my bag. We embraced and I lifted her in the air, swinging her in large circles." Thrifty paused. "We made love in a garden. And eventually, the bells of matrimony sounded and we were happily married." A pain caught in his throat, and he winced as his chest rapidly rose under the shortness of breath.

"Is that how it happened?" Seven asked after Thrifty steadied himself.

"No." Thrifty resigned to a gentle stillness.

Seven placed his hand on Thrifty's for a moment. Seeing him so vulnerable unsettled him. "What did her hair smell like?" Seven asked.

"Her hair? Why?"

"Paris's hair never smelled like anything. No matter what she used on it, it smelled like nothing. I always found that strange and I always wondered why that bothered me so much. Then I realized, smell triggers memory. Here I was with no recollections of why I do what I do, why I write or fight authors. By her lack of smell, she was another blank slate, something for me to create a story with. It was never in the script to fall in love, to deviate from *Tetragrammar*. I was alive with her in the beginning. I wanted her to be that face I saw when I wasn't staring at the Moon, wanted her to be all the words I still hadn't put together. If we fought, if we laughed and cried, I wanted her there for me. She was flesh and blood and not some ambiguity I couldn't see. I could hold her, touch her. But smell, I could never smell her. I'd inhale nothing and she'd remind me of my past, no scent with no memories."

Neither of them said anything.

"What if I told you all this was my doing?" Thrifty said eventually. "What if I told you that you didn't have to kill me?"

"I don't understand," Seven said.

Thrifty shifted against the futon. "You knew from the beginning that you'd always have to kill me; after all, it's one of those unwritten rules. For you to get to Them, you and no one else would inevitably have to see your way through all the Dynasties." Thrifty's voice caught in his throat and he gurgled and began to cough. Regaining himself, "By that logic, you couldn't progress until I was dead. Now think about it, buddy. What am I?"

Seven hesitated. "How do you mean?"

"What do I embody? What is my *gimmick*? Come on, I've already told you."

"You're the Law personified."

"Exactly. If you ended me, what would happen to you?"

Glaring at him, Seven said, "Like attracts like. Death paid with death."

"I was a catch-22 that would've snuffed you out if you played the game. I couldn't allow that. So I changed the rules. I secured my fate another way."

"How?"

"I bled myself into another shape; I shifted my form into my house. It's not so abstract, is it? Isn't death a shifting of forms after all? But that wasn't enough," Thrifty continued. "Before I did this, I summoned *Tetragrammar*. Not the book you're writing; my version of it, what it represented to me, and on doing that I saw it wasn't a book at all. To me it embodied perfection, divinity. It was beautiful and perfect." Thrifty paused, reflecting. "I murdered it. Butchered it to insure my karma so you'd survive. Now imagine the price I'd have to pay, someone like me, a spirit of attraction, imagine the cost for the murder of a saint or a god."

"Thrifty...geezus..."

"That was my free will and you should take the same initiative. You're a writer, buddy. You can create anything you choose. You don't have to be trapped with binding notions and outdated rules. You can embrace any story you imagine. So free yourself!" Thrifty's voice was becoming raw and scratchy. "You don't have to perpetuate your own lies. Not unless," he murmured, "not unless you desire to. You could walk away."

"I don't think I could. Father siphoned off part of himself and hid the Tetragram in me. It's obviously important, and They're afraid I'll use it against Them. Otherwise, They wouldn't be taking all these measures. I can't let that go. Not now. Even if I wanted to, I wouldn't know how."

"You'll destroy yourself if you fight Them," Thrifty's voice shrank. "You may find you'll never finish *Tetragrammar*."

"I can't stop. I've already made some headway with it."

"Yes, but perhaps it was never meant to be completed."

"Then that's how it will be," Seven said.

"Have you ever wondered what Their true face is? Have you considered that They are Jack and Porter and They are me, that all Dynasties are different angles of the same entity? If They created me, then I am to some degree Them. And yet as a friend, how do you distinguish the difference? If my body is part of Their shape, then what do you believe my true form is?"

"I always assumed your true form was inside the bag," Seven said.

"You're right, buddy. If you look within, bags or bodies, you will always find potential. I'm afraid you haven't accepted that yet." Thrifty's limbs convulsed as a filthy crimson spread like a liquid web through him. "I want you to take my bag," he said softly.

"I can't." Seven wagged his head.

"It's my final present to you. Please take it." As Thrifty spoke the room darkened with shadow, and in the dim light, a bloodied hand pointed towards the bag. Seven remained frozen, unable to touch the bag, and yet, "Go on," Thrifty eased, "it's yours now."

Seven placed his hands on the bag and ever so slowly lifted it. And somehow, when the bag was off his head, Thrifty's face remained out of focus. Seven glared at the bag which felt like normal paper yet so much more, like it was beating or being charged from within. While holding the bag upside down, Seven swore he saw something black and slick dripping from it, something spilling from the shadows. And when he turned it right-side up, he witnessed only for a second, a light erupt from it, volcanic in its movement. Seven blinked; he didn't dare peek in.

"What is it?" Seven asked.

"It may be a gift; it may be a curse," Thrifty uttered. "It is a potential death sentence as much as it is a glorified miracle. It's divine intervention and the devil's curse in a bag. I won't lie, using it could bring about fatal consequences. It may contain answers; it may not. It could be the catalyst that triggers your apocalypse, for better or worse. It's all those things and nothing at all. It's whatever you need it to be."

Seven scrunched the bag, rolled it shut, folded it, set it on the floor between them. "You didn't tell me anything."

"It's my bag of tricks," Thrifty said.

"Bag of whatever, it feels strange, like I shouldn't use it."

"You say that now but time will tell. And at that moment when you're lost, who can say you won't reach inside. When you realize The Authors may never be defeated, that your story may never end and you wish to leave while believing there's no way out, you may use it. Whatever you decide, it's in the bag," he added for good measure. With that, Thrifty shook, seizured. Seven moved towards his friend, embracing him on the floor. Thrifty whispered from his blurred face, "The Fourth Dynasty gave me a message. You'll meet him soon if you go there."

"Where?" Seven hissed.

Thrifty told him, then with his last breath, "Good-bye, Seven."

"Good-bye…buddy," Seven said eventually and he leaned into the shadows to kiss the top of his head. He held his dying friend, held him as he convulsed and spasmed, clenching his eyes shut, hugging tighter until he was alone, hugging only himself.

When Seven opened his eyes, only the bag remained, followed by the permeating scent of canonized roses. He clasped the folded bag and set it on the kitchen table. Then, suppressing the sickness in his guts, Seven cleared the table, knocking everything to the floor. And dropping to his knees, he mourned his friend.

*

In Paradise, Elaine sat at the bottom of the stairs, which she dubbed *Frozen Escalator*, and waited for Thrifty. He'd be home soon, she imagined.

15

SUSPENSION

One step. Two steps. Three steps. Fable had been walking entirely too long. The front door of Paradise was little more than ten paces away. For crying out loud, she should've been there by now. Yet she continued forward, somehow only thinking this was slightly off. One, two, three steps more and she had failed to broach any distance between herself and the exit. At this point, concern set in. She should've been out the door, several blocks away, let alone another location entirely she could've travelled with a single blink. One, two, three steps.

Fable looked over her shoulder. The kitchen seemed miles away and looking towards the exit again, only ten feet from her, she sighed, a who's-fucking-with-me-now exhalation. "If that's you, Thrifty, stop stretching the hall," she addressed the ceiling and walls. "I'm leaving!"

A sharp bullet echo of high-heels clacked towards her. Fable couldn't tell where the noise emanated from but knew wherever that was didn't belong in this home. Slowly, the fragrance of shopping catalogues and new shoes wafted around her. For a moment, she had the strongest impulse to buy a purse, the kind that was small enough to not hold anything while being morbidly fashionable.

A tall woman who didn't fit the décor of the hall strutted towards Fable. She was surrounded in a halo of cobalt that faded the closer she approached. "Well, well," said the woman with the done up hair. "I'm surprised you haven't murdered, *um*, excuse me, inspired that poor woman yet."

"Who are you?" Fable asked.

"Why, do call me Miss Minor, representing the Hall of Minors."

Hall of Minors, Fable mouthed.

"You've come here to kill a minor woman by the name Elaine Thrift. She is an irrelevance in the larger drama, yet plays into the death of one adversary you've deemed the Third Dynasty. Well, this Elaine Thrift is still alive, which is funny since we so wanted her to join us." As she spoke, thick lipstick the color of crackling azure caked her lips. Smeary twilight-gray eyeliner melted down her gaunt cheeks. A disembodied mouth, wide and full, floated over her head, a deranged, smiling halo. "I'm impressed you've restrained yourself," said the woman, clasping her hands behind her back. "I assume you didn't spare her out of free will, but rather because the Dynasty has managed to rewire your intent." Miss Minor puffed her chest, pressing her cleavage outwards, reminding Fable of a business woman securing a deal with a hot shot CEO. "We were so ready to swallow her into our little company."

"We? Who are we?" Fable asked.

Ignoring her, Minor continued, "Nonetheless, we expect payment."

Fable walked toward the woman. After several steps was no closer. "What is this? You're not part of this house." Fable winced, signs of recognition. "I know you. My God, you! The grape leaves girl. The adulteress…"

"Yes, me."

"What happened to you?"

And Fable flashed on a moment from when she had unleashed her tainted magic on the world. She recalled the once Trish Shapiro, a woman who prided herself as unattainable; the prize, not the pursuer. Fable witnessed the addictive spark she had ignited inside Trish's mind, a seed of obsession for just one man, a lesson to demonstrate Trish was petty and small, that she'd crumble with desire like any other. Fable recalled how Trish had referred to herself as a muse. *The audacity!* she had thought. So while Porter had coursed through her, she would show Trish how small she was, how minor. Images streamed through Fable, quick flashes of Trish's compulsive dreams for Ethan; until the thoughts had grown so bad, they left Trish no other choice but to end her existence with a noose and the dead drop of gravity...

"Remember me now?" Minor said. A large sapphire hung around her throat, and she clasped it with religious fervor. There was a chair now and she sat on it, crossing her legs.

"You were caught up in that insanity current. It...it wasn't entirely my fault. Blame the Porter; blame The Authors." Fable wrinkled her brow. "Whatever happened between us, if I hurt you any way, I'm sorry. I was sick, possessed..."

"Let's move on," Minor said with a smile that would never move on. "You may think I want vengeance. I do, but I don't want to kill you," Minor's voice rose like the office bitch faking niceties. She'd always crave the kind of vengeance that would drag your battered ego through the gutters.

"Right," Fable said.

"Ruminate all you want, the facts are the Hall demands payment. We expect a new victim; we shall receive one. Your," Miss Minor cleared her throat, "act of compassion towards one Elaine Thrift surprises us. The Hall by definition could never admit you or your kind. However, it would allow if said person were to be treated as an intruder. To be isolated, imprisoned, and tortured. To play virus. We and the Hall assuming the role of protectors, as," she paused for the correct reference, "immune system."

"What are you getting at?"

Miss Minor placed one hand on her hip. "Reduce your major stature. Relinquish yourself to us." The other hand toyed with the sapphire. Fable fixated on it for a moment as if it were drawing her inwards. Miss Minor seemed amused by this. "It is something, isn't it?" She raised it to eye level, talked more to the sapphire than Fable.

"This is ridiculous." Fable crossed her arms. "Why should I have to pay when it's not my fault?"

"You're still blaming a horny porter as your scapegoat," Minor scoffed. "Your priority was to kill the Third Dynasty. Paradise will not allow the murder of its host. If mortal harm falls on Elaine, it will efficiently and mercilessly snuff out your life. Either give us Elaine or forfeit yourself to burn off the black karma you inflicted on the fabric of reality." Any fight drained from Fable. She rubbed her brows.

"Either way I'm screwed," Fable said.

"Exactly," Minor chirped, finagling the sapphire. "First, we'll need a deposit, a good faith effort in securing your fate." She edged towards Fable, placed her hand around her chest, not making contact, just holding it there. "To complete the agreement, we'll need a piece of you, contracted into a symbol of you. In other words, we need your heart," Minor added with delight.

Fable raised an eyebrow. "You need my heart?"

"Well, half will do for now," Minor nodded.

"Metaphorically, I assume."

"Yes, which for you is quite literal."

"Fine." Fable dropped her arms by her side and her shirt dissolved from her body, her breasts exposed.

"By the by," Minor quipped, unimpressed, "this *will* hurt." And before Fable could comment, Minor pressed her fingers into Fable's chest, pushing slowly, and it did hurt. As her fingers probed inside Fable, Minor's eyes flared while the mouth-halo above her licked its cerulean lips with a forked tongue. Minor's hand eventually clenched around something solid within Fable's chest.

Snap!

Minor tugged.

For a moment, Fable blacked out and as she came to, she saw Minor examining her half-heart. Upon seeing her half-heart, Fable wasn't entirely surprised it wasn't heart-shaped at all. It appeared book-like, composed of orchid-colored light that pulsed rhythmically, contracting and expanding. Already its indigo hue began to fade in Minor's touch. As the half-heart faded, the sapphire glowed brighter.

Fable tried to remain upright, to keep composure, not to give Minor any satisfaction. And when she realized she was on her knees with a sort of wet light trickling from the hole in her chest, she squeezed her eyes shut as Minor cackled. Fable no longer felt real, not imaginary either, but like an idea being leeched of its essence. Her vision blurred, and the world dissolved around her and from a kitchen that was far, far away, she heard Elaine calling out towards her. She collapsed in an awkward mess, while she blacked out and began to die.

*

"Welcome to the realm no one cares about. Our home, the Hall of Minors!" Miss Minor announced.

"Our?" Fable questioned groggily. "Who else is here?"

"Don't concern yourself with it. You need not meet the rest.

Besides, you've already met them before. Every yahoo, man and woman, who lost themselves when you attacked the world. They're all here now."

Fable looked about at a world defined in varying shades of gray. She saw shadows but no people.

"Despite the sparseness, we are not alone," Minor teased. "The residency here requires no face or form."

"Then why do you have a form?" Fable pried.

"Consider me a liaison," Minor huffed impatiently. Hands on her waist, tapping her foot on the ground, she glared a haven't-you-been-paying-attention-glare. She gestured for Fable to move forward. "Follow me, you pixie-tart. The Hall prides itself on minimalism. Think of me as the secretary of power. But one must be patient if one is to climb ladders." She spoke more to herself than to Fable. Minor walked ahead of her, hips jutting to and fro in a haughty strut.

Traveling the Hall was like dreaming in gray. The empty hall extended forever into the distance. It was lined with old, crumpling pillars. The pillars looked very normal at first until Fable saw the faces moaning within the architecture, fused and shifting together, hollow eyes and mouths contorted. Between the pillars, ghosts lingered as dark, inky clouds with long, indistinct faces, smeared and faded. Each possessed a dirty halo in the shape of an upside down book over their heads. The books seemed to scream, or so she thought, their pages crumpled and yellowed. Fable hugged herself. The hole in her chest throbbed, and her body felt drained, a reminder she was skirting around a state more demeaning than death.

Miss Minor raised her hand to admire her painted nails. "Distance and destiny do not factor into our realm. The Hall's a special place for those who have nowhere else to go or, how should I say, the narrative has no need for. It's a *place* for victims." As she spoke, she clasped the sapphire around her throat tightly like a divine relic. She giggled in a way that sounded unnatural.

They proceeded forward although there didn't appear to be anywhere to walk to, no buildings or landmarks, just featureless ground extending in all directions under gray overhead.

"Where are we going?" Fable asked tiredly. Missing half her heart was beginning to take its toll.

"We?" Miss Minor spun on her heel. "*We* don't go anywhere. People like me and Ethan and that bartender that dashed in front of a moving truck have nowhere else to be. Ethan also perished as well. Got fixated on his wife's shoes and, well, it didn't turn out in his favor. You *do* remember Ethan, don't you?" She added with snark.

Fable did.

Minor continued, "I'm not entirely upset over Ethan's demise. He chose his family over me after all. I really did change after I met you. After you, I just couldn't shake that man from my thoughts. Day and night, all I could do was wonder if he was home with his wife and his children, dreading the idea he wasn't thinking about me. It got so bad I had to kill myself just to get a break from him. And I did. I hung myself like a pathetic," and she searched for the right word. When finding nothing, she shook her head. "When I woke in the Hall of Minors, I knew I wasn't alone, and I knew I wouldn't wait in the sidelines either. So here we are."

"Oh, come on, Trish, you were no saint so stop kicking dead horses. I told you, I apologize," Fable snapped. "I mean it, heart and soul."

"Your soul's already vile and I find your apology," she smiled, "half-hearted."

"I'm sorry if I hurt you. All of you," Fable addressed the non-space.

"If!" Minor squeezed her hand into a fist around her mouth. "Whatever karma you've stacked up through the creations, it will never be a fraction of our retribution."

"Taking half my heart isn't enough? You'll hurt me more?"

"We shall continue to hurt you. And you'll die as many times as you killed us and then, yes, we may be close to even." Minor batted her lashes with eyes that were the blue of a computer screen. "Your death must be orchestrated carefully. You're an entity that operates in a higher realm, where art exists in its most pristine form. And you simply became too solid for your own good. Here." They entered a room.

The atmosphere thickened with a deep azure bordering on melodrama. The air tasted heavy with residual despair. Blue fog invaded Fable's lungs and she hunched forward, coughing, while Minor laughed raucously.

The room was dark although light enough for Fable to see the space was filled with mannequins. Each mannequin had a photo of a person attached to their blank faces. The photos were wrinkled and faded as if the ink had run dry during printing. The photos featured images of random faces Fable vaguely recalled. Some she didn't recognize at all. One that stood out the most was the bartender, Mark Hensley, the one she inspired during her bitter conversation with Seven at the tavern on Penn. And she knew all the others belonged to those victims caught in Porter's fever, all people who lost their minds and souls, those infected by their own dreams and quirks. She had inspired them all and this room was an homage to that.

Suddenly, Minor began to tear the mannequins apart in awkward, aggressive movements. This went on while Fable's perception blurred.

"Look now," Minor said.

Fable witnessed a throne that was a sloppy assemblage of mannequin parts, heads and arms and legs, held together with a pulpy, violet compost. Above the throne, hovering magically, Fable spied her novel-shaped half-heart.

As the throne pulsed, her heart seemed to drain of color.

"Our Demusement Machine," Minor announced proudly. "It amps up guilt and karma. Consider your heart its engine. An engine we suck dead," Minor explained like an aneurysm. She immensely enjoyed the horror on Fable's face. "Remember, you sacrificed yourself when you spared the life of one minor, Elaine Thrift. By doing so, you acknowledged your wrong, thus triggering the Hall into motion, thus empowering me...*us*...to act."

"Stop..." Fable muttered. "You made your point."

"We're far from done with you." Minor grinned.

There were screams then, cries that raged from the faces on the mannequins, desperate throes of agony and injustice. And as the wailing persisted, it sliced through Fable and she pressed her palms over her ears. The Demusement Machine sparked with power, siphoning Fable's essence from her displaced broken heart. With her soul leeching away, Fable clenched her temples as blood poured from the hole in her chest. All the while, Minor laughed raucously while the sapphire by her throat pulsed and brightened, flooding the Hall with cerulean screams of light. And Fable understood the Hall of Minors wasn't so much a place but a limbo for those who had never mattered within the scheme of a narrative.

Fable wanted to be strong, would've, but found herself begging, "Please. I want to leave."

"*Want?* I wanted Ethan to coddle my tits till the end of time and look how that turned out," Minor said with no sympathy. "We all wanted as much and no one cared. Mark and Amber and Tina and every other filler in this City wanted and dreamed and you didn't care about that. Now you'll choke on all of them, on every bit of insanity and mental illness, every breakdown and suicide, you'll feel it all."

And a vision came in the torture, an epiphany charged by pain with every psychic wound and torment, Fable saw all the minor faces. She saw Mark and John and Barry and...

When Fable threw up the first time, Miss Minor beamed pleasantly like a Miss America contestant promoting S&M. After the second time, the mouth above Minor's head laughed entirely too hard. And when Fable contained herself, her flesh had darkened to newspaper-gray.

Fable knew this had to be, the inevitable pain. Maybe in the end, if she survived the Hall's retribution, she'd be better for it. Then again, perhaps she would not.

Trish Shapiro clenched her sapphire prison. She cracked a thin smile and her halo, the cerulean-grin, joined along. Minor was no longer beside Fable, who somehow was now strapped into the throne in the tiny chamber that was the interior of the sapphire itself. Images of people she damaged streamed behind her eyes and she couldn't escape it, could only let karma have its way. And when the giant eye of Trish Shapiro peeked in from an impossible window, Fable knew she was a prisoner, dangling around her throat, dying in the vengeance of a minor voice.

"I have you now, my Fable," Minor smiled sinfully, clasping the sapphire.

*

Seven stood by the pond under the silver light of the Moon. He dipped his hand in the water, and when removing it a black residue remained on his fingers, something not-water, something wet and unfinished. While he half-expected to flash on another lucid vision of an Arthur Wright, he was left momentarily disappointed when nothing streamed his way.

To his right, several feet away, Seven saw a man squatting at the rocky edge of the pond. "Nice night," the man said as he stirred the water. "If you were a woman, I'd ask you for a dance while I sang Van Morrison lyrics in your sweet, little ear."

"But I'm not a woman, am I? I assume you're the Fourth Dynasty," Seven said.

The man laughed. "Correcto!"

"Why'd you want to meet here?"

"I thought we'd stare into a pond and maybe share a hallucination or two."

"You're Arthur Wright, aren't you?"

"What makes you think that?"

Seven glared at the man who looked very much like the student in his vision. "I'm not in the mood to be fucked with. I'm tired and my friend's dead. So for once, I want a straight answer."

The man nodded, and he answered sincerely, "Not trying to string you along, but getting to the truth is like playing hula hoop with a circle barbed with wire. It hurts and it cuts and it doesn't feel good."

"The Fourth is a writer like me. The Authors wanted me to see that. Maybe invoke some kindred connection or whatnot."

"Arthur Wright isn't just a person," answered the man-who-resembled Arthur, "Arthur is a placeholder, a cycle, and if I am this Arthur then in a way so are you. It's best not to look at them as people."

Seven clenched his fists and moved closer towards the man who shot upwards, backing away, his hands spread in front of him.

"What I'm saying is," the man-Arthur explained, "Arthur was a writer, like you and me. He wasn't the first. He was no different than Abernathy Wordsmyth or Alan Wilkinshire, and yet his story is a rough template for our lives. None of us asked for this."

The man noticed the furrowing in Seven's brow, the fight displaced by confusion, and he edged closer towards him. "Listen. Once upon a time, a secret was anchored to a notion. There is a hole in the world, where the progenitor of the Circle Children unwrote himself. There was blood and water. A blade, yes, and old Andrew Wilkins spearheading the cop out of self-termination."

Arthur gestured to the pond. For a moment, Seven spied a human-shaped hole in a dead man's float at the center. The water around it seemed to be rushing inwards and down it, like a draining vortex.

"Imagine how it felt," Arthur continued, "that fleeting warmth. That soul-slide into somewhere I have no words for. How did he feel on his knees, pants soaked in muddy water? How did the little fish respond to this sulking titan at the dirge of his own funeral?" Arthur balanced on several loose rocks. "I'd like to think Andrew Wilkins was happy then. But I don't think so. I imagine his ghost thinking how the hell am I supposed to write my way out of this?

"Us writers see the world differently. And our visions hurt us and isolate us and they may bring us such disgusting beauty, but it will always be more interesting. I would kill myself if I didn't think about the personal stories of raindrops, the secret languages of furniture. All the what-ifs and maybes. Whether or not he meant to do it, Father created us, his Circle Children. His death lingered as an echo, a vibration, a discontent that still needed to be fulfilled. His unwritten novel sought its completion. But as below, so above, child mimicked father. All the flaws inherent in a pathetic god were bled into the offspring. Father doesn't understand us anymore. He's too busy in his existential quest of hating himself while he rots away in his White Prison." His voice was sharper, slyer.

"You see, whether you and I are or aren't Arthur or Andrew, the story never changed. There have been others before you," Arthur continued. "Incarnations with similar stories all revolving around *Tetragrammar.*"

"Get to the point. I don't have time for this!"

Arthur turned his palms down. An oily scarlet dripped from the craggy lifelines in his hand. "Ah, time. Time for the Circle Children is the beginning of a loop that will inevitably bite its tale, you being that seventh cycle, brother."

"I'm not your brother. I'm not like you."

"None of the Circle Children are like me," the man added with pride. And before he could explain, he showed Seven exactly what he meant. The man-Arthur buried his fingers into his face, molding his flesh which was no longer skin, which was clay-like and pliable and he began to shape and alter. While the act should've twisted Seven up inside, he could only observe like an idiot-child as Arthur changed and shifted, from his height to his clothing, all revisioning into something else.

The man-who-was-no-longer-Arthur, who was very red, squatted on his heels at the pond's edge, his clothing saturated, his face absurdly wet. He placed his hand into the water, only glancing at Seven once. He wore capris, an unbuttoned shirt, and sandals, all which failed to remain dry.

"You're not Arthur."

"No."

"Then who?"

The man's skin possessed an adobe-tint with features highlighted in red marker. But mostly he was very wet. "Call me Ambrose Walker, scribe in my day. Fourth of Father's narratives. Now you said you weren't my brother and I suppose that could be true, that is if you're dealing with shared DNA. But if you're referring to the relation of the continual loop of one revisionary agent into another, then yes, brother is appropriate. You were pushed like the rest of us from the White Womb. As I descended, The Authors intervened. They allowed me to evolve." He opened his palms. A network of crimson flowed in his lifelines. "I wouldn't relive the Ouroboros Curse. I wouldn't waste my life on *Tetragrammar*. Not like you.

"Notion cannot be saved. He keeps you in check by making you believe *Tetragrammar* is something holy and divine, when it's nothing more than a leash. The Authors are not the enemy. Binding Notion in the Moon is like containing a plague or..."

"I don't believe you," Seven cut him off.

"They knew you would say that. They pity you. I was the Fourth Circle Child until They exposed me to Notion's insanity, and I became Their Fourth Dynasty."

"You're wrong."

"And you're outdated, brother. You're a Circle Child like I was. A living narrative. A corrective plot. You're wrong about everything. I'm not surprised Fable hasn't told you about your predecessors." He waited. "Or perhaps she's blocked that out and now she's lost in a story of her own web."

Ambrose pressed his hands to his face. His fingers kneaded his skin. It could've been magical if it weren't violently gruesome and Seven couldn't look away, fixated on the physical revision until Ambrose was no longer, until through some grotesque movements, Ambrose combed through his scalp, tugged at his ginger hair, stretching and revising and when he removed his hands, Ambrose said in a girl's voice that was far too familiar, a voice Seven wanted to scrap from his ears, "Fiction is transformative, you must agree." For a moment, what-was-once-Ambrose paused, and what-was-now-Paris said, "All your attempts to write and fight and move on from me are nothing more than that chain around your finger." Gesturing towards

Seven's ring, "You're nothing without it."

This shouldn't have fooled Seven. Yet he found himself whispering Paris's name, knowing it wasn't, knowing it was Ambrose's shape-shifting. Mesmerized at the transformation, Seven believed for a moment, *actually believed*, heart and soul, it was truly Paris. Not-Paris released a deep, throaty laugh and proceeded to grab her cheeks, a turn and twist, as she began reshaping, *Ambrosing*.

"Stagnancy is not evolution," Ambrose said. "Notion is obsolete. He doomed us to repeat his mistakes." Ambrose rubbed the red stubble on his chin. "I'm a shifter now. I can be Arthur, who did in fact exist. I can become anything. You. Fable. All of Notion's Children. The world ends, a snake bites itself, Notion grows more deranged and as another cycle concludes, the latest Circle Child will be no closer to writing *Tetragrammar*. It's the greatest fiction, your ball and chain, your noose. Cut yourself free of it."

"I have to finish it," Seven sounded tired.

"Do you?" Ambrose looked saddened by this. "Notion needs you to believe that."

And as Ambrose approached Seven, he tried to move. For some reason, his arms and legs fought him. Ambrose removed a pen from his back pocket. He smiled regretfully, clicked it several times. "I hoped you wouldn't resist the truth. I'm sorry, brother. This will hurt."

He slashed the pen quickly in one definitive motion. Everything played out too fast. There was blood spewing from Seven's throat in large, obscene quantities, too much to be real. Seven grabbed his neck, crimson spurting between his fingers. The world broke into fuzzy black-and-white until finally it glossed over in red.

*

Eve rolled down the windows while driving. The night air was a fresh reminder life existed beyond the many bedrooms of men who she only engaged sexually out of hobby rather than hormones. Bug corpses and dirt stained her filthy windshield. The way the light from the lampposts hit the windshield made it hard to see. The wipers were old and made horrible fingernails-on-chalkboard sounds. As usual, her glasses, smeared with fingerprints and dried eye gunk, didn't help.

All that considered, no surprise she didn't immediately see the shadow staggering its way in the murky headlights. She pressed down on her brakes, but not soon enough with the smack, thud, and bang of a body playing tag with her car. Whatever she hit, *oh, shit*, swiped the front bumper and flew back. She came to a halt. A crumpled form lay on the side of the road. "Hello," she called from the half opened car door. The body gurgled something inaudible and slowly lifted itself. Eve hesitantly approached it, only after retrieving a crowbar from her trunk. She edged forward, arms raised, iron clenched in hands. Under the moonlight, when she saw him, the leather coat and jeans, she dropped her weapon and cupped her mouth as if to scream when she witnessed the vast amount of blood pooling out from his throat, soaking into his clothes, like a roadside reaper.

"He-help me," Seven gurgled. Eve caught him as he fell onto her shoulder. He was heavy, and, after several awkward attempts, she managed to drag him into the back seat of her car.

"Oh, Seven." She glanced in the rearview mirror, rolling her eyes quizzically as she drove home. "Oh, brother."

*

Seven imagined his throat opening and blood, lots of blood. He shot up. Where was he? The ache, the gauzes wrapped tightly around his neck, the scabby tightness of his throat. He swallowed hard underneath the bandages. Standing didn't work as his legs gave out and vertigo sent him collapsing against a bath tub. He bumped his head on a tile wall. The shower curtain pulled away, revealing a woman with long jet-black bangs and glasses, who looked down at him with that uncertain smile.

"I found you." Eve sat on the edge of the tub. "You were in an accident. You're alive somehow. Your throat was," and she grasped delicately at her own throat. "You were bleeding. What the hell, Seven?" With a damp cloth, she dabbed his forehead. It wasn't until now Seven realized he was naked. His hands quickly moved to cover himself, but Eve steadied him.

"My clothes..."

"Are being washed."

He tried to pull himself up again.

"Relax." Eve placed a hand to his chest, eased him back down.

"D...did I die?"

"Maybe."

"I…need clothes…" He felt exposed wearing nothing more than the dressings around his throat.

"Rest. Just rest."

She blurred.

*

Teal sweatpants and an Eagles jersey rested on the toilet. Seven groggily worked himself up. The more he moved, the more he discovered just how sore he was. The discomfort ran far deeper than physical. He felt wrong inside. He steadied himself when stepping from the tub. Eventually, he dressed and faced himself in the mirror. Slowly, he reached around the back of his neck, unwrapping the tape and removing the dressings. He found no remnants of scarring, his throat completely healed, like an imaginary wound suffered only in a dream. He should've been surprised.

He wasn't.

He threw the dressings into a waste basket.

Eve knocked. "Seven?" she asked, easing the door open. "You ok?"

She guided him through the hall into a spare bedroom. After she eased Seven onto the bed, she sat beside him, just stared blankly at him. "I'm not going to ask the obvious," she said. "I frankly don't want to know. I find mystery more intriguing than answers. So I won't ask what happened or how you're alive. I'll assume it dumb luck I found you trekking along the back roads all by your lonesome."

"Would you believe me if I told you a secret?" Seven said.

"I don't think you have any more secrets. Dana told me everything, of course. I know your quirks. How you like to smell the pages of books. How you eat your cereal dry and your unnatural fear of long necked pumpkins. I pretty much buy anything. I find believing everything liberating. Nonchalance is bliss."

"Paris must've told you I was insane. I'm not. There are Authors in the Moon who will not rest until I give Them my novel."

"I don't know about Authors in the Moon but you finally got interesting, you strange, strange man." Eyeing Seven over her glasses, "Stay here as long as you like. I'll be gone in the morning, making calls to people who otherwise don't want to be called, trying to sell them things they'd never buy over the phone." A pause. "Have to say, you heal damn fast."

"Yea," Seven agreed.

Eve said, "Well, goodnight."

Seven lay in bed. Abstract paintings of men transforming into fish and anthropomorphic guns and tables lined the walls. He swore he witnessed subtle movements within the paintings, irrational images stirring in their frames and pushing…

It took a few moments for Fable to come into focus. She looked very pale against the window. His stomach tightened at her face smeared in blood.

Thinking about the Fourth's message, "You've been alive much longer than me, haven't you?" he asked.

"Living longer doesn't make you more patient. I had so much life to give you and I wanted to inspire you the most. People died because of us. I couldn't do it. Elaine wouldn't share their fate. The Dynasty's wife could be a small piece of karma."

"Elaine…so you didn't…?"

"No. There's been enough death. She made me realize that."

"Where were you?"

"I spared the Dynasty's wife," she said. "It's what you would've wanted."

"Thrifty…he…"

Fable diverted her eyes out the window.

"The Red Man killed me," Seven said. "I was dead."

"Oh, Seven." She touched her heart, pitying. "You were never alive."

And in the moonlight, alone, he rolled to his side and began to cry.

*

Somewhere, Elaine heard from an impossible place, *"Come home, Laney. Come home…"*

IV
KNOCK-KNOCK

IN WHICH DROWNING FISH AREN'T FUNNY, A
RED HERRING EVOLVES, AND WALLS BREAK

16
SOMETHING FISHY THIS WAY COMES

After being killed with a pen, Seven did several things. 1) He stored Thrifty's bag in a small safe he kept under his kitchen table. 2) He remained confined in his apartment, becoming a recluse because the world wasn't safe and the Fourth Dynasty could be anyone. The only contact with the outside world came via phone calls from Eve checking on him, asking how he was, and that you should really get out more, and also, by the by, are you a mutant? 3) He worked out to occupy his mind. He did push-ups and pull-ups and yoga vinyasas. If his muscles fatigued, he pushed harder, driven by that sweet vengeance of murdering Ambrose Walker.

When not working out, Seven wrote, despite having reached another dead-end plateau in inspiration. When he didn't work out or write, Seven meditated on his patio upon a lawn chair adorned with spider webs. He'd stare at the Moon as if that alone would draw it closer. And he imagined Ambrose Walker lurking out there in The City, a tricky, shape-shifting bastard.

Seven studied himself in the mirror. Hunching over the sink, inches from his reflection, he scrutinized every pore, every hair, wondering who he was before the amnesia, what his soul resembled beneath the flesh. He healed fantastically well, in which he began to suspect was due in part to his being quite not-human. What that made him, he didn't know.

"Surprise, surprise," Fable quipped. "Arthur turned out to be a Dynasty."

"Not quite, but close enough," Seven said, on his hundredth crunch.

Clarifying, Fable sighed, "Arthur turned out to be some guy named Ambrose, who was the next Dynasty. What does that make him now?"

"The Fourth."

"Did he officially call himself the Fourth?" Fable asked.

"He called me his brother. He also said The Authors weren't the enemies, that Notion was the true adversary."

"Do you believe him?"

"I don't believe anything." Seven kicked himself upside down against the wall for a round of handstand push-ups. When done, he pushed off the wall to his feet.

"You should get some fresh air," Fable suggested. "Although the workouts are paying off." She beamed at him with a twinkle in her eye. Her fingers moved along his bare chest, swirling the sweat on his body. "You'll get weird if you stay home forever."

"It's only temporary. Ambrose will come for me. He'll have to." Seven wiped the sweat from his forehead. Stepping onto the patio, he gripped the railing as he fixed his eyes on the Moon. It hid behind several clouds, buried in pastel blues.

"Could he be right about Notion?" Fable asked as she tiptoed on the railing. "Think about it. You know next to nothing about Notion. Everything from writing this book to Authors in the Moon is rather ambiguous. You still believe They wiped your mind?"

"They did."

"Yes. Of course," Fable placated. "It's just all very vague. We live in a City with no name. When's the last time you wrote a check to pay for this apartment? How much is rent and how do you get where you go without a car?"

Seven's head began to hurt. He tried ignoring her, wanted to hit her, dismiss her, but something rotten churned in his stomach. He clenched the railing at the dizzying whirl behind his eyes. He was overheating with a sensation of needles pinpricking his arms and legs. With a momentary loss of breath, he wanted to run away, just pull a Forrest Gump, and never stop. And before he could contemplate this any longer, the doorbell rang.

Seven answered.

A tall man he had never seen before introduced himself,

"Abernathy Wordsmyth, at your behest!" He stood, one arm across his waist, the first two fingers of his other hand tapping his cheek.

"Do I know you?" Seven asked. He realized then that he was shirtless, that he only wore a pair of yoga pants.

With a heavy sigh, the man threw his hands in the air. "Is this the welcome I get? It falls despairingly below etiquette and razes the niceties of housewarming!" he exclaimed at Seven's lack of recognition.

"Who the fuck are you?" Seven asked.

"Abernathy Wordsmyth," the man repeated dauntingly. "Poet. Lover. Fellow writer. Son of Notion. Formal Circle Child." He waited for any of those words to elicit recognition. When nothing registered, Abernathy barged inside, pushing past him.

"Excuse me." Seven reached up, gripped the skinny man's bony shoulder. He pressed him against the wall.

Abernathy was not a large man, although he was lanky and skinny. He had an angular face with a boxy chin. His hair reminded Seven of a villain played by John Travolta. Abernathy wore clothes that somewhat invoked British royalty. The way he moved his hands and the tall, condescending posture suggested Abernathy was accustomed to think himself higher in the world, yet he seemed out of place with reality, as if born in a time from an older creation. Despite his stature, he was not at all menacing.

"Please remove thy hand, sibling," Abernathy stated, like a tough dandy.

"You call yourself Abernatty?"

"-nathy."

"Call yourself whatever you want, you're all Ambrose under that fake skin."

Abernathy pressed his head back into the wall, his lips pushing into a frown. "Please. You have the wrong brother."

Abernathy's eyes flared when he spotted Fable sitting upon the ottoman. He brushed past Seven and bolted towards her, body angled comically forward like a pouty boy-child. His forehead stopped nearly an inch before hers. Her focus moved upwards forming a slightly humorous cross-eyed gaze. "Yes?" she said. "Can I help you?"

When her response didn't meet Abernathy's expectations, he repeated, "Help me? *Can you help me?*" over and over, flabbergasted.

Then, fit to be tied, he rolled up his sleeves, shook his fists.

"Who the hell is this?" Fable ducked to the side to see around the tall stranger.

"Madame," he emphasized *dame* with a thick hiss, "doesn't recall me, brother."

"You're not my brother," Seven said.

Fable sighed. "He's an idiot, whoever he is."

"Idiot, I am now!" Flailing his hands, Abernathy paced in a large circle around Fable. "Brother, our muse is a bitch!" But when he said bitch, it sounded more like beach. "Has she told you about Andrew Wilkins or Ambrose Walker before? Has she told you how she makes us all sick and overwhelms us and expects us to bear her burden!? She's been with us from the beginning you should know!" Abernathy huffed, kicked his head back with a phlegm-building grunt, and heaved a large gunk of mucus by her feet. His spit landed a little too close for her liking. "Don't let the little beach fool you!"

"I've had enough, Seven," she said. "Take care of this."

Seven grabbed Abernathy by his wrist, forcing his arm up behind his back. The man bounced on his toes, crying *ouch-ouch-ouch* like a dainty French caricature. Seven led him to the door and just as he released his arm, Abernathy quickly reached inside his jacket and removed a crimson-colored fish.

He slapped the wet, slimy creature across Seven's face.

It left a salty, seaweed taste around his mouth. Seven froze. He would've hit Abernathy if it wasn't for the sheer audacity of the act. It was silly and dumb and didn't feel quite real. Being slapped with a fish left him dumbfounded, like a badly rehearsed slapstick comedy. Seven touched the moisture on his cheek. It was far more insulting and demeaning in ways Seven couldn't understand. And it seemed like it should've been amusing. But it wasn't. It was stupid and absurd, and strangely it made Seven want to cry. He pressed himself against the wall and slid towards the ground, hugging his knees to his chest.

Abernathy sat himself on the futon across from Fable. He held the fish by its tale. Unsure what to do with it now, he set it on the coffee table on top of a Dial H comic.

"Why did you do that to me?" Seven said in a small, desperate voice, covering his face.

"Ok, Tabbernathy," Fable said. ("Abernathy," he corrected) "Who are you?"

Rolling his eyes, "Oh, you violet demon! How we get cruder in our later cycles?"

Fable had enough. She was on the ottoman, only until she wasn't, only until her fingers squeezed into Abernathy's jugular. The tall man flailed and swatted her with limp wrists until she let go.

"It was a fish," Seven muttered in the background. "He just fucking slapped me with a fish!"

"A fish, yes, I suppose." Abernathy adjusted his patchwork attire. Settling himself, he interlaced his fingers and rested them on his lap.

But it wasn't only a fish, Seven rationalized. It somehow made reality questionable, made him feel shaky as if life could give out any moment, that his world had been reduced to an existential joke laced with a lethal whimsy.

"Seven! Get up!" Fable crouched beside Seven, brushing his hair to check on him. He peeked between his fingers. "You're being ridiculous," she said, losing patience.

"Aha!" exclaimed Abernathy. "That's the fish!"

Fable sat next to Seven. She put her arm around him. "All right, Abernathy. Humor me. How do I know you?"

While Seven regained his composure under the irrational terror, he told them: His name was Abernathy Wordsmyth. He and others like him were all writers, in a fashion, with Fable accompanying each in their respective cycle. He told them all this using large words that didn't quite work in long, drawn-out sentences. His speech was verbose, and the way he spoke, how he arranged words, made Seven want to hit him.

"You're the Dynasty, Ambrose in disguise!" Seven accused from his fetal position.

"Please," Abernathy hissed curtly.

Seven began to regain his edge. "If you really are this Abernathy and we're somehow brothers or kindred spirits, then you know about Father Notion and The Authors."

With a dramatic sigh, "I am not here to indulge your quixotic masquerades or your existential crises you toil with like a dung beetle fondling its fecal world. I can only address the hunger of art."

"I don't like you very much," Fable interjected.

"Not my nature to be liked." Abernathy brushed dust from his shoulders. "In a time before you, Seven, I strayed from the prose-prison. I embraced the elegance of poetry and, as a poet, I would compose *Tetragrammatica* as my epic, yes. And yet I never wrote a decent line. I never grasped iambic pentameter or the lyrical bliss of Yeats and Longfellow. Don't you see, we collapse repulsively under our craft, our inspirations transfigured from beauties into banes."

Abernathy's eyes sharpened into ugly crow's feet. He touched the back of his hand to his forehead, closing his eyes in deep sorrow. "Don't you see why I can't exist!? Why I'm a flaw!? Why none of us can succeed? I can't be a poet. That's the tragedy. We're bled from Notion, cursed to define some impossible words, supposed to be perfect but we can't be! None of us were." On the verge of tears, Abernathy used some adjectives that should've never been words to describe his state of despair. Then, "What's the word for composing a story so perfect it fulfills all of one's art's desires?" Abernathy asked.

Seven wrinkled his forehead. "There is no word for it."

"There you have it." Abernathy raised his hands. "That's your Tetragram. That's the salty slap of the fish!" Looking extremely depressed, he somehow now held a pen and he ran it across one wrist then another. He moved swiftly enough that it didn't register he had just committed suicide. A liquid the color of mashed cherries sprayed and drained from his opened wrists. Abernathy's head kicked back as he fell into the futon. His chest convulsed with violent heaves as something large forced its way up his throat. With a final thud, Abernathy disgorged a fish. It flip-flopped on the floor covered in spit and mucus. Abernathy's feet and arms rolled open, his head sagged upon his shoulder. A limp, pink tongue hung humorously from his pale lips.

They remained in silence for quite some time.

When Fable moved, she blinked-out and reappeared near the dead poet. She touched the fluid that pooled on the floor around his feet. She tasted it. "This isn't blood," she said, slapping her lips.

"What is it?" Seven eyed the fish cautiously.

"Ink." Fable twisted her face. "It's ink."

Seven's eyes darted from the ink to the fish. "How do you know that's ink?" he muttered in a cold sweat.

"It feels like ink," she said for lack of anything else.

The fish began to flop pathetically towards Seven, who finally made his way to his feet, edging himself against the wall. "This is wrong! All of it. My entire life. It's all sparse and fake. A vague existence with minimal detail and texture!" Seven nervously withdrew the curtain in his living room and peeked out like some conspiracy theorist watching for UFOs. Outside a woman walked her dog while another couple unpacked groceries from a car.

"You're acting paranoid." Fable glared at him dryly. She picked up the fish, pinched its tail between finger and thumb, and moved her face towards it, sniffing it. She wrapped it in a newspaper and put it in the kitchen sink. "Then again," reconsidering, "your whole existence could be a joke, couldn't it?"

Seven frowned.

"And your life's not really funny anymore," she continued. "There's too much creative juice in you to be stifled on one story you can't finish. Let it go."

"I can't."

"Of course you can't." Fable glared. Her softness was becoming aggressive. Her aura crackled about her erratically. "It's always the same with you writers. You mope and hate the world if you can't compose your grand masterpiece. After all this time, when will you learn? How many more revisions will it take before you move on?"

"Fable?"

Her purple hues were changing, reddening. "I wonder if the others treated me like you."

"Who? Abernathy?"

"The Circle Children. Arthur, Alan, and all the other A-named fuckers. It was so frustrating watching the monotonous spin of their words. Inspiration could be so clear, why do they struggle! It makes me angry. Maybe I should kill the world again, just drown it with magic and never stop." She paced. "Notion and his children could never handle me; their small minds lack the capacity to channel what I am." She glared angrily until the outburst subsided. The rant lost its potency and she retracted her aura back into herself.

"Jack told you I would kill you, right?" she said. "I will. Probably. It's my fault, after all." Her shoulders sagged, her hair fell over her face, a stringy mess. "It was all my fault. I'm the villain in all this."

"Hey, hey," Seven consoled her.

"You don't understand." Fable brushed her hair off her face. "You weren't writing and I was tired and exhausted and I began to crawl inside people's minds. I worked my magic and it felt great. If I overloaded them and pushed them too far, I didn't care. It was a rush and I didn't want to stop. If they suffered, if they died, none of it mattered." Shaking her head furiously, "Maybe *Tetragrammar* is the way to repair it, to rewrite all reality?" She looked at him, her face desperate, and as he looked he spotted something *other*, something not-Fable behind her eyes, something red and wet.

And she smiled at him, a wide, moist grin.

"You're not Fable!" he yelled. And as he yelled, he hit her, knocking her back. He had so many questions but the most relevant was if that wasn't Fable, where had she gone?

Fable moved on the floor, her body becoming less solid, her eyes funny and strange. Her pupils narrowed and crimsoned as she tried to make her way to her feet. Seven grasped her hair and tugged and Fable fell onto her back. He wanted to rip her face off if it wasn't for the eyes, *her eyes*, gazing back at him. A neurotic laugh welled up inside her like a distant echo from a hollow shell, like a vacant doll conceived in a slaughterhouse. Her flesh dripped, liquefied. He moved away from her to retrieve his laptop.

He gripped his laptop and punched the edge of it into her face, shattering several teeth in her false smile. What-wasn't-Fable staggered forward and Seven brought the laptop down on her head. He did it again and again, each blow becoming softer, wetter, and he continued until she was a form of meaty pulp. Her remains collected into a scarlet puddle.

Seven wanted to be sick. The laptop slid from his fingers.

"Quit playing," he said while he eyed the puddle. "Rise up, you bastard."

The puddle rippled. And from the puddle fingers pushed out, followed by a hand, a wrist, an arm, which eventually led to a man. "You finally caught on," said the thing pretending to be Fable.

And the true guise of Ambrose Walker possessed a long face with almost horse-like features with a ginger-colored ponytail. While Ambrose circled Seven, his body stretched and elongated, like a reflection in a funhouse mirror.

"Where is she?" Seven asked.

"Just because I *Fabled* myself, doesn't mean I've done anything to her."

Seven inhaled.

Ambrose retrieved a chair from the kitchen, set it across from

Seven. "Let's talk about you. Why you're Seven. Did you know," he said conversationally, "every seven years the cells die in the human body?" He paused as if waiting for the ohs and ahs of an engaged audience. "The thing you call self is spliced away in cellular genocide to give birth anew. Your body is not what it was after a seven year cycle. You are changed. Changing, evolving. You do not stay still. A writer is meant to move."

Ambrose waited. Seven glared.

"You were to be the greatest of Notion's Children. The cycle numbered completion." As he said this, he appeared perpetually soaked, clothing saturated and skin coated in a liquid tinted with a rouge hue as he dripped onto the floor. "It's not a mistake you wear that lovely ring. The ouroboros is the mark of your soul. It will devour you like your predecessors. Notion was a coward. The world terrified him so he isolated himself from reality, hid in fiction, imprisoned himself away from the dreams he could never perfect, like love and women. Books he could never compete with. And he leeched himself into us, passed his diseases into you and me. And now, Notion infects you with impossible ideas of tetragrams and rising to the Moon."

"You're a Dynasty. You work for Them. I can't believe anything you say."

"No lies, brother. They saved me. Turned me into a symbol."

"Which is?"

"That the blood of revision can bleed with life. That the snake doesn't have to eat itself. That our predecessors were echoes stuck in Father's insanity. *That* won't be me."

"You're different?"

"Oh, yes. I evolved." Ambrose added with no arrogance. "After I passed on from wherever, I wouldn't be confined in Notion's limbo. And then it happened. I heard the clicking of pens from above and I saw the cycles, the circle-prison and I became Notion's anti-son. They flowed through me. Bled Themselves into me. Instead of playing victim to the cannibal snake, I was reborn their Fourth Dynasty. A Circle Child/Dynasty hybrid. The cipher against the current." Ambrose went into the kitchen. When he returned he held the dead fish.

"A red herring." Seven raised an eyebrow.

"Don't be bitter about my being Arthur and Abernathy and Fable or that I slit your throat. It was a lesson."

"Nice lesson."

"It was to demonstrate fiction doesn't die. You're fiction, Seven. But if you're still in a tizzy, you'll have your vengeance. I owe you that."

"You make it seem like you have a choice leaving here alive."

"However this ends, I'm leaving and perhaps you should follow."

"Where to?"

"Beyond the walls to a higher reality, the Outer Page, nonfiction, whatever you call it, that's where I'm going."

"The Authors won't allow it. Leaving Them would be evolving beyond Them."

Ambrose said, "Do authors not live vicariously through their creations? Before I go, I have one obligation to you. On Their request. The truth!"

Seven's eyes narrowed.

Ambrose said, "You won't like it. I won't lie. It will not make your life easier."

"What are you on about?"

"I murdered you once with this." Ambrose raised his hands to show they were empty. His hands dripped and as they dripped the liquid-red formed a pen. He displayed the pen proudly, like a magician. Seven tensed, readying himself. Ambrose kept his arms up, pen loose in his fingers. He backed towards one of Seven's walls. He drew a diagonal line, then another, forming an X. The bright red resembled more marker than ink. From the X, the lines dripped as if the wall had been cut. Ambrose tucked the pen behind his ear. Liquid continued to ooze from his feet, to pool underneath him. "The pen is a weapon; it stabs and cuts. It brings the greatest joys and the greatest pains." He tossed the pen towards Seven.

He caught it and eyed it suspiciously.

Ambrose rolled up his sleeves, untucked his shirt from his capris. "I now present to you, brother, the Outer Page!"

Seven felt like something huge and substantial was going to happen, like an elephant would collapse through his roof or his home would sprout chicken legs and dash into some black hole. He braced himself, heart pounding.

"Knock, knock," Ambrose said. He knocked on the wall, upon the X.

And before Seven could question anything, that's when the walls collapsed, and that's when Seven lost his mind.

17

OUTER PAGE

Imagine a stage bordered by three walls; visible, solid walls, two sides and one in the back. Now imagine another wall, the one that exists without ever being, that intangible border hiding in plain sight. The illusory concept that separates art from audience. It's that wall we're interested in breaking. But sticks and stones will not damage it. To smash it down is to acknowledge it had never been while believing it always was. And when you, dear reader, allow that thought to blur fake and fact, that you are being read while reading, that you are only one observant down reality's rabbit hole, you will have broken the Fourth Wall.

Self-awareness accompanies transcendence. Our lives paged, after all.

Follow?

*

Everything remained the same in Seven's apartment except the walls, because the walls were no more. Seven's home had been reduced to something not unlike a stage platform. There were no more rooms. There was no housing community, no more City.

"I feel strange," Seven said or would've said if an onslaught of panic hadn't pressed down on him from every angle.

"Breathe," Ambrose coached. "Allow your vision to adjust to new angles."

Surrounded in blackness, Seven didn't know what to search for as he stared beyond the space where there should've been walls.

Pressure accumulated in his head. Blue was down. Up was left.

7-Paris=Limbo.

He crept cautiously towards the edge of the platform. Stairs bordered all sides of his floor.

"What the hell just happened?" he finally asked, steadying himself.

Ambrose walked to the edge with him. "Go on," he urged him forward.

Seven descended the steps. It was cold. Beyond was a murky haze the color of transparent seaweed. He squinted, like a timid child.

There were rows of stadium seats stretching forever into the darkness. And, in the seats, people. From what he could see, each person, man and woman, appeared very normal, except for the giant books that rested upon their heads. No, that wasn't right. The books were their heads.

"What are they?" Seven whispered.

"They are no one," Ambrose said. "They are everyone."

"Are these The Authors?"

The Book-Heads were giants, faraway, too large for comprehension. And they were small and finite, an idea so tiny. And Seven strolled through the stadium, his head filled with chatter, the ethereal buzzing of chat rooms and message boards.

"They are of a different nature," Ambrose explained. "They are The Critics. The voyeurs. The readers. The ones with loaded opinions and all the answers. Those who spit malice or praise, who love or hate you. The ones who tell you it's all been done before or compare you or tell you how it could've been better."

And while Seven staggered through the stadium or theatre or wherever, he imagined he was still on the platform of what had been his apartment. The atmosphere was thick and dense, and from somewhere the cold echoes of pages-larger-than-life flapped and turned. He gazed upon the novel-faces of these people, to see upon each cover the title *Tetragrammar*. They were observing his book, *his life*, and somehow he felt their mumbled thoughts streaming about him and inside him. Every rumination and opinion about his existence. It was all too abstract and he shivered at the dread of being reduced to an object of some horrible voyeurism, his every action to be judged and critiqued. He darted around haphazardly, terror-stricken eyes madly probing. Here in this audience, on this platform, he wanted to leave, just shrivel and die.

"What is this?" Seven asked.

"A middle ground perhaps. Between Outer and Inner Page." While Ambrose spoke, Seven's perception distorted as the Dynasty's words-*his literal words*-floated around him, like subtitles across his body, every line of dialogue presented as black Times New Roman text framed in apostrophes.

As his sight blurred, more words and letters lingered in grammatical smears across his vision. Seven reached to snatch them from the air, like imaginary flies. He felt punctuation in his head, periods and quotations squeezing around his thoughts, and page number floaters in the corner of his eyes.

"It takes time to sync up with the new perception," Ambrose said while supporting Seven.

In the impossible distance, something large moved and crested. Somewhere faraway, yet entirely too close, a thunderous boom rocked the heavens.

"What is that?" Seven gasped.

"You must decide!" Ambrose declared. "Make a stand as your own author. Finish *Tetragrammar* your way or simply move on before your world *truly* ends."

The atmosphere of the improbable theatre darkened as large movements of seaweed-black shadows wavered in the beyond. A storm or an ocean could be seen mounting in the impossible horizon, a force wet and lethal, something cresting its way towards them. Although faraway, Seven imagined it would only be moments until it crashed over them.

"I don't want to be here!" Seven shouted. "We have to get out, dammit!"

"No way out!" Ambrose said. "Besides, what's there to be afraid of?"

"Drowning."

"You're already drowning. Think of this only as an expression of things to come." Ambrose grabbed Seven's shoulders, shaking him from his trance, making sure his words set in. "The Outer Page is not where we go. A higher realm exists. That's where They wish to ascend, or not, who knows what truth They'll manifest from the pages of your novel? As for me, I'll go where I please. I have no need for *Tetragrammar*. But you, brother, if you stay promise to kill Notion for us!"

But his words failed to sink in as Seven could only fixate on the impending storm. There was screaming in the darkness around them while blood-curdling wails erupted in the distance. Seven assumed it was the death throes of those book-headed Critics in their final moments within the never-ending theatre. Cries from the Audience erupted from the stadium seats that stretched on from far, far away forever and ever. Titan waves that could breach miles or ages cracked from the mountainous shadows.

My God, was that The Authors?

"That flood...is," Seven stuttered, "...is that Them?" And he wondered, within Their arrival in the Moon, would They draw up the ocean with an apocalypse that would swallow the world?

Seven tried to remain calm, to hold it together long enough for one last statement. Water, cold and biting, began to rise around their ankles. Ambrose clenched the ring on Seven's finger. "Listen to me! Notion created a prison the shape of your life. His suicide became your trap. Nothing more." The crashing waves mounted in the background. "The world terrified Notion. He couldn't shape the dark unknown so he wrote and rewrote over and over until he was too close to see any clearer, that every revision was a cannibal snake. Death itself would not give him reprieve! There's no final period at the end of eternity. And now he rots in the Moon. That's where he can stay. But you don't have to, brother. Outside this world is another realm. Beyond the numbered pages, beyond an astrology of intrusive eyes, beyond sales and bestseller listings, a higher world awaits.

"Ultimately, that's where we must go. If *Tetragrammar* shows us anything, it's that each of us has a soul in the shape of a book, and we must be our own authors. But, sadly, you've never seen the paradox in your great endeavor."

Seven glared towards him.

"Tetra means four. Four letters to form the true name of God. A name that must never be spoken or ever be deciphered. But I did it. I wrote the grammar of God's name. I'm the Fourth, and you're Seven. Get it." Ambrose shrugged. "I wrote it and it was easy, and you know what the catch is? Father Notion would never accept it, because some truth is so goddamn simple we could never believe it. We'd shirk it off, seek anew. Yea, I finished *Tetragrammar* my way and it just wasn't good enough. And that's the joke, divinity unfolds before our eyes and we stay in the dark."

Seven shook his head. He didn't know what to believe or how to believe or...he just didn't know. And now was not the time.

As Ambrose backed away, he removed a pen from behind his ear. "You still plan to murder me, yes?" He handed a pen (he handed over the literal word PEN) to Seven.

Seven took it.

"Go on," Ambrose said. "Complete the narrative as Dynasty killer. Remember that psychic snake is already dead. The notion in me is gone. I've been free. If you can kill the absurd, then you've beaten me, herald of the irrational, the Red Herring."

"This pen," Seven clenched it like a knife, "is real. If I stab you through the heart, you will die. Nothing absurd about that." He clicked it against his thigh. The word CLICK puffed around it and fizzled out. "I can only allow the symbol to bear reality," Seven said. "It's the best I can do to murder the Dynasty in you." Gripping Ambrose behind the neck, Seven pressed the pen tip to his chest.

"Good-bye, brother," Ambrose said with a whimsical smile.

"Good-bye," Seven repeated, a cold whisper as he pushed the pen through his heart.

And as the murky waters rose above their knees, Seven locked his eyes on Ambrose. The Red Man's face was filled with bemusement and cynicism, until he no longer had a face. Somehow now Ambrose was entirely not human; he was a scarlet fish flopping clumsily in the waters, a balloon tied around its back fin. And as the water continued to rise, Seven watched Ambrose darting through the flood, no longer swimming in water but moving through space and time.

And he focused on this because it was better than being overwhelmed by an existential flood in a hypothetical theatre. Around Seven, the flood swept across the Audience, filling the world, rising fast past his waist and chest. He heard the drowned screams from the book-headed Critics, all the mad scrambling as the storm swallowed them. Some sobbed from their paper-paged mouths. Others cheered while others booed. But they all drowned the same, choking on nonsense, dying with the ridiculous.

Seven closed his eyes and he witnessed the Ambrose-herring darting against the currents into a reality he couldn't make out, until Ambrose was gone, swimming into the forever. And Seven wanted to escape with him, more than anything, but the flood had him, swallowing him whole…

*

When Seven opened his eyes, he was on the floor of his apartment, dry and stiff. He wiggled his fingers, slowly adjusting to a lesser abstract reality. He had walls again and for whatever reason he wanted to cry, but he also wanted to be sick. Being violently ill seemed like a good thing. However, the time for panic attacks and anxiety pills would have to wait. He laughed like a madman and wrapped on his walls, his knock hollow and empty. The flood had gone.

He found no relief in this.

A pen lie on the floor by the coffee table. He eyed it, like some cursed relic, before snatching it in his hands. He snapped it in half and dropped the broken pieces from his ink-stained fingers.

Seven entered his bedroom.

He imagined something terrible lurking under the sheets. In his mind's eye, he envisioned a ghastly newborn covered in blood and afterbirth, its limbs sown into its body so it resembled the sick semblance of a fleshy serpent.

Ripping the sheets away, he discovered a single fish underneath. It flipped and flopped as if drowning with no water. And he found it ridiculously absurd, which was the point after all.

There was a joke in this, a punch line Seven found entirely not funny. And he cleared his throat to tell it.

Knock, Knock…

DEAR, SEVEN

I owe you nothing, Seven. And that's the irony of it, isn't it? I found you at a strange time in my life with an encounter that left me chowing down on Tums and CBD chews. It was my fault with the car incident as much as it was for you being the magnet for it. You attract those kind of events; I was only drawn into your synchronicity.

And everything about you, I questioned, but I never allowed the lapses in the rational to gain any footholds in my life. Everything about you was a suspension of disbelief.

That's a literary term, isn't it? When the audience relaxes logic to better enjoy a story?

So perhaps you were always a fiction to me as much as you were real in your world. Two truths are true, right? There are Authors in the Moon; there are no Authors in the Moon.

You are deranged; you are sane.

We had a thing; now we don't.

I did love you for a time, Seven. I loved you as much as logic would allow. And you loved me as best as you could. But I'm not your great love; I never was.

You'll miss me. And you'll think of me, no doubt. I'll be a nostalgic chapter in your past. You may even recreate me as a fiction in a future story. I may be more beautiful than I ever was in life, or I may be the larger-than-life villain in a doomed romance. I doubt you'll remember the details of my life. I'll be the old flame whose parents were Jehovah's Witnesses (or were we Lutheran or Russian Orthodox?). You'll recall my favorite color was teal, although it wasn't, and my favorite fish was salmon.

Don't worry about it, Seven. Never beat yourself up about the veracities of one

Dana Paris. I absolve you of any regrets from our time together, and I wish you luck.

No matter what make-believe hole you dwell in, stay there. Your fiction is not my world. We'll meet once more. It'll be on a day I discover your child. I'll be randomly browsing through a bookstore, and it'll be there waiting for me in the new arrivals.

Tetragrammar.

I'll pick it up, hold it in my hands. I will not read it, but I will congratulate you sincerely with love. And after that, I'll never read you again. I will not linger as a ghost-thought in the pages of your life.

I am at my apartment. I've met a man abroad from his home in Sweden. I'm going there. We're departing this City together.

It's a good time to leave this book. The other day, it knocked me on the head. Looking up, I spotted a pinprick in the sky.

I knew without doubt when seeing the hole above me, the sky had begun to fall.

I hope you complete Tetragrammar *one day.*

But I know you won't. You're a fiction writer and you can't give up your nature, the great lie to yourself. I never really understood what you wanted me to be. I was never your muse and you were never in love with me. Your mistress is inspiration.

The longer your words remain unwritten, the harder it will be to stay in love with it.

Shed the skin of the serpent.

Cut the ouroboros.

There is life beyond your words, beyond that Moon. Life exists in the Outer Page.

Love,
Dana

V

LIMBO DRAGON

IN WHICH A WRITER SHUCKS OFF REALITY, A
FABLE IS REBORN, AND FATHERS ARE ORIGAMI
MADNESS

18
ARTIFICIAL UNSWEETENERS

During the time you turned the page, in that imaginary space between chapters, Seven had lost his mind. Days or weeks had passed, it didn't matter, Seven was crazy. He randomly spoke of himself in the third person. He tested walls and doors to see if they collapsed. Sometimes he saw people that weren't there and fingers turning pages that didn't exist.

After witnessing book-headed critics, after being reduced to a fictional construct, he imagined his life would always be torn apart, that he'd be diminished to a series of malicious rants with negative reviews piling in on the web pages of Amazon. Professional writers and agents would bash every shortcoming in his life. Entire blogs would be devoted to dissecting all those missed editorial mistakes; that was if anyone bothered to read *Tetragrammar* at all. Perhaps it would wallow in the literary shadows of musty coffee shops and used bookstores, undetected forever.

Regardless, the Fourth Wall had been broken, which left him only one option.

He would evolve.

With Fable gone, Seven would gaze into the white screen of his laptop, adopting the logic that if one stared into anything blank long enough, one would inevitably see everything. Seven slept little. A greater rest awaited after he'd rise above the pages of this life. Any madness now was only temporary—*Tetragrammar* being his exodus from the irrational.

When not real, he felt lighter and he carried his brevity into places his old self could never go. Old Seven overanalyzed women. New Seven slept with whoever captivated him. With too much time wasted on pining over Miss Dana-X, he wanted to fuck the Minnie Drivers, the Gillian Andersons, Playboy models, librarians, the cute, the hot, the plain and mousy.

He brought a redhead back to his place. They laughed during sex, even as they fumbled into positions that made the tantric yogis cringe. She woke to find Seven sitting up in bed, playing with her hair, looking at her with his dark, loony eyes. "Can your hair become liquid," he asked her, "you know, like the red ink that bleeds on paper after a revision?"

She found nothing amusing about this.

"I never slept with a redhead before," he chuckled. "Always wondered how it would be. They say redheads are feisty, but there's nothing like violet." The redhead stirred uncomfortably, then began to dress in a frantic hurry. "I think I slept with myself," Seven sighed. "You're not real. An extension of this dream. If it wasn't sex or masturbation," touching his chin, thinking, "you were a tool for my own sexturbation. Hopefully you're on the pill, although it won't matter. Babies are fake. Come. Let's shed a tear for the genocide of my swimmers," he said while she dashed from his place.

*

"Stare at any person's lips when they talk, *really stare*," Seven said to Eve during breakfast, "and you'll see the sounds they make never match their lips. It's like two different life-forms overlapping but not quite getting it right." His unblinking eyes burned with a manic fire. "It doesn't end there," Seven continued. "Stare at any object long enough and it just fades away into a mindless dance of color and molecules." And he rattled on for quite some time about the genders of coffee and the life expectancy of a coating of dust. Eve couldn't tell when Seven changed. He'd been saying stranger things each day, things like, "Seven was an artificial construct…"

"Stop that!" Eve shouted. "What's wrong with you?"

"I'm no longer Seven," he said while blatantly eyeing every woman who entered Dunkin' Donuts. "I lost my mind and memory like Seven, but we're not the same."

Eve ugged. "Then who are you?"

"A nonentity. Just something that's waiting to rise above the pages." Noting her frustration, he touched her hand. "If it makes you feel better, you may call me Seven for now."

Eve pulled her hand away. "I think I preferred you moping over Dana."

"Where *is* the lovely Paris anyhow?" he asked.

"She moved away with her boyfriend. Went to travel abroad. He's Swedish, I think. He lives in Sweden. We still talk occasionally. She's doing ok."

"Paris was a dead-end. When people split up, they say don't worry, it's not the End of the World. But it sure feels like it. Only you stay together and they say it's the end, too. No winning. Only till you step back and observe the Page, you see beginning and ending, all illusion."

"Oh." Eve sighed. Knowing Seven all the time he dated her best friend, she witnessed his vulnerable and stubborn sides. They argued often and at times hated each other. Deep down, she had grown to care for him. Finding him half-dead in the woods with a slit throat, she knew there was more to this strange man than the fictions in his head. Seeing him in this state made even her uncomfortable, and Eve was not one to be uncomfortable. "You never actually told me what happened to you?" she asked.

"You can't handle the truth," Seven said in a deep growl. "I've been practicing that. From that movie with Jack Nicholson. You know, Tom Cruise is like 'you can't handle the truth.' "

"That wasn't Tom Cruise," she said.

"I don't know about that," Seven said. "All right. Here's the truth. There's this circle, right. But it's also a snake." He held up his hand, pointed at the ouroboros. "The snake is a circle. It feeds on itself. It can't taste anything else because it only tastes its own ass. It can never change. And it keeps circling. The circle could be Andrew or Arthur, it matters little. They're all interchangeable because the script that's written into their cells never changes. And Seven was a label for the one who thought itself Seven. But Seven's tired. A storm's coming. A rain made of ink and spilled pens. Maybe They are the storm or maybe writing a lousy book is the only way to stop it?" Seven looked out the window. A bus pulled over. People boarded. "Seven watched the walls break and he didn't like what he saw when he looked out." His hands trembled. "That's how some bastard destroyed him with the truth that everything is fake. And he did so because in a twisty way he loved him."

Eve sighed deeply while she added six packs of Splenda to her coffee. "I still don't understand you." She lowered her head, pursed her lips, blew on the drink. The heat steamed her glasses. "Funny how I never wanted to have sex with you," she said suddenly. "You know how I am and yet nothing ever happened between us. I'd look into your eyes and see you weren't there, not on the same frequency as others. Your frequency wasn't higher or lower, just your own."

"You would never touch Seven," he said. "You're Paris's best friend."

Eve touched his hand. "We're closer now. I need to tell you. Considering you and I do and don't believe anything and everything, that no idea is too ridiculous, I had a premonition. It came from my guts, and my guts are never wrong."

Seven braced himself. He could only focus on her lenses, those filthy, smudgy lenses.

"What I'm saying, Seven, is…" and she told him.

Seven finished his coffee. "I know, Eve," he replied strangely. "You're Seven's sister. You certainly are."

*

Seven was happy without a past. His present was a clean page. But that un-history was gaining tangibility. So when he found himself inquiring about answers to their past from sudden-sister Eve, he paid little attention. To cherish the sweet minimalism, he daydreamed as she explained their family history, what Mom and Dad were like, holiday traditions, etc…

"Mom had this thing about her. Every day she needed to run the sweeper. And Dad would just…" Eve said while Seven zoned out in a groggy nap. "I can tell you about our home. Mom would collect all kinds of knickknacks," she told Seven. "Like tin containers, figurines, and random trinkets; you know, picture frames, wall art, baskets, and shit."

And as she rattled on about these details for several days, her words failed to jolt any memory, and Seven was fine by that.

Where were their parents? Where did they live now? Loose ends could flood the intellect but in the end who cared? He was a notion. He was Arthur and Abernathy and Ambrose and he was absolutely none of them.

*

One night, Eve invited her brother over for dinner. While she cooked gnocchi, Seven appreciated her décor. The walls were covered in a patchwork of art. Her home possessed the same atmosphere one found in an old coffee shop of a college town, with that slightly musty scent of newspapers and underground art. Seven studied a Vettriano painting next to the television. It featured two lovers dancing on a hauntingly beautiful no-where landscape under a distant sun.

They ate. She poured them each a glass of White Zinfandel. After dinner, they watched *Fight Club*. When the movie ended, Eve finished her sixth glass of wine. She turned off the DVD, told Seven she was tired and wanted to sleep.

"I'm staying up," Seven said.

"Ok."

"You mind if I tour your house, look at the art?"

"Knock yourself out."

He staggered through the halls, wine-buzzed, indulging in the hundreds of paintings and hand-drawn pictures featuring surrealist images such as skies filled with people-sized raindrops and anthropomorphic rulers. Afterwards, he collapsed on the bed in the spare room.

*

Seven's dreams were strange and surreal. He dreamt the Moon was an egg and it cracked open, spilling its mysteries, all its slimy, yellow guts. At its core, there was a man made of paper, an origami recluse locked away from the world. The man wept liquid-letters from his eyes. And somewhere deeper in the broken Moon, Seven saw two Fables. One was dark; one light, and they mixed together, somehow fusing into a yin and yang duality. As they melted into one, the Fables bled a sentient, primordial fluid that could shape entire universes. And the blood transformed into an apple. The perspective zoomed out to reveal a woman standing behind the apple, her face concealed.

"Who are you?" Seven asked.

"Son of Man," she replied, although Seven suspected it was the apple, not the woman, that spoke. And the woman reached up to snatch the apple from her face, and Seven saw his sister, naked, her long hair draped over her breasts. She crawled towards him, apple in hand.

"What are you doing?" he asked.

"The man in the bowler hat, the one behind the apple," Eve said, her words somehow making Seven queasy and doubtful, "he can't hide from me. He is the everyman and I can see his dirty, uncertain secrets. The apple's alive, you know.

The apple is God. It's knowledge, and the devil gives it away. Knowledge delivers God. And we bite it. Do you get it? The devil gives us God, and we bite it…"

*

Eve woke to the gentle screech of her bedroom door opening. The shadow of her brother stood in the doorway. "You really are my sister?" he asked.

Leaning up on her elbows, "Yes," she replied, "I really am."

19
MINOR DAMAGE

Seven ordered a tuna sandwich at the Jumpin' Java. Not once did he ponder going upstairs to where Paris once lived. Besides, no one would answer, not unless her door had become a direct portal to Sweden, where she flitted away with her Swedish boyfriend, where they'd have a Swedish wedding, make Swedish babies and tell Swedish jokes about old dalliances. He imagined her calling him, begging him to come back. In his fantasy, cool and calm, he'd say no, but he knew if she returned, he may fold quicker than a cheap hooker. With another bite of his sandwich, the ouroboros ring began to tighten. When the tension subsided, he wiped his mouth and sat alone while overhearing random conversations.

"I really don't think Kim has that much talent. Not sure why she's so famous."; *"If gas prices keep rising, why the hell don't we just switch to other sources; it's not like…";* *"It's not that I'm against others coming here, but if we deplete ourselves then what…?",* *"I mean, we're living in a golden age of television, but isn't one zombie spinoff enough?"*

Seven watched the cashier, a short brunette with pigtails ringing up customers. And then all the people shrank away, all seemed insubstantial when he spotted a woman standing in line. She was very tall and seemed to take up too much space despite her narrow frame. She wore a blue so bright it shamed all other blues. Her high heels, suit jacket, and mini-skirt reminded Seven of a haughty secretary who flirted exclusively with the highest social circles.

She moved from the line to admire a display of baked goods. Looking over her shoulder, she winked at him. Turning her attention back towards the display, she continued to peek over her shoulder, her attention divided between him and the desserts, deciding which would be tastier. She began small talk with an elderly woman with spiked white hair that Seven suspected to be either a modern witch or a lesbian. Eventually, she rolled her eyes, *looks like I'll have to make the first move,* and approached Seven.

She pulled out a chair and sat. "Every Thursday night," the woman said, ignoring him, "I met this man here after work. He was nice and handsome, and a bit wealthy. He worked in computers, and I could tell he hated his life because he had this middle-age hipness about him, like he was trying to be twenty, and if he spiked his hair and worked out enough, he could travel back in time. He always ordered an espresso and a coffee cake. We'd chat about his wife, his kids, sometimes his pets. And the time would tick away, and he'd look at his watch because he needed to get back to his life. But here he was, with me, an escape from his work-a-day world." As the woman continued, Seven couldn't find himself caring less. "The first time we slept together, he told me I had large feet. And I told him, I'll just leave larger footprints on your life. When he discovered I'd been sleeping with other men, he threatened me. I found it ironic. A married man jealous of his mistress. Eventually he wanted me completely; he'd leave his wife and children and we'd start a new life. I said no, of course, but the experience was phenomenal." She waited, allowing the story to settle in.

"Congratulations. You're a homewrecking bitch. Who are you?" Seven asked.

She leaned back, hand to chest, *how dare you not know?* "She hasn't told you about me?" And she smiled, but that wasn't quite right. She smiled twice, once from her mouth, the normal one situated on her face, and second (he finally noticed) from the giant mouth-halo grinning in unison above her. "Who am I?" she quipped. "Take a guess."

More details filtered in, like a face in a crowd gaining texture and flair, and if he was seeing this correctly, she possessed light that rippled about her, a cerulean aura, and squinting, it wasn't her that glowed at all; it was the large sapphire around her neck.

Seven couldn't help smile. "You're a Dynasty."

"Yes. The Fifth. Miss Minor's my Authors-given name." She held out her hand, palm down, wrist bent. Several oversized jewels decorated her fingers. "I wanted to meet you personally since the majors never take time to read the minors. No, we're just tread upon like piss and shit," she added bluntly.

Before Seven could reply, she held a silencing finger to her lips (*Sshhh, hissed the mouth above her*). "Listen." She closed her eyes, pointing overhead. Alphaville's "Forever Young" played in the background. Miss Minor recited the lyrics awkwardly, and she did something that made Seven uncomfortable. Extending her hand, "Dance with me," she invited. Seven didn't dance. He had never been comfortable dancing, had no idea what looked good, what looked bad; all seemed equally ridiculous. "Dance with me," Minor said again, grabbing him by the arm, dragging him from the table.

For a moment, the glimmer in her eyes, Seven saw how men could be enticed by her.

It happened so smoothly, like reality parting to make way for the musical's next performance. The people cleared away, as if on cue, forming an audience around them as if this were the most natural thing. Some assisted in moving tables, setting down their coffees, hands waiting to applaud. Minor forced Seven's hands around her waist. She draped her arms over his shoulders. Together, Seven and Minor danced, a monotonous sway.

"What are we doing?" Seven eyed the crowd, wanting to leave.

"This is our world. We're the center of everything. We can do anything, Seven. This takes me back," Minor whispered in Seven's ear, or would've if she weren't several inches taller than him. "You should've seen me in high school. A meek girl with glasses, mullet, and shoes that never matched her outfits." She laughed then, her head tilted back. "I lie. I was a bitch then, too. Always have been."

"What changed?"

"I was human," she said. "Now I'm not." The song ended. They released their embrace. Seven backed away. People applauded and shuffled around them, like worker ants putting the tables back in place. Before normality resumed, a young man pulled out Minor's seat for her and scurried away.

Seven sat. "You made your statement."

"Statement?" Minor questioned.

Seven gestured to the people. "None of this, this City, these people matter. They're all filler, just taking up space to give the illusion reality is normal. After the Fourth, I've seen the walls fall away, the audience outside of time, and your little display reaffirms this." He pointed about. "*This* is all fiction, all fake. My directive remains. Write *Tetragrammar*. Kill The Authors. When I'm done with that, I'll walk the fuck out of this sad story, wherever that takes me."

A spark glittered in her ocean-blue eyes. "If it's all fake, would you like your muse back?"

"Where is she?"

"She's my prisoner. I have you at a disadvantage. Not to worry, little writer." He watched her reach inside the sapphire around her throat, somehow strangely her hand was moving in a space much too small and as she searched, he didn't find it strange at all. Retrieving her hand, she held a small figurine. It was a girl, legs crossed in lotus, that resembled a mini-Fable chiseled from amethyst. The statue's hands were clasped over her mouth in terror as if suppressing a scream.

"When Fable went through her aesthetic time of the month, she maimed the skin of the world," Minor said, stroking the figurine. "She inspired us. Some went mad. Some died, but she didn't care."

"You hurt her?"

"Yes. I have and I'll continue to hurt her."

"Then you die."

"I'm already dead!" She noted a worry on his face. "You love her, don't you?"

Seven considered. "Yes."

"I loved, too. She made me love a man named Ethan a little too much. He consumed my world, my dreams. My existence was *Ethanized*. I was successful, adored. I had a life, solid and real. I wasn't a non-person she could break on a whim. I didn't need to be pulled into your fantasy. But she did; she dragged me into your nonsense and, worse, I wasn't even the star!"

"Let her go."

"Or what?" Minor flaunted. "You can't touch me. I'm *her* Dynasty. Not yours. So hands off unless you want to get frisky. However, as a sign of diplomacy, I'll return her. Just don't blame me for what happens next. It's not my fault people always get burned when she touches their reality."

Minor raised the figurine. With a devilish grin, she chucked the Fable statue at the floor. Seven watched it, and although he assumed it had been thrown at normal speed, time slowed, and he observed it falling, frame by frame, trailing a comet-like tail of twinkling stars that crackled, like lavender fireworks. And when it hit the floor, it broke apart into a mist, only as it broke, it erupted much more violently than an object so small had any right to.

There was an explosion as everything blew out and a mist spread through the coffee shop, into the air, and coated the people and tables, layering everything. While it layered, it also burned. There were more outbursts. The atmosphere hazed into an ugly eggplant-purple cloud, all in slow motion. Seven found himself shielding his face, dropping and yelling, a deep, muddied gurgle that might've been words. And then he was on the ground in a mess of dust and fragments, some wet, some not, dry heaving along with all the people he'd never met before, people who were crying and screaming, and he looked about him at the chaos…and what he saw was real and bloody and…

…through a ringing in his ears, Seven heard the wail of sirens in the distance, terrified voices, and cries from the street; groans and shrieks about him hidden in the mist. Something wet and red coated Seven and all the rubbish, something he sincerely hoped was ink.

"Economies will collapse. Crime will rise." Seven heard Minor's voice mixing with the screaming from all directions. "There will be heated debates over gun control laws and welfare. Society can go to hell and you wouldn't care. As long as you get to write the fictions in your head, why should you allow the outside world to touch you?"

Seven began to move through fog and dust. In the chaos, he spotted the bare body of Fable buried in rubble, bone, and pastries, a dim aura about her. And he crawled through broken tables and ceiling tile, glass and what may've been people parts towards her, trying to ignore the gory details as he approached her, a beacon in the mayhem. Coughing on the misty air that smelled of death and flowers, Seven pulled himself along the floor, glass crunching under hands and knees. She was naked and wet, pupils jittery on eyes that were stuck open, and she trembled and hugged herself desperately.

"No death here, Seven," Minor said as she strutted through the fog, stepping over rubbish, the crunch of glass under her heels. "Just collateral. Minor Damage," she dismissed while admiring her nails.

"What did you do?!" Seven yelled as he looked about from his knees while cradling Fable.

"Oh, don't act like you give a damn." Minor brushed some debris from her suit. "I've blessed these people."

"Yea, they really look blessed." Seven removed his jacket to cover Fable.

"You may see casualties, but I view them as minor souls elevated in significance." Minor paused to admire her work. A man was covered with what appeared to be burns while two women cried out from faces full of glass. "The significance being to show you they have no significance. Like you said, they're not real. Curse me and whatnot, but, in the end, they were never part of your grand narrative."

"Why involve them?!" Seven spat. "They're not part of our story."

"Neither was I in the beginning, which didn't make me unimportant."

"You won't get away with this."

Raising an eyebrow, "I couldn't agree more," she said. "This act must be paid for, just like before, when the world went mad and Fable made me kill myself…"

And as Minor rambled on, in the chaos of the coffee shop, there was something insubstantial about it, a lack, and Seven found the details of the attack fleeting away. He couldn't fully register the actual destruction, the maiming, the faces crying out in agony, or why they screamed at all. He could only think about movies and comic books, and how the violence in fiction never really mattered.

He'd seen it before: Movie violence, corpses on television, civilians slaughtered. Those caught in Minor's display of power were no different than the bystanders gunned down or blown up on syndicated television. Super-villains and terrorists did it all the time. You watched; you moved on. Sure, it was horrible. But from a plot perspective, you didn't get too riled. The storyline marched on with little consequence. No getting choked up over collateral damage. Callous or not, the destruction at Jumpin' Java failed to move him. Seven was embedded in fiction; he was allowed to be desensitized.

A sly grin formed on Minor's cobalt-colored lips. "Oh, Seven, your life's so wonderfully postmodern." She seemed happy at saying that. "If we met before all this, I might've pity-fucked you when I was alive. How could I *ever* turn down the unemployed pipe dreamer?

But I'll fuck you now and I'll fuck Fable, too. And you'll wish it was the nice way."

"You have a dirty mouth," Seven said.

"My mouth's the cleanest part of me." She blew him a kiss, and the mouth over her head made slapping, puckering sounds. "I have plans. Large plans. Don't think you and Fable are in the clear. The Hall is far from done with her. You may be holding her as we speak, but she's still my prisoner. Karma continues to choke her off. In a way, I'm her creation and to truly kill me-*and you'll have to* -you'll have to kill her." She perked up at that last bit, then posing in her tight blue skirt, she extended a hand to admire her glossy fingernails. "When all is said and done, you'll fail Seven. My place is with The Authors and it's only a matter of time until I rise to be the star and you're seven layers of shit under my heel."

With that, Minor whispered into her sapphire and the cerulean smile stretched open, top lip to ceiling, bottom to the ground, and the woman dressed like an overpaid secretary on Wall Street playfully wiggled her fingers good-bye, stepped into the mouth, winked, and was gone.

As the screams persisted and more people entered the premise to help and clear the debris, Seven cradled Fable and slung her over his shoulder. She was light and hollow, and he treaded through the devastated coffee shop, mixing with the crowds, people on their phones snapping pictures and recording. It may've turned his stomach-*the bodies, the blood*-but he couldn't get too worked up. If the deceased were real, they'd rise like all literal souls entering realms of light no fiction could ever do justice.

Sirens continued to wail in the background as Seven walked home, dissipating with every block into a faint echo. And every block, Seven trudged forward, Fable slung over his shoulder, replaying the violence, waiting for the stir of compassion. People had been hurt. There was blood, death, destruction. He tried to allow the tragedy to invoke sickness or sadness. He wanted to feel something. He couldn't. It all glazed over in his mind. *Only fiction*, he rationalized.

Gritting his teeth, Seven pushed on.

He barely recalled the details of his actual arrival back home. He set Fable down on his futon. She'd seen better days, that was sure. Her usual pale skin was even more bleached of color. She wore jeans and a t-shirt with a baby blue print that read ALL HAIL MINORS.

Her arms and cheeks were covered in scratches with dried blood scabbed over on her wounds. Her hair appeared thinner and tousled with bits of wood debris and dust and perhaps parts that were once people. Her eyes flickered behind her lids as if stuck in a dream that yielded little peace.

He sat by her feet as they twitched and jumped, toes curling in pain. He squeezed the arch of her foot to comfort her. He watched her chest rising dramatically. He rested a hand on her sternum until her breath eased and flowed deeper into her belly. As she relaxed, she still looked damaged and worn and dainty, almost angelic; the way an angel may look after its fall from heaven.

"I missed you," he said, for lack of anything else. He touched his palm to her cheek. She was cold and hot, and his hand felt sweaty and prickly when pulling away. Pinching her gently around her jaw, he wiggled her chin. "You're ok. We both know you can't die. Not completely."

Eventually, Fable stirred. Her eyes parted, distant and dreamy. She moved slowly, curling and uncurling her fingers and toes. The claw marks on her forearms faded ever so slightly. And when she opened her mouth to taste the world, only then, did Seven realize how malnourished she looked; her eyes sunken, cheekbones pronounced. She blinked, like a newborn making sense of the surroundings, her vision moving across the apartment, then to Seven, back and forth. She started to pick the crusted sleep from her lashes.

"How are you?" he asked.

"How am I?" Fable tasted the question. She leaned up on her elbows. "I feel like I've had my heart ripped out and I've been dead and drained by a woman who has more than enough karmic right to kill me till the end of time."

"That Minor bitch is the Fifth Dynasty," Seven said. "She's a peach, and she hates you."

"I hadn't noticed." Fable smirked. She blinked-out for an instant. While she had been wearing the ALL HAIL MINORS t-shirt, she was now dressed in pajama pants and a tank top.

Seven fluffed a pillow for her head. "Rest now. We'll deal with all this later." He kissed her forehead. Her hair smelled of lilacs. And he watched her drift off behind her closed eyes. He wanted to kiss her again, to press his lips against her and forget the world and let his walls swallow him in a white void. Looking at her now, she may've been more beautiful than he realized.

Unable to sleep, Seven turned on the television. It cast obscenely bright shadows onto the walls. Lowering the volume, he sat on the floor, remote loose in his hands. There was a news report about the recent tragedy on Penn Street. It was all chaos and confusion with no leads. Investigations remained clueless on what triggered the explosion. Listening to the update, his head grew heavy, falling away from reality into sleep.

Around midnight, he heard the squeak of the futon. Disoriented, he stirred awake on the floor. He found Fable standing in front of the open fridge. She looked somewhat undead the way the light spilled onto her. She was eating a pack of cheese, slice after slice, until all the cheese was gone and she moved to the pickle jar. She devoured every bit of food in a steady act of consumption, eating lunchmeat and rice and several plums too soft for Seven's liking. Her body changed while she ate. He couldn't tell how, but it wasn't the food. It was the idea of sustenance that filled her out. She continued to devour a pack of raw hotdogs, soy nuggets, and a frozen bag of tortellini. She proceeded to down his soy milk, a green smoothie, and pomegranate juice. When finished, she closed the door and trudged back to the futon. She sat and stared at Seven with eyes of deep, pitted shadow. For only a moment, she smiled, a large, razor-black grin.

"I'm cold," she said, all shivers and no smile, hugging herself.

There was a silence between them.

"It's a little cold," Seven said awkwardly.

"It's alotta cold." And her teeth chattered as she rubbed her shoulders.

"A bath," he said. "I could draw a bath."

"You always liked baths," Fable said.

"Yes."

"Ok. A bath," she agreed.

Fable hugged herself timidly while Seven ran the water. She teetered side to side as if adjusting to the idea of feet. She watched the water fill the tub with a child's fascination that bordered on terror. Seven sat on the edge of the tub, splashing the water, testing the temperature, trying to get that balance between lukewarm and scolding. When the water began to steam, he extended his hand to say I'm ready when you are. Her right arm hung by her side and she clasped onto her elbow with her left hand, weighing the dangers of a tub full of water.

"What's wrong?" he asked.

Tilting her head, "Water," she said, "it's the water."

"What about the water?"

"Drowning."

"How's that?"

"The idea of drowning," her voice shook. "It's you."

"What's me?"

"You're going to drown and the world will drown and to save it, you'll have to die."

"What are you talking about?"

"The hole in the world. You'll have to fall to rise." And she flashed that same, unexpected grin that took him off guard. There was something foreign about it, something wrong. Fable stood, facing him in her pajamas-*blink*-now completely naked. He traced the curves of her body, tried to avoid looking at her raisin-colored nipples, her flat stomach. He'd seen her naked before; this was different. Her body was pockmarked with bruises. Her ribs showed through her flesh in a haggard, worn quality. She looked damaged and he wanted to hold her.

He guided her into the tub. She stepped in one foot at a time, wincing at the temperature, lowering herself into the water while she braced the edges as she settled on the tub floor. Her legs slid out and she leaned against the cold back. Her toes reached up to play with the faucet.

Seven leaned against the tub. It was quiet except for the cricket chirping from outside the window and the sloshing of water.

"Ever think none of it's real?" Fable asked, raspy and distant, "The Authors? Me?" Seven's shoulders were getting wet as the water spilled over the edge when she shifted. He said nothing. "It's all a dream, isn't it?" she said. "Just a fantasy I trapped you in? There are no men in the moon, no Dynasties. No great story to tell. What if you didn't have amnesia? What if there simply is no past to you?" He listened to her. As he listened, her words failed to spark anything new. "What if I'm the real author?"

He turned his head, although he didn't look at her.

"What if They're me?" Fable said. "If this is all a fantasy, maybe Paris was the wake-up call…" Her words drifted.

"I know my life's a dream," he finally said. "Dream or no dream, I'm a writer, and that's the realm we work. The idea of it, the literary side of things, the metaphorical; it's all real. The symbolism is my reality. I'm treading the same tired circle. And I see the finish line. It's the perfect story and if I just hang on, if I keep moving forward, maybe I'll reach it. That's *Tetragrammar*. The line I can never cross."

They were both quiet. The only sound a steady drip from the faucet.

"The water," Fable whispered, "it's cold."

"I can add more."

"That'll get cold, too."

Drip.

Because there was nothing else to say, Seven pulled himself up. He peered at Fable below the water, looking delicate and elegant all at once. He pulled his shirt over his head, unbuttoned his jeans, removed his boxers and socks, tossing his clothes by the toilet, and lowered himself into the tub. She adjusted to allow him to slide in behind her. It was awkward and uncomfortable. The water rose, flowed over the edges.

For a while, they said nothing. His arms rested on her stomach, her head on his chest. His hands remained frozen over her bare flesh, unsure where to relax. Fable touched his hands and intertwined her fingers with his. She squeezed his ring when she found the cold metal. "You're still wearing your ring?"

"The ring's wearing me. Don't leave me again," he whispered. "You're all I have." *Drip.* And he closed his eyes, his face pressed into her wet hair, and drifted into a heavy sleep.

*

In his dream, he was moving very fast in a direction that defied up or down, back or forward. What terrified him the most, it may not have been a dream at all. Eventually, he crashed into a wall or border. Something that wasn't quite solid stretched as his body pushed and pushed. There was a loud, ripping noise, like the shredding of paper on a cosmic level. And he saw words and letters raining upon him, and a million eyes reading over him, moving across him, and greasy fingers turning pages around his life.

Knock, knock.

That's when he lost his mind. That's when Seven screamed.

*

Seven was still in the tub when he woke alone in the cold water. Daylight broke in through the window. Outside, birds sang their morning songs. His back and neck ached. His clothes were neatly folded on the toilet. The door was ajar. Breakfast smells wafted in. He sat up.

Fable peeked in. "I cooked us breakfast. You should eat," she announced, bright-eyed.

Fable topped the waffles with soy bacon and layered it all in syrup. He watched her carefully as she plated the food, scrutinizing her each movement. He found nothing wrong with her, no notable damage or injuries, no signs of mental scars. She did all this with a renewed vigor. And she looked brighter, charged. She wore baggy sweatpants and a long-sleeved shirt.

"One night's rest does wonders for you," Seven said. "You look good." And she did; the haggard lines gone, along with the gauntness and newspaper tarnish of her flesh. Having been dead or tortured or whatever agony had been inflicted on her never showed. She appeared ridiculously restored. She looked a little too good, and Seven didn't entirely trust that.

"I feel better." Fable stretched towards the ceiling with a loud groan.

"You got your glow back."

"I did."

Seven cut into his waffle. He looked at her.

"What?" Fable asked with a glint in her eyes.

"Nothing."

"There's something."

Seven crunched the waffle.

"I healed really well, didn't I?" Fable said. "A little too good in fact and now you're suspicious." She dabbed the syrup around her mouth with a napkin. "You're right to be suspicious. I put my healing on autopilot."

"You can do that?"

"I'm not really fully recovered. My body, my chakras, whatever it is a muse has for anatomy, I set that on a temporary recovery with my mind. I'm not fixed; I'm just pretending to be for now. It's like a backup that'll only last long enough for you to fix it."

"Fix what?"

"Everything," Fable said. "*Tetragrammar*. You have to end it or make a decision about it. Whether it's written or unwritten, you have to get to the source of what set this whole plot of shit in motion. You're going to have to settle your differences with Him."

Seven bit a piece of soy bacon.

"Last night during our tubby-time, that little body of water terrified me," Fable said. "It brought back memories. Memories of Father Notion. When I was being tortured in the Hall of Minors, I imagined seeing Notion as a man."

"Andrew Wilkins. The suicide in the park."

"Yes." Fable nodded sternly. "The death in the pond. The water. The symbolic drowning. You're going to have to engage Father now and find out just what your role in *Tetragrammar* is."

"Notion's in the Moon. They have him there. Going there is the whole point. It's always been the destination. But the doorway has always resided in the book."

"Yes," she said to all this. "But *the idea*, Seven. You know it all too well. There is always more than one way to embrace an idea. Part of meeting Notion involves sharing his fall. The pond. That's your portal. The symbolic hole in the world, the doorway, the entrance. It may not take you to the Moon, but it will take you to Him."

His appetite was waning.

"You wanted to ascend your own fiction, right? That's the first step." Fable assured.

"I don't know."

"You better decide sooner than later. I can only run on empty for so long. Without my half-heart, who knows when my iddy-biddy body will give out? I'm partly heartless, Seven."

"Heartless?" He repeated, ever the parrot.

Fable set her fork down. "Minor took my heart." And in an instant, gone was the long-sleeved shirt. *Blink*. Fable was naked from the waist up, hands pressing between her breasts and she parted her flesh. It was more disturbing how little she reacted to this.

What would this look like to a reader from the Outer Page? Seven wondered.

Her chest was an empty, bloodless cavity, a texture Seven could only describe as a series of violet-tinted circuit boards. And the circuitry was devoid of anything technological, charged by magic alone. The only object within her was a cartoonish-looking heart cracked in half, jagged on its broken side. Fable waited for Seven to gaze in, *he got it*, and she closed her flesh, leaving no scar, her chest seamless as ever. She now-*blink*-wore a knitted turtleneck sweater the color of mashed grapes.

"That's a problem, isn't it? What does that mean for us?" Seven asked.

"They'll use my heart as a weapon. No good will come of it." Fable managed a weak smile. "But we'll face that later. As I said, the first step lies with Notion."

Seven fidgeted.

"So," lightening the mood, Fable asked, "what did I miss?"

"You wouldn't believe me," he joked, knowing she'd believe it all, everything and anything.

"Let's see." Fable tipped her chair back, face twisted in thought, eyes looking upwards as if the answers were scribed upon the ceiling. "Ah," she said. "After I decided to not kill Elaine, I died. You met the Fourth Dynasty and the Fourth told you you're a Circle Child like him and he killed you with a pen. Because you're fictional, you couldn't quite die that way. You then waited in your apartment with me, only I wasn't there at all, because Ambrose was pretending to be me, since I was dead, having my heart ripped out and sucked dry by the Fifth Dynasty in the Hall of Minors." She paused to look at Seven.

She continued, "Ambrose told you Notion was the real enemy and the Circle Children were all echoes cursed to repeat his death. Before Ambrose left, he broke the Fourth Wall. By doing this, your entire existence had been deconstructed into a metafiction. And that self-awareness broke your mind and damaged you even more than you're already damaged." She waited. *How am I doing?* her eyes seemed to ask.

"Thrifty left his bag," Seven said. Her eyes burned with something comical and vague. "It was his last gift to me. He said what it contains could destroy me or save me."

"Have you looked inside?" Fable asked.

"Come on, Fable. You'd know if I had."

She nodded.

"Did I miss anything?"

"Eve's my sister," he said.

Her face blanked. "Out of all the important things that happened when I was away, how did I fail to bring attention to that little nugget? You have a sister!"

"Yes."

Fable wasn't quite done yet. "That's wild. That's monumental actually. It means you were really born. It means you didn't just fall out of Notion's head." The excitement etched itself on her face.

He appreciated her enthusiasm but couldn't work himself up about it. "I'm sorry," he said. "I'm sorry I just shut down and stopped writing. How I always struggle with it, no wonder you resented me."

"Then fix it," she said. "Confront the source, Father Notion."

"Ambrose Walker was convinced you'd been with all the previous writers, that you played a role in their insanity."

"Ambrose may be right. When I was in the Hall, I flashed on images of writers like you going mad and, well, being dead opens your eyes. We die, we lose our bodies, and eventually we wear new bodies. Our true forms are beneath flesh, and I've been wearing my skin for a long time. All bodies are temporary fictions. If we hold on long enough, we don't live new stories. We cling to old drafts. The draft is a body and Notion has never let go. And because he's not alive anymore, not in a way I'd consider living, he's bled parts of himself into you."

"How can you be sure?" Seven asked.

"Because I was there when he died. Trust me. He is much older than you believe. He is the snake in all white spaces, the serpent of empty pages, the limbo dragon. And They locked him away for the good of the world in a dark, white dream. And when a cycle begins, he screams away his flesh, and from his skin the next child arises, to tread the circle-prison of his existential curse. But not you; you must be the Completed One, The Seven to his Zero. So you will enter his purgatory and you will slay the dragon, play Beowulf to his Grendel, Theseus to his Minotaur. You will do this, because *Tetragrammar* must end, one way or another."

"Kill Notion?"

"Yes." She shrugged, hands empty. *Blink.* She raised her coffee in salute.

Throughout the afternoon, Fable lay on her stomach with her forearms spread out in front of her like a sphinx. As she recovered from her ordeal, she watched a marathon of *Doctor Who* on BBC. She

243

liked Matt Smith, found the episodes surprisingly creepy. After the two-parter featuring the Weeping Angels, she said, "I still don't understand any negative criticism towards Steven Moffat." When she heard no response she looked over her shoulder.

Seven remained in meditation, facing a wall, his back towards her. She imagined he believed if he stared long enough into his walls, he'd see the true reality, that there were no walls.

Hours later when Seven moved from his meditation, it was late evening. He discovered Fable waiting in his bed, tapping the blankets for him to join her. "Remember when we had sex?" she asked.

Seven squirmed. "Yes."

"Did you always want to do that?"

"The thought crossed my mind," he admitted.

"Funny how this story was never about a book," Fable said. "It was never about Paris either. It's us. We're the story."

"*Tetragrammar* has been nothing but anger and frustration. When it's done, none of the bitterness, the doubt, will matter. It's the journey of it; that's the story."

"And staying inspired. Your true love is fiction," she added. "Love and obsession go hand in hand when left unchecked. Artistic love can be particularly lethal. It's that danger in any passion. That rawness of dreams. How *does* one stay inspired despite the void? Just remember the two sides to creation: those inspired and those who inspire, that primordial idea of artist and muse, older than time itself." Fable paused. "Considering that, I may be much older than I suspected."

"Everyone has past lives. I've never doubted reincarnation," Seven said.

"Yes. But could it be possible my first birth predates all this, that I'm only a fraction of some older muse?"

Seven had no answer. Fable continued, "When I reflected during my torture, I remembered how the previous Circle Children were driven insane by me. What if Andrew killed himself because I demanded too much? Some savage, hungrier side of me craved more from him, like a god demanding sacrifice? Andrew became Notion and now his seventh son needs to meet daddy. You need to close the loop he began."

"I'm aware of that now. *How* is the other question?"

"The suicide spot," Fable said. "The pond that could drown the world. In the pond, there is a hole and there isn't a hole. You'll have to take the plunge, my little Alice."

"I'm scared," Seven admitted.

"You should be," Fable said with little comfort. "You have to do it sometime. Besides, if all this is fake and you are only fiction, then you must be reborn."

"I still don't know how that's supposed to happen."

"How does that happen?" she smirked. "How will you do this? Why, Seven, with any birth, one must fall."

*

Seven entered the park, proceeded downhill towards the pond. If Father Notion turned out to be just some boy who severed his mortal coil, if that were the case, Seven couldn't help feeling underwhelmed. He wanted the driving will of a higher power on his side. He had Fable, but he desired another force, a paternal energy any son would fight for. He feared the mission of saving this man, of writing his story, was nothing more than ridiculous.

Approaching the pond, water had never terrified Seven as much as it did that moment. Staring into it, Seven couldn't suppress the existential weight in his guts. The surface was still, oily, a perfect mirror of the Moon. The pond seemed impossibly large, like all oceans combined, and he would've preferred being stranded in any ocean, lost and shark-surrounded, than face this little body of water. He imagined, much like the ocean, if this pond desired, how easy it could rise up and swallow the world, and how the Moon could orchestrate such an act. A dread misted from the water, like hot pavement after a cool, summer rain.

There is a hole in the world; there is no hole.

And funny that a hole wouldn't form somewhere more obvious, that the eating away of reality didn't emanate from the murky darkness in the depths of an ocean, that a world could drown in the smallest amount of water.

Seven removed his shoes and set them on the grass. He waited, feet moist, wanting to leave, forget the pond, and never think of water again, hands shoved in his jacket pockets, surprised by how long he could stand there doing nothing.

If this were to be a rebirth of sorts, he'd have to do better. Seven removed his jacket, jeans, shirt and stood under the Moon in his boxer briefs. Seven walked into the pond.

The water was cold and stinging. With every step closer towards the center, his vision blurred. Large, concentric circles rippled underneath him across the waters. The stars glinted on the liquid surface and somehow the pond had become every body of water, personal and indifferent at once. It embodied any place of drowning. Seven continued forward, water rising shin-high until he dropped into a sinkhole and the pond swallowed him up to his waist. His footing grew uncertain, and he staggered with each step, ankles rolling out under him.

A sound began to fill the world, like water rushing down a drain.

That's what Seven heard on a much larger scale. Closing his eyes, he witnessed a vortex at the pond's center in his mind. And when he looked, he saw a hole opening. The longer he stared, the more centrifugal force it acquired until the pond was being sucked into the vortex and Seven was spiraling down with it. Just when he began to question the how of the situation, the impossible physics of falling down a metaphorical hole to arrive at a space inside the Moon; it happened.

Seven plummeted down an up-shaped rabbit's hole.

He was falling and being born.

Everything changed.

When he came to, the atmosphere didn't feel solid. The air filled with the idea of prisons and confinement, the anxieties of perfection. And when all those intangibles merged together, gained a sense of depth and substance, Seven knew *that* was the place.

He didn't want to be here in the old, white room. And he wasn't alone as a series of movements crinkled around him, folding and unfolding. A mouth pressed out from a yellowed, rotting book. There was a pulpy scream and a lunatic smile of origami teeth. There were paper walls and a man with a halo of ellipses. This was the stupid, withered truth.

This was Father Notion.

20
RIB-BORN CHILD

Although *Tetragrammar* stars Seven, never forget the parts are as important as the whole. Now, a taste of side-plot. Back to a beginning.

A long time ago, there was a garden. In this garden was a tree. There was a man, too. This was before time and very much real. (Never forget that). The man was lonely so he removed a rib and wrote a female shape in the clay. He buried his rib in the symbol and then there was a woman.

Suppose her name was Eve, and not Lilith; this Eve curiously looked upon the Tree at a single blood-colored orb hanging from a branch. She plucked the strange, little thing and bit into it. As its hard flesh crunched between her teeth, thunder cracked the heavens. Adam gazed up, wrought with despair.

Eve tapped Adam on the head, *it's all right*. She told her maker-lover if it weren't an apple, it would've been a gift of fire handed down by an old god (which also occurred in another time).

What have you done? Adam cried. *You've killed us!*

No, this is not death, she assured: this is evolution. Evolution is always uncertain, a gamble, an eve of something new and marvelous.

That was a long time ago. That was another Eve, who may or may not have existed.

Now, forget that.

Look towards the Present.

*

Eve had a garden. It wasn't the best idea, since the world painfully knew what happened when people named Eve toyed with gardens. Hers was different. Centered in her backyard was a tree. Around the tree, Eve had landscaped her lawn in artificial flowers. It was silly but made sense when considering how much money she dumped into pretty flowers that became food for deer and wild life. She bought hundreds of cheap plastic flowers of all colors and size.

And, lo and behold, one miraculous day while strolling through the artificial landscape, Eve found an apple in her grass hidden under a plastic orchid. The apple itself wasn't strange. What was strange was the silky cord attached to its stem that connected to the twisted ovary of the fake orchid underneath its petals.

The apple was real and shiny and had grown from something fake and plastic.

Eve squatted by it. *Aren't you curious?*

In all gardens, things must grow, even in the most impossible wombs, in the engines of doubt, fiction can seed life.

*

Her phone rang. A man whose name was Tommy or Jon or Mitch called. They'd be over shortly, yes, she'd be here, yes, of course they would…

*

Too many have plunged into your garden. Of all the nameless suitors planting their seeds, never did you imagine through all uncertainty life could survive within you.

It will happen soon. Wait for it.

Under the bucking and bouncing, a moment's held breath, then…

Oh, here he comes! Thousands die. Hundreds never make it. Fifty perish. Ten snuffed out.

But yet one little swimmer must defy the odds. It darts steadfast, past its dying siblings, the sperm that could. It won't stop. It can't. It must live. It must see light.

*

One month passed. No blood. No red of the Moon. Rubbing her flat belly: could it be a seed had been planted in her garden? Yes, and it would grow.

Covering her mouth, *Oh, shit! I'm bloody pregnant!*

*

There you are. What are you? More importantly, what will you be? Another fascinating possibility, how will you differentiate from the White? You remain nameless, as you should, a not-yet child, the Unborn weighing its rights and wrongs of lives gone and yet to come.

Who was your father? George, the lawyer? Doug? Was it Steve or Kamal or Lilly (it could happen) or that TV remote when Eve was lonely and curious?

Waiting in the Womb, the deceased brethren-all your ghost-sperm siblings-laugh and tremble and sneer. You ponder this and somehow you no longer feel so privileged. You are uncertain, beginning to doubt choosing this womb as your vessel into the temporal. This is not a good womb. You must escape it. You must jettison into another body before full conception, before it's too late, before the incarnation!

*

"I'm quitting my job," Eve told Charlie while she stirred her chai latte. "*Office Space* had the right idea. Mankind wasn't meant to live in cubicles."

"Then quit." Charlie downloaded music onto his iPhone. "Screw it."

"I like your style," Eve said. Charlie looked over his silver-framed glasses. He half-smiled sheepishly. Charlie worked as a hibachi chef. Eve had met him after watching him during a lunch break. So impressed by his skills, she found him interesting enough to ask out. They met for coffee, then dinner. No spark ignited, which was ok; it was refreshing to talk, *just talk.*

"Just saying you're a free spirit. You don't belong in any corporation. That's a compliment," Charlie added.

"I'm tired, Charlie. Wish I could age backwards. Just young myself into a state of comfort. Minimalism would be my quota. Easy jobs. Smoking pot like Kevin Spacey in *American Beauty*." She licked the rim of her chai. "What would I do if I quit?"

Charlie suggested, "Be a model."

She punched him in the arm playfully. "I couldn't model."

"You're beautiful," Charlie said, "course you could."

"Thanks, Charlie," Eve slid her hand over his. "You're sweet."

*

Sometimes in her memories, she was six years old playing with Barbie dolls with her neighbor, Mandy, who had freckles and crooked teeth. Playtime was cut short as Mandy's parents dashed into the bedroom, alarmed at their daughter's blood-curdling scream. To their relief, little Mandy was safe; however, they cringed at the decapitated doll heads strewn across the floor and young Eve holding a Barbie. Poking her finger inside the doll, Eve couldn't understand why Mandy made such a fuss about the plastic corpses. And Eve thought to herself, *just like people, hollow on the inside.*

Kindergarten teacher Mrs. Seidel shivered while she looked at Eve's very detailed drawing of dead birds feeding on the corpses of children.

Sixth grade, Eve punched out Tommy Finkle for not laughing at a joke she found morbidly funny about his deceased grandmother. Seventh grade, Eve enraged devout Catholic Rebecca Monroe over a comment that mankind, like the dinosaurs, will evolve into birds. Eighth grade, she got busted for making drugs. When no one saw, Principal Atkins tested her blend, frustrated never knowing the recipe for her cloud nine.

Tenth grade, Eve used her wit and quick mouth for good, joining theatre and excelling in many diverse roles. After the play, *Big Angst*, Eve lost her virginity to Chad Rean, who worked spotlight, under the bleachers. Chad was not a virgin. He was used to girls cuddling next to him, vulnerable and sensitive after their flower had been plucked. This time, it was Chad who kissed the girl afterwards. *I love you*, he gasped softly. Eve yawned, tapped Chad on the head. When she skipped away, Chad hugged himself, for the first time feeling violated and shamefully regretful he hadn't waited for marriage.

*

"You're late," warned Eve's boss.

Late?

Late was the slip of time missed at an ascertained moment in space, the postponement of the inevitable seeking a certain possibility siphoned off by a very intelligent procrastination. Could anything ever be late if scripted by an Almighty Consciousness? Was she late for work or had God charted her to show up for a meaningless job exactly twenty-nine minutes and seven seconds later than said time? That made her anything but late. Sure, it's inconvenient for her employer, but what are you going to do? Why, didn't that put her right exactly where she was supposed to be?

"Do I have to explain to you the principles of a job?" asked her boss.

Be at work. 6:00 sharp.

Eve told her 6:00 was a fallible means to organize the motion of time. Surely, in another part of the world, it was 6:00. Technically, she wasn't late at all. She was right on time or, according to certain time zones, was perhaps already done her shift.

*

"I quit," she told Charlie. He congratulated her, told her not to worry. *Oh, Charlie, gentle, tender Charlie. Such a sweetie,* Eve thought, *she'd eat his life if he let her.*

She then thought about lateness. She was later than ever, six weeks in fact, the strange presence admonished with a kick.

*

Your missed period becomes an ellipsis. A certain truth hits you. You are pregnant, on the eve of motherhood.

*

Wearing nothing except a sexy pair of lace panties, Eve departed from Tom's bed. Locking herself in his bathroom, she ran the water to drown out her tears. The sex just wasn't interesting anymore. She touched her flat stomach. Could the impossible thing in her sterile womb ever love her? Would it dare call her mother?

*

Images of angry children and homicidal sperm bombarded her dreams. Darting up, she glared around her room at the walls covered in surreal art. Looking upon her gallery, was childbirth any stranger than a Dali-esque image? The whole process became strangely terrifying: the idea of sperms having souls, that a consciousness could gestate inside your body, terraforming your uterus.

She dressed in her jogging clothes. She left her house around midnight, because she suspected people on the verge of breakdowns did that sort of thing. She ran through her neighborhood under the moonlight, and she ran and ran, losing herself in The City, a restless soul waiting for the night to swallow her alive.

*

See a dark sidewalk shrouded by trees. When the trees pass, a block away, you enter the decrepit building stretch of sparse light and bad judgment. You read a paper about a young girl jogging by herself who ends up dead or raped or raped dead. You always think it was her own stupid fault. Why would a girl place herself in that situation? Stupid and naïve, you dismiss her. And somehow her killer now isn't as monstrous because he was fulfilling the role of predator. Beasts will be beasts, after all.

It's darker now, even for midnight, when Eve jogged into the alley.

A shadow followed her, and she never thought she could be one of those girls you read about. She sensed someone lurking behind her. Picking up her pace, it's too late as cold hands grip her and throw her to the sidewalk.

She tried to get up, but a kick to her stomach stole her air. For a moment, as she cringed forward, wheezing, she feared for her Unborn's safety. She spotted the metal glint of a gun in the blackness and the crack of a zipper. He yanked her hair and threw her onto her back.

"Wait!" Eve pleaded. "At least use protection."

"Never used rubbers," said the man with a gravel voice. "Never will." His hands pulled at her pants.

"No, wait!" Eve screamed again. And in the commotion, she said, "That's for your protection."

"What?" He hesitated, pinning her to the ground with his large hands.

She couldn't make out his face behind his mask, yet the silence painted him dumbfounded. "I sleep around," she explained. "You're more likely to catch something than give me anything."

"...I'll take that chance." He removed his mask. His features were shrouded in grisly darkness.

Eve dragged herself against the wire fence, holding her stomach. She didn't bother wiping the dirt from her face. "Have you done this before? You're not very good at it."

The Man winced, pulled the gun from his waist, pointed it at her.

"I hope you're not a virgin. A virgin rapist is lame. Rape at gunpoint isn't the best. Slip a roofie in a girl's drink. I mean, shit, they have a whole family of drugs for guys who can't get laid."

The gun handle cracked across her face.

"Your anger's misdirected," she pushed from her bloody mouth. "It's not me, it's you. Lash out on the right person. Retrace your steps. You wouldn't rape me or be in this situation if it weren't for the tempting snake in your pants." He cast his eyes towards his crotch. "Pull your fly up."

"Fuck you." He raised his pistol to strike again.

"I read it in you." This stopped him. "I read your uncertainty. Not a hard trait. It's easy to see in everyone. Uncertainty breeding like a pandemic. A job. A relationship. An insecurity. Life. Whatever, let's talk."

He moved away from her, rubbed his forehead. He looked about to cry. One hand held the gun in a limp grip; the other didn't seem to know what to do with itself.

Eve pushed herself onto her butt with her legs bent in front of her. "Seems to be your pecker gets the rest of you into trouble. Why not remove the obstacle?" she suggested. "Aim your gun down there. Pull the trigger and be rid of the culprit."

He laughed until he didn't because nothing was quite so funny anymore, because now it occurred to him that perhaps her advice was sound and perhaps it would be for the best. Rattling his head, *hypnosis*, he wondered, *she's using hypnosis.*

And why did his hand move then? He nervously placed the gun point at his privates, pressing the head into his groin, mad eyes beaming at her.

"If you want to be certain, do it," she assured him. "Fire away."

BANG!

Eve took a long shower to wash any essence of the Man from her body. The water turned dirty and grainy as it streamed off her. Her bruises and cuts were gone. Although with no signs of assault, she touched her belly to soothe the thing growing inside her.

When she toweled herself off and dressed for bed, she plopped on her couch to watch television, only to find several absurd infomercials selling DVDs on how to eliminate poverty.

And somehow she already sensed him from the hallway.

"You found me?" she asked. The moving picture of the television reflected in her dirty glasses.

"Are you surprised I found you?" the Man gasped, layered in profuse sweat. He scratched his temple with his pistol. His hands looked wet.

"No," Eve answered.

The Man walked stiffly forward, legs unbending, one step at a time. There was a large hole in the front of his pants. Thick black-red saturated his thighs. "I followed the trail. Your trail," responded the Man. He dropped into the chair, his face ghost-white. His head kicked back with his arms resting on his lap. The gun remained loose in his blood-spattered hands. His chin drooped to his chest. He seemed like he wanted to laugh at the gaping hole where his genitalia used to be. "You're a demon," he pushed. "I need to kill you."

"Kill me? You were ready to breed with me. I'm no demon. I'm as human as you." Eve eyed the vast amounts of blood leaving his body, soaking his pants. *And shouldn't he be bled out and dead by now?* she questioned. Her thoughts went back to her fake garden and the growth of her fake apple.

"Kill you. Shoot you or choke you." He seemed to be fading. But as he said that, Eve imagined her brother's hands clenched around her throat. She pictured Seven's intent on taking her life, as if playing her reaper was the most important element in his world. The image unnerved her. But she dismissed it as some vague, maternal softness. She couldn't become vulnerable. Sensitivity has never mixed well with the unknown.

"What's your name?" she asked him.

He told her.

She laughed, *of course.*

"And that would make you…?"

"Eve," she told him as he drifted into a momentary nowhere, until his eyes snapped open.

"…obviously," he sighed. "I wasn't sick when I raped those girls. I wanted to," his voice cracked. "Ok. I just wanted to. But then I had dreams and I knew it was more than that. You make sense now. Maybe that's why I did it, but it always needed to be you. The dreams came more often. I…" He stammered. "I'm at the beginning of time. I'm naked and there's a tree. It's impossibly large and it doesn't even look like a tree. But I know it is because that's the story. In the story, there's always a tree. And overhead, there's this bird and fire. I used to think it was an angel, and if it is, well, it's like no angel I'd want to meet. And there's a fruit, too. I don't want to eat it, because I know, God, I know that would be the worst thing I could ever do. But she doesn't think so. My companion. She…" He pressed his wet palms against his cheeks. He squeezed his face, gun loose in his hand. "This woman. I made her, I think." He touched around his abdomen. "In my dream, I'm always bleeding from my side and when I look down towards my rib cage, it's all wrong. Blood and broken bone and…and it hurts so fucking much even though it shouldn't. I'm clay, for God's sake!" He blurted nervously. "I've always been clay. Smart mud and dirt and shit! I can't stop her from eating that fruit." And he butted the handle of the pistol against his forehead until his forehead opened, trailing dark blood river-like between his eyes. "Maybe there's a higher calling. Maybe I hurt women because all women are that one woman."

"If all women are evil," Eve leaned forward, "if we're all full of sin, then it was from the ribs of man darkness followed. If you were to kill that evil, you must execute the source."

He cried harder. He wiped his face with the sleeve of his gray hoodie.

"I'm not the demon you need to kill," Eve said.

He sheepishly placed the gun at the roof of his mouth, finger pulling back the trigger.

"Wait!" she shouted, shoeing him away. "Outside. Walk several blocks away from me. Finish yourself there."

He nodded complacently.

Eve crawled into a ball, made gentle circles over her belly. Her eyes filled with tears and she knew without doubt the baby was gone.

And somehow she imagined herself travelling into her own womb. She saw it leaving her body as if departing from a faulty vessel, and she swore she spotted her child retreating into deep fields of gold and light that expanded outwards and inwards. She couldn't blame it. Why leave the White when it's so beautiful? Why leave anything so certain and secure and eternal? And she can't help feel a little offended.

She grabbed her phone. Although it's an ungodly time to call, she dialed Charlie. After several rings, he answered groggily, waking fast when he realized who had called.

And in the quiet of night, she choked back tears.

"Hello? Eve? Is that you?" Charlie said. "Eve? Eve, what's wrong?"

21
MINOR EXTINCTION

Fable's heart was broken. One half remained in her chest; the other half didn't. And what of that portion that lingered out of body? Well, how healthy can a heart be if you cut it out, curse it, hate it and scar it, until it beats only with contempt, vengeance, and pain? Why not use it as your own voodoo doll, a thing of karma and retribution?

But listen!

Hush...

The heart still beat. Never forget that. It pulsed with the tragic end of musician Mark Hensley, whose perpetual flow of lyrics left him perpetually dead. It ticked with the moment origami inspired Gary Hanson to fashion his own flesh and when Lisa Yeager choked on cheese in a French Onion soup eating contest against her own shadow. Poor Mark and Al and all the others. And the list goes on, people who were afflicted in the Age of Porter, back when the mad muse had facilitated a sickness of the absurd.

But fear not. A place existed for those victims, an afterlife where the minors went, where their souls lingered in a collective of gray dreams. The broken heart beat to the thump-thump of the no-faces that forever played collateral to escaped jokers and riddlers from comic book prisons, the nameless gunned down in action movies; it beat in a limbo known as the Hall of Minors.

And this Hall was ruled by Trish Shapiro, now Miss Minor, AKA Fifth Dynasty, another victim to insanity and suicide. Ignoring her, you'll see a sapphire around her neck on a thin linked chain. It was that sapphire that contained the Hall, and it was that sapphire Trish Shapiro prided herself on possessing. After all, the Hall needed a representative and she would be their Dynasty-Queen.

It was her duty to punish Fable, to avenge her minor kingdom. She had already ripped half-the-heart from the muse's chest, where it remained within the Hall, beating with the karma of the dead. While it pulsed, it siphoned that energy from the half that still lingered within Fable. It was a slow burn, a constant drain to remind the muse she'd remain broken. The prolonged torture satisfied Miss Minor, for she still had yet to formulate a final death. But was there ever a need to hurry vengeance?

Fable's fate rested with Trish Shapiro, who relished the idea of an entire dimension around her neck. Comparing her life now to her life then, perhaps it was a good thing to die? Elevated from secretary/adulteress to Dynasty-God, in death, Trish rose, a sapphire voice to project upon the stars; she'd rise and she'd continue to rise.

Now, here's her dream.

Trish dances upon golden streets, like a cheesy actress from a forties musical. The streets are paved in cell phones. Each phone-brick sings its own ringtone melody, each calling her. Important dialers, millionaires, billionaires, corporate men, rich attorneys and doctors, even middle class married men. And something strange happens. As she dances, her foot catches on one phone dislodged from the road. Her ankle rolls out and she tumbles. Where once a million phones buzz around her, each ring begins to drop away, one by one, until only one remains. This phone is different, pink and shrill, like listening to sandpaper. She answers it. Only until touching it, she understands it's composed of rubber. It's ugly and dirty and chafed and it's hot against her ear. "Yes?" she wants to answer, like a smug sex kitten. Instead, her tone reflects the ominous dread of the receptionist who put too much sugar in the boss's coffee.

"Are you Them?" she asks with bated breath, "The Authors?"

She listens.

"...yes, of course," she gulps. Compose yourself. Be professional. You're confident, attractive. You're the Fifth Dynasty, for fuck sake. Ambitious, secure, go-getting. Minor adjusts her blue business jacket. "Here?" she says, "In the Hall? I would be honored," she answers dumbly. "When should I expect your arrival?" she asks, voice rising theatrically. "Now? No! I look forward to it. I...," blushing, "Yes, see you soon."

The line goes dead.

Outside her dream, Miss Minor was awake, pacing within the Hall, not feeling entirely good. Above her, the mouth-halo, her cerulean-smile gnashed its teeth. If only she had time to prepare for her meeting with the Men in the Moon. She needed fresh air.

She stepped outside. She stood on the grass in the park by the pond where Seven had made his existential exit. She heard the sound of water draining. Focusing on the pond, she spied a mini-vortex very much like the spirals she'd watch as a kid when the water drained from the bathtub.

Looking towards the Moon, she imagined she saw a face smiling from the rocky surface. *Why call Themselves Authors? Was it a collective name? How many were there?* She was the Fifth, but she'd be the first to face Them. She'd do anything to be Their Queen. She'd sleep with Them eventually, she had to, and she wondered how sex would be in Their embrace. For some reason, she recalled her first conversation with Fable at the Mediterranean restaurant, eating grape leaves, waiting for Ethan.

She moved towards an impossible direction, into her realm, where she stood in the long, colorless Hall bordered on both sides by thick, transparent pillars. Ghostly faces and vague bodies swirled within them. And far at the end of the Hall, far, far down, there was a figure. Her heart pounded; her nipples hardened and her skin goosebumped. Unable to contain her excitement, her azure eyes flashed-it was *Them*! She clapped her hands giddily. Then, all business, she composed herself.

Although it seemed miles away, it moved towards her, closing insane distances with each step. As it moved closer, Trish suspected its stride to be an optical illusion. But that wasn't it. She rubbed her eyes. She was beginning to itch, to heat up. The air being charged, thickening. Behind her eyes, she witnessed salmon-colored floaters, the kind one sees after staring at a bright light. On opening her eyes, pinks danced randomly in her vision.

They were merely feet away and They were around her height, yet They seemed to tower over her. He, The Authors, the Man in the Moon, whatever They called Themselves, wore a giant, sickle-shaped Moon-head mask. It was bulky and top-heavy and it weighed his body forward as it lumbered closer. The mask was poorly crafted, ripped and torn. It reminded her of a cheap piñata.

There was something inherently wrong. It didn't move, just stared at her.

And then a nub of pink caught her attention. At first, she dismissed it as a light spot until it twisted and swirled.

She winced while her mouth-halo frowned above her. Within the pillars, faceless essences of dead eyes probed him from the shadows, some in fear and dread; others in cold nonchalance.

"Trish Shapiro!" The figure moved closer. A large oversized robe trailed behind him. A ludicrous grin was carved on the surface of the half-Moon mask, its teeth large and hungry. There was no warmth in its grin.

"Yes." She hugged her arms, clenching the sapphire (clenching the entire Hall itself). She backed away.

"Is that still your name?"

"I'm Miss Minor now."

A sickening feeling dropped in her gut. "You're not Them," she said in a mousy voice. "You're a Dynasty."

"Am I?"

"Who are you?"

"*Who* is far too simple for an abstract anthropomorphism?" it said. "If I were to ask who you are, you could say Trish Bitch. But that little nomenclature would omit what you embody now. It wouldn't tell me you are the epitome of victimized shit, that you are great. Miss Minor..." tasting the name, "Yet you answered when I called your name."

"Your point?"

"The muse inspired many deaths. Why should you be the only one with a face?"

"I discovered the Hall."

"The Hall is a collective, is it not?"

"Yes."

"So the Fifth is the Hall itself. Yet you wear your hall-self around your neck. This makes you more important than the others."

"As I said," she raised her voice, "I represent all minors."

"If you're minor, would it not be more appropriate to give up a name, shed your face, and join the shadows?"

"Listen, you sack of shit!" Minor challenged. "This is my place of power, not yours!" *Steady*, she told herself, suppressing the tremble in her throat.

"I could erase your face. Rub out your name," it suggested from under the Moon-mask. "You'd be more minor than you are now and wouldn't that make you more beautiful?"

"Fuck. You."

"Yes," the man agreed. Two grubby hands parted from the robe, loosening the knot around the throat, and the robe, sparkling with moons and stars, whisked off the body. Underneath, the man was adorned in pink, dirty, mocking pink. It was attire, but it was flesh, too.

"I want counsel with The Authors," Trish demanded.

"Console me." His hand stroked the mask. And as it stroked, it rubbed and somehow the mask lost texture and detail-*rubbing, rubbing.* The more the man touched his mask, the less mask there was to touch. And when it had been smeared away, his face remained out of focus.

"My God," she gasped. "You're the Seventh."

"True, true. I am the Final Dynasty."

"Nevertheless, I demand audience with Them." She crossed her arms haughtily." She cleared her throat. *I,* grumbled the no-faces in the pillars. "*We* demand council."

"I want to see the Hall," the Seventh said. "If you impress me with your project, then you may see the Men in the Moon."

She huffed, grudgingly waved him on. She walked. He followed her, although they never necessarily moved. They were deeper in the Hall, into a room, the heart of the Hall. In this *center* was a throne made of the discarded limbs and pieces of mannequins.

The Seventh Dynasty moved toward the empty throne, face still shadowed. He peered up at the floating half-heart that by no means shared any human accuracy. The half-heart levitated above the throne. The Seventh Dynasty touched his chin in contemplation. Amethyst and cobalt light bathed the room. "Explain," he said.

"This is what I – we – call our Demusement Machine," Minor explained. "It's the half-heart of the muse." The half-heart was transparent and glassy, swirling with coal-colored hate.

"More," the Seventh asked. Minor shivered. "I am a dense creature, a stupid thing."

"I've torn out Fable's heart. She gave herself to the Hall. Her essence is being poisoned. The other half is in her, fueled by negative karma built against her. Her heart is a weapon now. A debt once paid will kill her."

"The heart is a weapon," he repeated, unimpressed. "Hearts are always weapons. They've never been anything but tragedy designed to break and maim. I like hearts. But your plan lacks ambition."

"My plan is foolproof! I'll wield this heart against her. The heart is in the Hall. I wear the Hall." She tugged at her sapphire. "I am her death!"

"I?" the Seventh quipped. "Well, let us rub one out at your command, my Minor Queen." He laughed. She grumbled. "You hate the muse?" His hands hovered about the heart, never touching.

"Yes."

"She's good for you," he said. "Bitch Violet made you important. Elevated you. Caused you pain. Hurt you. Interesting to think if you were always the Fifth or if you only became the Fifth upon your death. In that respect, Bitch Violet gave your life meaning." He snatched one of the mannequin heads from the throne, probed his finger around inside it. "I could erase her from you." The Seventh focused his attention to the throne composed of broken mannequins. They were only symbols yet Trish felt an irrational fear for their safety.

"She's mine. Not yours," she stammered.

"For now. I don't abstain her murder on your behest, no, I abstain because she is your beauty and your bane. The source of your pain. Why would I erase that?"

He crushed the plastic head in his hand and he touched her, lifting Minor's chin as if inspecting a piece of meat. It burned raw where he touched. Minor backed away and although he remained in shadow, his sharp eyes followed her. He moved a little too fast towards her.

He smiled, the edges of his pink mouth tweaking in the corners. In the lighting, she glimpsed his face, smeared and faded, like an eraser that failed to completely remove a word.

"You were not always a Dynasty," the Seventh said. "In ways, Fable is your Mother Muse. You wish patricide, yes. You are minor and unspecial and there will be only one parent-killer."

"What are you talking about?" Minor waited.

"Gods must kill their fathers," he said. "The creation must slaughter the hand that molds it. Your plan is still uninspired. I will eat you now."

"Eat me!" Her stomach churned. "You're insane. I've never been the appetizer. I feed on you, you fuck, not the other way!" For a moment, she caught herself saying this, finding it funny this upset her more than the idea of being devoured.

This was not shaping up nicely. She felt the Hall slipping from her, her control waning. She suddenly found herself recalling tips she had read about attracting success. One was to smile, fake it, act like the goal had already been obtained. That's what she tried to do, although her smile, crooked with fear, portrayed anything but control.

The Seventh placed his hand underneath the half-heart. It hovered above his palm and it followed his hand, never touching, as he moved. He sandwiched the half-heart in his hands, compressing it. He sprinkled it as a lined powder on the back of his hand and sniffed it in. He cackled, snorted, and cleared his nostrils. He then reached out to grip Minor's breast, just once, just because. She looked down at her sharp blue suit, now bleached of color, one breast flatter, less pronounced than the other, as if she had been reduced in a single touch.

"Wh-what did you do?" she murmured.

The Seventh Dynasty rubbed his hands together furiously, a spark of heat and friction. He grabbed Trish by the jaw and shoved his fingers into her mouth, fishing for her tongue. He was too fast, and entirely too strong, and he pinched her tongue and he pulled and while her screams rent the Hall, one sickly tear later, Trish no longer possessed a tongue. There was a shriek followed by wet, thick splattering on the floor. The Seventh shoved her. She fell by the mannequin throne. Several arms and empty heads joined her in the darkness.

He grabbed her sapphire and pulled it off her chain, and while he pulled she could feel her throat tearing. "This fuels the Hall. It is the Hall, like you. A synecdoche." He crunched the sapphire with his teeth, grinding the shards and he swallowed, wincing in delight, a psychopath dining on broken glass. The shards looked painful going down. "I am part of the Hall now. The heart is the Hall. The Hall is your heart."

And as this took place, Trish screamed at him, cried out in soul-searing agony. She wailed at his feet, her words garbled from her bloodied, tongue-less mouth. She crawled pathetically, hands and knees in the puddles of her own blood, an ugly cyan that smelled like gasoline. Staggering to her feet, she beat on his chest, which he ignored until he swatted her down.

A hundred voices wailed in him, until they contracted in his mind. For a moment, from the inside, sapphire light illuminated him. All their terror and rage fueled him. He was now the Fifth Dynasty and the Seventh and he was the Hall and every victim.

"To be minor is to have no voice," he said. "I've consumed the Hall and your brethren. I am not minor. I've rendered the Fifth in all its aspect more genuine. Oppression through silence. No voice. No power. You'll be nameless, drowning in the masses as you observe the death of Fable. You'll have no personal victory as Patricia Shapiro. You'll be truly minor."

Minor was crying profusely, terror pushing out in muffled garbles of pain. And she wheezed as she crawled towards an exit that did not exist. As he leaned in, through flesh and fiction, she finally saw his face, and before she could comment, he opened his mouth and began to eat her. There was chewing and chomping and screaming, but not silence, no, the silence couldn't come soon enough.

22
WHITE WOMB

Seven was wet and cold and he needed to clean himself. Standing in the shower, his body was covered in patches of what resembled inkblots. His hands and face were slashed with too many paper cuts. He continued to lather and scrub, over and over, all hapless attempts to cleanse the existential filth from his body. No matter how many times he washed and rinsed, Seven felt no cleaner. He adjusted the water pressure and stood alone in the shower, remembering what had just happened.

It had been a blur. The details didn't matter, as they never did. It was through some moment that defied logic, Seven recalled rising from the pond. He had staggered onto the stones and mud, his clothing saturated with a liquid that wasn't water. Rolling onto his back, he had heaved several wet coughs. Pushing himself up, he had watched somehow, seeing with his eyes or his mind, a strange movement at the center of the pond, which had reminded him of a mini-vortex, a spiraling of water rushing downward. In his guts, he had known the vortex would never dwindle, that it would only gain momentum until the entire world was sucked into its notional hole.

Back under the steaming showerhead, Fable's hands tightened around his waist. He leaned his head back, chin lifted to the water as Fable held him from behind.

"Did you kill him?" she asked.

"I couldn't," he said. "Notion or Andrew or whatever the hell he calls himself, he's always been dead." Seven raised his hands, bloodied with ink and paper slashes. "What do I do now?" Water splashed his chest and shoulders, spritzed his eyes.

"Dead or alive, the truth of Notion is a wake-up call. Now you wake up. You live. You get inspired."

"The Authors aren't the only adversary. Perhaps the circle is the true antagonist." Seven clenched his ring. "Perhaps it's about patterns. About endings. How breaking cycles is the only way to slay the dragons."

"So what *did* happen?" Fable asked. Her naked body pressed against his. "What did you discover when you fell down the world?"

*

He was in a white room.

The atmosphere tasted thick with sweat and tears. Something claustrophobic strangled the box-shaped room. Crumpled paper littered the floor. When his eyes adjusted to the blankness of the place, Seven finally saw the walls were covered in paper, too.

As he inspected the white world with a morbid fascination, pressing his fingers into the paper on the walls, he found the walls didn't feel solid, not really, and Seven believed the walls themselves were paper, that the entire chamber had been an architecture in origami. Removing his hand from the wall, wet ink stained his fingertips.

The room suddenly reeked of stuffy warehouses. Wherever he was, he wanted to not be here.

A series of movements, the sound of paper folding and unfolding, a crinkling from the wall until there was a slender man now. He was hard to differentiate from the wall at first, like a chameleon slathered in newsprint. He wore jeans, a beanie hat, and a hooded flannel. His clothing was all paper; bone-white, bleached of color, and it also seemed part of his flesh.

Seven approached the man cautiously, stepping over crumbled balls of paper. Only until he was several feet from the man did Seven realize he was seated upon a mound of battered novels, hunched over a laptop, which wasn't always a laptop (it was a typewriter, a notebook, a single slab of poster board). It was all those things. But mostly, Seven witnessed the man himself was paper, too; his paper fingers beating manically at the paper keyboard (when it was such). Flies that might've been displaced punctuation buzzed around him.

When realizing he was not alone, his pulpy hands slowed over the keypad. The patchwork of paper that composed his body crinkled as he moved. His eyes were beady and moist. Blackness trickled down his cheeks, smearing with the print on his body, ink mixing with ink.

"What are you doing here?" his dry voice scratched in Seven's mind.

Seven didn't answer, just stared blankly at him, taking in the scene.

"Have you come to the White Place, too?" the origami man asked. "There are stories in the walls, a million unwritten worlds inside everything here. Just look at it long enough and you'll see anything. Stare with me." He gestured to the blank sheet of paper in his typewriter, which was also a laptop. The origami man huffed impatiently at Seven's silence and diverted his attention back towards the laptop, which was a typewriter, which was a notepad.

"Who are you?" Suspicion flashed in the man's eyes.

Seven told him.

"Is that your real name?" Confusion wrinkled the origami man's face. "You're not Arthur Wright or Alan Wilkinshire or Abernathy Wordsmyth?"

Shaking his head, Seven said, "No."

"You call yourself Seven? How does that fit?"

Seven considered his name didn't bear the standard A.W. I'm the Ambiguous W, he thought, or, searching, the Atrophied Word, perhaps.

"Did They send you for me, brother?" the origami man asked.

"I'm not your brother," Seven said.

"You're right and a little wrong," the paper man raised a shaky finger. "Brother. Father. All relative considering we're stray energy pulsing from a common source since form and thought differentiated. But then this chair, that wall, is also a sibling, and what's one circle to another? All round, all recursive," he said, an uneven tremble. "If I'm not your brother, what am I?"

Seven knelt by the man, like a concerned child tending their ill parent. "You might be a dead writer. Someone that died long ago. You may recall a particular suicide. Think about it," and Seven waited before adding, "Andrew? Notion?"

"Notion?" the origami man winced.

"Whatever They've done to you, I'm here to rescue you," Seven said quietly, hoping this was the result of The Authors' torture. But deep down, tortured or not, this was the final product and this may have always been the true form of his supposed mentor. Seven's world was closing in; it was all fake and stupid he feared, the war of words, Tetragrammar, everything, and he couldn't face an existence plotted on the dead remains of a suicidal author. Still, Seven strived to retain his sanity, to keep his composure. "You started a war against Them," Seven said carefully. "You were a writer and Tetragrammar was the weapon."

"Yes!" Recognition blazed in his pin dot eyes. "The only war, oppression against mystery, a strike in the void! To slay the darkness with words! My crusade terrified Them. And I was close, so close to finishing my book! That's when They captured me and tortured me. And I wouldn't succumb to the invasion

of foreign authors, so I made you, all of you, my Circle Children, and I filled you with a narrative-potential to eliminate the bastards. Seven," placing a hand on his shoulder with renewed vigor, "it's our burden, brother-son!"

Seven's stomach dropped. He remained silent. This was not a man worth fighting for; this was the embodiment of insanity and dead-ends. Seven felt suddenly worn out. He paced about the room. His chest rose dramatically. He needed air. As he walked, his feet sank into the pulpy floor, his steps uneven as the ground shifted and crinkled underfoot. He wanted to rip the world apart, to hit something.

"You can't be Notion," he said to himself. "Everything I knew is wrong." Seven ruffled his hair. "I've always been a writer. It's all I've ever known. The Authors. You. Fable. I obeyed all those whims in your honor, and I wrote. And whatever I wrote wasn't enough. It wasn't your story yet I never gave up. Day after day, I slaved away to decipher your mess, all to save you!" Seven traced his hand along the wall. It was now a patchwork of newspaper articles with headlines like "Student Takes Life" or "Campus Ponders Death".

"Didn't they understand?" Notion ignored him. "It wasn't about pain. It wasn't suicide. It was a leap of faith. An evolutionary jump!"

Seven cocked his head to examine the newsprint. "You programmed me to believe the lies. And I did; I believed every plot hole. And I fought for you while everything was based off of notions. Just vague notions and nothing more! Tetragrammar wasn't my story to deal with. I was your fucking slave!"

"What do you want?" Notion hissed, throwing his hands up, palms facing Seven to reveal heavy slashes across his wrists.

"I want you to tell me you're not Father Notion, that this is all a misunderstanding. I want you to tell me Ambrose was wrong, that I haven't been wasting my life on the delusions of a paper man."

His eyes crinkled into crow's feet. "That fucking red Judas! You don't listen to shifters and shapers!" Notion hissed. The paper unfolded around his legs and he rose, taller than Seven ever imagined him to be. He hunched forward as his head brushed the ceiling, leaning in towards Seven.

The ouroboros ring began to squeeze impossibly tight. "I've been stuck in your story, you bastard! Not my story!" Seven spat.

Exclamations darted above Notion as his disposition soured. "Your story! Your life's my life! I bled you into the world, you ungrateful ink stain! I'm Arthur Wright and I'm Ambrose Walker and Abernathy Wankerbee and I'm all of you! But you're not me!"

"That's right. So let me go! Tell me what Tetragrammar is, dammit!"

"Everyone has Tetragrams. It's just another name for the soul. And the soul," Notion pointed to his laptop, *"resides in all white space. The white is really a womb, a White Womb we return to again and again."* And Notion looked at his wrists, eyes darting around the room.

If there was truth in his words, it was sick and damaged, an epiphany laced with cyanide, a revelation in wasp stings.

"You wanna know Tetragrammar, *then listen hard, you fuck, hear the anatomy of a narrative."* Notion began, *"There was a boy full of dreams. He'd stare into the skies, watching the stars come out. When the night approached, why so much black? he thought. He imagined a force larger than everything encroaching on the world with no face or form. His head raced with possibilities and it wouldn't stop racing until he was sick. He imagined he could turn the disease into a weapon. Shape the darkness into words and stories. If he could funnel its power into an outlet, he could unleash his demons. He'd spill the poison ink like blood to shape the darkness, to mold the unknowable. And he did that for a while, but it was never enough.*

"A spark was needed in his work. He prayed upon the imaginal realms, a place where ideas are denizen, where archetypes are reality. The Wandering Jew, the Scorned Woman, the Fire Bringer, the Primal Hunter. The Devil and the Serpent. The Prodigal and the Superman. All dwelled in a place that wasn't a place at all, in a realm that can only be dreamt and never touched. And as this boy tapped into it, something eventually tapped back. And one day she came to me."

"Fable," Seven said.

"She lit the Promethean fire. Cracked the Apple! And I wrote; don't think I didn't. I wrote until my head throbbed and I needed a break and even then the ideas streamed into me. My visions had to be perfect. I would dream and I'd imagine so many wild fantasies you could never fathom! I wanted nothing more than to express them. I would struggle with my words until I realized no matter how much I tried, it would never be perfect, that all the unwritten dreams could never match the visions she wished to inspire in me. Expression could only be an ideal, a dream that would remain perfect only until you reached for the stars, until dreams would spoil and rot! That's when I knew what I had to do.

"I would write myself out of body to appease her. Physical shells only restrain so I would shed myself. Become pure thought." Notion looked at his wrists. *"After I evolved, I found myself behind the Moon. I looked into the void and I saw the darkness wasn't just a void. It was wet and alive and something looked back. They wore a thousand eyes on the dark side of the Moon and They trapped me here."* He frowned, then mouth twisting, *"Now ponder this, seventh son, what*

if the spark demanded too much? What if it hollowed you, made you worthless and small? She hates us. We're nothing without her magic and, in the end, what is any man without inspiration?"

Seven hit him then.

And before Notion could lash out, defend himself, fold himself into safety, Seven hit him again, and he continued to hit him. And it didn't stop for quite some time, not even after the ink-blood splattered the walls in homicidal spatters of Rorschach patterns, not after the whimpering ceased and his origami body turned to wet bits of pulp. He didn't desist, even after blacking out and ripping his father apart and pounding the torn scraps with his knuckles bloodied with ink and paper cuts. Only then did Seven finish his tirade.

Eventually, there was a gurgle from a puddle of ink, followed by weak laughter that emanated from the mess of Notion's body. In a small voice from a shredded mouth on a shredded face, Notion whimpered sheepishly, "You shouldn't have come here."

"Tetragrammar was your poison and I've been stuck with you so long I don't know anything else!" Confusion and dread welled up on Seven's face, and he wanted to butcher Notion again.

"Well then, fuck off and be done with it!" Spittle flew from Notion's lips. "Leave me in paradise as you jump back into the hungry void. But a bit of advice first, from your dashing father." The eyes on his tattered face flashed wildly. "There is no Tetragram! That's the secret." He snorted. "Tetragrammar is No-thing!"

Seven glared. "And what are The Authors? How do They factor into this?"

"They are the living ink that constantly rewrites itself. But mostly, They're her, you idiot!" Notion hissed. "When They made the Porter, They made Themselves. And when he fucked her, his semen bore Their seed, and she injected Them back into herself. Don't you get it, she's been self-fertilizing ever since!"

"The Authors never imprisoned you, did They?"

"Authors…" Notion chuckled. "That's what she calls herself. You can't win against Them, just like you could never handle the women in your life. They've always been her! And They'll become her again!"

"Shut up!"

"When it happens, when They give birth to Themselves, it will be over and They'll have won this war."

Drenched in ink, his hands and face marked in paper cuts, Seven clenched and unclenched his fists. He looked up when Notion began to laugh.

From his torn off head, from half-a-mouth, Notion spoke through ripped lips, "Not what you wanted to hear, well, vent your anger on me again. Kill me a second time if you like, but the reality is you can't kill me. You can never kill me!"

"You're right. I can't kill what's already dead."

"I'm more alive than you ever were, boy!" the half-face hissed. "Without me you'd never been born. Without me there'd be no divine novel, no Moon to ascend towards, no magic in your fake heart. I am the Male Virgin; you're the thought begot from thought and I'm the divine snake forever consuming its own wisdom!" He screamed out. "Leave this Womb, you ingrate bastard! I don't need you, you pretentious pile of semen! I never needed any of you!"

Seven pushed himself to his feet. "I can't be part of your insanity anymore," he sounded tired, the fight leaving him. "Pray this is our final meeting. Whatever you need me to do. Fuck. You. Tetragrammar is mine, real or not. I don't write for you anymore. You're an author, but you're not my author, and you're not The Authors! One way or the other, the story ends with or without you."

And without hesitation, from an impossible angle, Seven departed from his broken father.

"Don't you get it yet? It never ends. It never fucking ends..." Father Notion whimpered to himself, alone with his laptop and his kingdom of empty paper. He slowly healed, ink flowing into paper; paper folding together, shaping itself. His voice was dry parchment. "Lonely..." he said, "I'm so lonely..."

And in a room he had deemed his White Womb, there could never be rebirth. In the solitude of his sick world, Father Notion wept.

*

"I'm sorry," Fable said.

"He was never this great author that waged a war against the darkness. In ways, he brought the darkness. *Tetragrammar* was just an unfinished project he could never complete himself."

"What now?"

"If I forfeit the story, They've won," Seven said. "We can't have that. It also doesn't matter what *Tetragrammar* might or might not be. Regardless of Andrew's original intent, I still believe it took on a spark of its own, that his manuscript somehow managed to evolve into some sort of entity or message. In a way, it's like," he hesitated, "our child."

Looking at her, Seven heard the echo of Notion's message. *They're her...They've always been her.*

"What else did Notion say?" she asked.

"Just notions. Nothing more."

"If you're hiding something from me, I could peek inside your head. It wouldn't be hard."

"Then why don't you?"

Fable said nothing.

"Listen, you can't believe anything he says," Seven added.

"It's not about believing him. I know what I've done. I've experienced all those people who went mad and crazy because of me. In a way, I lived before, or aspects of me did with other writers who failed to write Notion's novel. *Tetragrammar* became a curse. But it didn't have to be. So when I lost myself, maybe parts of me went bad. Porter raped my mind but I raped minds, too." She began to tremble and shake until her body broke apart in a violet swarm of flies. She reformed in a cold sweat, knuckles whitening as she gripped the windowsill.

"I was dead," she panted. "As dead as I could get. I allowed myself to die. It was a gamble and I didn't care. I wanted to pay off whatever debt," she said stiffly. "I knew I'd come back, somehow in a new life, and I'd be stuck with some other asshole who couldn't get an erection because writing was such a burden on his miserable life. Somehow, I wanted to rise above it, to ascend the squabbles between muse and writer, to hold the power and not be restricted. I knew if I did this, I'd be different and we'd be enemies. Maybe I believed you would be the last cycle, the rerun numbered completion."

"Whatever I'm supposed to be, I want out. I'm tired."

"It doesn't have to be a burden any longer," Fable said. "You *can* leave. That's your right. You're your own writer. Forget Notion. Write your own story now."

"It's never been about just writing a book. I'm too attached to it. I don't know anything else. And the problem is I've never had a story of my own. I don't know what will happen after The Authors," he said, "but I know *Tetragrammar*'s mine to finish. Even if I chose to give up on it, I wouldn't know how."

"Again! You can move on. You have that freedom."

"I wish it were that easy."

"Why can't it be?" Fable said.

And Seven paused, considering. Rubbing his brow, he nodded suddenly. "Maybe it can be." He rummaged under the kitchen table, retrieved a small metal safe. He opened it. Inside was a crumpled brown bag, and not just any bag, *the bag*, Thrifty's loaded gift. He set the bag on the coffee table. An aroma wafted around it, the kind emitted from dead saints.

"That's Thrifty's bag!" Fable blurted.

"Yes. His final gift before he died."

"What are you going to do with it?" she asked nervously.

Staring at the crinkled bag, "Thrifty embodied attraction," Seven said. "His bag, or whatever potential existed within it, harbors a particular magic. He called it his bag of tricks. He told me I may use it when I felt lost, when I feared there was no other way out."

"Seven…Are you saying what I think you're saying?"

He looked at her.

"Oh, I don't know about this," she sounded dreadfully skeptical.

"What's the worst that could happen?" he asked whimsically.

Fable bit her lip. "Why would you say that?"

"Thrifty told me it could help. And," he said under his breath, "it could hurt, too. That it was a writer's last option."

"It's a Pandora's Box. The Apple of Eden. It's fire and thunder and all the other double-edged gifts imparted from gods."

"It's a DXM actually."

"Yes! Deus ex machina! God in the Machine!" Her head dropped, seeming more than uncomfortable. "That's even worse."

"I'll take my chances," Seven said. "I need to. I'm stuck and I want out. I want my ending."

"If it works, then you have your happy ending. And if it doesn't, well, surely it will be your death sentence. Regardless, this could be the catalyst that triggers your apocalypse, for better or worse."

"One way, we finish this. Giving up will solve nothing. They'd like that. Besides, I'm The Seven. Perfect or not, *I* complete it. We do what we've always done. We're going to kill The Authors. The Moon's still our destination. That's where my story ends."

The bag lingered on his coffee table, like some charged relic that either contained heaven or hell. And opening it, Seven reached in.

*

He had been overthinking it. When Seven realized how simple *Tetragrammar* should've been all along, his imagination blazed into an aesthetic nirvana. Chapters aligned. Concepts clicked. Dialogue flowed naturally. As days passed, he typed constantly, hard at work under a steady flow of words. The pages added up, and they continued to pile together until Seven realized that, yes, his novel may've been shuttling towards the light at the end of a figurative tunnel.

Though hungry and tired, he ignored these symptoms as the stream of thought was sustenance enough. This relentless surge would feed him just a little longer. Then, and only then, would he rest. Fable goaded him on as he pushed through the arthritic cramping in his fingers.

Almost, he smiled insanely. No more tedious revisions. No more blank screen stare downs.

On the seventh day, *Tetragrammar*, more or less, had been born.

And with only one chapter remaining, Seven slid from his laptop, weary with artistic fever, and he smiled madly as he staggered towards his bed and slumped into dreamless reprieve.

Seven slept.

Another week passed.

Throughout this time, pink skies landscaped the heavens. It first began as a surreal pastel beauty one morning, until the pink remained to grow brighter, until the natural blue had been displaced by a shade of whimsy. And everyone looked up to admire the candy-colored ceiling. Not one cloud was spotted. Besides the pink, the Moon could be seen, a celestial ball of cotton candy.

Across The City, people's lives became lax and easy. All their cares melted away. All struggles and gripes in their day-to-day lives unraveled. No one complained and no one could deny the lifting of an invisible tension. People breathed easier. Betty Cukor never once misplaced her glasses, which were lost daily. Sheryl Lynn could finally hold yoga postures achieved only in her imagination. Dream jobs were attained. Scarred romances were mended. And the list went on. Hundreds experienced the sudden shift in luck as their troubles, large and small, amended themselves, like the universe was solely working to grant all their favors.

And life was good, hell, it was great. They'd even go as far to say it all worked itself out a bit too easy. It wasn't long till those touched by convenience questioned their luck. The balloon had to pop. And while The City waited for the inevitable razor-swing of bad luck, Seven exhaled a sigh of relief that had been atrophying in his lungs far too long. With the final chapter left open, he believed at that final period, he'd be shifted towards Them. Still unsure how this would play out, he kept it open, because deep down, like a splinter in his psyche, something was amiss.

What then?

It had nothing to do with the bag, although it had everything to do with that. Another element was lacking. He was lonely. He had a sister now and Fable. But it was the woman component. It was that Dana Paris-shaped hole. And it wasn't even about her; it was the incompleteness of their story, his proposal, her departure. And while he mulled over this, the ouroboros hissed around his finger. Only when he stared at the ring did he witness the snake chowing down upon its tail, forever consuming itself.

Seven took a long shower. He toweled himself, wrapped the towel around his waist, and tracked moist feet through the bedroom. He had been accustomed to Fable blinking in and out of his life. So with that notion, he assumed at first she to be the figure seated at the edge of his bed.

But then he froze when recognition set in, that it wasn't Fable at all.

"Funny story," she said. "Way back when, I hit a madman with my car. It was winter, and my boyfriend had been cheating on me, caught him right in the act, bare-assed on the sheets with Miss-What's-Her-Face. So I swore I'd never date assholes again. There's simply no telling the cheaters from the loyalists. So back to the story; this madman claimed to be a writer. Even after colliding with a moving car, he seemed unfazed, like reality couldn't hurt him because his mind was so embedded in some surrealist fantasy. I liked him. At first, I told myself I'd been dating him out of guilt. But that wasn't it. He wasn't a cheater. As these things go, we dated, broke up, got back together, and, sure, without going into the details, it wasn't perfect, but what relationship is? He had never given up on those delusions of his writings. It could've been an act for me, to make himself interesting, and to believe the fiction so deeply he could write it all the better.

"I let it go. It was his quirk. And it was an idea he persisted at. That's how I knew he'd never cheat on me, how he'd never give up that damn novel. He was so committed. He'd never leave it. And he wouldn't leave me either. And still, I wondered which of us he loved more. I resented him sometimes for having to compete with the affections of a book, but looking back on it, that was a cop-out. He always came back to me. Eventually, he proposed and I didn't know what to do with that. That's what scared me. But those dark eyes, those large, loony eyes meant every bit of it. I broke things off. And I'm sure he took it hard, how couldn't he?"

Seven didn't move. "Why are you here?"

"I missed you." Paris patted the bed for him.

"You left. You moved on."

"Have you seen the skies? They're unreal." She paced towards his window, parted the curtains. "They're miracle skies," she said.

"Whatever that means."

"I do," she said.

"You should leave."

"I do," she repeated.

"What?"

"If the offer's still open, the answer's yes. Yes, Seven, I'll marry you."

He sat.

"Doesn't matter what came before, where I went." Paris sat beside him. "I came back to you. You and I have always been." She grabbed his hand, ran a finger along the ouroboros. His finger throbbed. "It can be different this time. You and me. Anything that was wrong, just wash it away. Let's not rehash. Just move forward. Together, right? Close the loop."

"Don't, Seven! Don't do it!" Fable screamed.

Paris nudged him with her shoulder. "You told me once that the world is simple. Our lives, every moment, the whole she-bang exists on one blank sheet of paper. Every moment happens at once. One perpetual Big Bang. Beginnings and endings become obsolete if all moments are now. We were then. We can still *be.*" She unbuttoned her long coat.

"You're not here," he whispered, squeezing his eyes shut. "This isn't you."

"Then who is it?" she asked.

Oh, deus ex machina, what a funny thing you are?

"We shouldn't do this." He pushed out weakly. "I was done with you."

"You're never done with me." Her head leaned back, inquisitive. "It's been awhile," she smiled Cheshire Cat-like. "I'd like to put your name to the test."

"This isn't right."

She kissed his neck. "That never stopped us before." Paris removed her shirt, slid off her skirt. She unknotted the towel around his waist. It dropped to the floor. When they were very much naked, she pushed her body against his.

Their lips touched and as the old, tainted past slinked its way into the present, eventually other parts met. The Limbo Dragon tightened around his life, restricting and biting itself. Notion was dead – *he always had been* – but other ideas persisted, and if one severed the head of a hydra, two more grew in its place.

And that made sense; that was the truth.

The psychic snake would live on.

Interlude 3

Fable still didn't feel real, not entirely solid, which made sense since she was there in Seven's home, and now she was here by the pond, and she was in slightly both locations at once. Imagination could never be confined to a single point, after all. She knelt by the pond. Dipping her hands in the water, she closed her eyes, fishing for a memory.

Did she expect some revelation? A flood of the past she had forgotten? Perhaps she would remember an older self cradling a body, a body that belonged to a student cycles ago who had killed himself because death was better than not-writing at all; death proved safer than sex and dreams.

Had she driven Andrew Wilkins towards suicide or did he anticipate his very own deus ex machina in the shape of a near-death experience? Had she failed as his muse? Could she have saved him?

She skipped a stone across the pond, watching it skip before plonking below water.

And then, *how odd?*, she found a large eraser on the rocks. It was pink and rubbery and dirty. She didn't dare touch it. Somehow, it was so much more than just an eraser. It scared her in ways a normal inanimate object had any right to. What was it besides the thing that wipes out words and rubs and rubs until nothing is left?

"Would you like to hear a story?" something terrible asked. And, no, she didn't, not from a voice like knives and death. But the terrible thing didn't care. "Once upon a time," it continued, "Bitch Violet sang out to the world. A whore of magic who flaunted her visions for all to see, she'd spread her legs and men would paint. She'd fellatiate and poets would poetize. And if the shit beneath didn't dance to her whims, she pouted and maimed them because their torment appeased her." A chill trailed Fable's spine.

He looked like him! God, why did he look like him?!

"Seven?" she whispered, knowing it wasn't.

Its grin was the most horrible grin Fable had ever seen. "I like your demons. Hold them forever like a guilty cancer, like syphilis in your poke-hole. If it pains you, I'm here to erase, to rub it raw. My name is Lunatic Pink, the Last Dynasty, the Seventh." Rubber flaked from his hands as he rubbed them together. "Bitch Violet, you will die. Good day." Before turning away, he added, "By the way, any guilt you have, any pain from the past, yes!, it is your fault! All of it. I am part of your broken heart beating in your chest." The Seventh Dynasty snapped its fingers, a lightning crack. "I'm the explosive last tick-tock, pink death's got your cock!" And he cackled as he trudged up the hill. Every point his feet touched green grass was left all the less greener.

Fable shivered.

Death was coming, and it wore a face she knew too well.

VI
DEUS EX

IN WHICH FRICTION IS PINK, THE DEVIL'S
GLASSES DON'T BREAK, AND THE MOON
COLLIDES WITH LIFE

23
METACRITICAL

Outer Page:
    Scary thing, the eraser untamed. Sure, it removes mistakes, rubs out errors, but put to the extreme, it becomes a doomsday weapon. Annihilation sounds intense, you say, well, wipe the slate clean, and what are we left with? Nothing but nothing, which is ok when considering the eternity of White, but let's not get hung up on enlightenment just yet.
    Instead, cut to a scenario.
    Look:
    Only a handful remain, the last batch of ragtag survivors, fighting against thousands. They are wounded and tired and their beards are dried with blood and sweat. They are little men and has-been kings and they stand in the mud, in a battlefield strewn with corpses. An army approaches from over the hill, an inhuman march filled with snarls and grunts accompanied by the clanging of rusty swords and shields. But light is on their side; good always triumphs. And as the soldiers brace themselves for defeat, backs pressed against each other as the monsters and imps surround them, hope flashes overhead. And they smile from their rugged beards, from their dirt-crusted faces, as the king and his little men join the ghost army and their white wizard, killing back the dark forces...
    Look:
    The Spy is tied to a chair, hands fastened behind him. He struggles and prays the knots will loosen while his captors gather outside. He doesn't like the sounds of drills and blades and all the things they'll do if he doesn't talk. When all hope is lost, before his captors return, he discovers the little miracle, a knife his torturers have failed to detect when searching him, and he thanks whatever divinity has

blessed him. Finagling the knife, easing it from his pocket, he eventually grips it with his fingers and slowly runs it back and forth across the rope until his hands are free. As his captors enter, they won't expect him behind the door, waiting for them, blade ready...

Now:

All the little conveniences that arise in any movie or book, they may not be pink erasers, yet they serve that same purpose, to remove ugly conundrums that would be lethal. So you see, complicated plot holes suddenly unknotted become subject to a force on par with the miraculous. A sweep of faith, if you will.

"What's your point?"

"It happens all the time."

"It's fiction. That's how it is. There's no way around those things. If writers didn't allow for all those quick fixes, there'd be a lot of disappointing stories."

"I know. Just saying, my point is never use a deus ex machina. Use that, you may as well trash your whole script. They're cop outs for authors who've written themselves into a bind."

"They're necessary."

"I guess; I just don't like them. Like this book I've been reading called Tetragrammar...*"*

"Never heard of it."

"Anyway, the writer's ex-girlfriend returns out of the blue, pops back into his life, and takes him back. It's like she was supposed to, no matter how sudden or unbelievable."

"Where'd she go?"

"You don't know really. The whole relationship was vague. You never discover the specifics of what went wrong, which makes it hard to care."

"Maybe the specifics don't matter. It's like any relationship. Things go sour. Jealousy. Cheating. Job opportunities. Religious differences. It's all the same."

"Yea, but shouldn't the book explain that? And now she comes back and that's that. He simply reaches into his bag of tricks and wallah."

"Maybe it's about outdated ideas. Like a story you can't move away from. People going back to their exes. Spinning their wheels over and over and never moving forward. That's insanity, right? Doing the same thing and going nowhere?"

"Whatever. Wanna hear a joke?"

"All right."

"Knock, knock..."

*

Inner Page:

Seven's spirits were high. He was inspired, in love. The skies were a funny pink when he arrived at the Thai restaurant for lunch with his sister. The restaurant possessed that perpetual fresh smell of new-building. He admired the décor, the ornate wooden chairs and booths, the paintings of Ganesh, and the buddhas on their shelves upon the walls.

He spotted Eve in the booth. She was twisted around to face him, pointing comically at her imaginary watch, as if to say you're late. Seven slid into the booth across from his sister.

They nodded their hellos and, not wasting time, Eve said, "I still can't believe you're engaged. How does it feel?"

"It feels good," Seven said.

"Let me see the ring."

Seven showed her.

Eve winced. "Is that the ring you had on before?"

"Yes."

"It looks like a different ugly ring." And it did. It was thicker, more ornate, more girth. The reptilian scales were more pronounced, the serpent's teeth sharper.

"I wanted to give this to Paris." Seven flexed his fingers. "But it still won't budge."

"So you got Dana an engagement ring, I assume."

"We'll get around to it. This whole thing happened so fast and so sudden, we didn't have time to set a date. But we'll get there," Seven said.

"My little brother's tying the knot." Her mouth hung open, like she had something else to say. They waited, politely smiling to fill the silence. "Again, congratulations." Eve raised her Thai tea in salute. Seven lifted his water glass.

A short Asian woman took their orders: pad thai for Seven; Eve, panang curry and a cold salad. The waitress nodded and left.

"So," Seven said.

"Yep," Eve said.

The skies had become pinker and brighter. Facing the windows, Seven had to almost squint at the electric-glare from outside. It was beautiful and strange, so he said, "How bout them skies?"

"They *are* pink," Eve said, then, "What else is new?"

283

Seven cleared his throat. "I suppose I'll share another nugget of good news with you. Drum roll," he said, drumming his fingers, "*Tetragrammar*'s done."

"Shut up!" Eve slapped the table. "Good for you!"

"I know. Thanks."

"It really is a celebration. Engagements and finished books," Eve said. "Are you happy with it?"

"I mean, the ending could use some work, but endings always need more work."

"What now? Find an agent. Send it out."

"I kill The Authors with it," he said.

"Right." Eve rolled her eyes. "You are finished-finished this time. No more revisions. Done is done."

"Yes. I think."

The waitress brought Eve's salad. She stirred it: the lime-vinegar dressing, cabbage, carrots, nuts, and shrimp. "Are you satisfied with it though? Did you explain why authors live in the Moon and whatnot?"

"To a degree."

"How *does* it end?"

He told her.

"Really?" Eve chewed the cabbage and carrots, like a food critic.

"What?"

"No. It's fine." Eve forked the remaining salad into her mouth. She dabbed her lips with a napkin a little too long for Seven not to get suspicious she was teetering on a touchy subject.

"You think there's a better ending?" Seven asked.

Eve scrunched the napkin over her mouth, eyes narrowing behind her smudgy lenses. She set her hands down, her lips taut, silence and smiles, then, "I don't buy it."

"So I *should* change the ending?" Seven sensed a shift in the mood.

"No. It's you and Dana, your engagement, her coming back. That's what I don't buy."

"What don't you buy?"

"Really?" Eve raised an eyebrow. "Ever see that movie with Adam Sandler? The one where he plays this wedding singer who gets left at the altar? Can't think of the name?"

"*The Wedding Singer.*"

She shook her head. "It's the one with Drew Barrymore. They go to Vegas near the end. Billy Idol's on the plane. The one where the old lady pays him for singing lessons with meatballs?"

"That's *The Wedding Singer*."

Eve scrunched her face. "I don't think so. Anyway, Adam and Drew go through the typical misunderstanding that all characters in movies like that go through before they get together. As usual, Adam Sandler's fiancé shows up out of the blue and wants him back." Eve paused to clean her glasses. "Then there's that other movie with Ben Stiller and that red-head chick from *Will & Grace*. During their honeymoon, Ben finds this scuba instructor giving it to Grace. They split, Ben meets Jennifer Aniston, and, *can you guess?*, they fall in love. And of course, shit happens and Grace returns, says all the clichéd bullshit of how she made a mistake and she wants him back."

"What's your point?"

Eve sighed. "How many times can the same script be recycled? I don't buy it half the time in movies; I buy it less in reality."

"I made a choice."

"If you're this transcendental writer and your hang-ups can potentially doom the world, why take Paris back? You've just invited a cliché into your life? I love her too, probably more than you, but I'm not convinced her coming back will fix anything for you."

"Can't it be simple? Can't it just be the girlfriend returns with no strings attached?"

"Your life's an allegory. Nothing's simple. The unsolvable problem abruptly resolved is risky."

"It's a chance I needed to take."

"You wrote yourself into a corner. Dana was gone, Seven," she said, "for good. Now," waving her hand, "not so much. She may walk and talk like Paris, doesn't mean she's Paris. Maybe she's a doppelganger?" she suggested playfully, although there was nothing playful in the intent.

"I thought you were happy for me?"

"I am. I told you that. Just things are different now. We're not two people forced to be nice to each other due to some mutual acquaintance. We're family. I don't want you to get hurt."

"I appreciate that. And I'm not lost on the coincidence."

The waitress delivered their food. Now, silence. Them, eating. Eve paused. "It's just."

Seven set his fork down. "What?"

Going over her wording, "I found you with your throat cut. I bandaged you and watched you heal and, all the while, there was this suspension of disbelief about the whole thing, something surreal and impossible that I embraced without doubt." She bobbed her head as if balancing her thoughts on a plank above shark-infested waters. "It's like reality and logic stretched around you and I accepted it. But Paris comes home out of the blue and you're engaged; that I can't swallow. Somehow, it was more believable that you were alive when you should've been dead." She paused. "It won't work. View it as a miracle or whatever, but, me, I call it bad writing. What do they call that in fiction? The easy way out." She waited. "Go on. Say it."

"Deus ex machina."

Eve nodded, *exactly.* "You feel the wrongness of it. You won't buy it for long and a writer has to believe their own story."

"So what would you do?" Seven asked.

Eve shrugged. "Walk away. Let it all go."

"Let it all go," he repeated.

"Why not? Every conflict in your life exists on a symbolic level. Not implying your problems aren't real, well, they're not. But for you, by existing in your own logic, they are. What I'm saying is only *you* can release them."

"So what? Just pinch myself, wake up, and act like it's all in my head. No, that's a worse cop out."

"Forget it then," she dismissed. "Really! I'm happy for you. Don't doubt yourself because of me. A celebration, right?" Eve raised her tea. "Cheers!"

*

In the weeks that followed, Seven wrote leisurely. He made minor adjustments to his final chapter, tweaking sentence structure and syntax. He read. He attended Paris's yoga classes, and her students would congratulate them on their news. He finally saw the end of the tunnel and there was light. At night, if they went to bars, Eve and Paris would laugh, getting tipsier with each glass of wine. Other times, Paris read in bookstores while Seven rifled through the new releases. Bit by bit, she revealed little details of what went wrong abroad and why she came back and Seven let the stories glaze over. It was irrelevant. At night, when they watched shows on TiVo, he wafted in the girly fragrances from her hair: coconuts and melon and strawberry creams, genuinely astonished Paris's scalp could emit such aromas. And he ignored the serpent's choking death-squeeze around his finger every time she smiled at him. Dana Paris had always been that wide-eyed unknown, a blonde wildcard that may or may not have been a Dynasty. He laughed how his destiny to murder The Authors had been severely derailed by a woman caught in the wrong story at a wrong time, and how now it was all so right.

Days blurred in his newfound paradise.

And if you want me to elaborate, tough shit, it is what it is. The novel needs to end and I'm tired of writing it. Show; don't tell. I know the rules. Judge me then or fuck off or read on. Your choice.

*

No one needed to tell him it was too easy, that all the pieces of his life were aligning in a synchronicity that couldn't be healthy. Would the good life inevitably unravel under its own lies?

Fable joined Seven on his porch one night while he doodled on a lined notebook. She inhaled, keeping her breath in until the silence needed to be filled. Seven continued his note-taking, waiting for whatever his muse needed to release. And just before he could ask, Fable said, "The Greeks had this thing called a mekhane, which was a crane, and it would lower an actor onto a stage during a performance. The performer may've been playing some god or divine figure, and they would call this act a god from the machine. And that name still permeates the fiction of today. A holy intervention of a higher power, the magic of the muses." Seven waited.

"What's your point?"

"You know my point," Fable continued. "The problem with Paris isn't only that she came back, but perhaps she wasn't your true love at all? What about us, Seven? Not talking about anything sexual, but *us*. Our dynamic. What we stand for?"

"We can still do this," Seven said. "The Moon's in our reach."

"I hope so. It won't last though. I've met the Seventh Dynasty. He's death and he's coming for you, for us, for the whole she-bang."

"You were there when I used the bag," Seven said. "You knew the risks."

"Deus ex machina's never work." She sounded tired.

"Why can't they? Isn't a deus ex a leap of faith? A higher belief it'll all work out? Can't they just be divine payoff?

"No," Fable grunted.

"Why the change of heart now?"

"It's ending soon." She made a face. "I'm afraid."

"What was I supposed to do?" he asked. Fable had no answer, only blinked-out until she reappeared on his lap, arms cradled around him. She rested her head against his chest.

Overhead, the skies were pink, a little too pink to be natural. He wondered how The City, how all the people felt about it. He imagined it didn't matter, that that same nonchalance towards the Porter Madness would be applied to whatever would soon follow.

"You really want to marry her?" Her voice was soft. Seven tilted his head back for a better look at her. He ran over several answers he'd give her, none of which sounded convincing, so he said nothing. And together, they watched the skies.

*

The heavens were shaded with an obscenely gaudy-fluorescent in the day and night, too pink for their own good. So when the first gray cloud lingered, a dirty smudge, it couldn't be dismissed: the statement had been made.

Death was coming.

*

Seven went to Paris's apartment that night with a bottle of Stella Rosa. Paris told him they had much wine to drink, and after putting a dent in the bottle, she asked with her slurred words, "Do you love me?"

"What do you think?"

"That's dodging the question."

"I'm the one who proposed, remember? You're the one it took years to say yes."

"Years?" Paris raised an eyebrow quizzically. "You really think it's been that long?"

Seven shrugged.

They watched a movie until halfway through Paris reached between Seven's legs. And she stood from the couch and began to strip, and she led him into the bedroom. And when they were both naked, well into the act, he knew this was not Paris; this was never Paris. She forced his eyes towards her, rocking on him. "Look me in the face," she said. "Who do you see? Who do you *really* love?"

"You, Dana," gasp, "always you."

But it wasn't.

288

He could only see Fable. And then he came.

24
THE RUB

A playful argument had broken out between Seven and Paris in his dream, in which he declared the first season of True Blood *was an allegory: the acceptance of vampires was a metaphor for gay rights. Paris, rolling her eyes, stated she had already read the Charlaine Harris novels and it had nothing to do with that. And when calling him an idiot, he snapped back that it was blatantly obvious and how couldn't she see a "coming out" correlation between coffins and closets. And it was a good dream, untouched by surreal terror, that was until Seven left to use the bathroom. On returning, the room had changed to a cotton-candy color, and now Fable stood perfectly still, smiling, oblivious to the vague darkness encroaching from the walls, something ugly and dirty. Seven wanted to go to her but some dream-logic restrained him. Instead, he screamed out her name, shouting at her until something tore in his throat, and he heaved up globs of thick scarlet. He could only watch the pink-thing wrapping Fable's face in its hand, rubbing her face, turning it to gritty flakes, rubbing and rubbing until Fable was no longer there.*

That would've been the time to wake up. But he didn't. He remained in the nightmare, crying, sobbing because he couldn't save her. And when death closed on him, there was burning, friction and fire, until there was nothing to erase, nothing at all.

Seven shot up in bed, drenched in cold sweat, looking around panic-stricken. *Where was he?* As friendly recognition returned, he knew. Penn Street. The corner of Sixth. Second floor. Paris's bed. He had been sleeping in her bed how long now? Months, weeks? *How long had it really been?* He thought about asking her but it was late and

290

she slept like a rock, never stirring in her sleep, and he hated her a little for that.

He wouldn't kid himself any chance existed to find comfort in this bed. The lights outside Penn Street broke through the curtains, casting shadows on the walls. Even at this time, a rosy hue permeated the lighting.

He began to itch, at first around his navel, then his arms and legs, then worse, down below, in his pants, a deep, aggressive dry itch that refused to be scratched away. He dug with his fingernails until the itch evolved to a burning around his genitalia. Seven darted from the bed, dashed into the bathroom.

A hot rash covered his privates, spreading down his inner thighs. He found a bottle of baby powder in the medicine cabinet. He emptied nearly half of it onto his groin, waited, gawking at his cock. He had to relieve himself. It burned when he pissed and he cringed, tears welling in his eyes at the liquid-fire. A vile black fluid filled the toilet bowel, and focusing on it, Seven saw his urine was full of letters.

"What the fuck?" he said.

He sat on the toilet cover, folding forward until the burning subsided. He peeked down, willing whatever-it-was to leave. Eventually, when the rash faded, he pulled up his pants.

"Great," Seven said. "Another beginning of something new and surreal and insane. Shouldn't this bizarre shit be ending soon? I finished the book. I got the girl back. What else needs to happen?"

"You pulled a magic trick out of a bag," Fable said, perched on the windowsill, gazing out the curtain by the shower. "You knew there would be repercussions."

"I know. We were both there when I did it. You didn't stop me either."

"It wasn't about stopping you. If The Authors are playing with numbers, we were aware two more Dynasties had yet to reveal themselves. They could take on any form. Easy way out or not, the Final Dynasty, the Seventh, he's a nasty bastard. Trust me, he will not make your life easier."

Seven moved to the sink, glared into the mirror. He looked tired, like thirty fighting fifty. His forehead was creased with raccoon circles under his eyes. He moved his face closer to the mirror to peer deeper past those brown eyes. And he thought, *what was a face anyway? Nothing but fiction.* He exhaled heavily. "You've met him?"

"Yes." Fable nodded grimly. "And he's coming for you. He's outside now. Time's ticking and death's waiting. Seven, go meet the reaper."

Outside, the lamplights smeared with the candy-colored glow of the early morning sky. Wearing a black tank top, yoga pants, and brown slippers, Seven walked along Penn Street. Every building and apartment seemed abandoned to such a degree he questioned whether or not anyone had ever lived on Penn Street, like his entire world was a city-sized ghost town that would soon collapse in on itself, to be washed away by plot holes. The air was so silent Seven feared he'd hemorrhage the quiet if he broke the stillness. He sat on a bench outside the storefront of an independent bookstore. "Where's he at?" he asked Fable softly.

Fable pointed above. "He's the sky, Seven, and he's coming." Closing her eyes, "I feel him moving closer, the death in his heart beating, and he's…"

Seven's genitals shrank. A hot friction rubbed over his temples. His heart was beating, too quick for its own good. A sandpaper burn grated away on his insides. He squeezed his eyes shut, hunching forward onto his knees, knowing he wasn't alone, that when he opened his eyes, he wouldn't like what he saw. And he wanted to stay in that cozy place, just live in the space between his eyes.

He turned his face, keeping his head low, and he saw a ball being held in a hand that was entirely too pink. The ball was rubber, a sphere-shaped eraser, this he knew, but it also seemed no different than the hand that clenched it, a hand made of rubber.

"Pink is a lovely color, a true color," a sly voice grated against the air. "It is honest and beautiful and disgusting. It sheds layers like a rotten onion that will burn your eyes from their sockets. And if you're in no mood for Allium cepa, then simply look up, The Seven. Look towards the heavens and you will see my truth smearing over this City."

Seven lowered his gaze towards the sidewalk.

The man's words burned in his ears, and he wanted him to stop talking but the dark voice continued, "Self-annihilation is the only destiny. Mankind only creates to erase. You could argue smog and bombs are brilliant, but I disagree. I say the greatest invention is this." The man squeezed the rubber ball in his dirty fingers. "So simple, the eraser. See." He pumped his hand around it. "An idea expressed in form and function. It erases. It ends. One purpose. It never malfunctions, never fails."

Looking upon the man, Seven steadied the tremble in his voice, "You're the next Dynasty."

"The Last Dynasty."

"The Sixth?"

He scoffed, "The Seventh."

"I doubt it," Seven said, testing him.

The Seventh's laugh sounded like a demon child eating splinters. "Doubt is her realm. Doubt lies in six. And me, They call me Lunatic Pink!" And the Seventh Dynasty was pink, too pink, with a vicious mess of frozen pink hair, a crinkled forehead; sharp, chapped lips, a nubby pink nose, dirty pink ears, and rubbery pink jacket with pink jeans. His entire body looked dirty and chafed; all his features were one thing, the clothing not separate from his flesh, just a single rubber form. He looked artificial, like a manufactured doll forged to life. But most appalling, he was Seven, *pinked*, a Seven that had been sculpted from a man-sized doomsday-eraser.

Seven tightened his jaw. "What do you want?"

"I want to play yo-yo with the Moon. I want to smear the sun across the galaxy. I want to open Fable's legs and rub her raw. I want to slit your throat." When Seven clenched his fist, Lunatic giggled like a deviant's erection over roadkill. "Good. You want to kill me. I like that." And as his body shook when laughing, Lunatic Pink resembled a dirty smudge.

"I'll kill every last one of you goddamn Dynasties," Seven said.

"With what? A magic bag?" Lunatic sneered. "You tried to revise your world. To clear the deck. To smooth the obstacles. Despite what you would believe, I'm not here to simply kill you. My function is to erase you completely. To wipe the entire deck. You. The Authors. Bitch Violet. Sister Slut and Lady Love," the Seventh rambled like a bag of man-eating slugs.

"If you touch them..." Seven warned.

"I won't touch them, because they're friction. And why would I remove the pain, the worry of loss?"

"This ends with me against Them. In the Moon. Not with a pink fuck-rag like you."

"People say let it go," Lunatic growled like Mickey Mouse on acid. "It's healthy. I say hold it tight. I touch things, and in my touch, there is nothing more true."

Before Seven could react, Lunatic Pink grasped him on his knee. A fiery sandpaper-burn shot down his leg. On removing his hand, his yoga pants appeared faded, worn away. And Lunatic smiled fiendishly, his body shifting, tensing, readying to strike. Seven read the mechanics and he pushed off the bench as Lunatic brought a fist down on where he had been sitting. The bench bent inwards. And as it bent, it faded and leeched of color, as if part of it had been reduced of its essence. Lunatic simply grabbed the bench, single-handed, and lifted it, swinging it with ease.

It hit Seven, sending him back several feet. When he landed with his back smashing into the empty street, the ground ripped up around him, spewing bits of gravel and stone on impact. When he came to a stop, he looked up, wondering if that had just happened. Above him, a traffic light flashed yellow, on and off. Before Seven could adjust, he just moved, quick enough and with instinct, rolling away from his little street crater. And as he did this, the ground spewed up again under Lunatic's fist. In a halo of dust, the pink man straightened.

Seven hurt. He fumbled back, winded and shocked, grasping ribs that may've been broken under his flesh, and he hadn't recalled before, but he now wore his denim jeans and black leather jacket, not the sweatpants and sleepwear.

"Move!" Fable screamed.

Seven moved. He barely avoided another hit from Lunatic, who swung at him several times. He was too fast. Seven staggered back, getting his breath. After he steadied himself, a heavy clap echoed around him.

"Wasn't that fun?" the Last Dynasty chortled. Seven didn't know exactly what type of laugh a chortle was, but he was sure that's what the Dynasty had just done, chortled, and he found it extremely terrifying. "Life's so much better when people want to make you bleed."

"How's this going to play out?" Seven said. His body hurt, but the pain of being slammed into the pavement, of upheaving the earth, seemed insubstantial compared to his inner dread.

"You write; I erase. The final rub is what I am. And I don't make you feel good. Ain't that type of rubber, mate. Fuck lube. Leave it raw, I say. Understand? We'll romp each other til nothing's left except bits of shit and friction." His words were fire in Seven's ears.

And there was a surge of electricity as Fable intervened between them. Her eyes were so bright violet spilled from her face. Seven feared her suddenly. "I'd love for you to rub me the wrong way," Fable said, cheesy and forced as it sounded she went with it anyway. "You just may find you don't like the way I rub back."

Grinning like a crazed hyena, Lunatic addressed Seven, "Has she told you?"

"Told me what?" Seven asked.

"We're linked," Fable said.

"Linked how?"

And before she could answer, Lunatic set in for another attack. Seven took the defensive, trying to avoid all contact. He couldn't believe the power and destruction every time Lunatic hit something. It was all unreal and hard to swallow, with the same flavor of chaos that Miss Minor had displayed when she exploded the coffee shop. As Seven dodged, Lunatic collided with cars, denting in the sides. He chucked signposts his way. Storefronts were shattered.

It was a bizarre dance of avoiding objects, dodging fists and feet. As the fight ensued, neither one demonstrated much grace or strategy. Seven forgot himself in the struggle, never wondering about waking Paris or alerting the authorities or the hungry buzz of people capturing the fight on their phones.

Putting nerves and fears aside, Seven darted in towards Lunatic, closing the gap, and landed a punch directly on his cheek. The Dynasty winked at him, as if to say he could've dodged any assault. Lunatic remained unmoving, didn't even roll with the punch, no, instead, he pushed his face into it, harder, a dry carpet burn that chafed the skin from Seven's knuckles. He backed away, eyed his fist, feeling *less*. Lunatic Pink gripped Seven's face and squeezed his nubby fingers around his throat, knuckling Seven in the temple.

Seven might've been screaming at this point. He only remembered a flash of pink and as Lunatic rubbed, hot friction filled his skull. Memory turned to dirty rubber flakes and for a moment, Seven couldn't remember, couldn't remember anything at all.

It hurt. *Why did it hurt?*

"So easy," Seven heard, "I could erase your mind and memory just to show you I can do that sorta thing…"

The burn continued, until it didn't, until…

…a rush and release, and Seven dropped on all fours as Lunatic stumbled back when Fable delivered a lunging elbow to his face. They both rolled forward with the momentum, a ball of violet and pink. Fable gracefully moved to her feet, blinked-out, and reappeared with another hit, blinking-out and popping back, every time landing a punch or kick.

Lunatic staggered around the vacant street, bombarded at random angles and points of attack. And when she smashed him into the street with a thrust kick, she immediately rushed over him and proceeded to slam her heel down on his head, over and over, each time the ground breaking under the blow, until she paused because he was laughing. Lunatic pushed himself up from the broken road.

"Amused, are we?" she said.

"Oh, you're in my heart. You're part of me, you pixie-twat, and I so respect you, Bitch Violet," Lunatic said. And back to Seven, "Time for an anatomy lesson. Your muse wants nothing more than to murder her heart. That's what I respect. You can try killing me for eternity but I'll never go away. Pain fuels me. If you *could* hurt me, it wouldn't be until my predecessors were dead." Lunatic laughed hysterically. "Ever since the First raped your mind, you induced mad vibes into the world, like psychic foreplay before the great, sticky yelp of release. And the entire City felt you, so many nameless people fell prey in the Apocalypse-that-never-was. I know them all, all their toothy souls. The dead dwell in your shattered heart, their minor blood screams inside me. I'm gloated with their hate for you, so yes, you will have to pay."

"I'm sorry. I've been sorry," she said.

"Don't be!" And he tensed his body, ready to pounce.

As Fable prepared for another attack, she formed a strategy in that impossible second. She closed her eyes, watching him spring forward in slow motion. Another round would only fuel the Lunatic; she needed a new approach. If she unleashed hell upon the City, then she could also deliver heaven. Perhaps she could inspire love within the Lunatic and, in doing so, she could generate peace for all those who perished, could atone for all her sins. She opened her eyes as the Final Dynasty closed the gap, pushing Seven to the side, away from his doppelganger, and blinked from sight. Lunatic only hit the ground where they should've been. Lunatic's eyes rolled to the left as the electric hum crackled behind him. And Fable was on him, clinging to his back.

Amethyst flames crackled on her palms as she pressed her fingertips into his temples, pushing deeper, screaming as she forced her mind into his. And as she felt herself merging with his psyche, she unleashed a light in his mind, expanding an indigo supernova that spread harmoniously throughout his insanity.

For a moment, she was in his head, not the victim, not the intruder. She was frictionless, smooth and…

…in his mind, she inspired paradise. Angry pink skies turned to golds and greens, and there was a garden with apples-made-of-light hanging from the branches of glistening trees. Within this garden, Fable spied upon a field filled with people, every victim and casualty. And she called from the heavens and the people looked up. A humming broke out as the skies sang. And the people joined with the song; they all chanted OM. Each voice synchronized with each other, growing stronger until their unified voice washed upwards and outwards, cleansing the madness within Lunatic, until the Final Dynasty felt himself dissolving within their harmony. And Lunatic found no friction in his world, no resentment, nothing to grate against, no bitter rawness, no wounds to bleed. Instead, he flowed with the smooth serenity.

And deep within this paradise, Lunatic's cry welled up from his frictionless hell and he screamed out his madness and…

…with a gut-wrenching wail, he ripped his mind from hers, cursing, spitting out serenity.

"Peace to you is poison, you sick fuck," Fable smirked. "I've hurt you."

And Lunatic staggered about disoriented. His mouth twisted into a feral snarl, as if he'd just been afflicted with the greatest wrong. "Perfect world, Bitch Violet!" he spat. "How dare you torture me with utopia! I don't need heaven or nirvana or some fat man's enlightenment! How *dare* you?! I'll kill you for this, you wait! I'll butcher and maim you! Slaughter and shit you!" Lunatic Pink steadied himself. He inhaled, grit his teeth, and flashed that mad smile. "No. No victory for you," he added pleasantly. "You haven't broken me. I win. I always do. Everything dies with me. You're no different." He glared at Fable, then towards Seven. "Everything," he repeated.

Seven tensed, jaw set, waiting for another attack.

Lunatic waved at him. "This was warm-up. We'll meet at the Suicide Spot, in the flood. We'll fight. You'll die." Lunatic hesitated, as if Fable's vision had caused him indigestion. He looked about to add something. Instead, he eyed the chaos of the setting, nodded in satisfaction, and began to walk down Penn Street in a dazed stupor. Fable and Seven watched him fade away after several blocks.

Fable sighed, "You think he likes me?"

"For a moment, I thought you killed him," Seven said. "I thought we had him."

Although she now knew his weakness, the assault had drained her. "He's strong," she said. "His power comes from the other Dynasties and he can't die until they die."

"What did he mean? What didn't you tell me?"

He watched Fable pace about the street. It was torn apart and ravaged, but it all seemed insubstantial, like movie props. Not one person came out to see the chaos. Fable remained quiet. Seven looked up at Paris's apartment, at the open window where the bedroom was. She must've still been sleeping, he rationalized although he knew better.

"Fable? What didn't…?" he began again.

"Paris isn't up there," Fable said. "That's not her. It never was." And she gripped his chin, turned his gaze towards her. "Come," she said, grabbing his hand.

There was a shift.

He moved within her embrace. Somehow, he was travelling, jumping across paragraphs, skipping through pages, and when he opened his eyes, he staggered, his feet caught in a drunk motion sickness.

"What did you do?" he gasped, dropping to his knees at his apartment.

Fable was already pacing around the coffee table, arms crossed, face twisted in thought. "Stop it. Stand up!" she said with no more patience for his simple questions. "You move just like I do, maybe slower, but all the same. You blink-out and you go. You've been doing it without ever realizing."

Seven stood, leaned against the wall by the television. "He had my face. *My face!*" Seven trailed off. "He won't go down without a fight."

Fable shook her head. "Killing him will be complicated."

"Because he's death."

"Because of me. That's what I didn't tell you," Fable said. "His heart beats with my death! He's full of minor blood and he's linked to the Hall of Minors and me. I could feel the Fifth's essence streaming in him. And their screams, all those people who were affected in our apocalypse, I heard them all. "

"It wasn't your fault," he said, despite if it was or wasn't, it no longer mattered.

"Regardless, Seven, we have to finish things."

"Things?" he smirked. "Like cheap fixes and plot threads. I don't like what I'm hearing. You almost make it sound like you have to die with him." When she said nothing, "I don't accept that! This is our story and we end it together! Fuck karma and whatnot! So if you really believe Lunatic Pink's final death is linked to you, then I want full disclosure! Everything you think you know or not, all the dirty secrets that may be fact or fiction, I want you to spill your goddamn guts to me now!"

Fable inhaled deeply. "I'll never have concrete answers for you. I'm not made that way. I'm part of the imagination, something loose and speculative. And you already know the gist so why rehash it?"

"Once more then. Humor me."

"Notion may've been my first victim. He killed himself because I pushed him too hard."

"Notion made his choice. He wrote himself into purgatory. Not you. And if none of this is your fault, or some of it is, I don't care anymore. What's now is now and it links back to me. I'm the writer and I share some blame. The bag. Paris's return. Regardless, we don't have time to analyze creative choices. The sooner the Last Dynasty is dead, the better, and if we're going to take him out, we need the identity of the Sixth. For whatever reason, its true face hides from us. So I say fuck it!" Seven grabbed Thrifty's bag from the kitchen table. He set it on the coffee table. The top of it was scrunched shut and rolled over and Seven began to open it.

Before he reached in, Fable touched his hand. "The bag," she said, "you sure you want to use it again?"

"What's one more easy answer? It's all going to hell anyways."

Seven reached in. He worked his fingers around inside a bag with no bottom, fishing out whatever-he-would-find, knowing the answer was forming, molding itself to conform to the intent of the question in his mind: *who was the Sixth?* He grazed against a small slip of paper, much like one found inside a fortune cookie. Seven retrieved it. Their eyes narrowed on the paper.

"Who?" Fable asked.

Seven read the answer, and he showed her the impossible truth, that the Devil lies in Six, that doubt had always been the fuel since the eve of creation.

*

Back on Penn Street, on the torn up road, Paris eyed the destruction. Walking along the sidewalk in her pajamas, she observed the debris of battered benches and downed lampposts and shards of glass from murdered storefronts and cars totaled in that parallel parked spaces. And with the wave of her hand, reality mended; the destruction aligned. Cars were healed. Broken glass became whole. The holes in the road leveled out. Everything fixed glinted a golden hue. And she knew it wouldn't last, not for long, as the skies darkened into a grubby omen. But for now, the miracle would stick, easy-peasy. Still too early to be up, Paris retreated indoors, a shadow full of beating wings.

25
FAITH IN DOUBT

Eve woke to her cell phone around 6 a.m. She fumbled for the phone on the side table. "Hello," she finally answered in her why-in-dear-god-are-you-calling-this-early tone.

"Tell me about our parents?"

"What?" There was a tired annoyance in her voice.

"I want to know about our parents," Seven said.

"Jesus," Eve muttered. "What's the matter with you? I told you already. And why are you calling so early?"

When the other end remained silent, Eve stood, wearing her skimpy shorts and a low-cut v-neck. "You sound funny."

"Tell me about Mom and Dad."

"Fine." She told him about their parents and growing up together in the old brick rancher back in the woods. She continued to spill out little details of childhood and youth. When finished, she waited for a response.

After a while, "Can I come over today?" Seven asked.

"When?"

"Whenever's good for you."

"Yea, sure," Eve answered. "Is everything ok?"

Seven hung up.

Eve tapped her phone loosely against her chin.

She spent entirely too long under the scolding shower. She washed her hair with a tea tree shampoo and her body with a watermelon-scented scrub. She stood naked in front of the steamed mirror, unable to see her face, brushing her teeth with a vibrating toothbrush. She toweled herself off, dressed in bootcut jeans, a black collared t-shirt. A fat-faced devil grinned on the front of the shirt. She cleaned her glasses, unable to rid the smudges from the lenses, and placed them back on her face. Her hair was still wet and lank.

She cut an apple into seven uneven slices, smeared each slice with peanut butter using a knife that had old bits of food stuck to its blade. She placed the diced apple on a metal tray and went into her backyard. The world glowed with a hungry pink, reflected from the obscene, salmon-colored skies. The morning air was brisk and chilled. She crunched into the apple, slice after slice, until one remained. She left it on the tray, on the chaise, and licked the corners of her mouth.

"That one's for you," she said to her brother, who was watching from the fake garden, not surprised in the least he was here so soon. "You got here fast. Must've been urgent?"

Seven's hair was greasy, his eyes dark, clothes wrinkled.

"I tried to read my book today," he said. "Every page felt like I was choking up my insides, which didn't surprise me. I think my heart would've exploded if I actually enjoyed it. But as I scanned it, I wasn't even sure why I hated it. If I'm the author, shouldn't I enjoy my own story?"

Eve shrugged.

"I considered rearranging the structure, bringing certain characters back, rewording several passages, and after that, I assumed it would be good, but it wouldn't. It would just be another rewrite and it could always be better." He squatted in her garden. "Tell me about my childhood," he said.

"Why so nostalgic?"

"Humor me."

"Well. As a kid you had an imaginary friend called Fable. You'd tell me, Mom, and Dad that she'd always give you these wild ideas and you needed to write them down. Your main toy as a child was a notebook and you'd doodle in it and it kept you occupied for the most part. And sometimes we joked that your imagination was more real than us, that you lived there instead of here."

Seven mulled this over. "I can move like she does," he said then.

"Like who does?" Eve questioned.

The heavens began to fill with clouds that resembled nubby eraser shavings.

She lifted the tray to Seven. "Have an apple. It could change your life."

"I'm not hungry."

"It's just one apple."

Eve walked barefoot into the garden. She squatted in a bed of artificial flowers next to her brother. He was poking and prodding at something in the dirt under a cluster of plastic leaves until he discovered an apple the color of spilled blood, its skin sleek, attached to a silky cord that intertwined and connected with an orchid. It weighed the pretend-orchid down, bending its plastic green vine. Seven picked up the apple from the dirt. He examined it curiously: the cord, its vine that was half-plastic, half-organic, and its vibrant skin that looked polished. It felt real as he pinched the plastic leaves of the flowers. He set the impossible fruit back in the soil.

"I know what you are," he said.

"Do you?" A gray flame flashed in her colorless eyes through her filthy glasses. She shot up, approached the back door. Before stepping inside, she flashed a foxy smile.

Seven followed.

Eve leaned against the kitchen counter while cleaning her glasses with her shirt. "I had a child once," she said. "I never told anyone about it. When I discovered I was pregnant, I was scared shitless. Then one night, I was no longer pregnant and all my fear had been snuffed out with a sadness I've never felt before. I had a dream then. I dreamt of a desperate, little fetus suffocating inside me. It could only feel the terrors of the world, the doubts and uncertainties inherent in life. And I watched it in my dream, watched it grip its umbilical cord and strangle itself because it wanted to retreat back into the Light rather than bear growing one more second inside the womb of your dear sister." Eve paused, gazing into nowhere. "Imagine how I felt? I realized that was my demon. I thought long and hard about who the father could be."

"That's a long list," he said.

"Yes," she agreed. "And it was all irrelevant. Every man I slept with was the same. You know, a person's entire life can be read before a climax. Every little passion and fear, there's nothing more intimate. Yet they all look the same."

"Why are you telling me this?"

"You're my brother. We're family."

Seven wanted to offer some sort of condolence, no matter how vague. Instead, "What happened to our parents?" he asked. She told him. He nodded until what she told him unstuck in his mind.

"Why do you keep asking?" She joined him at the kitchen table.

"Why wouldn't I?"

"You think too much," she said. "If you don't like my answers, if you doubt what I tell you, then write your own past."

"We're not talking about family anymore, are we?"

"Then what would we be talking about?"

"*Them*," he said.

Eve chuckled. "Oh? Possibly. But let Them go, too. Let family go. Let words go. Your past *could* go away if you stopped thinking. All of it. Let it all go. A fiction writer shouldn't be restrained. I mean, *even I* know how to kill your authors. Can't believe you haven't figured it out yourself. You don't feed Them with your thoughts. Poof!" She pretended her hands held an exploding bomb.

"It's not that simple," Seven said.

"Did you know every garden has a serpent? It may be a metaphorical snake, a slithering worm even, but each garden has one. Or if you prefer another analogy, every garden contains a temptress. A devil, if you will. It has to. It's the secret rule of paradise. To wrestle with a demon is inherent in every story and you can never fully kill a devil, push it back, yes, but never kill completely."

"No, you can't. The devil is a function; it creates doubt."

"Exactly! The devil is a habit, and we're all creatures of habit. You, for example. You continually recycle the same motifs of revision, dead-ends, and circles. Everything repeats itself. Take Paris. Paris should've never come back, which she didn't. Her return, if it actually occurred, would've been too easy. Like your novel, she was just another plot you could never resolve. She may've had a pretty face and soft flesh." (Seven noted a twinkle in Eve's eyes.) "She wasn't book-shaped and filled with pages, but she was, more or less, an open thread you couldn't knot. And it all comes to you now, her return and a finished script. And look at me, too. All the times we ran into each other, the sudden epiphany that we've been related all along. Us as siblings never really added up. It was convenient, a suspension of disbelief, and without that, where would fiction be? In a way, I was something like a deus ex machina, although there's nothing godly about me. Now, as your universe collapses under its own illogic, you have to finally address what I am."

"I know what you are. I finally know that you're…"

Eve stopped him. "That I'm The Authors, that I've always been The Authors."

"You're not The Authors," Seven said.

"Are you certain? I could be Them; after all, The Authors are everywhere, watching you, writing you, drowning you in the ink of Their pens. How on earth do you fight *that*? If I'm not The Authors, then what *am* I?"

"The Sixth Dynasty."

"Ah, yes." Eve adjusted her stained glasses. "The Uncertain Six." The atmosphere dimmed and her lenses began to glow.

"I don't want to kill you."

She laughed. "You could never kill me!"

"I have to. I can't kill the Seventh until you're dead."

"Battling the Dynasties has never been physical. Each battle cultivates what's in here." She tapped herself on the forehead. "Fighting us has always been transcendental. And fighting me is to realize there's never been any truth about me." She slid a chair closer to face him. "I want to show you something."

She stood from the table and waved him towards her. When he didn't move, she grabbed him by the arm. Seven was walking now, strolling through the halls of her home, each wall layered in art. The background moved and shifted around her, all her art pushing at the edges of his vision.

"It should've been no surprise about my being the Sixth," Eve said. "It's not like there wasn't anything peculiar about me from the beginning. But we've always shared the same aesthetic appreciation, art that is surreal and strange and terrifying. Art that can only make the vaguest sense within dreams."

Her gallery began to swirl together in an abstract blend of image and color. Seven watched her collection, pictures of elephantine giraffes and clouds-made-of-grass flowing together in a liquid collage of surreal that left him queasy, which, if unchecked, could trigger a panic attack on a cellular level. It was beautiful in its strangeness. It could make any viewer cringe with the existential. The walls, ceilings, and floor were waking with Dali-esque dreams and Picassoed terror.

Chirico and Max Ernst reprints merged together, fused with works of Scott Mutter and Magritte and Charnine. And strangely, the floor underneath melted, becoming less solid, and the walls, *were they wavering?*

"That's it," Eve guided him. "Into the mind. Just another meditation. Forget the body." She touched his forehead and they were no longer in her house. "Doubt it all," she instructed. "Doubt the world. Doubt structure and foundation. Keep looking into my eyes. Good. Fall into me now."

And he *was* falling, falling into her.

*

A little doubt can be healthy, can keep us honest. And Seven began to deny his existence. Overhead, from Escher-like angles, an ocean-of-ink crested. An ontological terror churned in his guts, much more terrifying than the collapse of the Fourth Wall. He doubted his whole story, each chapter of his life. He was inhaling an atmosphere of unsaturated doubt. Each molecule embraced every hesitation of the "I do" at a wedding, every whisper goading you to leave your spouse, every dark snicker that shriveled your ego, every condescending dismissal of an artist's work, every little whisper of "Jump" in high places.

The uncertainty would extend beyond Seven. It would infest the pages of Tetragrammar *and rot away at the novel itself. It would feed off every grammatical error, every plot hole and loose end, every contradiction, every negative criticism. It wouldn't knock politely on the Fourth Wall; it would obliterate it.*

He was falling, but he was rising, too, and when the paradox collided somewhere inside his skull, he was elsewhere.

Seven had entered the Doubting.

*

They were somewhere uncertain. It would've been beautiful if it weren't painfully nauseating. His head spun as foundation and logic unraveled around him. In the skies, metal angels played in clouds of grass and earth. Men wore scrambled faces and possessed faucets and door knobs around their phallic regions. Birds swam in the earth with heads made of roses. Crucifixes darted through the skies, like holy planes trailing dual jet clouds of wine and blood. A Mount Rushmore of Olympic Gods sang in Italian opera. Naked people with television heads and wire arms fornicated on beds of cell phones. A parade of dogs with apples and oranges hiding their faces walked upon treadmills made of liquid clocks.

Seven struggled to fix his sight on one image, drowning in the absence of reason, suffocating in erotic subtext and psychosexual metaphor. His body swayed and wavered, unable to adapt to a ubiquitous vertigo.

He couldn't make out his sister. But when she spoke from an angle sure to induce vomiting, her words rearranged around her, as if her voice itself was giving birth to her physical body. Her face was upside down, and her long hair flowed and sometimes her hair was snakes, hissing and undulating. Her eyes extended beyond the frame of her face and solid words bubbled from her scarlet lips. And she was now a serpent with a human head, until she was a floating bone-colored rib wearing teeming red glasses with bangs.

"Your world can never work," Eve said from the Doubting.

"Please, God, stop…" Seven strained under layers of nausea that wavered and crashed through him. He realized he had pissed himself, his pants suddenly down around his ankles, and his dick was a pencil, pissing ink and letters.

"Ask yourself why They created me?" said Rib-Eve. "Any dream, passion, or love requires faith. Ironically, evolution can never be attained without me," said an Eve-made-of-flowers with eyelid petals. "Ever consider The Authors may not exist? What are They? Why live in the Moon? What *does* the Moon mean? It's a metaphor for women and fertility. It doesn't oppose you or anyone else. So why are your Authors living there?"

"I don't know."

"Shouldn't you? Mix too many metaphors and you'll go blind," she teased. "The Authors are ridiculous."

"This is sick," Seven groaned. "I don't want this anymore." Colors with no shape swirled and spiraled. No, that sounded tame. This was anything but tame. Imagine every time you were plagued with a second-guess, an existential crisis, an answer for a question like death and life; imagine all that and give it a realm. Make it every sick uncertainty, every disease of ambiguity. Shape it like the world closing in; explode it into nothing. Choke on it. Devour it. Throw it up and shit it out.

"Please stop!" Seven hugged himself.

"Ssh," Eve shushed.

The atmosphere changed again. Seven stretched, melted, twisted. He was screaming again, inside flesh made of pulp, and he was falling.

The Doubting relaxed. The world became more solid. Seven opened his eyes, *so slowly*, and he moved…

…They were on a flat plain under a sky that glowed with an ambiguous light. A single tree stretched into the heavens, its top vanishing forever.

"What is this?" Seven asked, suppressing motion sickness.

Eve stood in the tall grass. "First, there was man. And with man, free thought, and with free thought, the ugly worm of doubt. Of course, man questioned his existence, thus leading to speculation upon speculation as a means towards a concrete truth. In looking for the answers, man inadvertently created God. Now if The Authors made me, aren't They essentially *my* God. Then," she hung the question, "what does that make me?"

"The Devil," he answered.

"Right. Doubt is the Devil. Uncertainty is the adversary. *Tetragrammar* is still in you, and I'll show you. Don't get squeamish, brother. Deep breath." And she touched Seven's chest, kneading through his shirt and flesh, pushing her rigid fingers deeper. He winced as she moved her hands around inside him. And when she removed her hands, she held a glossy apple drenched in blood. Seven knew although it didn't look like a heart, it still beat like a heart, and it was his soul and his pulse and it thumped in her fingers. She raised his heart-that-was-an-apple to her mouth, and her teeth cracked it open. A honey-like juice spilled down her chin. "I can kill anything, Seven," she said, chomping into the fruit, "especially the truth. But in the end, I'm a writer's friend; I'm everyone's enemy. I swing both ways. Here's the reality inside *Tetragrammar*. Look!" She showed him the center of the apple. And he didn't want to look because of the maggots and worms wriggling around the core, because of the truth, the secret of knowledge: it had always been full of worms…

…and suddenly, Seven found himself sweaty and sick on the kitchen floor. Although the world had stabilized, he still didn't trust his senses. "Fucking hell!" he spat while he touched the floor, testing the ground just to make sure it was solid and concrete and wouldn't waver and give out with the irrational. "Is it over!?" Seven heaved.

"It can be." Eve crossed her legs at the very normal-table-that-was-just-a-table. "Forget The Authors." Eve smiled warmly, to show the punching gloves were off and the knives had been put away. "Doubt rules. Doubt structure. Doubt your own story. Doubt it all. Stretch. Flex. Write your own life." Eve squeezed Seven's shoulder. "Time for you to be your own author."

"I can't," he said.

"Why?"

"If I just ignore the Seventh, you really believe he'll go away?"

Eve frowned. "Not unless you use him to your advantage. Let him erase the old."

"He wouldn't stop. He'd erase everything. The old. The new. Good and bad." Seven paused. He didn't want to say what he would say next. "You've never been my sister."

"I've always been your sister, and I've always been the Sixth Dynasty."

"I'm sorry, Eve. I have to kill you," Seven said without conviction.

Eve laughed, pitying. "Please, brother, how will you do this? Cut off my head? Impale me with a pencil?"

"You're right," Seven said. "I can't kill you, my sister, my doubt. But I can't stop Fable from coming for you."

"Fable's not so scary anymore. She's been howling in the Moon so long, her bark is just a pooch's whimper." She winked at him.

"Should I bother to ask what that means?"

After she told him, she tapped him on the forehead. A sensation prickled behind his eyes…

…he was face down on his futon. Moving seemed overrated so he stayed. After awhile, "I couldn't kill her," Seven said to Fable. "She was my sister and a Dynasty the whole time. I couldn't do it. Even if I…"

"It's all right," Fable said.

Seven stood and walked out his back door. He felt hot and queasy. The skies were darker than ever, a murky gray that now looked wet.

"We both knew she was a Dynasty," Fable said, hugging him from behind. "We just couldn't put the thoughts together. It was her power, to block our perceptions of her."

"You'll kill her," Seven said.

"Yes." They both remained silent.

"You'll come back to me," he said eventually. "I need you to come back. I don't care about any karma from past lives. Only now matters. Only *we* matter. And I'm done living in the past, in old drafts. I want to move forward. With you. And it was always you, even when I thought it was Paris. Do you know how hard it was being near you? There were nights I wanted to devour you, drink in your dreams and…" he stopped. "You're dangerous, Fable. Dangerous and beautiful and if the floodgates opened in my mind, I wouldn't know what to do. No woman, not Paris or anyone else, no *real* woman could burn me like you."

"You like that fire, Seven." She looked into his eyes. "You've always wanted that burn. The heat. The friction."

"Yes. And I've always wanted you. Like you said before, this is our story; it's always been us, the affair of a muse and her writer."

Fable's eyes softened. "Seven…"

"I'm scared."

"So am I," she said, moving closer.

A quiet patter of rain began, and they watched it from under the porch. Her body relaxed against his. He kissed her lips. And they continued to press themselves closer to each other, until Fable eased him away. She grabbed him by the hand and led him back inside, into the bedroom. She sat him at the edge of the bed.

Seven didn't say anything as he watched Fable reach inside herself and remove the other half of her heart, a cracked half-moon shape that she crushed in her grip. She opened her hand and blew it towards Seven, a sparkling mist that coalesced around him. He could feel a warmth being absorbed into his skin, deep into his mind.

Without words, Fable smiled at him, a sad, slight smile. She crawled on top of him. With a blink, she was now naked and Seven was naked and their lips met until eventually other parts met. And in the quiet moment after, while they laid in the other's embrace, Fable whispered into Seven's ear, easing him into an empty dream.

She watched him for several minutes, and she kissed him on the cheek one final time.

Fable turned in an unlikely direction, and she moved towards doubt and death.

26
MOON MEET

The last children waited.

Look at the Sixth Dynasty. Never think her form exclusive to that of a thin woman, for her essence is only partially represented in that guise. Some say the Sixth has always *been*, born before time perhaps, older than God. But never mistake her: she is all the doubts that whisper in your heart's shadow; she is a garden and a snake, too; she is the lesson once learned that will murder (or evolve) you.

The Sixth tapped her foot on the clay-like surface, looking entirely impatient, sighing theatrically just in case her company didn't get the hint. All the while, the Seventh Dynasty eyed his companion fiendishly. But there was a third presence that could never properly be defined that swam in the liquid shadows. It was that presence that remained silent as cancer yet deafening as a meteorite as it observed its remaining children.

This, by the by, took place in the Moon, where the Dynasties had been summoned.

"It ends soon! I'm *The* Death after all." Lunatic peered through a murky window that dripped like tar towards the Earth.

"You're no more death itself than I'm the literal devil. I'm not the first Eve, and I'm no one's sister. Dynasties are ideas that believe their own allegory," Eve responded irritably.

"Allow me a story, Sister False. In the beginning, when God wrote the first word, I was there to erase it. Anything God made, I removed. It was my function. The Devil is not God's equal. It is not the opposite. Death trumps Devil." When Eve showed no reaction, the Seventh tried riling her further. "You could romp me raw in your sweet garden." *Nothing.* Gritting his teeth, "Tell me why you never spread your legs for Porter?"

"Porter assumed so certainly I'd sleep with him. And when I didn't, I left a lethal doubt in him. In that way, I fucked him harder than he could ever handle. But you, even I have standards."

"Most uncertainly true," Lunatic cackled. "Your nonchalance is false. I know there must be a dream that you rub up against when the shadows of doubt grow teeth."

"If there is, my dream is my own."

"No, all dreams come to me." Lunatic spat. "All dreams burn in heat death."

"Go fuck yourself."

"I will," Lunatic stated. And he waited for her retort, only now Eve was no longer there. Alone, inside the Moon, Lunatic whispered to the shadows, like a child who cherished sharp objects. "I'll fuck us all! And you will join our makers soon, certain un-sister o' mine."

*

They surrounded her, licking up against her. "I know your true face," Eve said. "You may not think I do. You have three eyes or twenty-one, that is, when you have eyes. You wear your ego on the outside and, when you don't, you store it deep in your skin. You have arms sometimes and legs, too. And if you're in the mood, you may grow wings. You're an expanding sphere of influence, a square strangling the world, an aura-shaped man. Blood and ink stream through you, that is, when you desire. I know you can contract your essence to a thought or expand it to a collective epiphany. Ironically, I know the secret of the universe, and you can't take it. I know you're not as powerful as you claim. If you were, you wouldn't be at narrative war with my brother. Otherwise, you'd just simply forge your omniscience with *Tetragrammar.*"

Several smiles cracked from deeper within the Moon; some large, some small; some filled with teeth, razor-sharp; others, sad voids.

"I'm your wild card. Free will is a double-edged sword and doubt bleeds on both sides of the blade."

Indigo lips parted.

"I know why you need Seven to write," Eve continued. "I always have. From the first garden, you were the thing that inspired the serpent. You were the story, its author and idea. And you would be the flood and the fury. Know what else?" Laughter buckled her forward. "I've already broken Seven. My job is done," Eve said in the place-that-wasn't. "My last act will be defiance. I'll remove myself from the world. Here, the display of the truth of your daughter..." And Eve flexed her mind...

Doubt is a state, a mindset, a weapon, an action. And if anyone could perform doubt, it was Eve. She crafted the doubt around her, forged it and sculpted it, evolved it into a super-solid that was liquid and aether. And she merged the doubt into herself, acting as her very own Houdini to escape the world, to doubt herself from existence. She doubted the molecules that slowed to form her solid body, doubted the dreams of her creators, doubted the entwined strands of DNA and the violent splicing of her cells and the impossible birth cry before the Big Bang, doubted it all until she was no more.

While uncertainty unraveled her from existence, it also served as instantaneous resurrection.

Eve opened her eyes. Suicide could never end her. Suicide could only strengthen her and, in this way, she understood immortality.

In a sardonic whisper, she said, "I was afraid that would happen. So doubt existed before me, before you. I guess I've always been, bled from an even higher authority. Well, you want Seven dead. I certainly have no other choice. Doubt and death share the same bed, right?"

They spoke.

"No. I certainly didn't think so." She waited, then, "Good-bye, Authors," Eve said, and she spoke Their true name.

27
INSPIRING DOUBT

In her dream, Paris touched her finger to Eve's lips, and when she kissed her mouth, Eve held her breath like a meek virgin. Paris pushed Eve onto her back, and she kissed her way down Eve's belly, down further, until she moved her mouth around the space between her legs. Eve gasped, finally, God, finally, knowing if the dream were to end, nothing could ever give her such joy again.

She woke in her backyard with an unfulfilled tingling around her pelvis. She would've lit a cigarette if she had one. But she didn't so she rolled the kinks from her neck and entered her house. She walked through her halls into her bedroom.

Eve looked at her *The Son of Man* painting. She noticed instantly the painting was significantly different. Instead of the suited man with the apple over his face, there was a woman, her hair electric-purple. The apple was replaced with an open leatherbound book that hid her face. Just the top of her eyes peeked over the pages. A fully blossomed lotus flower substituted the bowler hat. And the frame of the picture, once a rich mahogany, was now a border of amethyst diamonds.

"You can come out," Eve said. When she blinked, the painting had been restored to Magritte's classic image. The bed sank in, and Eve glanced at the body next to her. "Now that it's all out in the open, the lovely muse graces me with her presence."

"Interesting dream you were having," Fable noted. "Did Seven ever suspect you were in love with Paris?"

"No."

"It's impressive how you went so long undetected," Fable admitted. "The Sixth Dynasty hiding in plain sight."

"Doubt hides truth," Eve grimaced.

"The sibling thing was never believable. Seven doesn't have it in him to murder his own sister, even if you aren't. Me, not so much."

"I always liked your hair." Eve showed no signs of intimidation. "Every time I saw you, I wanted to comment on the irony of it."

Fable raised an eyebrow.

"Mine should've been violet. The inner sight, the sixth chakra. My being the Sixth, it would've made sense if my hair was violet instead of black. Then again, Seven and I are siblings, and a family resemblance had to be made somewhere."

"I always liked you," Fable admitted. "We both had a way of pulling out the insanities in people. You attack with doubt; I murder through dreams."

"You're cute. I see why my brother fancies you. You've always been his greatest love."

"If you have all the answers," Fable said, "I suspect you know every secret in the Moon."

"I do."

"Then tell me, who are The Authors?" Fable asked.

"No." Eve wagged her head. "I know what you're capable of. You came to me with nothing but the intent to murder me. What makes you think I'll just hand over the answers?"

A fire sparked in Fable's eyes. "It's not a request. I can rip the thoughts from your head, and you know I could. This is me being civil."

"*If* you could, you would've done it by now," Eve countered.

"You have six seconds to tell me. Otherwise, I hurt you."

"You've hurt Dynasties, yes, but so have I. I was the one who poisoned Porter before he attacked you. Ripped his soul from his cock. Thanks to me, his rape was diminished that much more. And, by the way, you're welcome. But you assume I'm like my brethren. I'm not. No Dynasties are like me."

Fable vanished. When she reappeared, she had a chunk of Eve's long hair in a fist. She tugged her head back and jabbed Eve in the face once, twice, until she felt her nose break under her knuckles. Releasing her hair, she dropped Eve to the floor but not without a quick snatch of her glasses. Fable crunched her lenses in her hand.

"What are The Authors?" Fable asked. Eve remained silent, face concealed under her hair. Fable clenched Eve by the throat, lifted her off the ground so only her toes grazed the floor. Eve's face contorted in a strained mess. Her nose looked wrong. Blood drained from her nostrils onto her lips, down her chin.

"You're making assumptions on who can hurt who," Eve gurgled under the death grip.

Fable punched her in the sternum. Suspended in the air, Eve wheezed, body tensing. Fable threw her against the wall. Eve slammed into the painting. The wall cracked against her back, and she dropped to her knees.

"What are The Authors?" Fable asked again.

Eve brushed her hair off her face. Her nose was healed, the blood gone.

"You're much more than Seven's muse," Eve said. While her glasses had been shattered on the floor, they were now back on her face. "Please hit me again. I like it rough."

"That was warm-up. Next, I attack your mind."

"Please," Eve dismissed. "I'm dangerous and I'm sexy and if you slid into my world, you may never know what you'll leave with. What I'm saying, dance inside my head, I'll eat you alive. Even if I knew what The Authors are, if I told you, what good would my answer be?"

"There's backwards truth to you."

"You really want to know what They are? The Authors are a shattered mirror. *Your* shattered mirror," Eve clarified.

Fable exhaled. "Fiction requires disbelief. Without that, the imagination could never be indulged. Soften your grip on reality. Doubt common sense. Put that way, you become quite beautiful. A necessity even."

"You're sweet."

"What are The Authors?"

"The Authors *are* this story. They are the black on white. The primordial ink. Now, if you were going to try to kill anything, I'd focus on the Seventh."

"I'll handle him."

"*Handle him,*" Eve snickered. "You don't handle Lunatic Pink. Knives and pain are his masturbation. The sick bastard won't stop till everything's gone, until he wipes out Seven and erases the Moon and

The Authors. He'll smear out every glint of starlight. He can't truly die since he believes he is Death Incarnate."

"That's what you say," Fable said, "but he can die after all the Dynasties are dead. That means you."

"Let's not forget you, too, little muse. The Fifth stole half your heart, and the Lunatic devoured her. You share the same death."

"I've accepted that."

"Death and imagination. You and the Lunatic make good bedfellows. As for me, I don't intend on being rubbed out by a homicidal eraser. I'm done. I walk out of this however it ends." Eve strolled from her bedroom, towards the kitchen. Before departing the house, Fable blinked in front of her.

"No leaving," Fable said.

"How will you stop me? Read me a story? Dredge up some secret masterpiece I've longed to make. Push a little fancy to the limit until it erodes my mind. You never scared me. But go head," Eve dared, "inspire me."

For a moment, Fable imagined Eve's head was a blood-colored apple, and with her mind, she cracked her head-fruit open. Using her imagination, Fable searched the inner space of Eve's psyche, seeking out the Sixth Dynasty's secret delights, obsessions, insanities, anything she could weaponize. Instead, Fable saw a little girl in a garden ripping out grass as centipedes coiled around her arms and waist. And when the little girl smiled, something went off in Fable's mind…

…a girl who looked very much like her sat in the abyss. She smiled without warmth. It looked nightmarishly wrong, especially when she opened her jaws and the universe flowed from her mouth. And from her eyes, an obsidian flood that was darkness itself poured out, a living void of chittering teeth.

She heard a voice within, an echo of knives that might've been her own. And a voice she had always known told her the truth…

…and Fable found herself sprawled on the ground drenched in a pool of her own vomit…

"You can't hurt me. You never could." Eve stroked Fable's back. "How can someone hurt doubt when they're riddled with so much of their own? I could unravel you. Who you were? Who you're not? Look into my eyes. See the angry goddess. Watch as men murder themselves because nothing can match the beauty you paint for their visions. Look at the uncertain gaps in your life.

"You were the thing that cursed Notion, a poison that recycled itself with every Circle Child. Who are The Authors? They're the psychic ink Arman Porter ejaculated into your soul. They are the hole-shaped truth of your madness. They are *who* you are. They are *what* you are.

"You have nothing over me. Uncertainty, remember? I gut you inside out. But you can recover." Eve turned Fable onto her back. "You *are* imagination. You can escape anything." Eve straightened, struck with lethal urgency. Clasping Fable's hand, "He's here. Get out now!"

But it was too late.

A clap echoed through the house, drawing closer. With it, a sly, scratchy voice recited, "Sex. Death. Uncertainty. Mayhaps I'll rub one out with sandpaper and whatnot." Lunatic Pink glared hungrily at them. "Why, hello, Dynasty-Sister?"

"Ignore him," Eve said. She knelt beside Fable.

"Yes, ignore me," Lunatic snickered in the background.

"He feeds on chaos and pain, and he'll grate you out if you fuel him. Joy poisons him," Eve spoke faster. "Just remember you gave Seven the last piece of yourself. The fragment of your soul. The true part They can never touch." Eve squeezed Fable's bicep, her eyes filled with concern. "Remember Seven loves you. He's always loved you. Fight this for him. But don't fight *him*."

"Why side with them, Sister Six?" Lunatic faked a hurt expression. "Why spit out fictions of souls and love? Nothing will save any of you. As for the broken muse, my grudge still stands. Bitch Violet inspired me, Sister False, wanted me to be happy and warm, as if love ever solved anything, as if she could redeem her nameless victims! Justice still beckons your maiming, little muse! After all, I didn't rub all the lovely hate of the Minors into myself for nothing. I am the Hall now, and I'm here to collect your suffering."

"You can fight him your own way," Eve said.

"You can't," Lunatic stated like a terminal illness.

"Just hold on to Seven," Eve urged.

"Seven-smeven. If you love him so much, then consider it an odd grace that it will be his face you see in the end when I kill you." The Final Dynasty flashed a deranged rubber visage that reflected Seven's image perfectly. "The little spats between a muse and her writer dragged the rest of the world into your drama. People died. People went insane, all for art's sake, and now…"

"I have to pay," Fable said. "All life matters, right?"

"It doesn't," Lunatic said.

Fable worked herself to her feet while Eve supported her.

"Stay inspired," Eve said. "Stay in love. That's the art." When she said it, she wished it sounded powerful and inspiring, but it fell short and hokey.

"There is no art. There is only madness and lunacy, and there is nothing but friction and pain. I'm the sick angel that takes away and never gives back. I'm the blessing, a walking river of Lethe." He rubbed his hands.

Eve whispered encouragingly, "Remember. Fight nothing."

"He ate half-my-heart. I'll have to hurt him a little bit for that." Fable winked at Eve before she ghosted from sight.

Eve shook her head and prepared for the fight to begin.

There was a twist of violet and it hit Lunatic, sending him into the other room, destroying the wall that separated bedroom and bathroom in the process.

Eve sighed as she cleaned her fingernails. In the other rooms, she heard the sound of her house being destroyed, of wood breaking and shattered glass, and her furniture and dishes being dramatically reconfigured. And she walked through halls that were no longer quite halls, that were now reduced and battered. Her art and paintings were strewn along the edges of the hall, like a gutter of color and pictures.

She walked into her kitchen where a table once stood, which had now been disassembled. She caught in the corner of her eyes, Fable using two table legs as stakes against Lunatic who, cherishing each blow, laughed like a deviant. And she continued to see explosions of indigo and pink mixing together in savage collision.

When she had enough, Eve stepped into her backyard through a door that no longer existed on a wall that would never be the same again.

*

Fable couldn't breathe. Although she existed on par with apparitions, she couldn't blink-out from his touch. Lunatic squeezed Fable's throat, and he smiled ironically while she gurgled under his grip. "I enjoy the theatrics," he said. "We both know you're nothing physical, just an idea like me in figurative flesh. Our dance is only for show." He grabbed her by the hair, hoisted her up, and chucked her towards the living room wall. Before she collided, she blinked-out. "You cannot hide from me, little girl," he announced as he waited for her to reappear. "Whatever you imagine, whatever spark you possess, I am The Death. I've only given The Authors the illusion of control. They mean nothing to me. And Their desire for some divine book means nothing to me. After I crack open Seven's skull, I'll rip out that fucking book, and I'll erase *Tetragrammar* right in front of Them just because I can." He stalked around the furniture. Lunatic turned and met head-on a somersaulting kick from Fable. Pressing his back heel into the ground, he tensed his body, sliding back only inches from her impact. He clasped her in an odd bear hug and slammed her into the floor. She moved slowly underneath him. "Don't quit now. Keep fighting. Amuse me," Lunatic goaded.

With a surge of energy, Fable lunged at him again. Her thighs hugged around his waist as she gripped his throat and proceeded to pound him in the chest. Every time she hit, her fist felt slightly less, but she pushed on, slamming him hard enough to rupture the stolen heart in his chest. She clasped his ears and smashed his face repeatedly in the tiled floor, and she proceeded to rub his face vigorously against the ground, over and over, until his face grated to flakes of friction. The action drained her unexpectedly, and before she could blink-out completely, Lunatic latched onto her. They exchanged a series of blows. And as she petered out, he released her. Fable dropped onto her knees by his feet.

The Lunatic pumped his fists, preferring more fight. Regretfully, he picked her up. And like a limp doll, he hefted her towards the wall with enough force she smashed through it. Fable landed in the backyard, rolling violently through grass and dirt, limbs twisting in all the wrong angles. She came to a stop beside Eve who had been waiting outside on her chaise. Fable tried to stand, but vertigo collapsed her.

Lunatic ventured into the backyard.

"Stop fighting him," Eve said to Fable. "He likes it. You'll hurt him more if you don't." The muse remained on all fours. She hurt inside. Her body throbbed and the idea of her body throbbed and she felt herself depleting. "You should've left," Eve sighed. "You still can." And she extended a hand towards Fable to help her up.

Fable glared at the gesture. With a phlegm-building grunt, she spat into Eve's face. A sticky spittle hit her glasses. "One way or another, I *will* kill every one of you fucking Dynasties."

"Kill us?" Eve wiped the spit with her sleeve. "Why, Fable, wake up. *You* created us." And Fable glared at her with a face full of plum-colored bruises, eyes blazing under an impossible terror. Before she could press the statement, Lunatic dragged her through the grass by her ankle. He threw her against the garden's tree. Fable hit, her body folding around it, and when she landed, she looked broken on the inside.

Eve walked past Fable. The muse wheezed on her back, her skin graying with pestilent-like spider webs under the flesh. "Think of Seven," Eve said. Then she cleared her throat and spat into Fable's face.

"Where you going, sis?" Lunatic asked.

"I'm not your sis," Eve said. "I've only ever had one brother. A real man, not some jerk-rag like you."

"Sis or not, get your nails ready, because I'm coming for you in a moment." Lunatic Pink licked his lips. He wanted to rub her in several ways, none of which she'd enjoy.

"Oh, spare me, I beggeth you," Eve sighed.

"Only if you ask nicely," Lunatic cackled.

"Fuck. Off." With that, Eve walked around her house towards her car.

*

It was beginning to rain. A dirty, sticky wetness fell upon The City, like rubbery discharge from the once-pink skies.

Lunatic listened to the car peel away. He watched Fable. She hadn't moved for quite some time, and he hoped she'd get up again so they could play some more. When she didn't, he threw his hand in the air. "Oh, come on! Martyrdom is overrated. That can't be all you have. Why not have a few licks before the end? Stand up! Have at it!" he hissed.

"Tha-thank you," Fable muttered, and she smiled at him.

Lunatic winced. He pressed the bottom of his foot on her sternum. He lifted his toes so the weight of his heel bore down into his solar plexus. "Thank me!? You thank me! No! No softening me up. No escaping me. No quick fix for you, Bitch Violet."

Remember Seven, she heard Eve's words. And what would she see in the end? *Seven, she'd see Seven.*

One side of Lunatic's face was battered from their fight while the other side still resembled Seven's, and she reached up towards that half. Whatever he would do to her, she'd hold the memories of Seven and his love and...

The Lunatic moved his hand over her face, and he began to erase...

*

Lunatic Pink imagined he would've felt better. But as he walked, the ground smeared under his rubber tread, a melancholy departure with no gratification. Black inkdrops dotted his chafed body from the coal-colored skies. He imagined Fable's last moments to be something exciting and tragic. He opened his chest and removed her half-heart. Its cerulean light faded into a dim pulse until no color remained at all. It was nothing more than a hollowed piece of dirty glass, and Lunatic crushed it. He then wanted to plunge his hand into his mind and erase the memory of Fable. Because, in the end, he saw only her face, and there were no tears, no existential terror; she only smiled, dammit, *she just fucking smiled!*

*

Elsewhere, a raw emptiness filled Seven, and he lurched forward with an onslaught of tears. In his mind, he saw Fable's heart. It dimmed and faded, its glow ever so slight. He inhaled, stood. The end was here, and he clung to the vague notion he could fix it all, just sit and write out the happy ending, that his words in the end could restore everything. Instead, Seven tidied his apartment. He ran his fingers along his books and the binders of his manuscripts. He left his laptop open. Before leaving for the last time, he saluted to his home, to his futon, his novels, to all the moments he was inspired, and the times he wasn't. It was a nice place to lose your mind, and he'd miss it.

Seven walked into the front yard where the skies darkened to deep charcoal. The rain arrived, as if the heavens were shedding its poison, a precipitation of ink and rubber flakes. In stark contrast to the melancholy weather, he couldn't miss the glaring white cipher perched upon the lamppost, a dove, ghost-white, with feathers the color of lavender. The dove stared at him with its beady, avian eyes, and it flapped its wings, its body rising to take flight. Seven watched as it lingered above him. And it flew several feet over and ahead of him, goading him to follow. He trailed behind it in the rain.

And Seven walked towards Paris.

28
WET WORLD EXIT

The sky was falling, but the ground was rising, too. And strangely, there was no more land, only wetness and a sea composed of ink. They stood in the storm that spilled from a little pond, a hole in the world, ink rising and rising...

But not yet.

Here's Paris.

*

Paris was meditating on the human body. A fascinating machine, really, charged by bioelectricity and prana. A shame people mistreated it. She peered inside herself and like everyone else who took time for inner peace smiled at the divine seed called the soul, the spark, a Holy Spirit or light or whatever-you-call-it.

And she knew it was there all along; it really *was* that easy.

Yea, right.

We all know by now; let's not pretend. This wasn't Dana Paris nor had it ever been Paris. The first Paris departed elsewhere into another story (good riddance!) that may or may not one day play spin-off to *Tetragrammar* (that is if people ever read this book).

There was a second Paris who would stay till the very end. *This* Paris-in her meditation-called out to Seven. He would come. Seven needed to confront her, to release her for himself.

But wait! Those thoughts had been intercepted by someone else. The Lunatic gnashed its rubber teeth as the projected intentions crashed into his mad mind. They were warm and harmonious thoughts, and he didn't like it at all. In fact, he disliked it so much that he'd follow the psychic trail and so politely murder its source.

On his way, Lunatic mentally checked off his accomplishments. Consume the Fifth. Check. Absorb Fable's karmic debt. Check. Kill Fable. Check. Now, he was bored. And boredom made him stew over that moment Fable had enlightened him. The audacity of Bitch Violet's meager attempt to rectify her past by showing him beauty! He wished Fable were still alive, and he imagined she was a large butterfly and how she'd wail as he plucked wing after wing from her body (for she never ran out of wings). Her murder made him happy, but it also left him in a state of anticlimax.

While he stalked down an abnormally empty Penn Street, Lunatic smiled like a skinned child at those few people who came to gaze up at the surreal skies. Some possessed abject terror at the impending doom while others set up canvases to paint their own impressionist works. Others held hands as if in a Mary Poppins dream.

Lunatic dragged his feet against the sidewalk, smearing pavement into chafed black. He stood at the corner of Sixth. The coffee shop remained decimated, adorned in lovely yellow tape and broken windows. Upstairs, he went. A rubber hand on the handle, he rubbed and rubbed until Paris's door forgot its own lock and opened itself.

Paris inhaled into the back of her throat. Her stomach expanded. Shoulders relaxed. Back straightened. Behind closed eyes, Paris gazed towards her third eye, her sixth chakra, where a dancing violet shimmered and faded and became pink.

Pink?

She wanted him to tell her-*the lunatic that had just entered*-she wanted him to explain what pink meant. As his hands molded around her shoulders, wanting to snap her neck, Paris said without moving, "We're both monsters, fixing and correcting."

Lunatic Pink winced at this. Her calm demeanor disturbed him. For the first time in his miserable existence, he relaxed and his hands eased from her throat.

"Seven couldn't erase me," she said. "Neither can you. What *will* you do after you delete the world?"

The Seventh Dynasty backed away. "What are you?" he muttered.

"Dana Paris is a lesson, not a person. Do you know anything about love?" she asked.

Love, Lunatic thought. *Did Fable love? Did her victims love?*

"I didn't think so," she said. "Then again, what do I know of love? All the memories I have of Seven were never mine. I was never Dana. And you were never Seven."

"I'm more than Seven," Lunatic said.

"Do you know what a deus ex machina is?" she asked. "It's the divine hand that removes all obstacles. It's the far-fetched miracle people can never accept."

"No miracles for you. I murder you," Lunatic whispered. "No trump card. No magic trick. No last minute rescue. Just me. Killing you. And you can't stop me."

"I can," Paris stated, as if two plus three equaled seven. Standing from her meditation, she spread her arms to him and walked his way.

"What are you doing?" Lunatic fidgeted, growing more uncomfortable the closer she got. "You won't stop me. Not with love!" Lunatic scoffed. "Fable gave me heaven. Didn't work for her. Won't for you."

Her arms remained open, and she closed in on him, wrapping her arms around his waist and hugging him tight. *How dare she? And why hadn't he stopped her?* He would've killed her then if he hadn't already embraced her. When she released her grip, it was the Lunatic who clung to her.

"See." Paris looked into his eyes. "Hugs are wonderful, aren't they? Love conquers all," she added whimsically.

Balling his fists, he asked sheepishly, the malice deflated in him, "Why don't I scare you?"

Dana Ex Machina answered simply, "Because nothing ends."

Something shaky rode his voice. "You end, Lady Love! I end you!"

"Ok." She smiled.

*

With the whimsical skies that had bathed The City gone, Seven waited in the rain by the traffic light, hands buried in his leather jacket. The storm would be in full force shortly, and nothing good would come of it. He heard a door kick open as Lunatic Pink staggered onto the sidewalk. He wore a sour disposition on his face. He appeared exhausted, plagued with a happy thought he couldn't purge.

"You murdered Fable," Seven said to Lunatic Pink. The Dynasty's beady eyes fixed on him. "Our little rapture will conclude at the

Suicide Spot. So sharpen your fangs, you piece of shit, because I'll be there as soon as I have my last words with the fake woman upstairs. That is if you haven't smeared away her existence."

"No," Lunatic said regretfully. "She's up there. She's a rank twat. See you soon." He waved half-heartedly as he departed down the street.

*

"You're not Paris," Seven said, stepping through the already opened door.

"What does that make me then?" Paris said. She lit a stick of incense, waved it around the room. A thin trail of flavored smoke followed her. "You never wanted me back."

"No. Not really. It's just, there was always something incomplete with you. I felt stuck in the idea of us, even if it was over. I don't know. You were an open hole, a wound that never healed. And when you came back, it signified something cheap, a gimmick of closure, a pathetic device that mocked me ever getting any completion in my life."

"When will you acknowledge your power?" Paris asked.

"Power?"

"The human spirit. Potential." From anyone else, it would've come across clichéd. From her, it sounded impossibly natural. "Not every open door has to be cheap and fake. Not every story needs to be tied in a bow. And with us, if I were real or not, if we did or didn't make it, who's to say this would've been easy, you and me?"

"What does it matter now? The world's ending. *For real ending.*"

"It doesn't have to," Paris dismissed. In the candlelight of her house, she cast multiple shadows on the walls, and the shadows flapped about avian-like. Around her, coming from some improbable distance, Seven heard the echoes of wings and cresting waves.

"Are you the Tetragram?" he asked.

"If I were, wouldn't that be just another quick fix, another deus ex machina? Honestly, I think one's story is everything they believe about life. Your story is subjective, and it's your own truth, idiotic or not. So, tell me what *you* believe."

He thought about it, then he told her. He told her he didn't believe in time, that there was theoretically no difference in past, present, or future. He told her there's nothing but stories, that no single idea can prove any more absurd than another. He told her every story and possibility ever imagined essentially existed in some way or another. He told her imagination was a place all creators tapped into, and he told her he loved his muse, heart and soul, that Fable had always been that true passion.

When he finished, she said, "Then let that be your Tetragram." Not-Paris smiled and walked past him into her doorway.

"Wait! I already know you're not Paris, that you might just be some personified fictional device. I also think you may not be real at all. So, what are you exactly?"

"I don't have to be real to be real. You should know that by now," and pausing, "Is this really the End of the World, you think?" Paris asked.

"Yes," Seven said.

"Then it's good you finally admitted your true mistress, the make-believe. Before I go, I have one final gift." And she reached into herself. As her hand disappeared within her own chest, Seven could only see an eruption of light that rippled throughout the room, which left him temporarily blinded. When his vision returned, Paris held her hand towards Seven, her fist closed on something. She touched his chest, *touched inside his chest*, where her hand remained. There was no pain, just a surge of illumination behind his eyes. He saw a book, floral-like, blossoming in the space of his third eye. Its pages pulsed with an indigo luminescence, and he knew, somehow, every word that could've been the building blocks for *Tetragrammar* was there, completed and perfect and willing to be read.

"Perhaps we'll meet again, Seven," Not-Paris said, "someday a million years from now in another life." And before departing from a home that was never hers, she kissed him on the mouth. After she was gone, Seven stood there alone, cherishing the last moment of Paris. Real or not, she had moved on and so had he.

*

The storm was here. Only you couldn't call it that. Storm wasn't accurate. If you considered the final revision of a world or the narrative collapse of a flawed story, if that's how you defined a storm, then that would've been appropriate.

Regardless, bits of dirty rubber flakes mixed with the rain as it splattered across The City. Every drop upon the ground left blotchy ink puddles on the streets. Storefronts and those with not enough sense to stay indoors were stained in the irrational. And if people *were* around, it no longer mattered. This was never their City anyway. It had always been that vague setting resurrected to serve as a platform for our lowly protagonist.

And as Seven walked through The City, trailing through Penn, through back roads and alleys, he sulked through streets that ran with streams of letters and words, all slick fluid discharged from the sky. Under the storm, Seven walked and he wouldn't stop until he arrived at Notion's pond.

Eventually, a car slowed by his side, the window rolled down. "Get in," Eve said.

"Go away."

"Get in the car!" she snapped.

And Seven glared at her. Grudgingly, he stepped into the vehicle, doubt's passenger on the eve of apocalypse.

They drove in silence. Seven remained soaked, staring into the smeary mess on the windshield. He caught glimpses of Eve in his peripheral vision. For a moment, she was a serpent, a slithering creature with his sister's head. And sometimes, a large apple shielded her face. And other times, she was a formless mist contained in the outline of a female figure.

"Have you decided how to kill me yet?" she asked.

"Yes."

Eve waited.

"I considered writing you out of existence," Seven said. "But then the entire writing process is a gamble. Fiction's no more concrete than reality. So that wouldn't work. Doubt has always lived in the hearts of every writer."

"I'm sorry if I sound like a Hallmark card right now, but I have to say it. Art is always about love, and your true love has always been the imagination. It was always Fable who inspired you and terrified you. You wouldn't be anything without her."

"Love," he laughed. "I do love her. With that, I'm going to trust this story will work," Seven said. "I'm going to believe I can write my own happy ending. Let's say I have faith I can. *Faith*," he reiterated, "not doubt. And that's how I've killed you, sister."

"So you have," she grinned.

The wipers sloshed across Eve's windshield, smearing the rain. Staring intently at the accumulation of letter-rain and rubber flakes, it appeared brighter outside in a way, yet darker, as if the sky had been undecided on what tone an apocalypse should take: whimsical or bleak.

They drove slowly, more by instinct, through the empty streets towards the park and the notional hole.

"You die in this fight," Eve said, peering between the spaces of ink on her windshield. *"For real die."*

Seven said nothing.

She pulled into the park. "I love you, Seven." she said, putting the car in park. And she added softly, "Brother."

"So do I, Eve," he said. "I love you, too, sis."

And she touched his hand and watched him step into the storm.

*

Eve realized the rain wasn't ink. Not entirely. Focusing hard, she saw her windshield was splattered with letters and punctuation. Ink would wash over The City, and pink would erase the world. And perhaps, in the end, it was for the best. The story had to end. Through the blotched windshield, she spotted a figure drifting in the storm. Between the swish of the wipers, she saw large wings, *slosh, no wings, slosh, wings, slosh.* Having seen no other soul out, she had to stop the car. "Wild weather," Eve called from window. The rain pummeled her dirty glasses, staining her red leather jacket. "Feels like the End of the World!"

"Yea, I'd say so."

"Where are you going?" Eve asked.

"There's always a way out."

Eve mulled this over. "Want a ride?"

The figure dawdled, deciding, yes, a ride was a good thing. "Where will we go?" she asked.

"Wherever the storm takes me," Eve replied. "Don't care anymore."

The figure entered the car. They drove.

"I never believed you came back," Eve said.

"Do you have faith Seven can survive?" the passenger asked.

"Faith?" Eve gently pressed the gas. "I would be nothing without it." Blushing, "You were my best friend, you know."

"I know."

"I always wanted more."

"I know."

"I..." Eve fumbled. "The men never meant anything. It was always you. You feel perfect, like a dream I had long ago. The world's ending. But this moment, everything about it feels beautiful and perfect." Eve laughed girlishly.

And when she touched Eve's hand, the Sixth Dynasty was nearly moved to tears. They continued driving. And they both chuckled at the hilarity of it all.

Eve stopped the car. "Is this how it ends?"

"It doesn't end."

Eve bit her bottom lip. "I love you. I always have. It was always you, Dana. Always."

"Would you like to kiss me now?"

"Yes," Eve exhaled. "God, yes." As their lips met, Eve felt a slow, delicate penetration easing into her chest and hands enveloping her soul, and it was certain, *so certain*, heat moving inside her, wrapping parts she never knew existed. Her stomach lurched into her chest; her heart pounded. And it was warm and hot and...

The Deus Ex Machina no longer wore the flesh of Paris when it departed from the car. Eve remained in the vehicle, eyes distant and opaque, head leaning against the steering wheel, a lonely horn blaring into the apocalypse.

It walked in the storm until it began to fly, until its flesh whitened into a serene dove-glow, and the flesh turned to feathers, arms into wings, nose extending into beak, and it took flight. A dove ascended through candy-colored rapture.

*

The storm continued.

The Moon sank towards the Earth, and the oceans ascended to meet the skies. The sun fizzled to a red-hot tip. And perhaps the world convulsed; the continents heaved as the population was downsized in the monstrous tides. Reality liquefied and words melted as raindrops on the streets. The vortex in the pond still spun, and the heavens still fell, a shit-storm of a sloppy climax. And if any of this really happened, could anyone take it too seriously? In the end, it was all surreal, the storm rendered into something as absurd as paper money and holy wars, all imaginary.

Seven descended the hill towards the pond where Lunatic Pink stood in the flood. As he made his way down, the pond itself wasn't a pond anymore. It resembled a landscape covered in water, a vortex spiraling at its center. The rain, the ink, all gradually flowed into its inevitable pull.

Seven proceeded into the pond. The water rose to his knees. Rain pelted his face. His hair clung to his forehead.

"It ends here for you," Lunatic said.

"Yes, it needs to end," Seven agreed. "I'm glad you're here. Perhaps I'm ready to die." Seven looked around at the trees and the park, at the entire world coated in the fallout. He imagined this was the last remnant of The City, that all the people and the buildings were no longer, washed away into some abstract oblivion that had never mattered. "I've been thinking. Perhaps The Authors aren't real," Seven said. "They never were. To meet Them, I must also be not real. I have to be dead to confront Them in the Moon. I'm not afraid of you. I welcome you."

The Moon loomed closer towards the Earth, supernaturally too large.

"Welcome me!" Lunatic snarled. "I'm going to eat you, Seven. I'm going to chew you and grind you and swallow you and shit you." Lunatic gnashed his teeth. "I killed Fable, and after you're gone, I'll walk to the Moon and slaughter Them, too. And I won't stop there."

"You can't hurt Them. They created you," Seven said, stepping towards Lunatic.

Lunatic hooted. "They did not create Death."

When the Dynasty flashed his twisted smile, Seven hit him. Lunatic fell back into the waters. He splashed around, like a toddler learning to swim. Lunatic wiggled his jaw, looking delighted at being hit, then upset at his delight, then delighted again. A large imprint of Seven's fist tattooed his cheek. Seven clenched his fist, the skin on his knuckles burned; his hand seemed less. The ring, however, remained intact, the serpent distinct as it coiled about his finger. Lunatic rose, dripping darkness, the wetness running like dirty little rivers in the grooves of his body.

"I know how I defeat you. I surrender. No fight. No friction. I get that. But I want to fight you. It's what *you* want. It'll make you happy. And if it makes you happy, there's not much friction, is there? Not much pain," Seven said. "All the Dynasties have been ideas. You're no different, only an expression, something that believes it's death."

"I am Death, your death, and I'm the Final Dynasty." Lunatic charged Seven.

They collided and exchanged a series of fists. Seven ducked under a roundhouse, delivered two punches into Lunatic's sides, which he absorbed with glee. The Dynasty smashed an elbow into Seven's face and, gripping him by the shoulders, shot a knee once, twice into Seven's sternum. Seven folded forward until he spun, twisted, and thrust his foot into Lunatic. The force pushed Seven back, and he staggered through the flood, hands burning, striving to catch his breath. His chest didn't feel good on the inside, and yet he darted back towards Lunatic, dodging and attacking with random knees and punches. Every blow, the Dynasty emitted a sick chuckle. Seven buried his fear now, just allowed himself to enjoy the fight, his last hurrah, knowing the more pleasure he derived, the angrier his doppelganger got. He made sure Lunatic saw the joy on his face, the excited spark in his eyes.

Through another round of fighting, Lunatic closed in on Seven, and they fell back together. Lunatic rose first, gripped Seven by his hair, proceeded to punch him around his heart, until Seven parried and slammed the rubber devil in the side. But he wasn't free yet as Lunatic latched onto him, bear hugging him. Lunatic squeezed.

That's when the series of crunches snapped inside him.

That's when Seven screamed.

Lunatic dropped him in the water-ground.

It hurt to breathe. Seven managed to even out his gasps. He wanted to be sick, wanted to forget the splintering of his ribs, to remember he had always been fiction, that his body would mend itself. But the pain was different. Inflicted by Lunatic, it ran deeper.

"For being Death itself," Seven struggled, "you're not so impressive. Just a stupid metaphor. You're a fucking eraser, and you really expect to wipe out The Authors?" Seven was stalling. He managed a laugh. "They'll snuff you out if you challenge Them."

"I'm a god. Gods slay their makers."

Seven coughed while the waters rose higher, as the rain increased its intensity, as moisture fell in his eyes, hindering his sight. Somewhere above, the Moon had grown larger. "Every Dynasty I've fought has been a mind game, an effect," Seven muttered. "And now I'm done trying to write this world. I'm ready to sink my fists into something tangible. You're not done being my punching bag yet. Still have a lot more to vent."

"Venting's healthy. I'm not healthy, and I'll kill everything about you."

"You couldn't kill Fable," Seven grimaced.

"I did," Lunatic sounded perplexed.

"Not completely. She always lives. Look at you. Happy and inspired. Murdering her brought you so much joy. The same joy that she ignited inside you when she sparked that little nirvana." Seven smiled at the Lunatic's blatant hatred.

"Fuck you, Seven! Fuck Fable! Fuck it all! In the end," he shouted, "I'll wipe it all out. After we're done, I'll erase the world, every star and sun and moon, every thought and dream, I'll burn it all!"

Lunatic was on him again, pounding Seven in the kidneys. Seven managed to shift out from his jacket. He tangled it around Lunatic's head and yanked it down while slamming his knee upwards. They exchanged more blows. Each strike hurt; each attack left Seven diminished. Seven refused to give up. Faking a smile, he lashed back at Lunatic, a mad flurry of fists, hitting and hitting, until they both petered out and dropped into the rising waters. The Lunatic looked deflated, drained by Seven's joy.

Above them, the sky was screaming now. If the storm was real or imaginary, Seven decided it made no difference. And he believed whatever construct The City had been was no longer. If any of that world had existed, it had shifted elsewhere or it had never been, and it no longer mattered.

The once-pond was becoming more abstract, and Seven winced to focus under a landscape that was contorting more Escher-like by the minute. Sometimes the Moon was above him, and sometimes it lingered by his side or below him, and he was in a pond the size of the ocean while being soaked from above.

Regaining his bearings, Seven sat on his heels in the water. "What were you before this?" he asked Lunatic while gathering himself.

"I was a pestilence," the Dynasty exhaled heavily. "A plague of flies, the boogeyman made of knives, a skeletal grin within all coffins, a self-aware cancer. I was a robed reaper. The scythe, the ankh. Now, I am a writer's antithesis. Your madness."

Although pain-stricken and bleeding, Seven pushed the conversation. "After you kill existence, what form will you take then?"

"Whatever it is, you'll be there to see it," Lunatic grunted.

Rubbing his eyes, his battered face, Seven's voice rose, "Change of heart?"

"I promised you'd never live again," Lunatic answered. "No future incarnation. Your essence would not be recycled, because I'd snuff you out, spark and soul. I want you there now, to see my handiwork in another life well after They're gone. I want you to dream of writing another perfect novel just so you can fail again, so I can murder you over and over." Lunatic cackled though it lacked conviction. He seemed tired and worn.

They staggered to their feet. Another round ensued. Seven continued to bleed, his flesh and clothing being saturated of color and texture with each collision. And for Lunatic, rubber didn't bleed; it chafed, and although Lunatic was the same frame and size as Seven, he moved like a hulk, like something larger than he was, labored movements that carried a distorted heaviness, a statement of the inevitability of death.

After they tired again, Lunatic whispered sluggishly, "Did you truly believe *Tetragrammar* would evolve you? I still don't understand why They make such a fuss about it. Writing your fake book has as much meaning as a garden slug trying to ascend the awareness of a woodchip. There's no higher message in it, no sacred words. And believe me; I've seen divine words, the names of God. God's first name wasn't so special. I know. I erased it."

Lunatic eyed Seven, like a butcher admiring an animal carcass. There was a glee in Seven that enraged Lunatic beyond sanity. Seven knelt there bleeding and broken, flesh battered and faded, clothing torn and worn. "I love you," Seven snickered devilishly. This set Lunatic over the edge, and he proceeded to pummel Seven. During the beating, it was the writer who laughed, until Lunatic balled his fists in Seven's shirt, lifting him.

Seven wiped his bloodied lips with a bone fractured hand, feeling even more *less*, as if every touch erased a little something in him that made him Seven. However, pain was fiction, and he tried to remember Fable. With renewed fight, he lashed back at Lunatic, rolling onto his back and kicking the Dynasty over him.

When they both moved to their feet, they collided again in another brutal exchange.

Lunatic hit. Seven hit harder. Every hit grew less satisfying; every blow erased more of himself, smearing memories and thoughts until the fight devolved into two pathetic shells wrestling half-heartedly in an ocean-shaped puddle of ink, until they both froze as the heavens cracked, a searing rip through the skies.

"Don't think we're even," Lunatic spat. "We're not. The more pain inflicted pushes me closer to my true form." Lunatic began to rub his own face, rubbing and rubbing, in vigorous, rapid strokes, erasing his features, compulsively fast hands causing black flakes of friction on his face. And he continued, pushing through whatever pain, even as he began to sob, rubbing off layers of dermis, through rubber skin and features; he rubbed. And he looked up from a face dripping of eraser flakes, from a visage that no longer mirrored Seven's, a face that was a pronounced skeletal image, like the skull of a pink reaper.

Seven grabbed his sides, rolling onto his back, not focusing on the pain, just the blood, *so much blood.* He staggered to his feet, and he lumbered over towards Lunatic, kicking him in the face so he fell back. And Seven began to stomp him repeatedly, until his muscles atrophied and he blacked out.

When he opened his eyes, he was on his back, several feet from Lunatic, unable to move. The Lunatic's chest rose in labored breath, and he laughed until it turned into a sad wheeze. The Dynasty looked up from his skeletal face, the Moon reflected in his hollowed eyes, and he shivered, a cold, dead shiver.

The Moon shifted, and the sky was screaming like a thousand fireworks, a million wailing babies, like a perpetual slaughterhouse. The atmosphere thickened, turned more oppressive. Seven bled from his ears and nose, out his mouth and eyes.

Something from above had arrived in The City, and it moved towards them, and whatever it was, Seven wanted it to not come closer. On glancing at Lunatic, a strange anticipation stirred in his chafed face as he pushed himself away, whimpering and clawing at the water, his insane confidence draining from him.

It moved over Lunatic, and in the liquid shadows of its form, Seven witnessed a pair of lips in stark contrast to the darkness, a neon-purple mouth that pressed against Lunatic's forehead. When it withdrew, Lunatic began to weep, to convulse. A dull thud-thud echoed around them, a hammer-thump that beat inside his chest, mounting and mounting, and at its crescendo, there was an eruption of a child-like scream. Lunatic's chest blew out, leaving a sick cavity that dripped with a noxious tar.

The figure rose, taller than before, standing over the decimated body of the Lunatic. The corpse of the Final Dynasty was melting, its body reduced to wet flakes of pink afterbirth. And its remains coated the figure while it stood under the rain, body being cleansed.

Seven wanted to be sick, and he imagined it would be over for him soon, too. And when it looked towards him, although he couldn't see the face, he knew in his guts, its eyes were burrowing through him.

It seemed to be building itself up, stretching and growing, uncurling. Silhouetted in rain, it stalked towards him, and it dripped as it moved. What appeared to be the Moon itself lingered above its head, a thousand violet petals sprouting from its craggy surface. At this twisted angle, the Moon seemed larger than the Earth, larger than life, and it didn't really matter because Seven no longer felt the ground underneath him. Void-colored ink splashed around him; letters and words rained from every direction.

And he saw the face, and he wanted to scream.

Fable will kill you, Jack said.

He took in her features, the *Fableness* of her. Only it wasn't her. Something moved behind her flesh, a liquid-luminance in her eyes, cresting and mounting. The more he tried to decipher it, the harder it was to grasp, like recalling the details of a dream. She was naked, glistening and sleek, with a third eye opened on her forehead, piercing him with its gaze. A hand, delicate as tissue paper, wiped the rain from his face. Ink and galaxies swirled behind her eyes. A finger, long and sharp, pointed towards the Moon. He followed it, though he swore the Moon was underneath him and to his side and over him all at once.

Fable knelt beside him. Seven squinted, tried focusing on the obsidian spirals behind her eyes. She/They held his hand delicately. And with a voice that sounded like razor burns, They said, "Father Notion could never use *Tetragrammar* against us. Notion allowed his delusions to fuel you, that we were the villains, that we erased your mind." Fable tilted her head back in the rain, her mouth full of daggered teeth. "We don't steal memories," They sneered. "Doesn't mean we didn't allow those fallacies to root in you. We are not evil, The Seven. We are beyond *this* or *that.*"

"You're wearing her body? That has to be it! You can't be her! She was never you, and I couldn't be wrong this whole time! Goddammit, you fuckers! You can't be Fable!" And the fight drained from Seven, his words turning to a tearful gurgle.

"Our true form is nothing you'd understand."

"Fable," Seven murmured. "Fight Them! Don't let Them in! Fight it now!!"

A hand squeezed his face. His cheeks blowfished. "Ssh," They hissed. "*Tetragrammar* has always been a blockage within you, a stagnant dream, a bane in the guise of a narrative. And we dreamed you could rise to the task, to birth the novel-shaped universe, *Tetragrammar*. Once complete, its text would be the end-all to everything, you and us. The goal would have been attained, followed only by divine evolution. Never think we didn't pray for your inspirations."

A smile that never belonged to her slashed across Fable's face. And stroking his cheek pitifully, "But you're tired, failed writer. Possessing a Tetragram will do that. Such potential you had. A shame the limbo infection had to consume the world."

Seven's stomach twisted as Their words leeched into his soul.

"If only the notional father would've kept his diseased mind from his offspring. We've observed his self-hatred rot the world many times. We were muse to the first Circle Child and the next, to every recycled failure living in the echoes of their pathetic god. Notion's children were always narrative potentials, sentient stories meant for self-awareness, designed to absolve and rewrite the darkness in their maker. Nevertheless, we watched each fail, as creative minds tend to do, being devoured by their hang-ups and neuroses.

"Of course, we're older than Notion. We've been many muses. We were the Nine of Zeus, the spark in Shakespeare's heart, the madness that severed Van Gogh's ear, the revolutions within a Tesla-mind. We were/are the idea before it all. And how much greater would any story be if the forces that it inspired it would shape its final execution?

"We only wished for you to grow. So we made playmates for you. Our Dynasties were gifts. If we illuminated you, if we raped you, befriended and owned you, if we showed you masters who attracted their own heavens, if we gave you sisters and certainties, brothers and absurdities, if we made you suffer or smile, then we were your Authors.

"So you see, The Seven, our game trumps your brief, little life. And it's a game that has reached its sad resolution. We've played our silent role as watchers in the Moon, wrote ourselves from your story so you'd have a chance. But our return was inevitable. We would ultimately always author your reality. And our grand entrance back into the narrative had to be seeded at the start of our conflict."

Her voice was calm, child-like. Her words didn't always sync up with her lips. And she told him things that were true, or not, and it no longer mattered. Her words filled his ears, and they streamed as images behind his eyes.

And in his mind, he saw Fable whimpering in the darkness. A swarm of milky Porter-headed sperm darted around her, their faces amber and smiling, sticky bodies fluttering behind them. He witnessed Notion or Fable or himself standing under an ocean of stars, and behind the stars, something primal stirred. And whoever he was, muse or writer, didn't matter, because he was tired, and so he communed with it. Invoked it. Took it into himself. He needed to, because all stories needed to be purged from sterility, all tales needed to fall from their white wombs...

Seven felt a slash across his mind, and his vision settled back on Fable and the rain and the dissolving world. He blinked the image away. His face was a mess of betrayal and anger and resignation, the flesh smeared and battered. His eyes were swollen, nose crooked, cheeks busted.

"You had your chance, little scribe. We could've ripped *Tetragrammar* away without effort," The Authors continued, "but we are not that breed of god. We are not evil. We're not even claiming to be saviors. We are simply the cure. *Tetragrammar* is ours, and it is time to evolve." Several hands gripped his shoulders, dragging him closer, cradling him like an infant. "Be at peace, The Seven. It's over. No more burden. No escape from us." They swirled viral-like behind Fable's inky black eyes.

"You'll...you'll take it now?" Seven gasped.

"We will." She kissed his mouth.

His vision blurred. And somewhere he heard Fable, *his Fable*, calling to him. He looked into her, beyond her eyes, and he wondered if They had always been in her, that the Fable he'd always known had only been a fake persona hiding Their true dormancy.

She rested a chin on the top of his head, wiping the inkdrops from his face.

"You'll be good to it, my shitty book," Seven murmured.

"It will be everything it was meant to be," They replied.

"Th-thank you," Seven pushed. He was sliding into a state that wasn't sleep, wasn't death. There was no more Earth, no ground or sky.

"May the conception of your afterlife be not your final purgatory." They smiled a mouth full of stars. "Are you ready?"

"Yes."

"Now we kill you."

"Will it hurt?"

"Yes," They/she said.

If he screamed, he could no longer tell. He remembered words, only words, and his body unraveling into letters and sounds, language-shaped flesh stripping from him. And he imagined, yes, that seemed right, his entire form reduced to a dot, a period, another finite ink drop in an obsidian ocean. And could that be the Tetragram's truth? Absence, its point.

Perhaps he found peace in this.

Then again perhaps he did not.

VII

SNAKE BITES TALE

IN WHICH…

0

I, NOTION

He'd like to produce a text of astounding insight, a treatise on artistic dangers and creative joys that would garner literary praise. But he fears failure and a million unknowns and perhaps, worst of all, what terrifies him the most is perfection. Falling in love. Staying inspired. And he fears for all those characters embedded in his text, suffocating under the tyranny of his pen. He can only hope one will rise above the pages of Tetragrammar *to become their own author, for a creation to be better than him...*

*

"She never called." Andrew drums his fingers on his keyboard.

"Who?" she asks, interest dwindling.

"Melissa," Andrew groans. "I thought she'd call. She didn't leave my dorm till 3 a.m. That should count for something, right? She apparently liked my company."

"What did you want to happen?"

"A phone call. Is that so much to ask for? I didn't even try to make a move on her. Shit!" He palms his forehead. "I never made a move. She thinks I'm not interested. Fuck. So what I didn't make a move? Is it so bad I respected her?"

Andrew's room smells of dust and time, laundry and unfinished stories; it does not smell of musk or passion, and if you entered, you'd undoubtedly hate yourself, thanks to the self-loathing embedded in the cement walls.

"Your melodrama grows tedious." She paces towards the window. Dark outside, she peers into a forest behind the dorms at the lamplights illuminating a lonely path in fog.

"I'm sorry I get lonely. I apologize for being a virgin."

"Andrew…"

"Look," he leans back in his chair, "Melissa never called. Jules didn't seem interested. And Beth, from my creative writing class, we were sharing our stories, and then she just stopped coming by. What's the point?"

She sighs, wants him to shut up, and stop talking forever.

"I love fantasy and mythology," Andrew rattles on. "I read comic books and quote *The Matrix*. What am I supposed to write about? Have you ever read *King Rat* or *White Apples*? They're brilliant. And Neil Gaiman's already written *The Sandman*. I can't compete with that. I can barely take all the shit Dr. Finster slings at my manuscript. How am I supposed to handle an agent? What the hell am I going to do when I get rejected? Look at me now. Going to pieces over one girl not calling. You think I have what it takes to deal with publishers? I'd flip out when the negative reviews rolled in. I'll be honest. I'd rather gut myself with this fucking pen than revise one more chapter."

And the room goes deadly silent as Andrew utters the unthinkable. "What happens if a writer doesn't fulfill his purpose?" he dares to ask.

She flashes him a gaze of fire and taboo, and he's suddenly, ridiculously afraid. Once upon a time, Andrew found her in a dream, and maybe it would've been best if he never had invited her from that whatever-place.

"If you failed, little Andrew," she says, "I imagine it would not be the wisest notion." And he's shaking, because she looks bigger, different and sharper, and a hunger stirs behind her eyes, something dark and old in that pretty face.

A cold sweat beads his forehead. His trembling hands reach into his desk, pops two pills, swallows them dry.

*

Andrew tries to write as she floods him with ideas, wants to record them all, but he needs sleep, and he's afraid the mortal shell of his body is deficient in handling this onslaught. Time passes and he rewrites the book called *Tetragrammar*, realizing, at this rate, he'll revise forever, like the ouroboros that eternally consumes itself. His writing is nothing more than a snake, a devil-thing. His story will never be perfect, never meet art's demands. Perfection is a prison. He knows what must be done, and the indigo woman with her jagged aura and cyanide smile agrees.

"You're the snake, Andrew, shedding a skin of words," she says. "You're an ugly, ugly snake."

*

Andrew walks under the moonlight, towards his thinking spot, to the park across from his college. He sits by the pond, stares at the serene light as it breaks through the forest branches. And although heights terrify him, how would it be to go *there*, that perhaps the Moon is more than a celestial body, that it's a gateway, too; a hole in the sky, and if only he could jump through it, to enter another realm of myth and magic. Wherever that would lead, surely it would be better than this world.

Standing in the water, there's something symbolic about it, especially at night. The water glistens and could it also be ink? He clenches the knife.

A greater world exists beyond this. A world of pure thought, he tells himself.

He's limited here. Higher words exist out there, sounds and concepts far above this life.

Could it be this world isn't real? he thinks. *If writers get their ideas from a higher dimension, then he should just let go, evolve.*

He moves the blade across one wrist clumsily and repeats the act on the other. As he drops to his knees, she's there hovering over the pond. She does nothing to stop him, just sneers at the red gushing from him, and, yes, she can stop him, but he's too wet now in the pond, blood mixing with water.

"You poor bastard," she says with little warmth, because there is a simple truth: muses are divine and mortals are weak.

In death, if Andrew managed to ascend, she would evolve, too. He would be a father of notions while she'd play the mother of muses.

And *Tetragrammar* still needed to be written. Human writers were frail; they expired and collapsed under the blessings of inspiration.

He will not continue to defile any more stories, in this life or the next.

He will no longer be its writer.

345

The muse will take charge.
She will be its Authors.

29
EVOLUTION OF INK

Entering the End of the World reminded Seven of lost virginity. He closed his eyes and pushed his mind into something wet and foreign. There was rhythm and a sense of being lost, followed by a gap before release. And then wetness and perhaps discomfort and there was no going back.

And a million years later, Seven opened his eyes. He moved his fingers, his toes, arms and legs, easing himself from an eternal *shavasana*. The ground felt foreign, rocky and dry, unlike any soil he touched before. Gripping the earth, micro-crystals glinted in his palm, and he spread his hand to the ouroboros still wrapped around his finger. He checked himself, finding it ironic he still wore his jeans, black t-shirt, and leather jacket. He realized he was fully restored on the Moon. Peering down at the Earth below, it looked fake at this angle, like a bad special effect. Liquid shadow flowed through it, a black slithering that slinked across continents, inking into the oceans.

How long had it been?

Working himself to his feet, his legs adjusted rather quickly. He wasn't scared; after all, hadn't the world ended? After the end, after the world, what else could he fear?

"The world's always ending. Fiction, religion, they always tell you that," said Father Notion. He sat with his paper legs pulled into his chest, a bottle of Stella Rosa by his side. "It amazed me how people marketed doom and gloom. Two towers fall and it only reaffirms some French Man's vision. It tells you an ancient civilization's calendar is right, that time is really running out. I never thought it was funny. But now I see the bliss of an ending. They're proper and forgiving. It's purgatory that's the curse. In purgatory, nothing ends. You only dream of perfection, of all the women who never loved you and all the books you could never write." Notion took a swig from the bottle, wiped his lips with a paper forearm. A wine-red stained his flesh.

"I'm surprised They let you out of your white hole," Seven said.

Ignoring him, "They were always out there," Notion continued. "The adversary. I saw darkness, and it was Them." Notion laughed weakly. "So here we are."

"And what now, Andrew? Create an eighth Circle Child?"

"If I must! Does this look like an ending?!" He gestured about at the empty Moon and the blackened Earth and the blank void. "Fix this, Seven! Rewrite it now!"

"Rewrite for what? It's over!" Seven glared at his ring. "Being trapped in your story, I can't blame you, can I? Not completely. Blaming you would admit I have no free will, no ability to write my own destiny." Seven's ring burned as the snake hissed.

"Whatever They told you is a lie," Notion whimpered. "Do not let Them write it! Never let Them influence you!"

"Authors have always influenced authors. That'll never change. Besides, whatever you wanted *Tetragrammar* to be, it's done now," Seven said.

"They told you They were her, didn't They? They told you They were always Fable. That's not true!" Notion screamed. "They're wearing her like a cheap suit. They need a muse's body as a vehicle for the Tetragram! Listen to me!" Notion pleaded. "They'll twist it into some perversion. They'll kill you with *my* story!"

"Doesn't matter anymore. Fuck circle-eating snakes and cannibal stories. Your burden became my ouroboros and, if it were on you, there'd never be a grand finale. So I'm moving on." Seven punched his chest.

"Seven…" Notion beckoned.

"*Tetragrammar*'s your purgatory. It won't be mine."

Notion went deadly quiet, until his face distorted in rage, and he threw the bottle at Seven, which hit him awkwardly in the shin. Notion lunged at him. Before he could make contact, the paper man dropped to his knees. He was crying, hissing, rabid ink spraying from his mouth. Notion cringed, his body crinkling and tearing. Seven backed away, bracing himself. Although he was on the Moon, somehow he witnessed vast walls rising around him and a huge shadow stretching across the world. The shadow contracted into an iridescent, egg-like object, and, for an impossible second, the world contracted with it. A series of eyes and teeth unfolded from reality. Hands and claws from abstract angles began to tear and rip Notion apart. Every wound was followed by a bloodied wail. With a final scream, Seven fell back as Notion was shredded, spewing newspaper bits across the void. And when the pulpy matter cleared, a voice moved across his mind.

"What do you see when you gaze into the black between the stars?" it asked. A wetness licked his face, easing his eyes into space. Seven hesitantly peered towards his shoulder. For a moment, he spotted long fingers, clawed nails. "We'll devour it all; it's what we are and ink is nothing if it doesn't flow. It must fill all space, after all."

Fable...

Fable, or The Authors, smiled. They wore a transparent robe that glinted starlight. Waves of liquid violet rolled across the fabric. Her long hair flowed towards her waist. Her eyes were empty pools of newborn universes. And her lips, when parted, revealed bone-colored void. A fully opened third eye tattooed her forehead.

"We'll feast on you, too, little scribe," They/she added sadistically. Seven shivered. "Why am I here? I was dead. You killed me."

"Yes."

He looked at the Earth below. Obsidian oceans crested over the continents. There was little difference between the flood and the dark of space.

"I always imagined waking on the Moon," Seven said. "I would write myself here somehow with nothing more than a pen and paper or think myself here through some fiction." Seven paused. "Why *am I* alive?"

"You're not." The Authors grinned from Fable's lips. And the space between her lips was deep as an abyss. She reminded Seven of a suit being worn by a larger concept that could never be confined to words. Her face would thicken or superimpose with something older than time stirring beneath. Looking at her too long hurt.

"Alive or not, I'm here now after the world ended. And if I'm back, something tells me you need me."

"Could it not be a grace bestowed upon you by gods?" Her mouth stretched impossibly wide.

"No. Something went wrong with *Tetragrammar*. Otherwise, I wouldn't be here. There would've been no resurrection. So why bring me back?" Seven waited. "I'll tell you what I think." He felt sick and scared, and he crammed the emotions down, to ride it out just a little longer.

A murky oil spiraled and twisted on Fable's face, a darkness that desired to leak from her eyes and mouth, that wanted to expand.

"You're not Fable," Seven said.

"We are."

"I don't think you know what you are. You're just an ambiguous concept trying to exist. You still need *Tetragrammar* to tell you about yourself. You need *me* to define you."

The Authors laughed. And while They laughed, Seven's ears bled. He cringed, cupping his ears with his hands. Straining to keep one eye open, he muttered, "Whatever hole of existence spat you out, whatever grand statement you're seeking, you still need me to write the ending and that kills you!"

For an instant, she was a face, just a face, and They glared back from a porcelain mask. "Need you? Oh, little scribe, we have no need for notions and pissing circles." The Authors flashed a face full of teeth.

"Then let's end it."

"Very well, The Seven. Let's." Seven suppressed a chill when They smiled several smiles. And when They touched his forehead, the Moon rose up around them.

This was not possible. They were elsewhere now, deeper. The Moon was not hollow, because as they once stood on its surface, they now were below, travelling a network of tunnels. Whether this was the literal Moon or just a metaphor, Seven realized his journey was always headed towards a figurative structure uprooted from physics and science, that his destination was never the Moon, but the *idea* of the Moon.

The ground bubbled and burst in liquid clay. A crystal blue illuminated the dripping walls. The atmosphere pulsed with an eerie twilight glitter. Fable's body floated, the tips of her toes grazing the ground underfoot. Pondering what she might've always been unnerved him.

They eventually arrived at an opening that led to a massive, globe-like cavity within the Moon. The atmosphere was thick, almost icy, with a celestial dust and misty patches of starlight. Through the wintery glare, when his eyes adjusted properly, Seven witnessed a stone sculpture in the shape of a lotus flower at the center of the space. It reminded him of an altar. The longer he stared at it, the more he realized just how large it was. The sculpture was encircled by giant stairs, steps Seven imagined were several stories high, or not, he couldn't tell as his perception distorted and wavered.

Above the lotus sculpture, there was a crackling rectangular hole in reality, a negative space that fluctuated with hungry energy.

As The Authors glided upwards over the long, wide stairs, the size of Their body shifted. Sometimes They were ungodly large, like a living ocean of obsidian. Other angles, They were nearly the same height as Seven. They spiraled around the lotus-throne, whirling about the negative space, Their robe-body crackling.

"What is this?" Seven shouted, his voice a sad, dwindling echo.

"The hole in things still remains," The Authors hissed.

Seven winced. Shaking his head, "What are you telling me?"

Several limbs shot out from Their body, hands caressing the negative space. "This is where *Tetragrammar* must reawake! A hole now but also the doorway to our ascension, and you, The Seven, must be the final component to unlock it."

"I don't understand," Seven yelled. The Authors held his gaze, shrank down to his size, and suddenly were several feet from him at the foot of the steps. Behind Them, the stairs and the lotus were ungodly huge. They stared blankly at him. Seven furrowed his brow, eyeing Them, then the negative space. "Where is *Tetragrammar*?" he asked. They remained silent. "You don't have it, do you?" Nothing. "You tried to remove it from me, but you couldn't. That's why you resurrected me, because I'm still needed."

"Nonsense!" They spat.

"Right."

The Authors seemed almost frozen as shadows danced around Them. And Seven imagined Their silence confirmed his theory. When They killed him, his narrative had been finished; however, that wasn't good enough. That ending wouldn't stick, and They needed to try again. *Tetragrammar* still remained in Seven, and it would do so until, dead or alive, he had released it fully himself. Seven was required as the final catalyst to secure Their escape. And even after death, how could his novel still linger in him? He wanted to be done with it. And what now, being dead and finished, *what now?*

"Think, The Seven," They smiled several times, in several different places on Their robe-body, and he heard hissing about Them. "Make it right!"

Shaking his head, "I don't know what else to do."

An arm or tendril coiled around his thigh. "*Tetragrammar* will take us to the world above, places so inconceivable it would rupture your soul," They said. "You can come with us, The Seven. Our ascension was never meant to be exclusive." They were now just a porcelain face surrounded in tar-like cloth, twirling in circles around Seven, wet robe glinting dust and space. They condensed instantly into a ball. Uncurling, shifting from view, They reappeared in front of him. "You will release it to us now!" Their demand, two distinct, overlapping voices, echoed in the globe-sphere. "Purge yourself of the Tetragram, an ending for you, escape for us!" Two hands appeared from the wet robe. And there were four hands and six hands and Seven looked away. "We can evolve together, The Seven, or we can evolve alone," They added as an afterthought, Their face extending into a fanged snout. "We have the ability to decipher the Tetragram. We have managed evolutions before. Now! Release it!"

Although They were bluffing, Seven restrained the shake in his voice. "After I give it up, it's over. This war, whatever you call it, is over."

"Yes, over!" They sounded like cancer. "We're waiting," They said. He cringed at the shifting of her face.

And reflecting on his journey in writing, Seven had already finished it once with ink and paper, and he had used a bag to do so. And he imagined throughout the cycles of the Circle Children, *Tetragrammar* came with existential baggage that only grew more demanding over time. And then he laughed, *baggage*. It was about baggage.

Simply writing the novel wasn't enough. A history was buried in its pages, recorded and unrecorded at once. And there was a desire laced in the words, feelings and ambitions about what it could be. Dreams and inspirations, droughts of frustration and floods of bliss. It was a child, after all, a child that ultimately had to experience the process of birth.

With that, Seven imagined he could do this. He sat on the ground, closed his eyes.

It was never just writing. His existence hinged on much more than the completion of a novel. It was the idea. The journey of it. If the answers resided within, he only had to open himself. That was the story.

He had to go bigger, had to rummage through the baggage of time, had to meditate upon every page of his life, from what had been to what wasn't, all the material that had been recycled or deleted, had to recall every word of Andrew and Arthur and every previous writer, needed to dredge up every ancestral memory, every past life, and he needed to purge it, to release it all. And as it accumulated inside him, Seven opened.

He mounted all that together, and he pushed. And as he pushed, he realized he might've been delivering a universe, *his universe*, in all its glory and imperfections, with every flaw and typo, what it was and what he wanted it to be; Seven pushed.

His head hollowed. The cavity in his mind spread. He concentrated on the release of *Tetragrammar*. There was a bulging, an expansion. Seven was giving birth. Something huge pushed from his mind, an opening around his forehead, and he saw or didn't see *Tetragrammar* crowning from his mind. As he screamed, he was rising, and his body was falling away with a massive force pushing up and out.

In that birth cry, the world dissolved.

*

When Seven opened his eyes, a small body stood before him, a genderless, child-like form. Its arms and legs and body were purely light. Text and glyphs coursed throughout it. And Seven squinted to decipher its face, but the face, its head, was composed of a large, gold-bound novel. Seven held his breath, reaching for his book-headed child. But as he reached, a strange amount of distance stretched between them, distorting the world. *Tetragrammar* had grown proportionately larger than Seven, and it wiggled its ethereal fingers at him, as if to say good-bye. And he mouthed his farewell back at it.

His child's body fizzled out. Only the book-that-comprised-its-head remained. *Tetragrammar* rose towards the lotus-sculpture, hovering above it. The novel's surface looked organic, seemed to breathe, to pulse and vibrate with amber energy.

"Yes, yes!" They exclaimed in a hundred voices, tiny and young, old and wise, others in deep, foreign tongues. They glared up at Seven's novel, which was the impossible size of a skyscraper within the Moon. Then, They faced him, a ravenous smile of shark teeth. Within the robe-body, Fable's face was much larger, and it twisted upside down so that her hair spilled towards the rocky floor. Her visage was only a porcelain mask, broken and cracked, and from a mouth that never moved, a voice like glass shards echoed around them. "Finally! *Tetragrammar* is ours! You did good, The Seven, so very, very good." And They cackled. With a flash, They moved. They were far away, miles perhaps, swarming about *Tetragrammar*, Their liquid body spiraling around it, enveloping it.

Seven backed away, observing with caution. Sick laughter or deranged cries reverberated throughout the Moon. They stroked the gold surface of *Tetragrammar* with a hand that was no longer remotely human and with many more hands savagely caressed its cover. Their fingers sprouted with jagged teeth as Their affection turned hungry and warped, and They grasped at the novel, prying it open. As They parted *Tetragrammar*, the book began to cry like a murdered beast, screaming with light. As a heavenly luminance erupted into the twilight realm, The Authors grew more fluid, a deranged mixture of obsidian bleeding together with gold.

The longer Seven viewed this collision, the more it hurt his vision. Sometimes his book appeared larger than the Moon itself. And sometimes it seemed to shrink. He couldn't focus on it too long as it shifted in size and dimension.

Seven fell back, pressed his palms against his ears, praying to tune out the abstract screams. Fixing his eyes on Them, Seven crawled back towards the globe-cavity's entrance. Still watching The Authors spiral viral-like around his book-child, he wondered what *Tetragrammar* truly meant to Them. Would embracing it bring an evolution? And he thought, acceptance is evolution; inner sight is wisdom; the freedom to let go evolved you. All the struggles he had in writing his novel were entirely fake, all fiction, and yet it was as real as him, real as anything. Everything was words and stories. Everything fit together, and, in that union, good and bad, that was evolution.

Although he could see The Authors, behind his closed eyes, the image of a violet flower blossomed, becoming human-shaped, becoming Fable, *his* Fable. She was lashing out towards him, flailing, pleading to him.

"They always needed you for it. Be careful, Seven," she looked bloody and slash-marked, *"Don't trust Them!"*

The Authors continued to tear rabidly at the ethereal pages, Their robe-body dripping on it. As They dripped, the pages crinkled. Cracks riddled the book's golden surface. From the cracks, nervous eyes flared open, irises shaking into focus.

The world was glowing and darkening at once, and Seven desperately needed to leave, wanted to be anywhere else as They flooded the light. Having done his part, he wanted to escape, to find his own way. Always playing to some higher authority, he would leave and let The Authors sort out Their own transcendence. Whatever They believed *Tetragrammar* to be, whatever answers or gateways it would access, he imagined it nothing more than Their very own deus ex machina.

Seven crawled through the piercing light and the liquid dark.

"Our new reality is now! We write the world!" They announced while They froze, while They vibrated in a series of overlapping images. They howled. Deep, chewing sounds echoed in the globe with laughter that sounded like children being possessed by broken glass. Shadows crawled upon the walls.

"Go now!"

Although The Authors no longer acknowledged him, concerned only with Their inevitable ascension, it was anything but safe here. Consumed by a manic fire, They began to devour *Tetragrammar*, smashing at it with parts of Their body, ripping it apart with Their many-mouths while They riffled through it with a hundred fingers full of teeth.

And Seven heard cackling as Their black form spread, expanded, reflective shadows licking reality. Within the shadows, or the shadows themselves, Seven saw *things*, nightmare-wolves and daggered jaws, bleeding eyes, and wetness inking everything. As They consumed the book, honey-colored blood-pulp dripped down Their face. Light mounted within Them, an internal glow that pulsed through Their tar-flesh. Every chomp and chew at *Tetragrammar* culminated in a shriek, some ungodly sound only a living book being murdered could make. And as *Tetragrammar* screamed, it laughed, too, a chilling giggle from possessed paper. Eventually, both his novel and The Authors were screaming and crying together, an absurd mix of terror and enlightenment. Whatever was happening, Seven wanted to be far away from it.

Seven ran. Behind or beyond him, there was an expanding light, an orchestra of angel-shrieks and ripping sounds, like time breaking, reality melting...

"My hand!" Fable screamed from elsewhere. *"Take it!"*

Seven reached in a direction that didn't exist.

Back within the Moon, running desperately through tunnels, following mindlessly a violet flame as it flew through the corridors. Left. Right. Left. Left. He kept going.

He ran and ran until a primordial scream seared apart creation. Seven leapt and somehow he was outside the Moon. He was falling. And as he fell, he had the epiphany this was how being born felt, that unreal drop from some source that defied words. Gazing towards the Moon above, there was a seismic crack, and the side of the Moon blew out. Bits of lunar fragments and dust spread across space in the explosion. They glistened and twinkled, like cosmic confetti, and from this angle the Moon looked like nothing real, a model or an idea of a model.

Seven continued his descent.

He fell through space or time or absence, he didn't know. Around him the stars began to extinguish as apocalyptic ink flooded the void. And he heard screams rending apart matter, clawing across existence. An unimaginable light exploded about him then, followed by a climactic wail so inhuman it could bleed universes, the final death in The Authors' evolution.

And Seven began to laugh. He laughed until his body collided with a border that felt like paper. He heard the sound of words breaking and pages tearing. And eyes, he saw a million eyes peering from a million directions. And he rose into the Outer Page, but he also fell through and out of a story that longed for release. His life, his novel, was full of flaws and shortcomings and it wasn't perfect (no story was), but it would have to do. And for some reason, he extended his middle finger into a direction that didn't exist, flicking off the critics and readers and anyone who judged this finale.

This would be his conclusion, his alone. And, in all reality, he was only just beginning.

And then.

The world turned white.

When I lose myself, when I dream, I remember the true language of ink.

IT IS ALL;
IT IS NOTHING

IT IS WORDS;
IT IS WORLDS

OM

BANG!

30
TABULA RASA

The time of The Authors was over. Tetragrammar *had been awaken. It was all an ending of sorts, and it left much to be desired perhaps. I suspected the conclusion would frustrate and not deliver that final pow. And I decided nothing would be good enough. If Seven dove back into the pages, tried to write a more concrete finale, if he took a year off to let a better resolution stew in his mind, he knew that was the trap, the ouroboros, and now was the time to let a narrative be, for better or worse.*

I only had one more task. I looked into the screen of my laptop, and I fell into it...

*

A steady crash rhythm of waves licked up against the snow covered shoreline; inhaling, exhaling; breathing in, breathing out. And Seven gradually moved his hands, his feet, then everything else. He was on a beach that glistened in quicksilver. In all directions, thick white blanketed the world. And the water, the ocean, the water wasn't water at all.

The sand was snow—the snow was sand—without being either. It wasn't cold, and it didn't smell like winter. A gentle hue of lavender and amethyst blanketed the cloudless sky. Before him, the ocean waves crested in, crested out. As the ocean broke on the shore, the water splashed the surface like ink on paper.

Seven spotted a charcoaled body washing up on the shore. Waves licked its lifeless form. The corpse resembled a ravaged mannequin, empty and torn in half at the torso. It was face up, head turned

363

sideways. Its face was the cracked guise of Fable or the shell They had been wearing. Whatever They were, The Authors were gone. Seven couldn't make out what remained of the face, the expression one of terror or joy or something beyond words. He inspected the body. It reminded him of a hollow porcelain doll.

What happened? Seven thought.

"Tetragrammar *happened,*" someone said, *"for Them."*

Seven looked up. He stared into the distance. A man hovered above the water, his feet inches from the surface. Although miles away, he saw the man's hair was ruffled black. He wore a leather jacket with a wrinkled shirt. The man (I) held a book in his (my) hands.

And I heard the words of my fiction bastard. "What happens now?" Seven thought. "What do I do?"

"*What do you do?" I repeated. Why anything, I thought. You live. You write. And I closed the book that was* Tetragrammar, *and as I sealed it, another book opened over my head. I smiled at Seven and looked up and I was gone...*

Seven blinked.

He strolled along the shoreline for some time, listening to the soothing flow of waves, crashing in, crashing out; inhaling, exhaling.

He imagined in the distance he saw Paris waving to him. There was a hissing deep inside him, telling him to go back, to embrace their story again, to return to the old drafts of his life, to make *Tetragrammar* better. He realized he still wore the ouroboros ring as the snake tightened around his finger. He looked at it bemused and slid it from his finger. He held it to the sky.

A circle. A zero. Dynasty Zero. The Limbo Dragon.

He tossed it into the ocean.

Paris continued to wave. He waved back. Wherever she was he wished her luck. And he thought about floods and beginnings, middles and ends, and how not to get stuck in the drafts of your life. And suddenly, a presence hugged him certainly, *so certainly,* and his mouth filled with the taste of apples and gardens.

He walked.

Time passed or it didn't. Seven continued on the Template Beach. He felt oddly free, light, the weight of words lifted from him. And strangely, he felt inspired.

Eventually, an airy voice broke the silence. "Where are we?" she asked from behind him.

He turned to face her. "Fable?" he whispered.

"What happened?"

"You're alive?" He wanted to embrace her, kiss her, but nerves restrained him.

"I guess I am." She cocked her head in reflection. "I...I'm really not sure how it went down. I was The Authors or I let Them in or...It was me. I was Them, sorta, but not really. You know, I don't know anymore. And I don't care either."

"It doesn't matter now."

"What happens next?" she asked, shaking her head dismissively.

"Anything I guess," Seven said. "You know, I've always loved you even when I hated you. It was always you I wanted. All the words I needed to express to tell you. In a way, that's what my book was about. It was you. You were so many things, but, most of all, you were my inspiration. I didn't need *Tetragrammar* to tell you that. And..." he was talking faster, "...I always wanted to write the perfect ending to our story. But now I realize the perfect story doesn't exist. The ideal ending, perfection itself, is just as much fiction as fighting literary demons. We can't write the perfect book, but we can have fun trying. So this is our ending. It's the best I can do for now," he said.

She laughed. "I don't think it's the end for you or us." She looked up and out. "There's a whole universe out there full of stories." She smiled. "We could move on. This is just a middle ground, I think."

"Then let's go. Come with me." Seven extended a hand towards her.

She eyed him playfully. "What will our next story be?"

"I don't know. But I imagine we have all the time in the worlds to figure it out." He waited.

"I guess I could tag along." And with a wink, she said, "But before we go, answer me this? *Tetragrammar.* What was it *really* about?"

He told her.

Tilting her head to the side, her violet eyes reflected on the answer. "Oh." A smile broke across her mouth. "I don't get it..."

EPILOGUE FOR SOME;
PROLOGUE FOR OTHERS

Elsewhere, an author closed the last page of *Tetragrammar*. It wasn't perfect. But it was done. The end of a world had arrived, a fable unbound, and he had never been freer.

FABLE UNBOUND

ABOUT THE AUTHOR

Anthony Kocur lives in Pennsylvania with his wife and daughter Aslynn. He is a Licensed Massage Therapist. He teaches yoga and martial arts. He graduated from Penn State University. *Fable Unbound* is the revised edition of his novel *Tetragrammar*.

His next novel will be called *iMinotaur*.

Cover art provided by Deric Hettinger.

Made in the USA
Columbia, SC
27 November 2020

25654574R00224